Sacrificial Princess and the King of Beasts

9

Yu Tomofuji

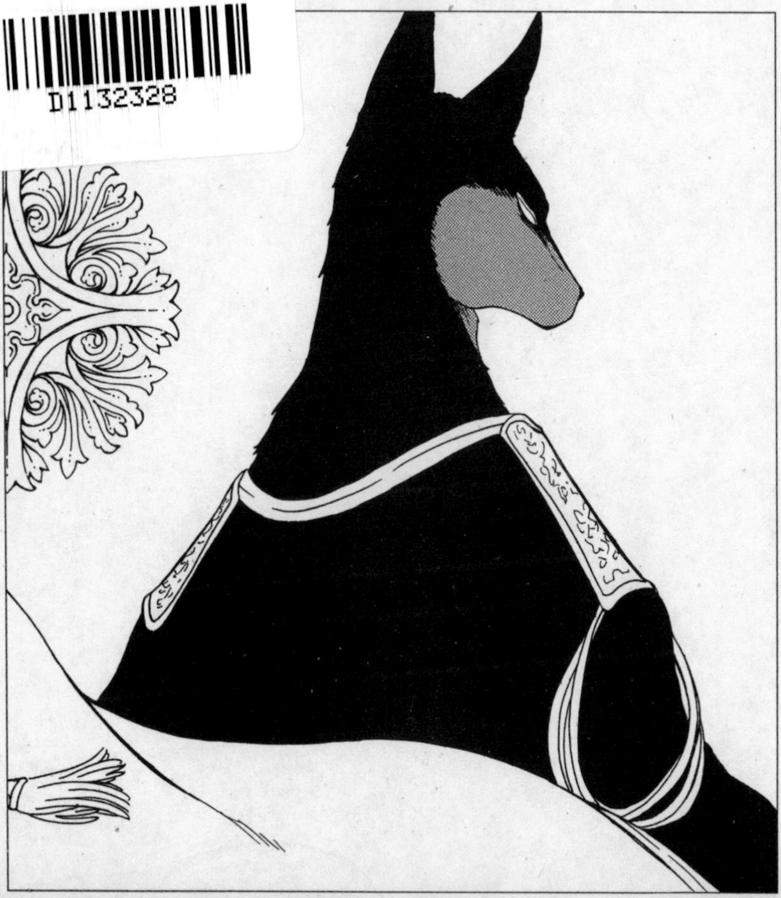

SACRIFICIAL PRINCESS
AND THE King of Beasts

9

c o n t e n t s

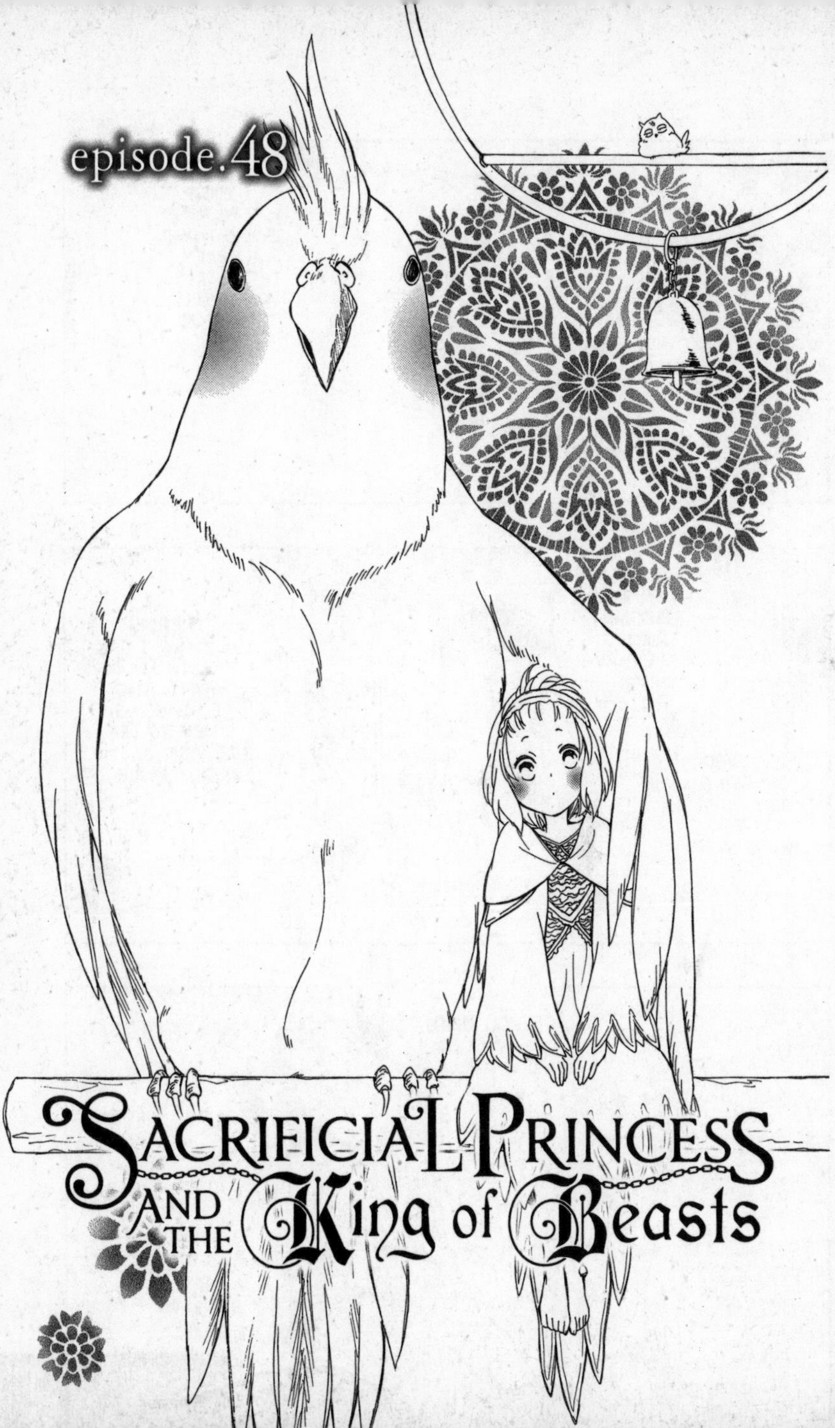
episode.48
SACRIFICIAL PRINCESS
AND THE King of Beasts

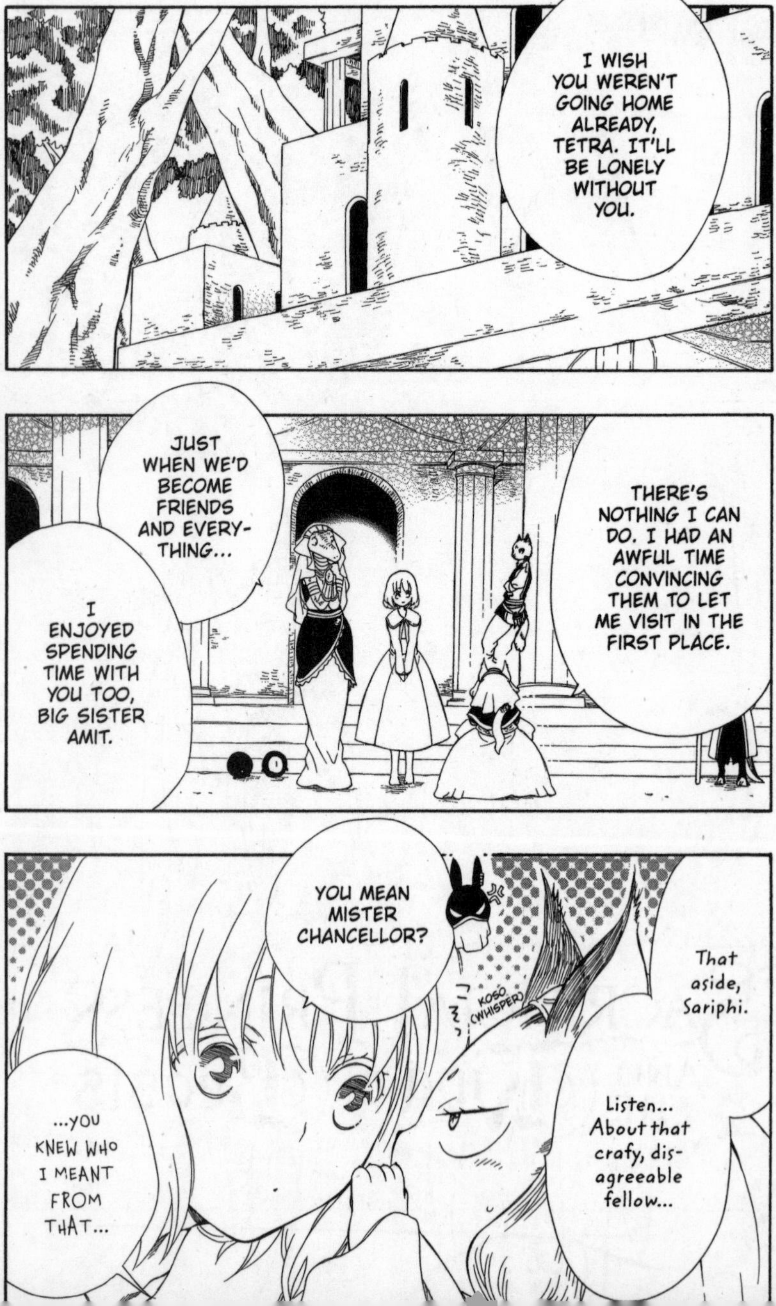
I WISH YOU WEREN'T GOING HOME ALREADY, TETRA. IT'LL BE LONELY WITHOUT YOU.
THERE'S NOTHING I CAN DO. I HAD AN AWFUL TIME CONVINCING THEM TO LET ME VISIT IN THE FIRST PLACE.
JUST WHEN WE'D BECOME FRIENDS AND EVERY-THING...
I ENJOYED SPENDING TIME WITH YOU TOO, BIG SISTER AMIT.
That aside, Sariphi.
Listen... About that crafy, dis-agreeable fellow...
YOU MEAN MISTER CHANCELLOR?
KOSO (WHISPER)
...YOU KNEW WHO I MEANT FROM THAT...

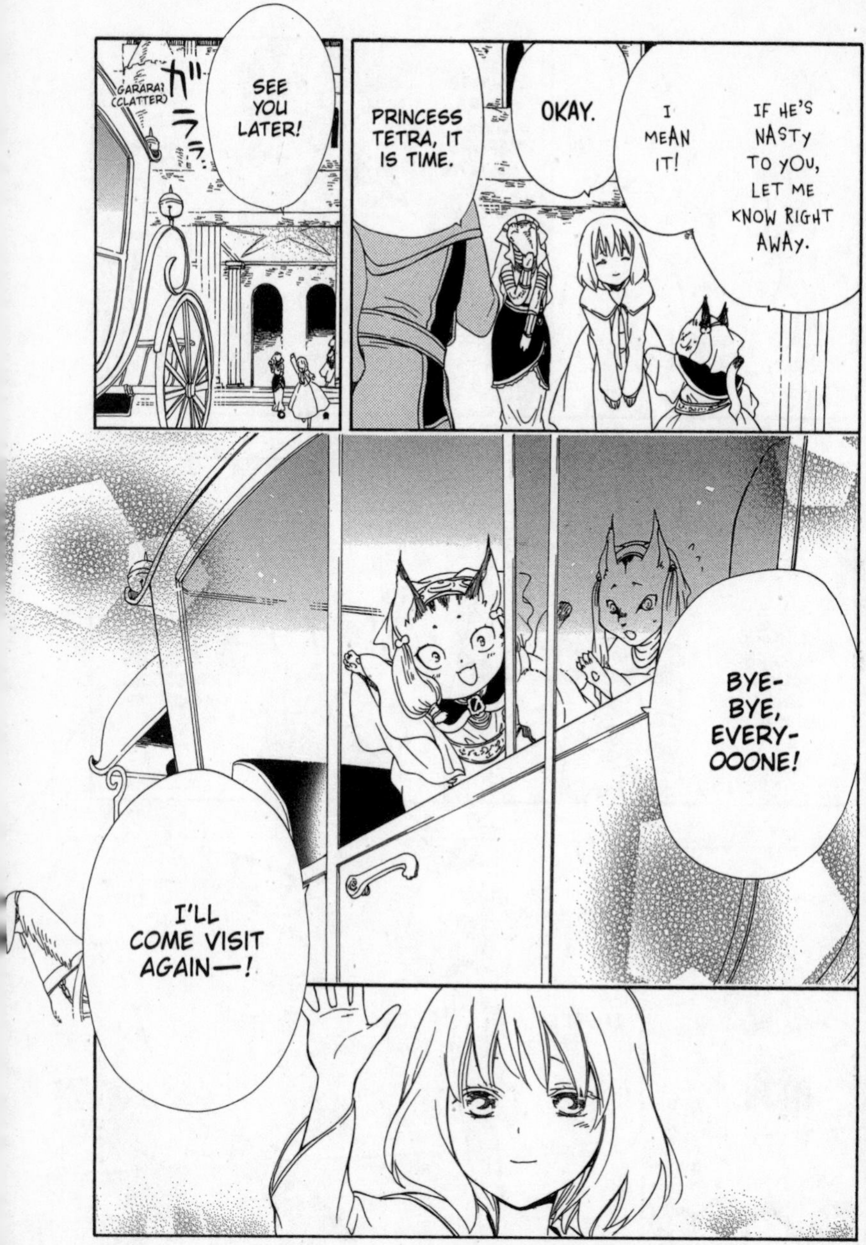
IF HE'S NASTY TO YOU, LET ME KNOW RIGHT AWAY.
I MEAN IT!
OKAY.
PRINCESS TETRA, IT IS TIME.
SEE YOU LATER!
GARARA (CLATTER)
BYE-BYE, EVERY-OOONE!
I'LL COME VISIT AGAIN—!

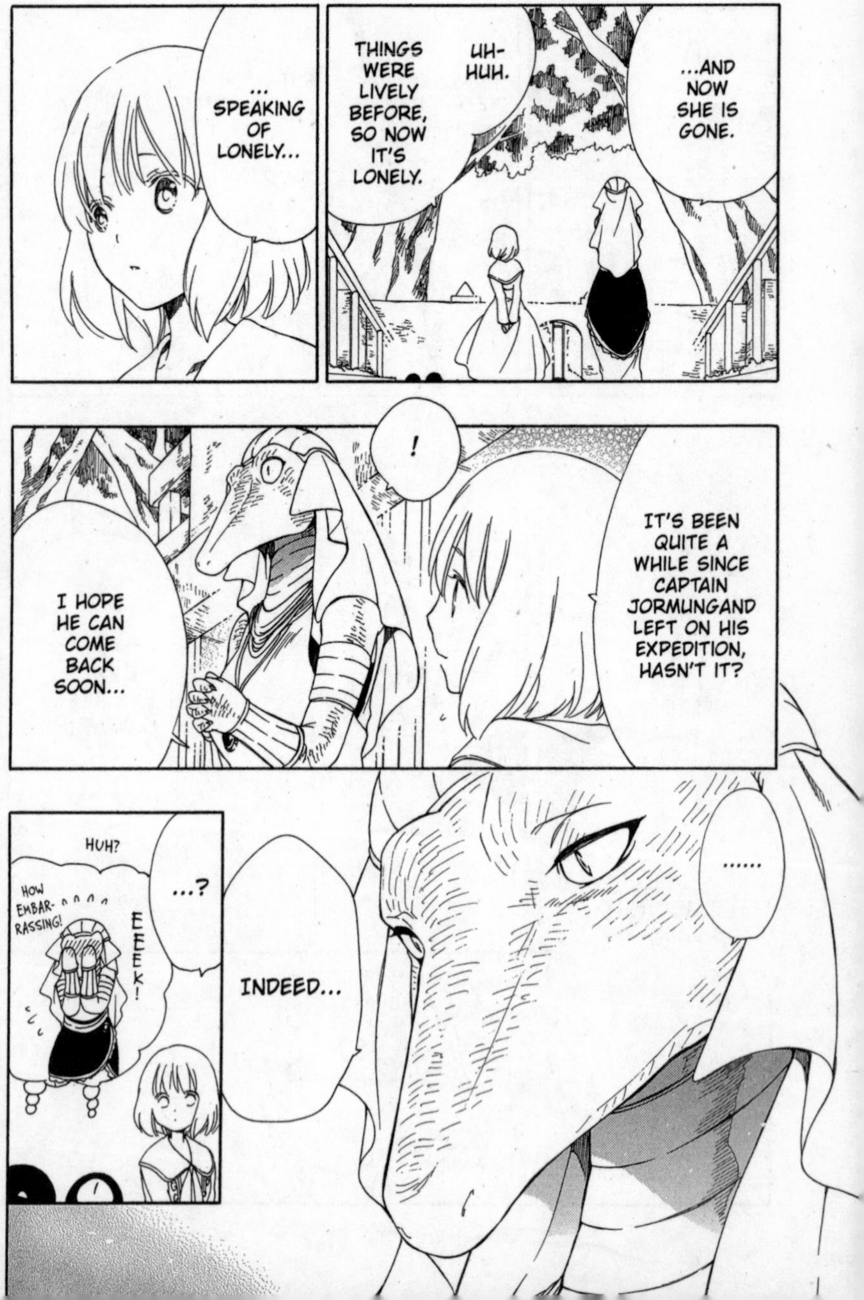

...AND NOW SHE IS GONE.
UH-HUH.
THINGS WERE LIVELY BEFORE, SO NOW IT'S LONELY.
... SPEAKING OF LONELY...
IT'S BEEN QUITE A WHILE SINCE CAPTAIN JORMUNGAND LEFT ON HIS EXPEDITION, HASN'T IT?
!
I HOPE HE CAN COME BACK SOON...
......
INDEED...
...?
HUH?
EEEEK!
HOW EMBAR-RASSING!

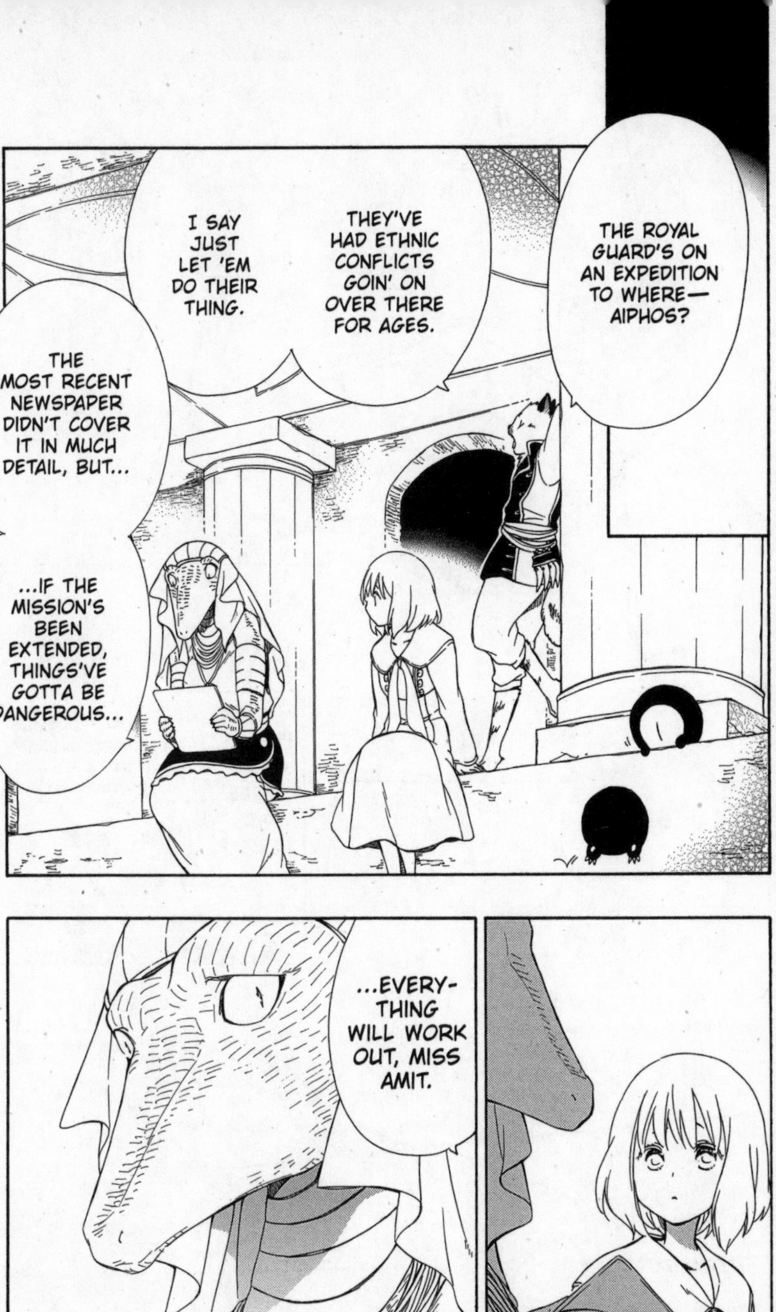
THE ROYAL GUARD'S ON AN EXPEDITION TO WHERE—AIPHOS?
THEY'VE HAD ETHNIC CONFLICTS GOIN' ON OVER THERE FOR AGES.
I SAY JUST LET 'EM DO THEIR THING.
THE MOST RECENT NEWSPAPER DIDN'T COVER IT IN MUCH DETAIL, BUT...
...IF THE MISSION'S BEEN EXTENDED, THINGS'VE GOTTA BE DANGEROUS...
...EVERY-THING WILL WORK OUT, MISS AMIT.

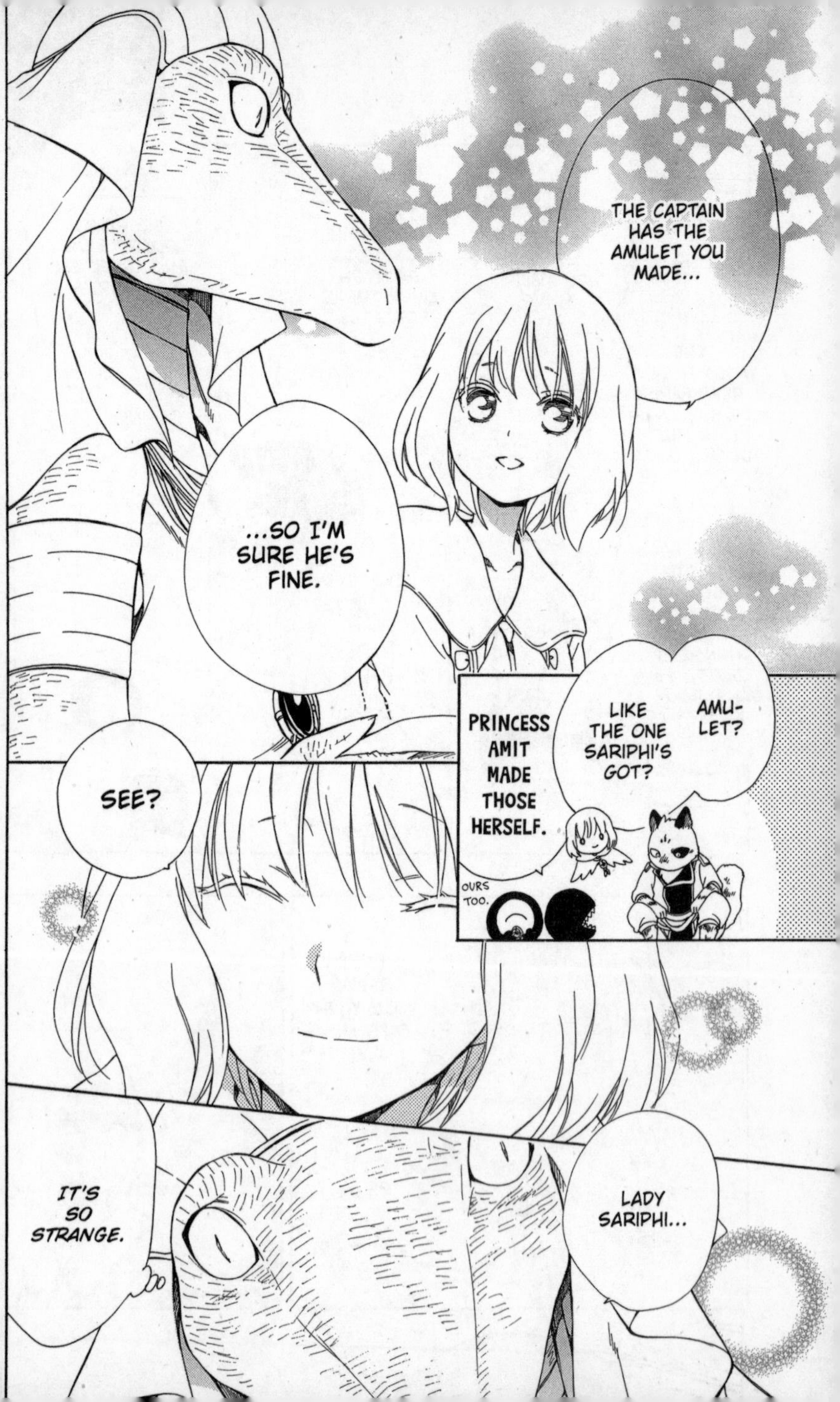
THE CAPTAIN HAS THE AMULET YOU MADE...
...SO I'M SURE HE'S FINE.
AMU-LET?
LIKE THE ONE SARIPHI'S GOT?
PRINCESS AMIT MADE THOSE HERSELF.
OURS TOO.
SEE?
LADY SARIPHI...
IT'S SO STRANGE.

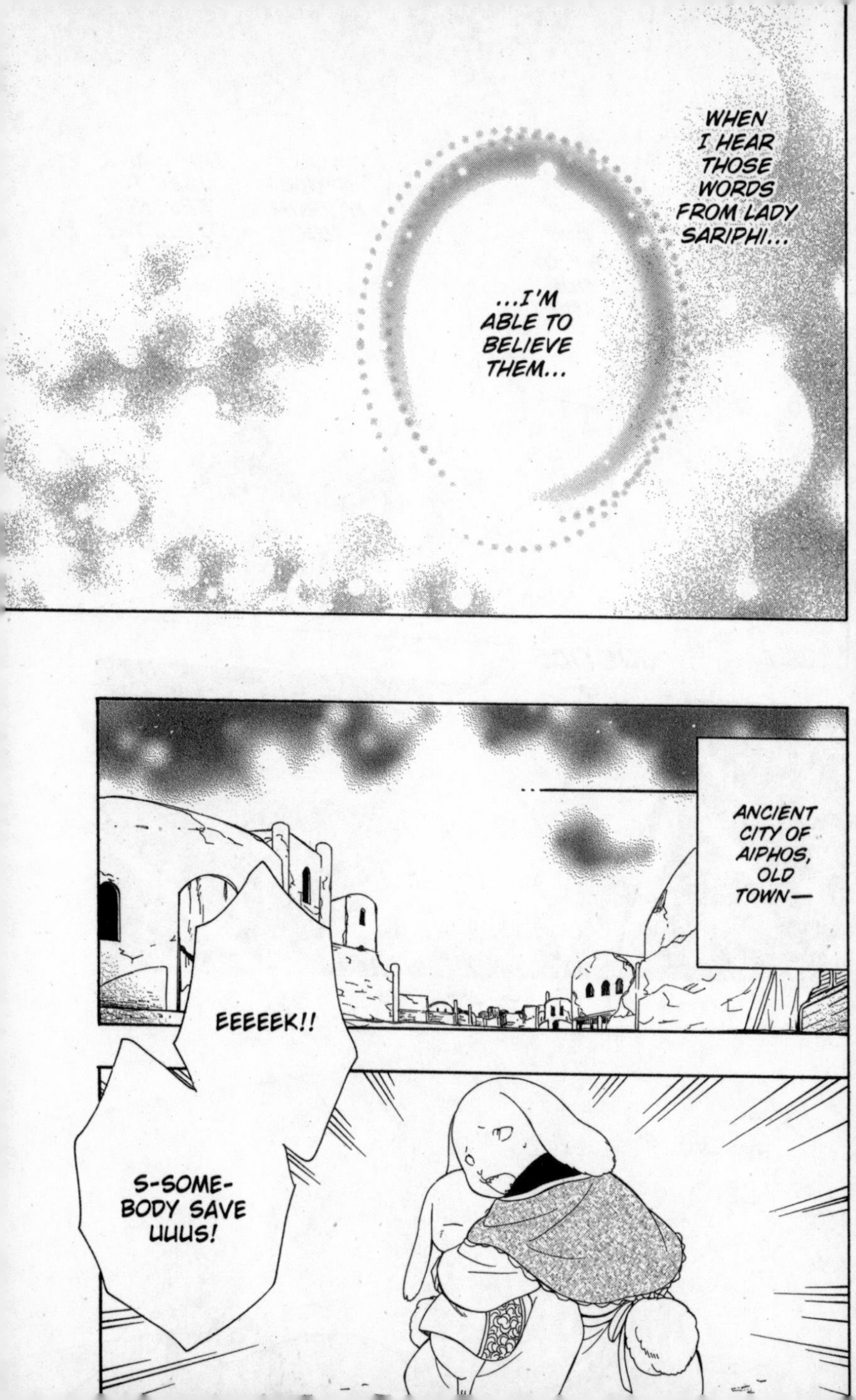
WHEN I HEAR THOSE WORDS FROM LADY SARIPHI...
...I'M ABLE TO BELIEVE THEM...
ANCIENT CITY OF AIPHOS, OLD TOWN—
EEEEEK!!
S-SOME-BODY SAVE UUUS!

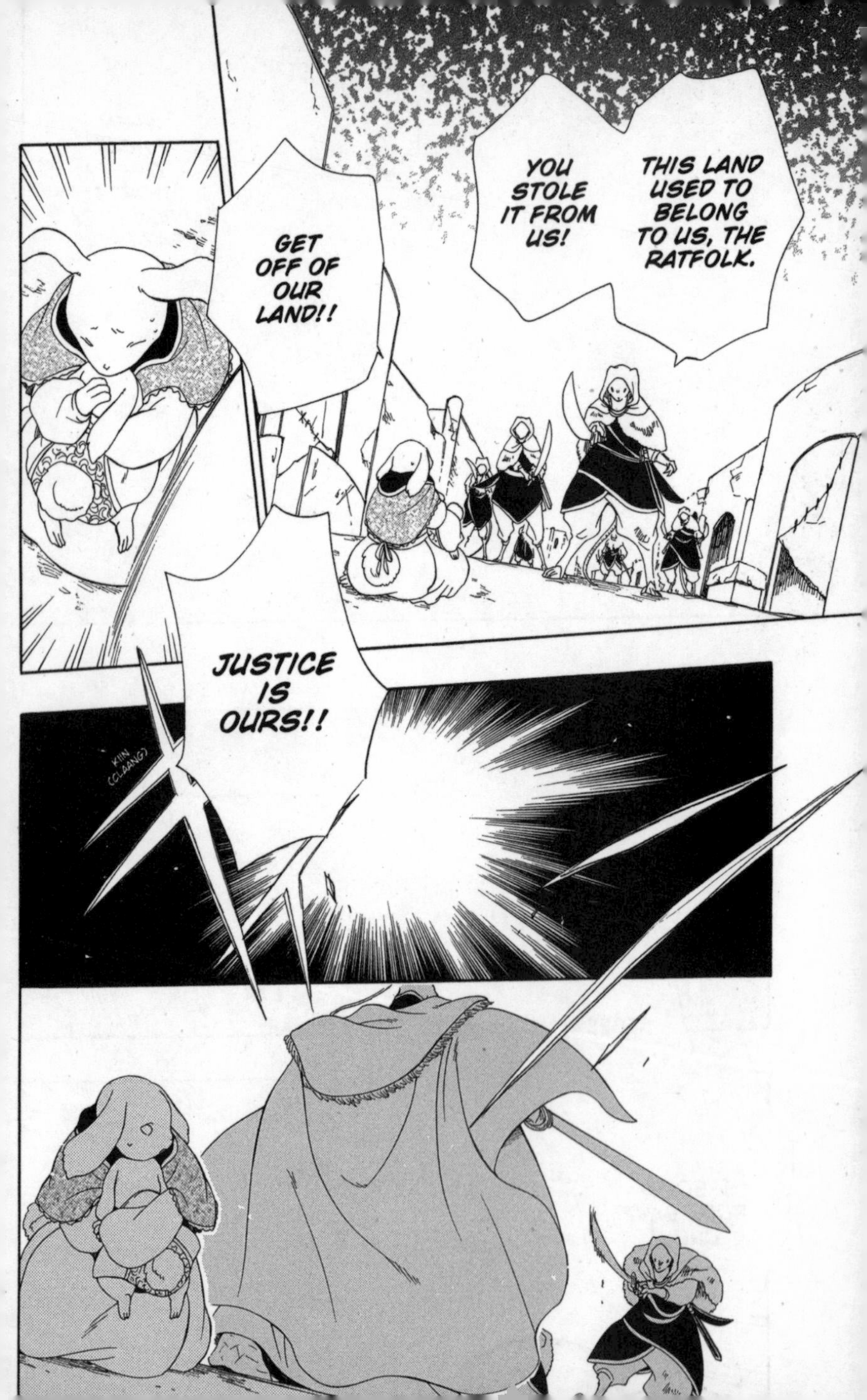
THIS LAND USED TO BELONG TO US, THE RATFOLK.
YOU STOLE IT FROM US!
GET OFF OF OUR LAND!!
JUSTICE IS OURS!!
KIIN (CLAANG)

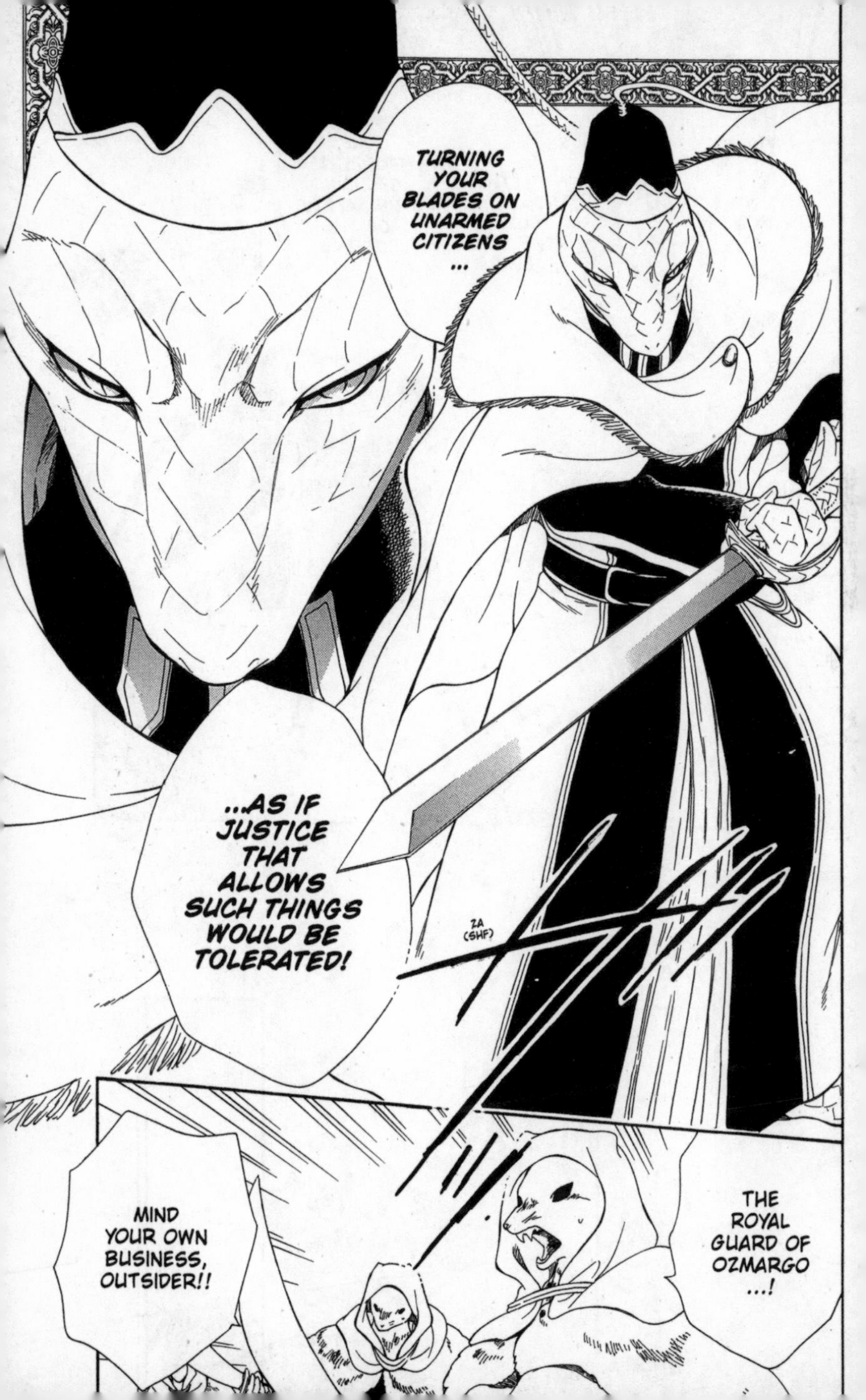
TURNING YOUR BLADES ON UNARMED CITIZENS ...
...AS IF JUSTICE THAT ALLOWS SUCH THINGS WOULD BE TOLERATED!
ZA (SHF)
THE ROYAL GUARD OF OZMARGO ...!
MIND YOUR OWN BUSINESS, OUTSIDER!!

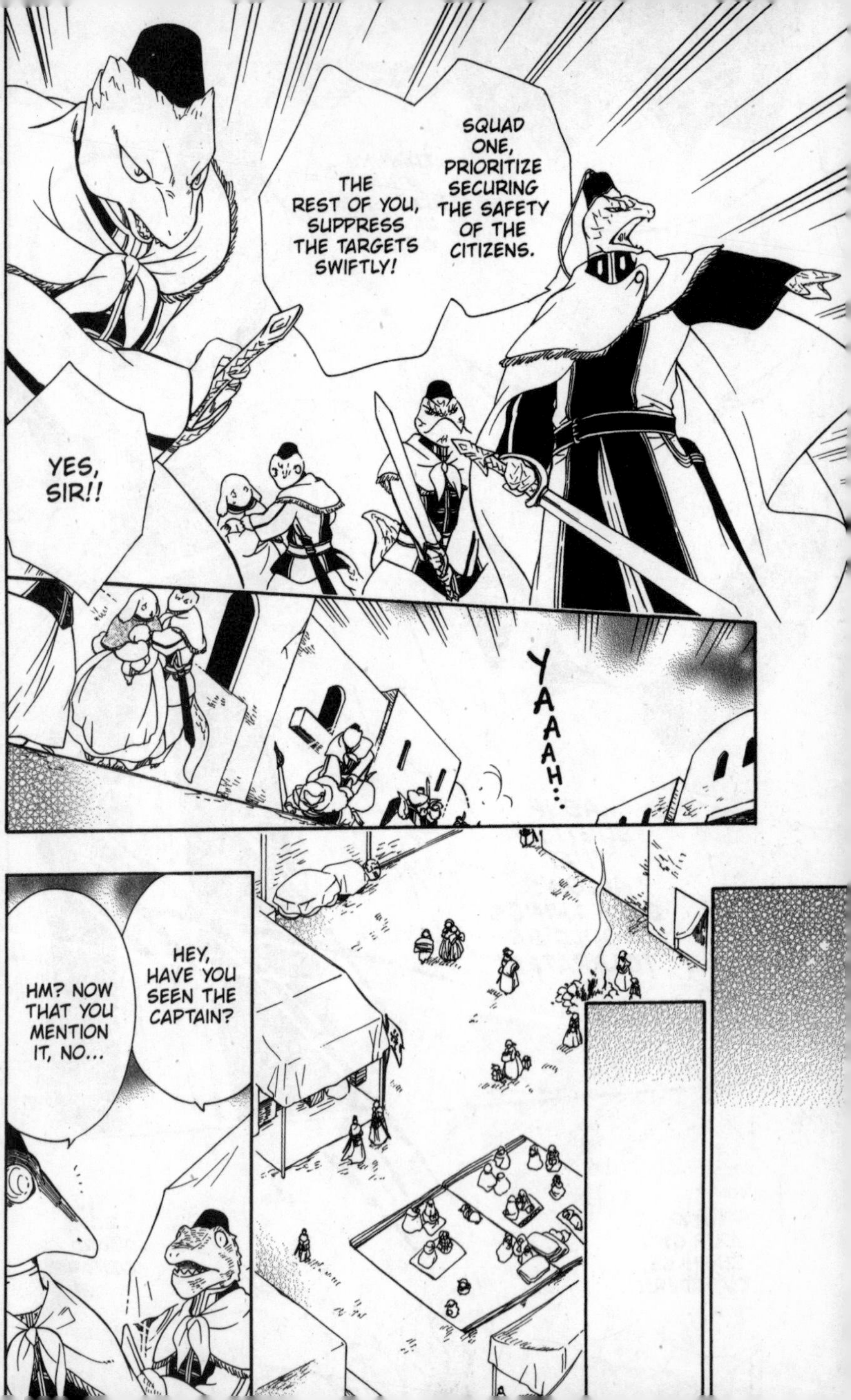
SQUAD ONE, PRIORITIZE SECURING THE SAFETY OF THE CITIZENS.
THE REST OF YOU, SUPPRESS THE TARGETS SWIFTLY!
YES, SIR!!
YAAAAH...
HEY, HAVE YOU SEEN THE CAPTAIN?
HM? NOW THAT YOU MENTION IT, NO...

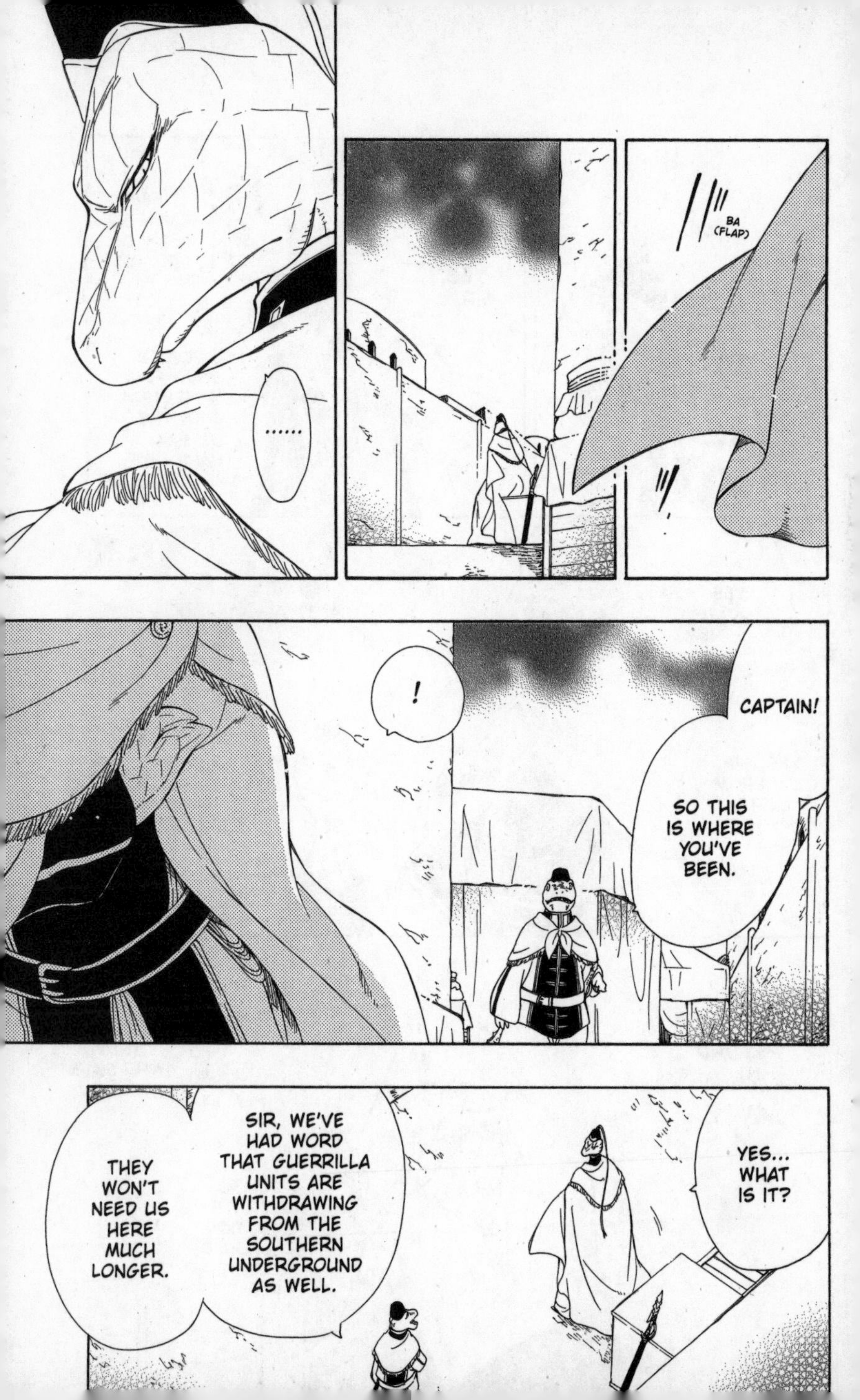
BA (FLAP)
......
CAPTAIN!
SO THIS IS WHERE YOU'VE BEEN.
!
YES... WHAT IS IT?
SIR, WE'VE HAD WORD THAT GUERRILLA UNITS ARE WITHDRAWING FROM THE SOUTHERN UNDERGROUND AS WELL.
THEY WON'T NEED US HERE MUCH LONGER.

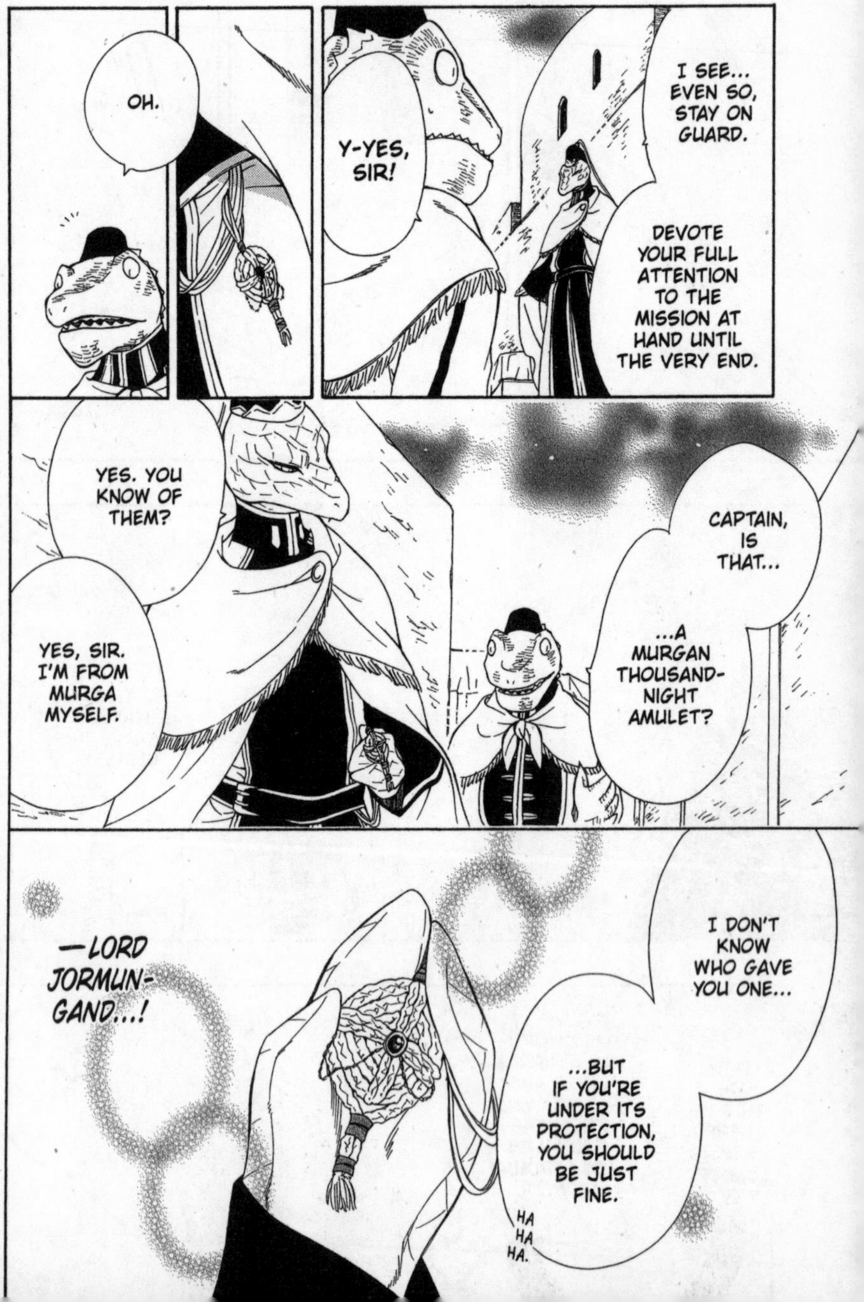
I SEE... EVEN SO, STAY ON GUARD.
DEVOTE YOUR FULL ATTENTION TO THE MISSION AT HAND UNTIL THE VERY END.
Y-YES, SIR!
OH.
CAPTAIN, IS THAT...
...A MURGAN THOUSAND-NIGHT AMULET?
YES. YOU KNOW OF THEM?
YES, SIR. I'M FROM MURGA MYSELF.
I DON'T KNOW WHO GAVE YOU ONE...
...BUT IF YOU'RE UNDER ITS PROTECTION, YOU SHOULD BE JUST FINE.
HA HA HA HA.
—LORD JORMUN-GAND...!

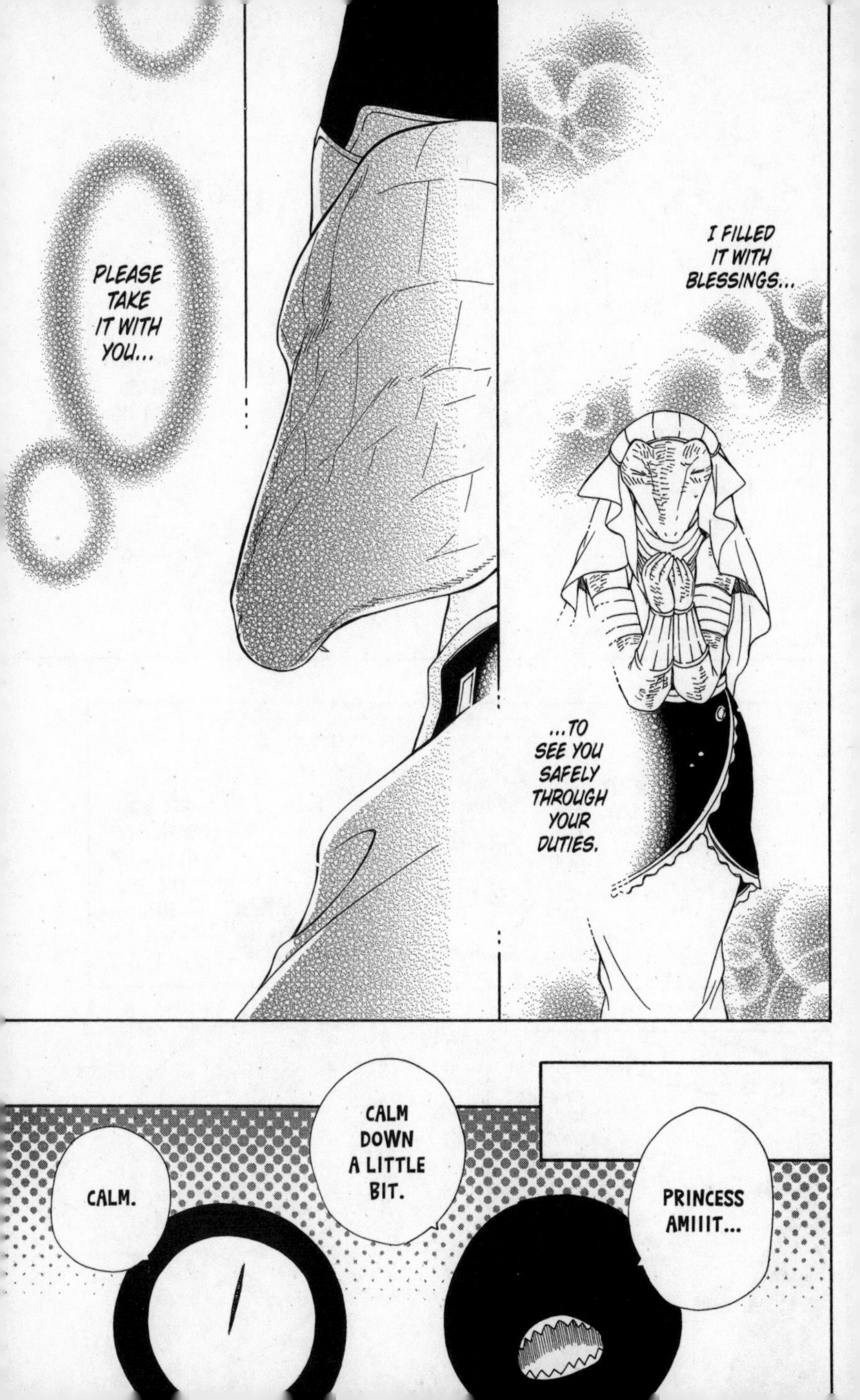
I FILLED IT WITH BLESSINGS...
...TO SEE YOU SAFELY THROUGH YOUR DUTIES.
PLEASE TAKE IT WITH YOU...
PRINCESS AMIIIT...
CALM DOWN A LITTLE BIT.
CALM.

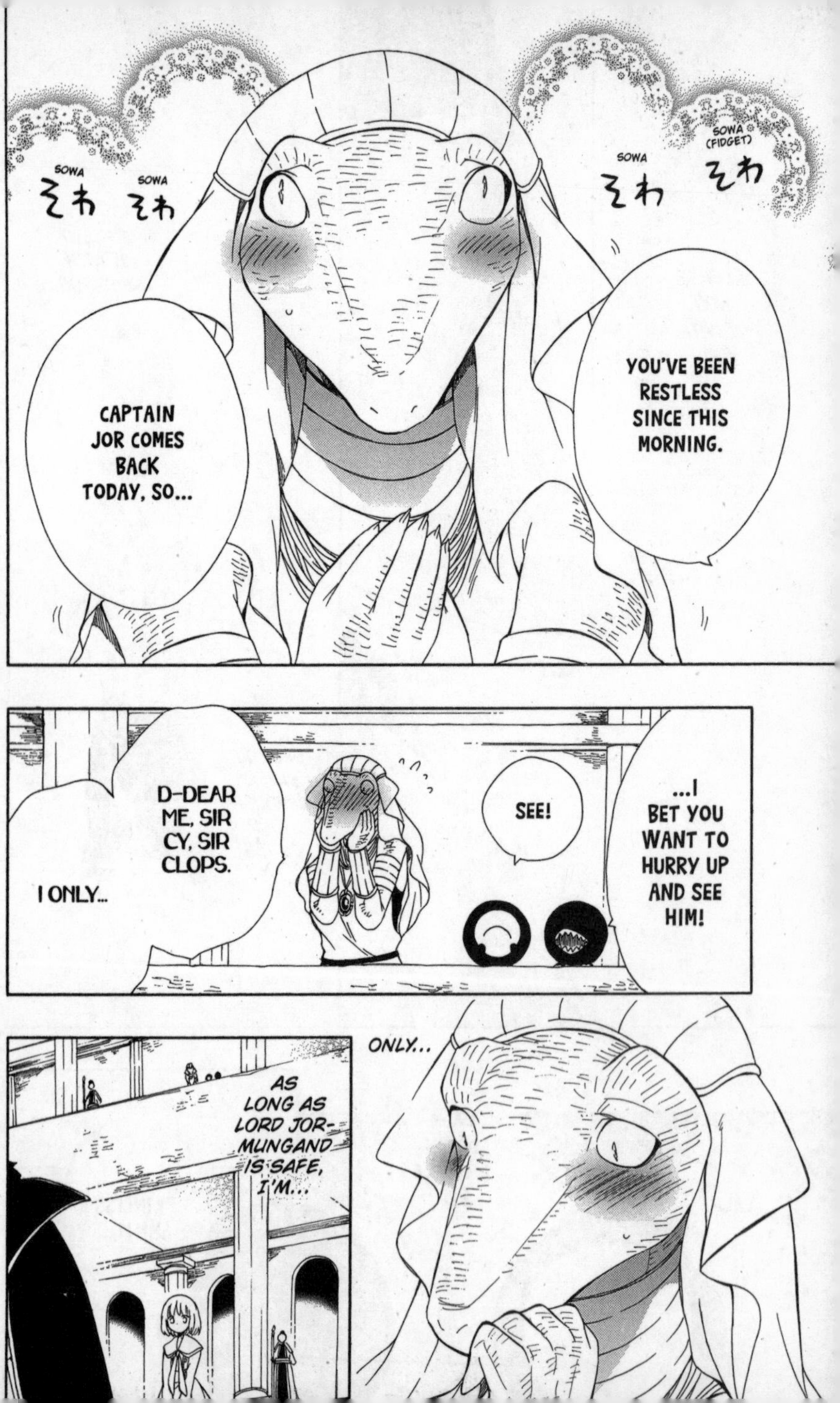

SOWA (FIDGET)
そわ
SOWA
そわ
SOWA
そわ
SOWA
そわ
YOU'VE BEEN RESTLESS SINCE THIS MORNING.
CAPTAIN JOR COMES BACK TODAY, SO...
...I BET YOU WANT TO HURRY UP AND SEE HIM!
SEE!
D-DEAR ME, SIR CY, SIR CLOPS.
I ONLY...
ONLY...
AS LONG AS LORD JOR-MUNGAND IS SAFE, I'M...

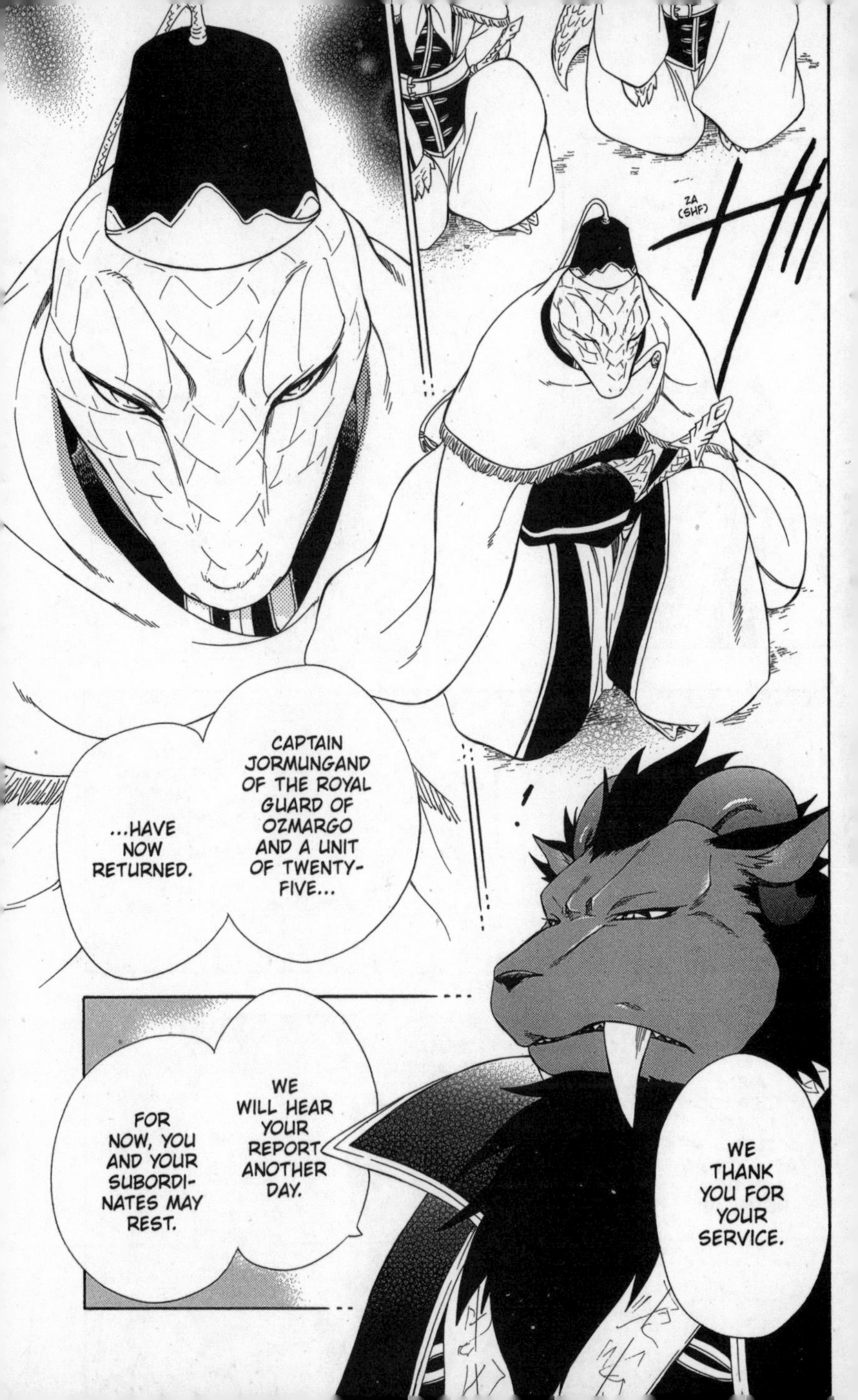
ZA (SHF)
CAPTAIN JORMUNGAND OF THE ROYAL GUARD OF OZMARGO AND A UNIT OF TWENTY-FIVE...
...HAVE NOW RETURNED.
WE THANK YOU FOR YOUR SERVICE.
WE WILL HEAR YOUR REPORT ANOTHER DAY.
FOR NOW, YOU AND YOUR SUBORDI-NATES MAY REST.

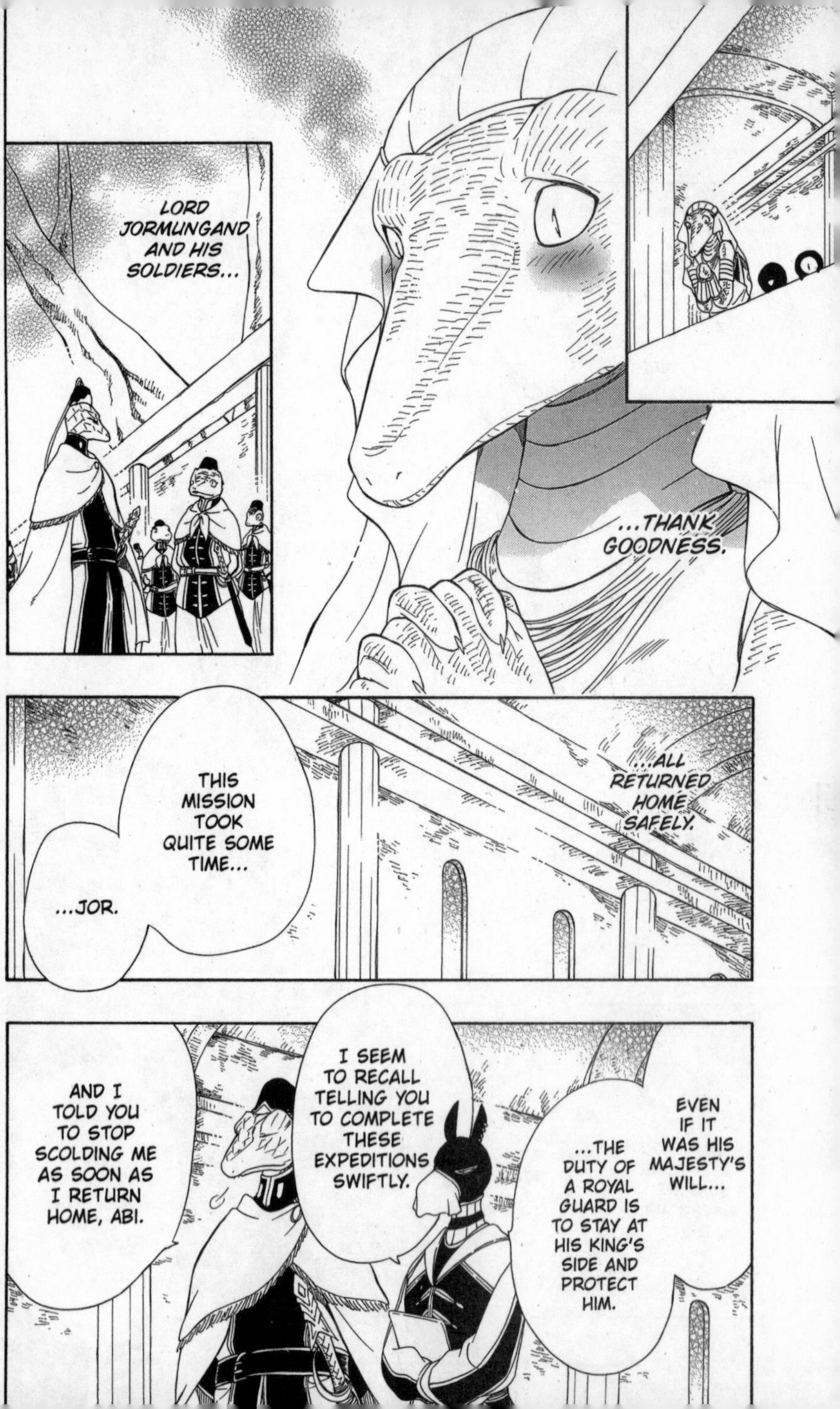
...THANK GOODNESS.
LORD JORMUNGAND AND HIS SOLDIERS...
...ALL RETURNED HOME SAFELY.
THIS MISSION TOOK QUITE SOME TIME...
...JOR.
EVEN IF IT WAS HIS MAJESTY'S WILL...
...THE DUTY OF A ROYAL GUARD IS TO STAY AT HIS KING'S SIDE AND PROTECT HIM.
I SEEM TO RECALL TELLING YOU TO COMPLETE THESE EXPEDITIONS SWIFTLY.
AND I TOLD YOU TO STOP SCOLDING ME AS SOON AS I RETURN HOME, ABI.

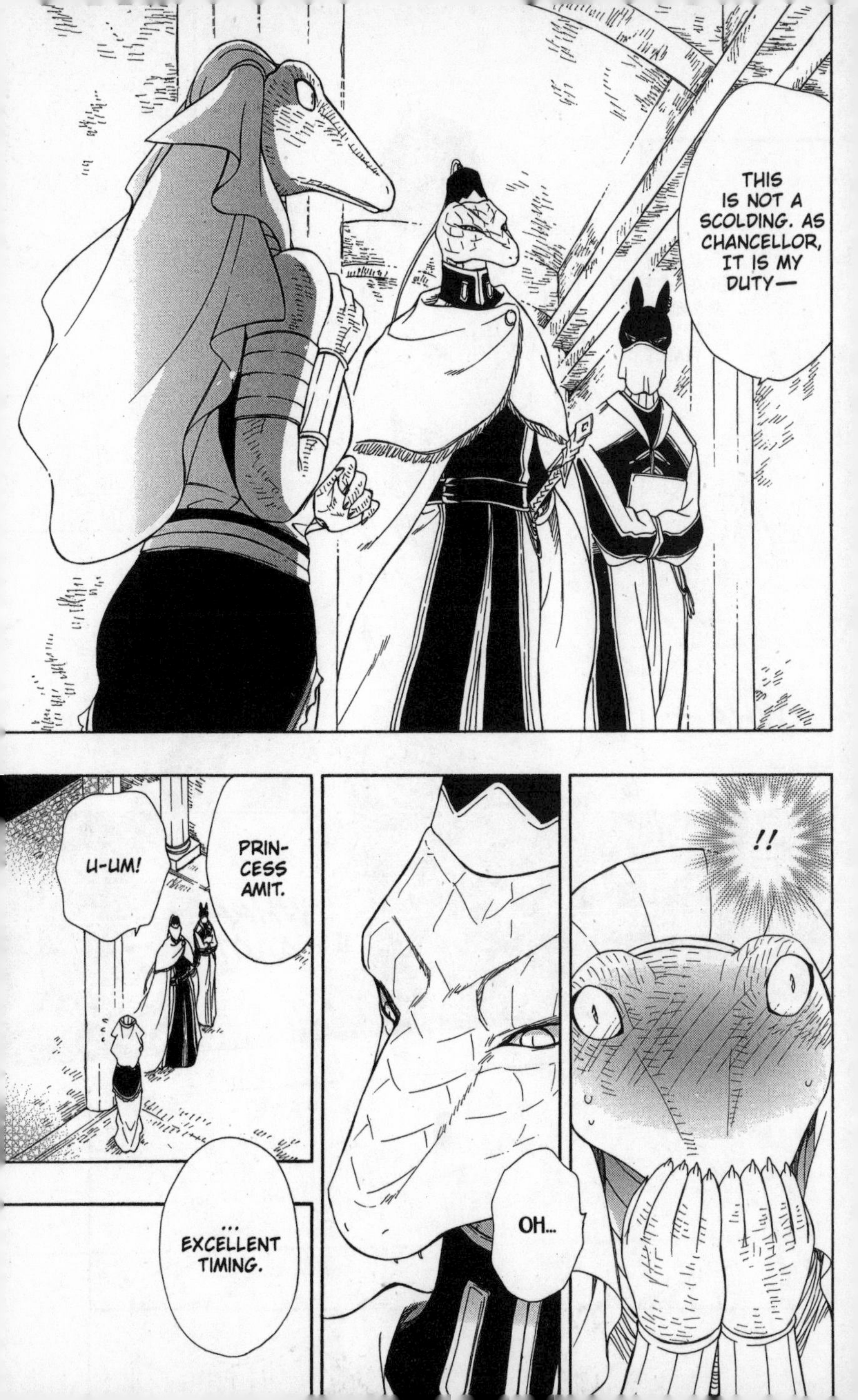
THIS IS NOT A SCOLDING. AS CHANCELLOR, IT IS MY DUTY—
!!
OH...
PRIN-CESS AMIT.
U-UM!
... EXCELLENT TIMING.

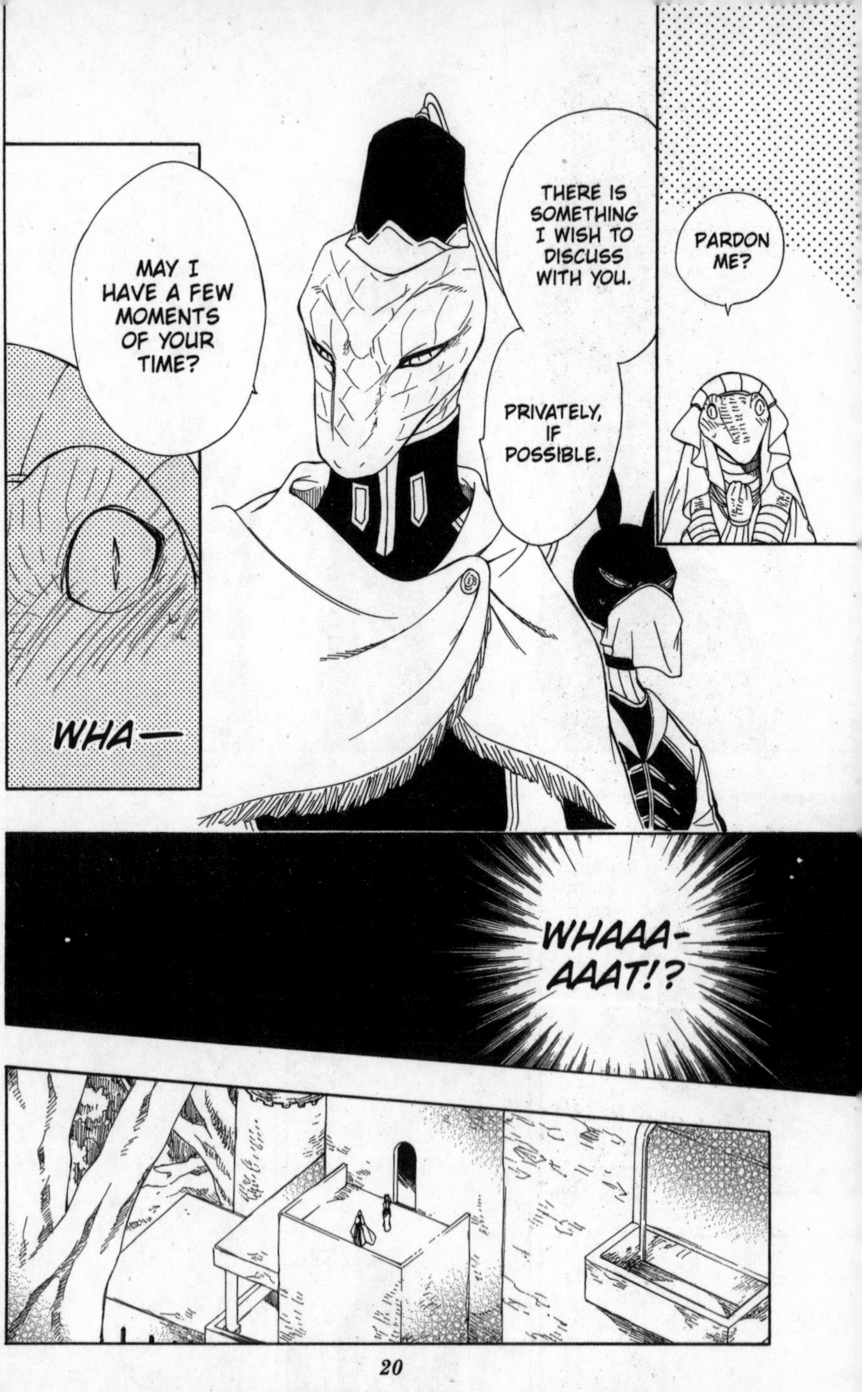
PARDON ME?
THERE IS SOMETHING I WISH TO DISCUSS WITH YOU.
PRIVATELY, IF POSSIBLE.
MAY I HAVE A FEW MOMENTS OF YOUR TIME?
WHA—
WHAAAA-AAAT!?

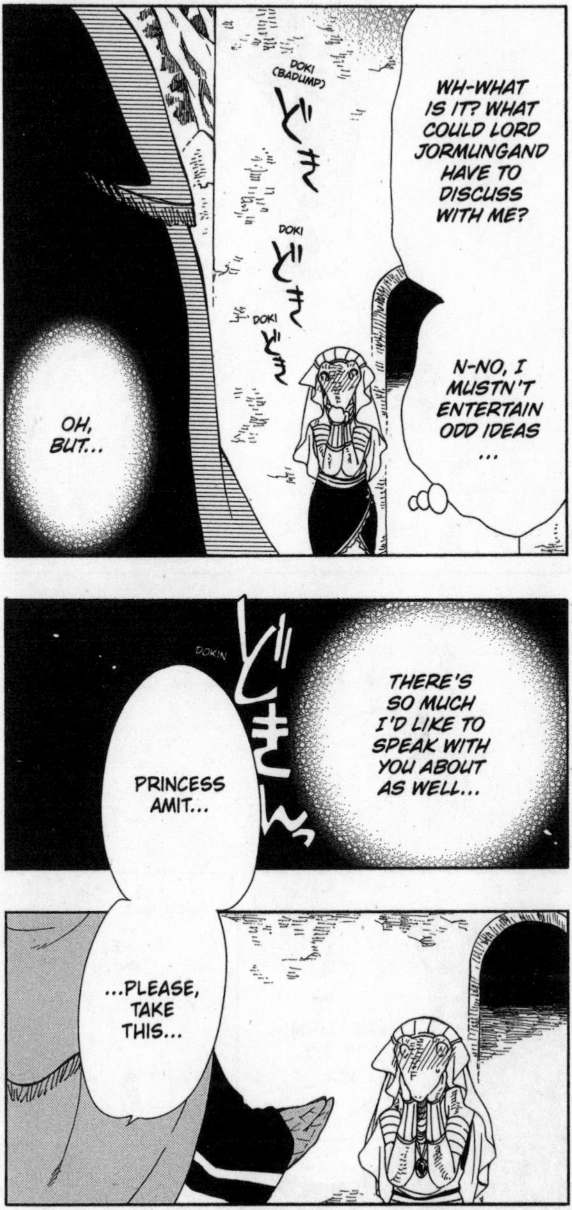
WH-WHAT IS IT? WHAT COULD LORD JORMUNGAND HAVE TO DISCUSS WITH ME?
N-NO, I MUSTN'T ENTERTAIN ODD IDEAS ...
DOKI (BADUMP)
どき
DOKI
どき
DOKI
どき
OH, BUT...
THERE'S SO MUCH I'D LIKE TO SPEAK WITH YOU ABOUT AS WELL...
DOKIN
どきん
PRINCESS AMIT...
...PLEASE, TAKE THIS...

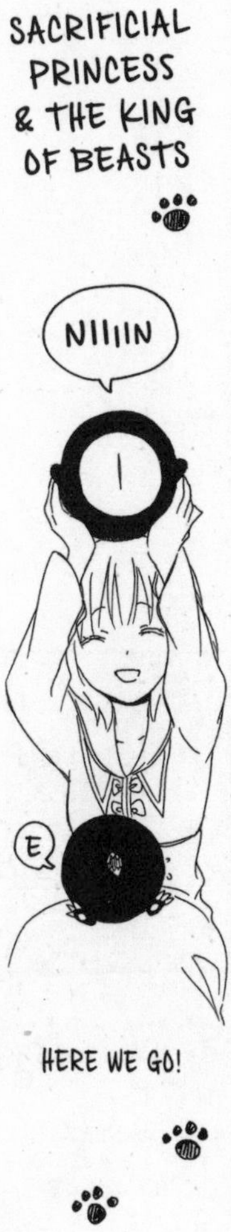
SACRIFICIAL PRINCESS & THE KING OF BEASTS
NIIIIIN
E
HERE WE GO!

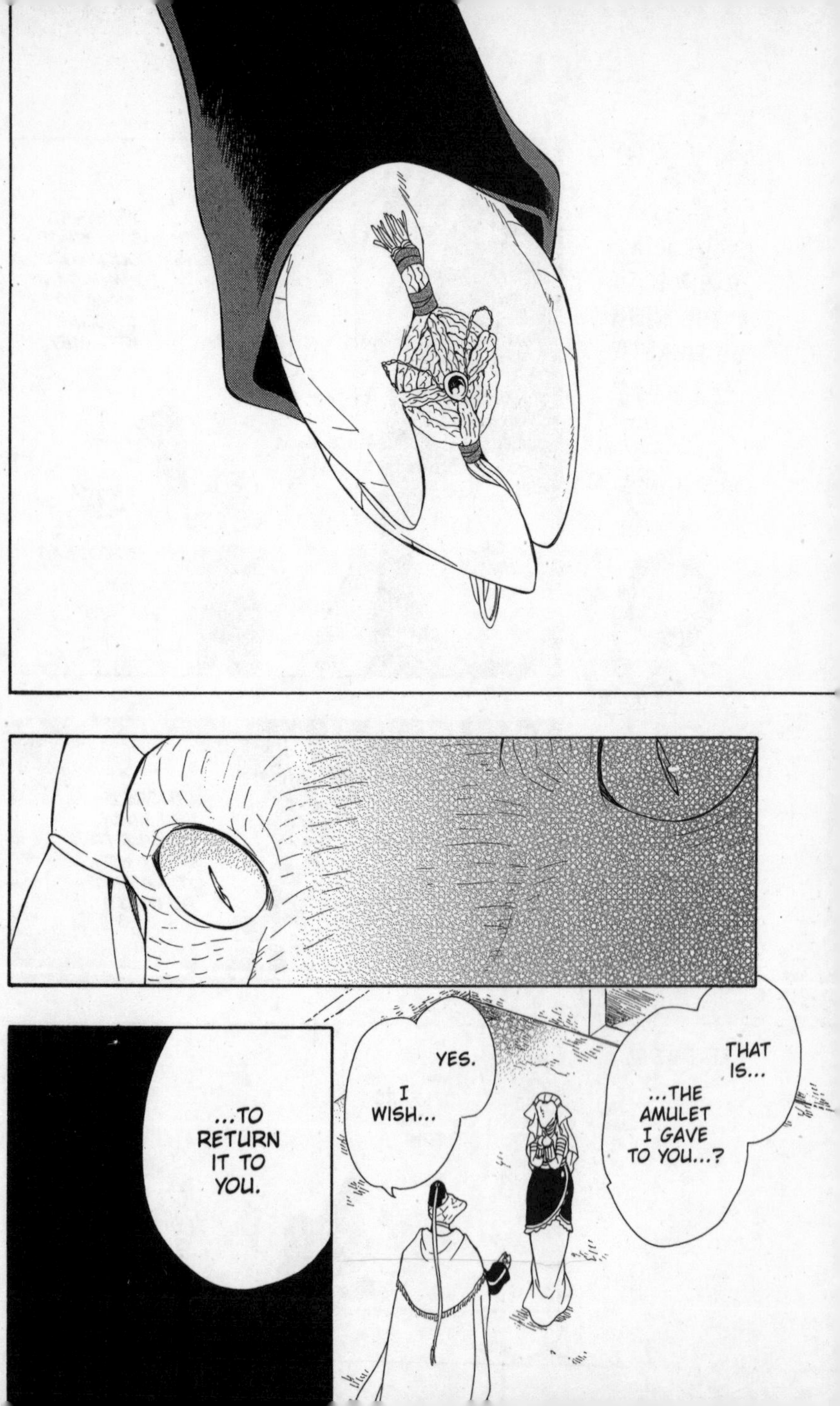
THAT IS...
...THE AMULET I GAVE TO YOU...?
YES.
I WISH...
...TO RETURN IT TO YOU.

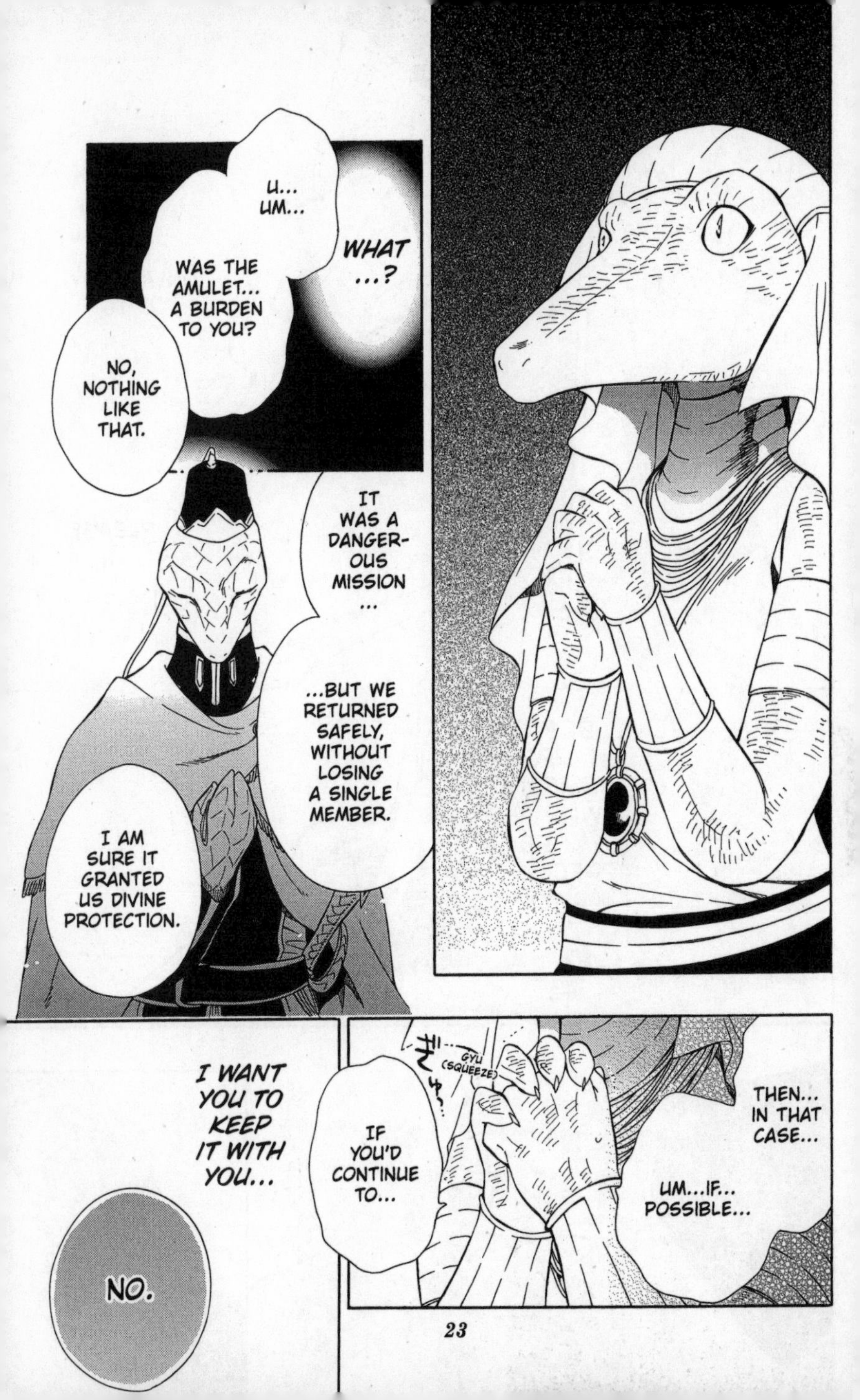
WHAT ...?
U... UM...
WAS THE AMULET... A BURDEN TO YOU?
NO, NOTHING LIKE THAT.
IT WAS A DANGER-OUS MISSION ...
...BUT WE RETURNED SAFELY, WITHOUT LOSING A SINGLE MEMBER.
I AM SURE IT GRANTED US DIVINE PROTECTION.
THEN... IN THAT CASE...
GYU (SQUEEZE)
UM...IF... POSSIBLE...
IF YOU'D CONTINUE TO...
I WANT YOU TO KEEP IT WITH YOU...
NO.

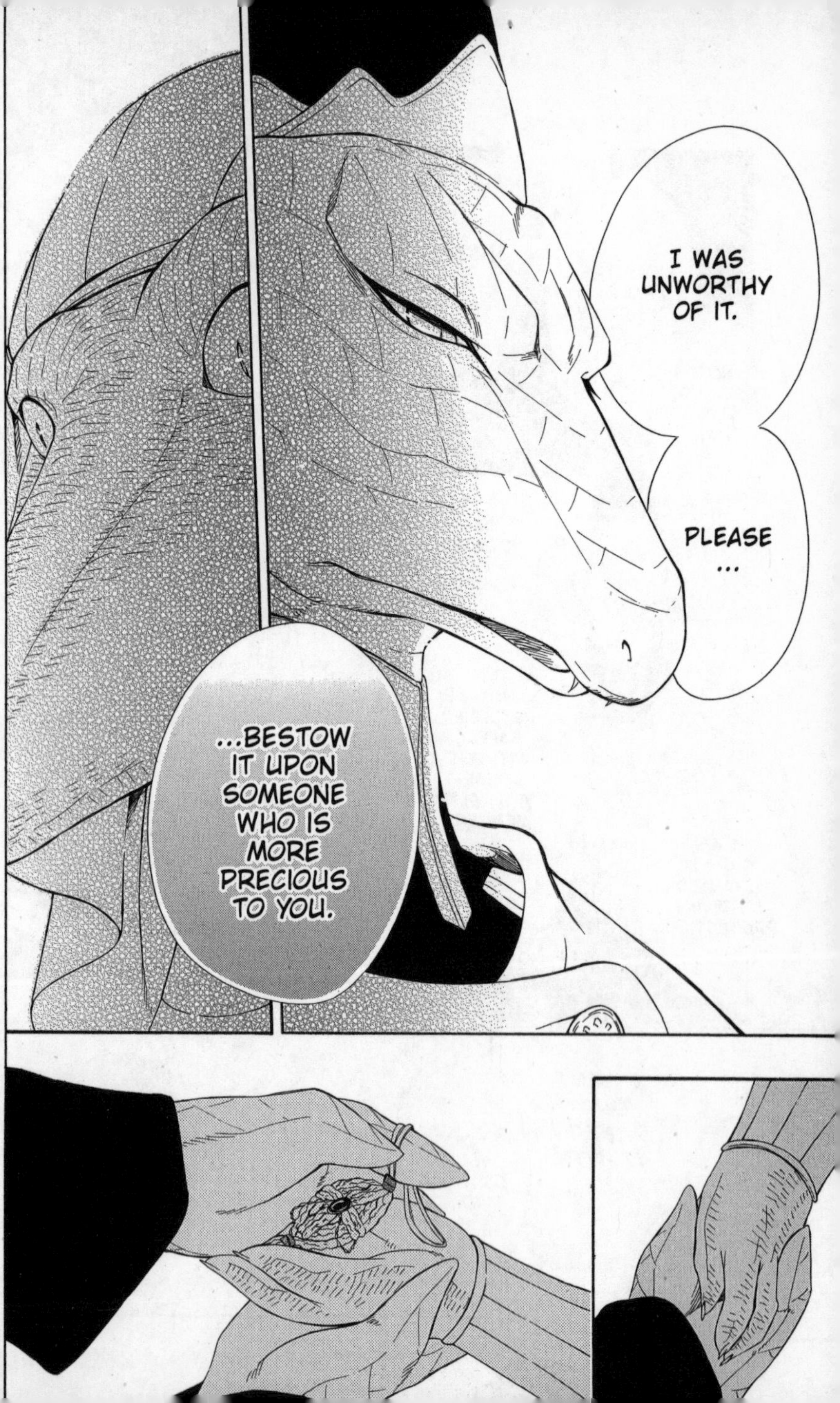
I WAS UNWORTHY OF IT.
PLEASE ...
...BESTOW IT UPON SOMEONE WHO IS MORE PRECIOUS TO YOU.

I'LL TAKE MY LEAVE, THEN.

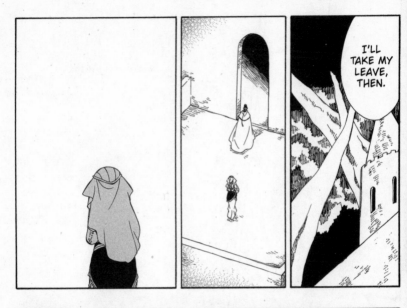

SOMETHING I CAN DO...

A SINGLE BLESSING GOES INTO EACH STITCH...

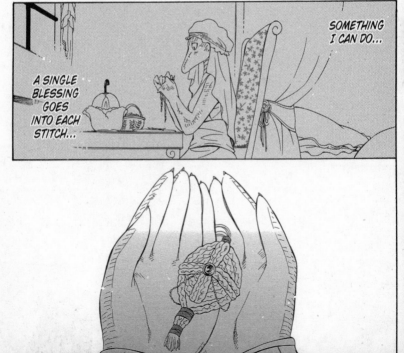

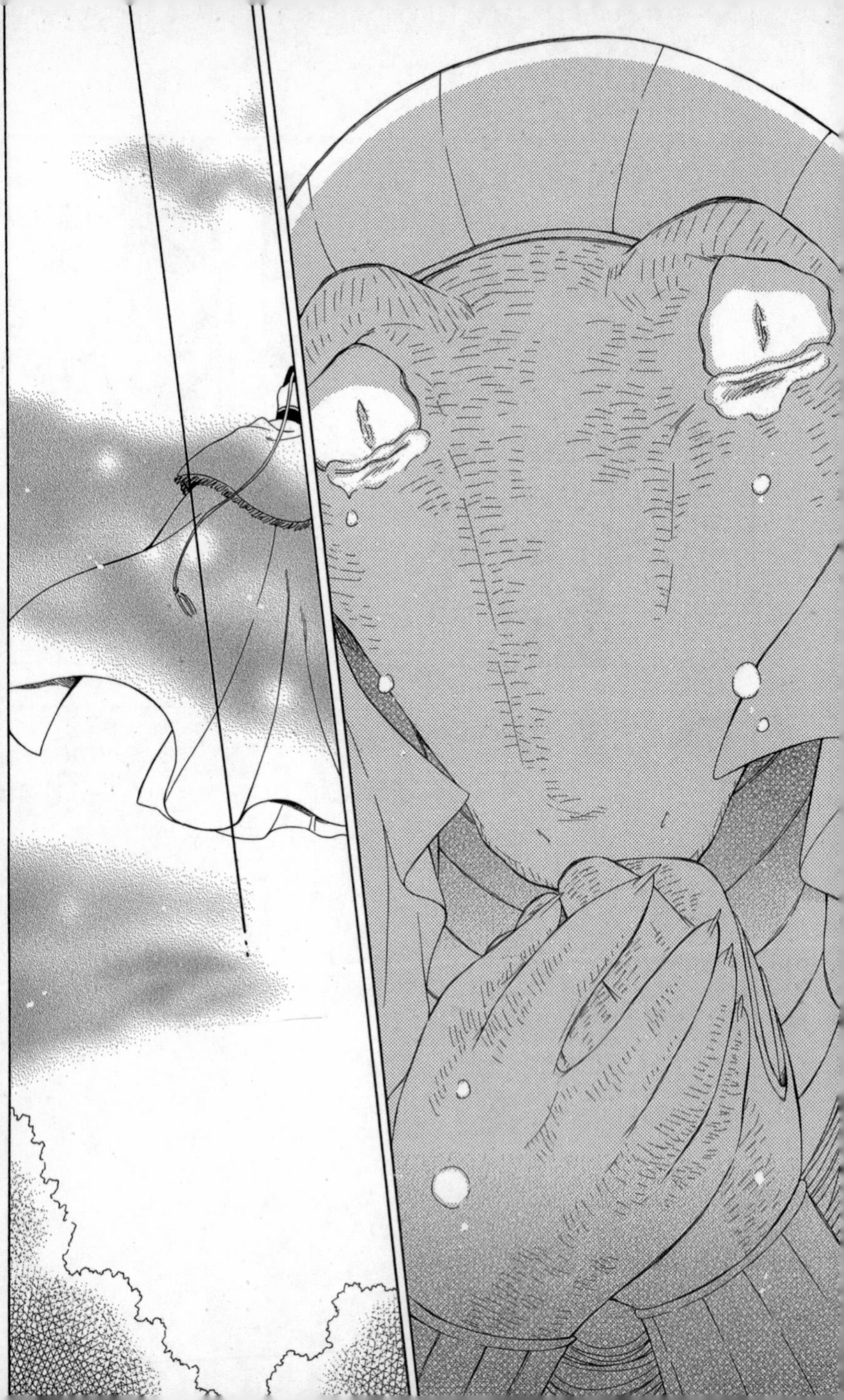

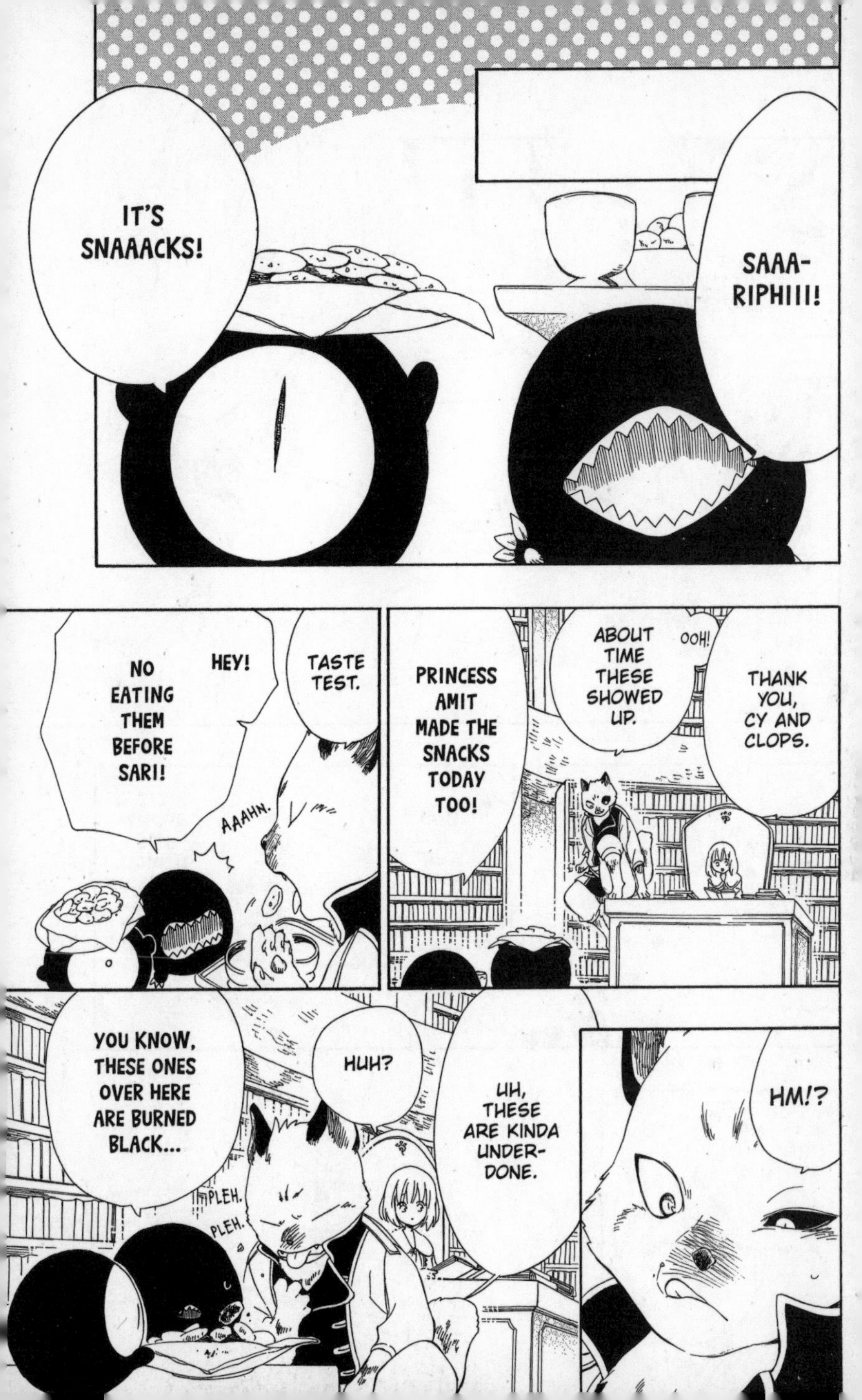
SAAA-RIPHIIII!
IT'S SNAAACKS!
THANK YOU, CY AND CLOPS.
OOH!
ABOUT TIME THESE SHOWED UP.
PRINCESS AMIT MADE THE SNACKS TODAY TOO!
TASTE TEST.
HEY!
NO EATING THEM BEFORE SARI!
AAAHN.
HM!?
UH, THESE ARE KINDA UNDER-DONE.
HUH?
YOU KNOW, THESE ONES OVER HERE ARE BURNED BLACK...
PLEH.
PLEH.

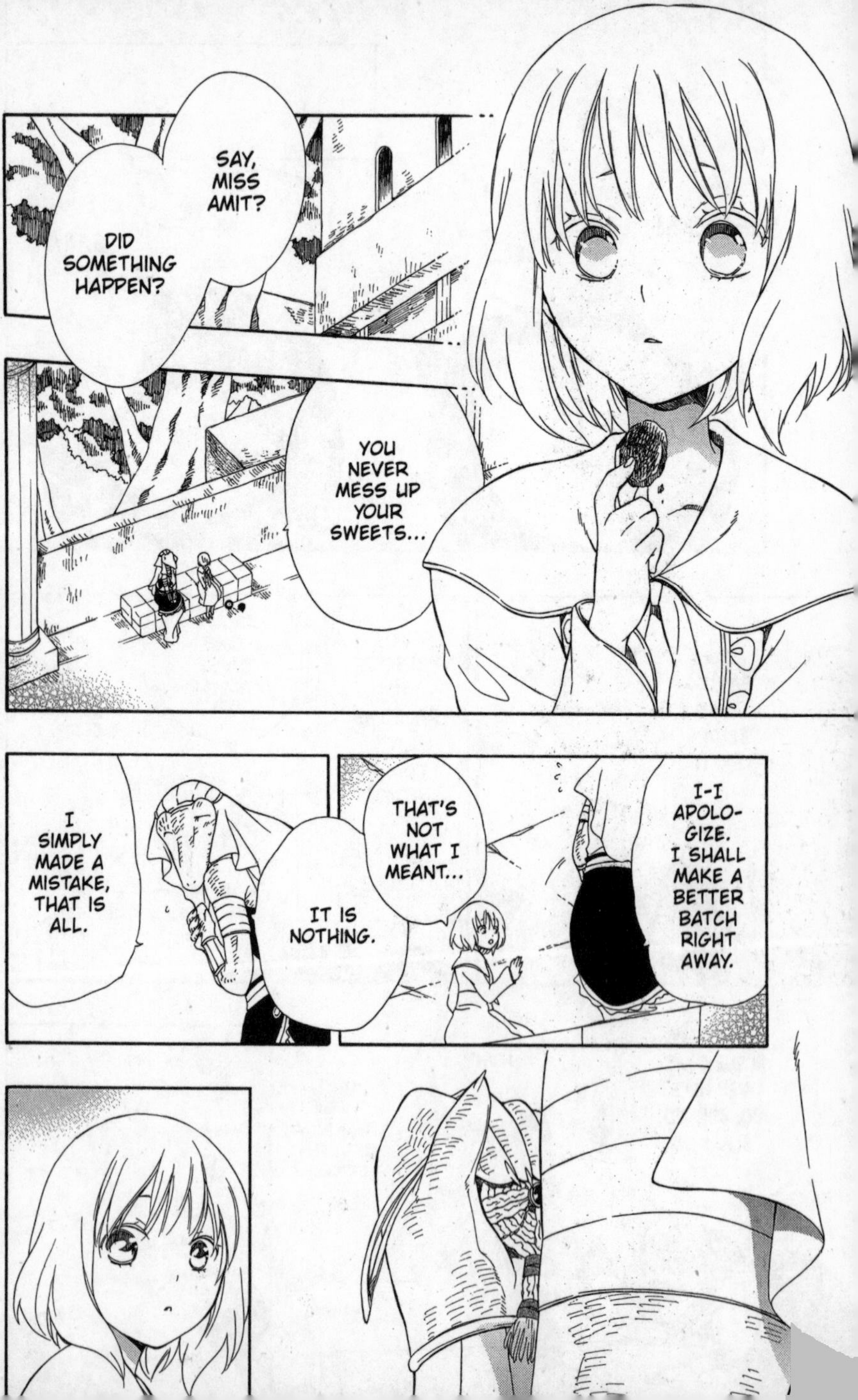
SAY, MISS AMIT?
DID SOMETHING HAPPEN?
YOU NEVER MESS UP YOUR SWEETS...
I-I APOLOGIZE. I SHALL MAKE A BETTER BATCH RIGHT AWAY.
THAT'S NOT WHAT I MEANT...
IT IS NOTHING.
I SIMPLY MADE A MISTAKE, THAT IS ALL.

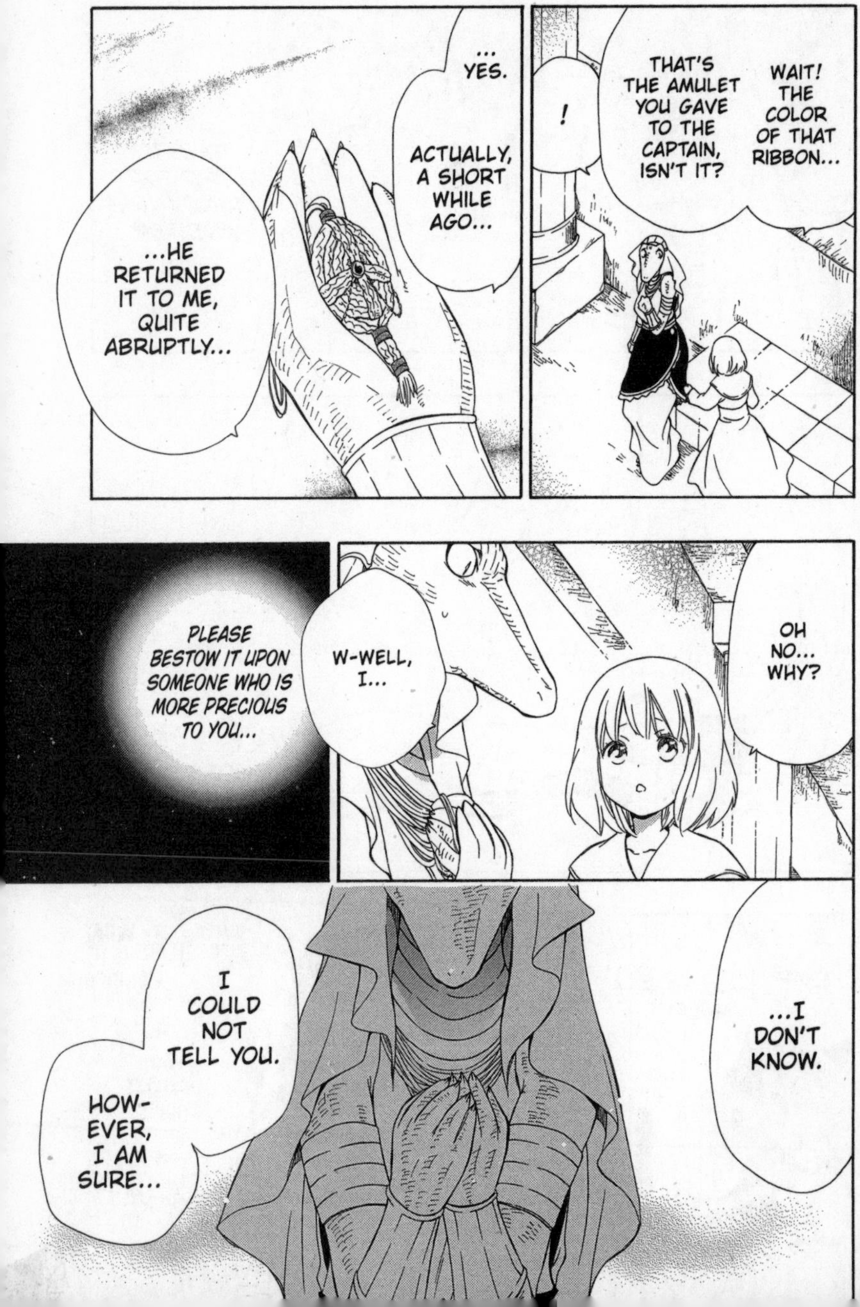
WAIT! THE COLOR OF THAT RIBBON...
THAT'S THE AMULET YOU GAVE TO THE CAPTAIN, ISN'T IT?
!
...YES.
ACTUALLY, A SHORT WHILE AGO...
...HE RETURNED IT TO ME, QUITE ABRUPTLY...
OH NO... WHY?
W-WELL, I...
PLEASE BESTOW IT UPON SOMEONE WHO IS MORE PRECIOUS TO YOU...
...I DON'T KNOW.
I COULD NOT TELL YOU.
HOW-EVER, I AM SURE...

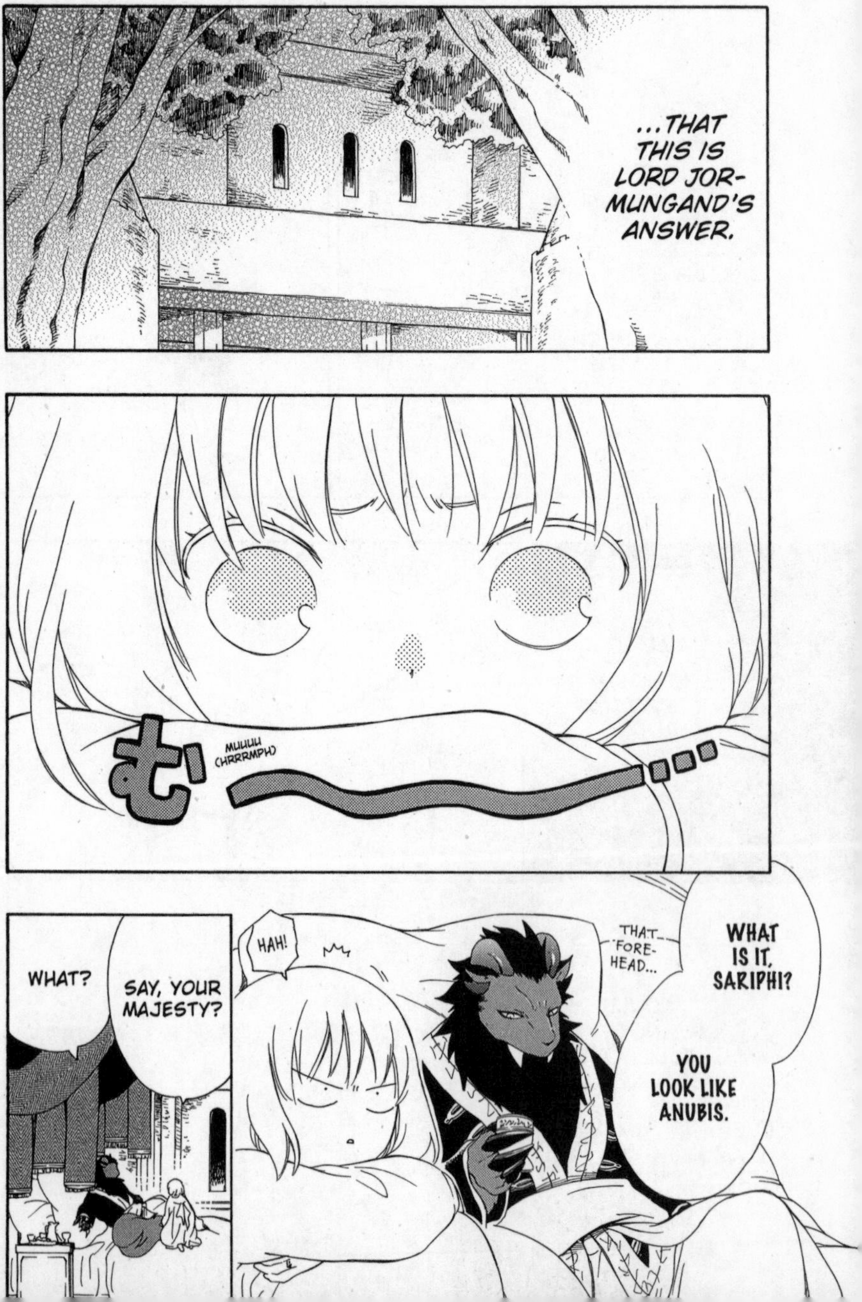
...THAT THIS IS LORD JOR-MUNGAND'S ANSWER.
む
MUUUU (HRRRMPH)
WHAT IS IT, SARIPHI?
THAT FORE-HEAD...
HAH!
YOU LOOK LIKE ANUBIS.
SAY, YOUR MAJESTY?
WHAT?

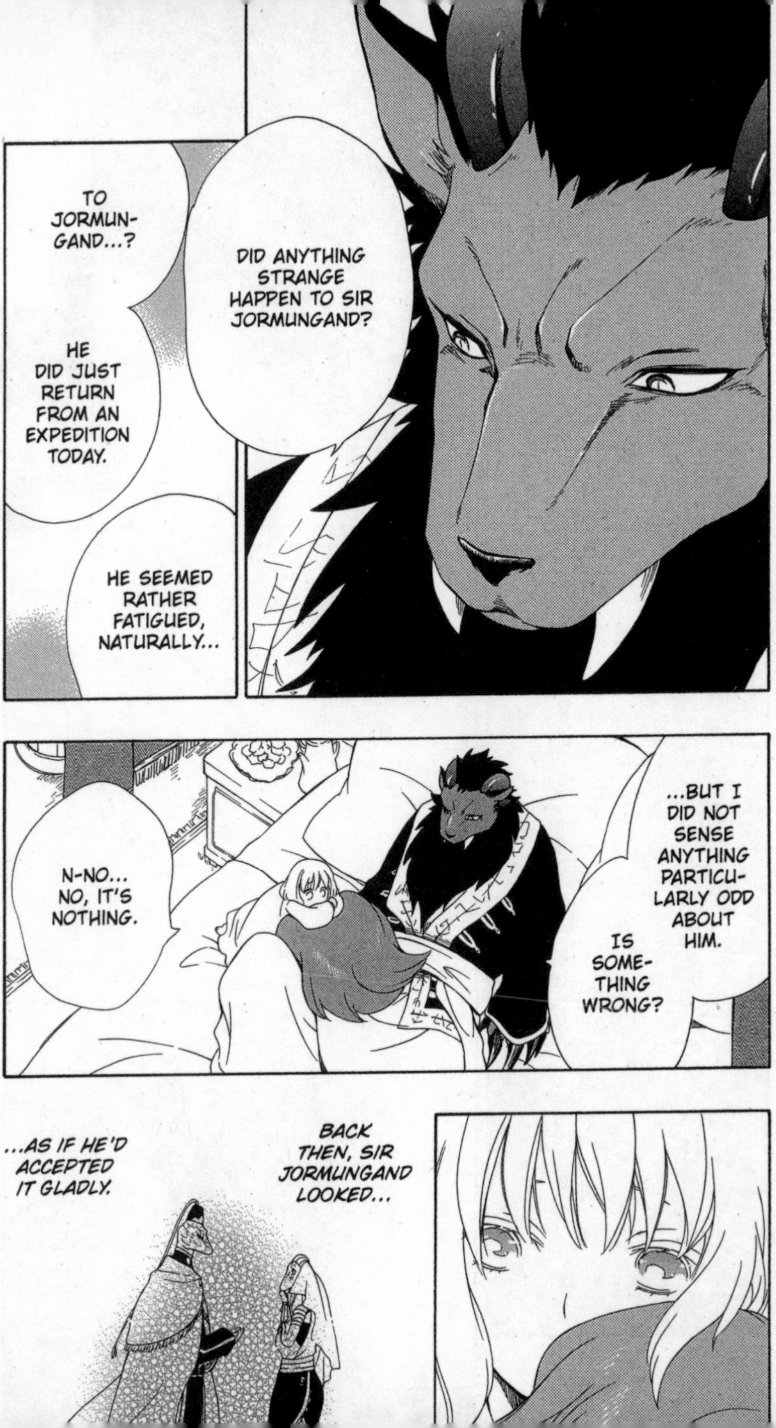
DID ANYTHING STRANGE HAPPEN TO SIR JORMUNGAND?
TO JORMUNGAND...?
HE DID JUST RETURN FROM AN EXPEDITION TODAY.
HE SEEMED RATHER FATIGUED, NATURALLY...
...BUT I DID NOT SENSE ANYTHING PARTICULARLY ODD ABOUT HIM.
IS SOMETHING WRONG?
N-NO... NO, IT'S NOTHING.
BACK THEN, SIR JORMUNGAND LOOKED...
...AS IF HE'D ACCEPTED IT GLADLY.

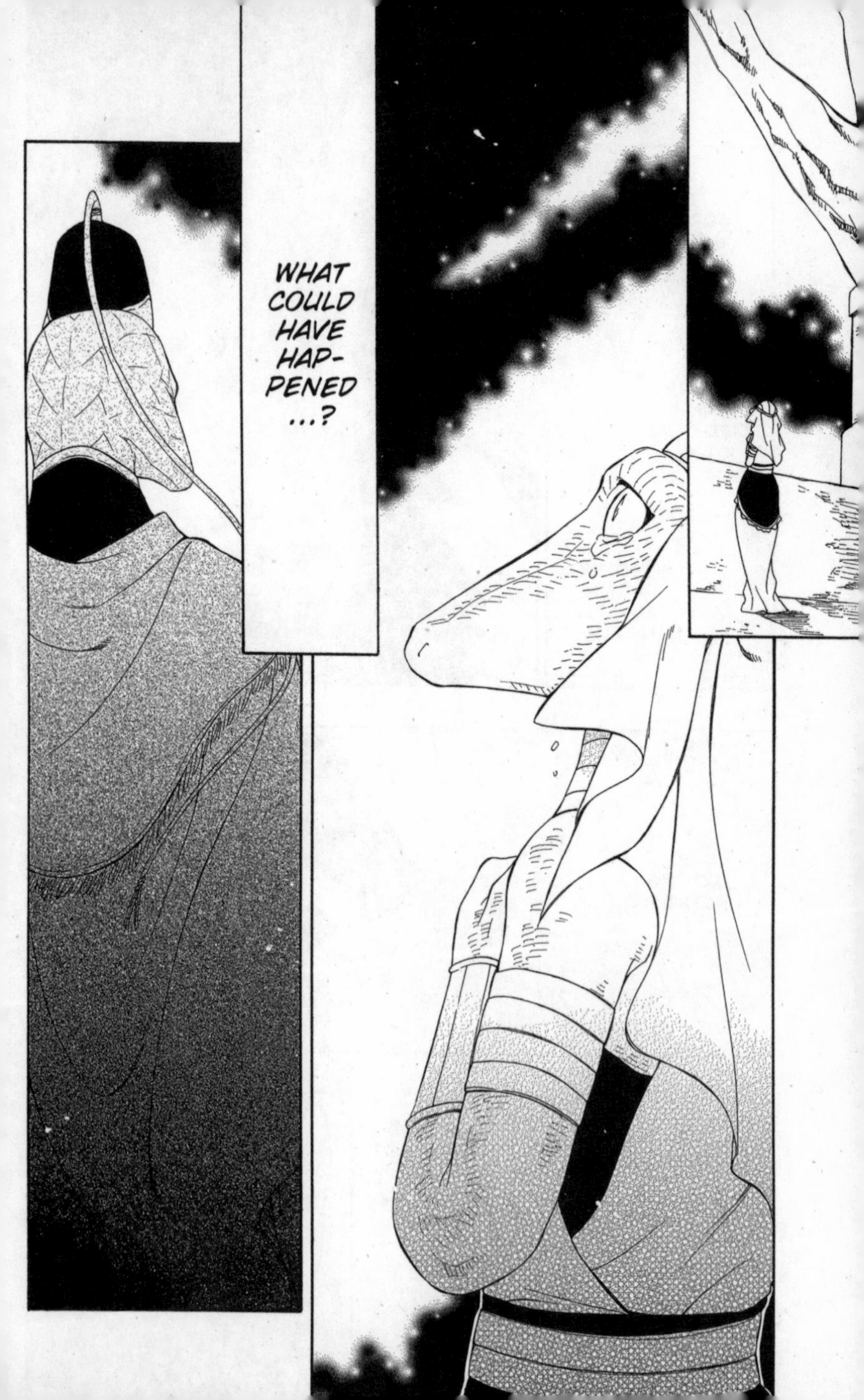
WHAT COULD HAVE HAP-PENED ...?

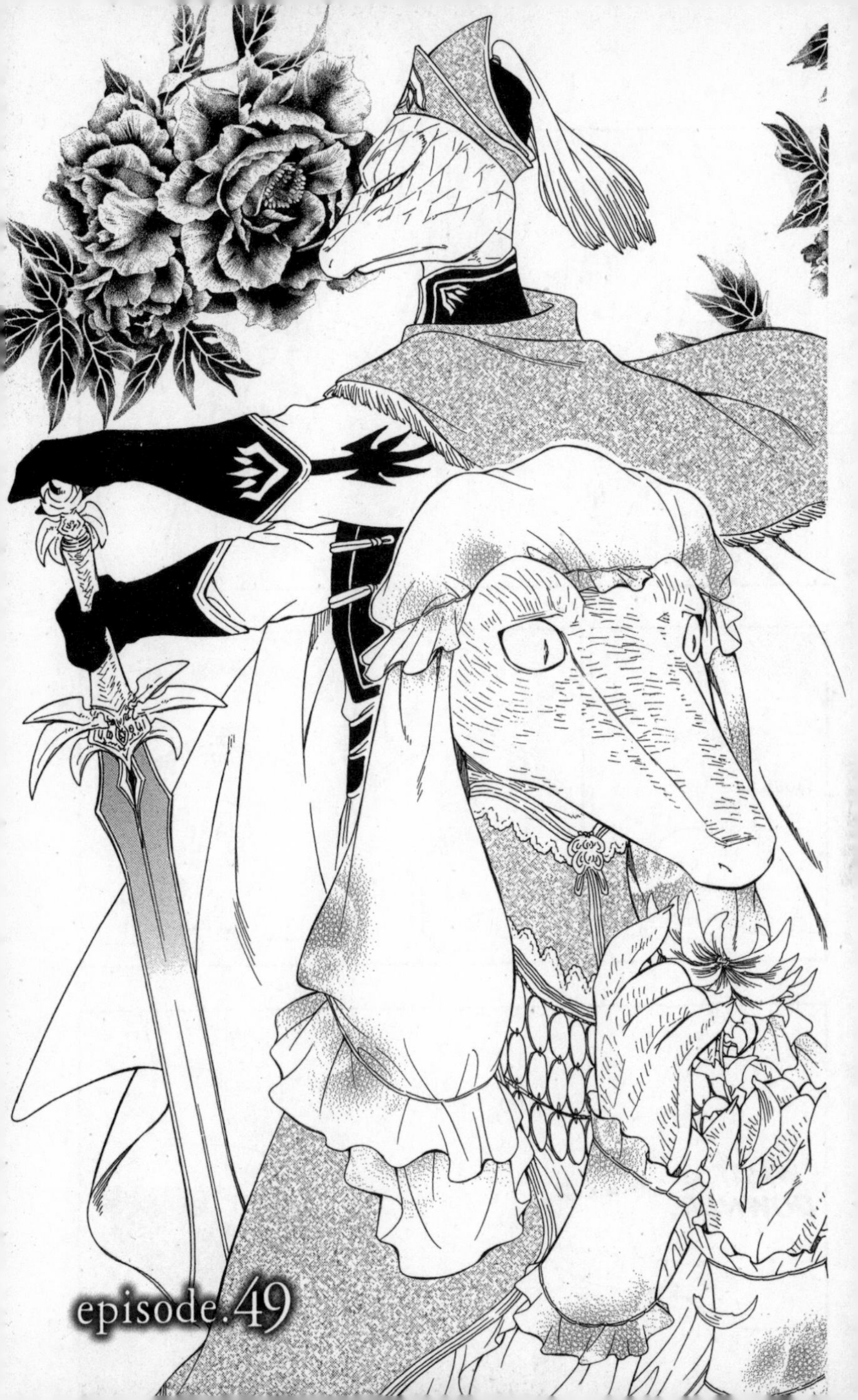
episode.49

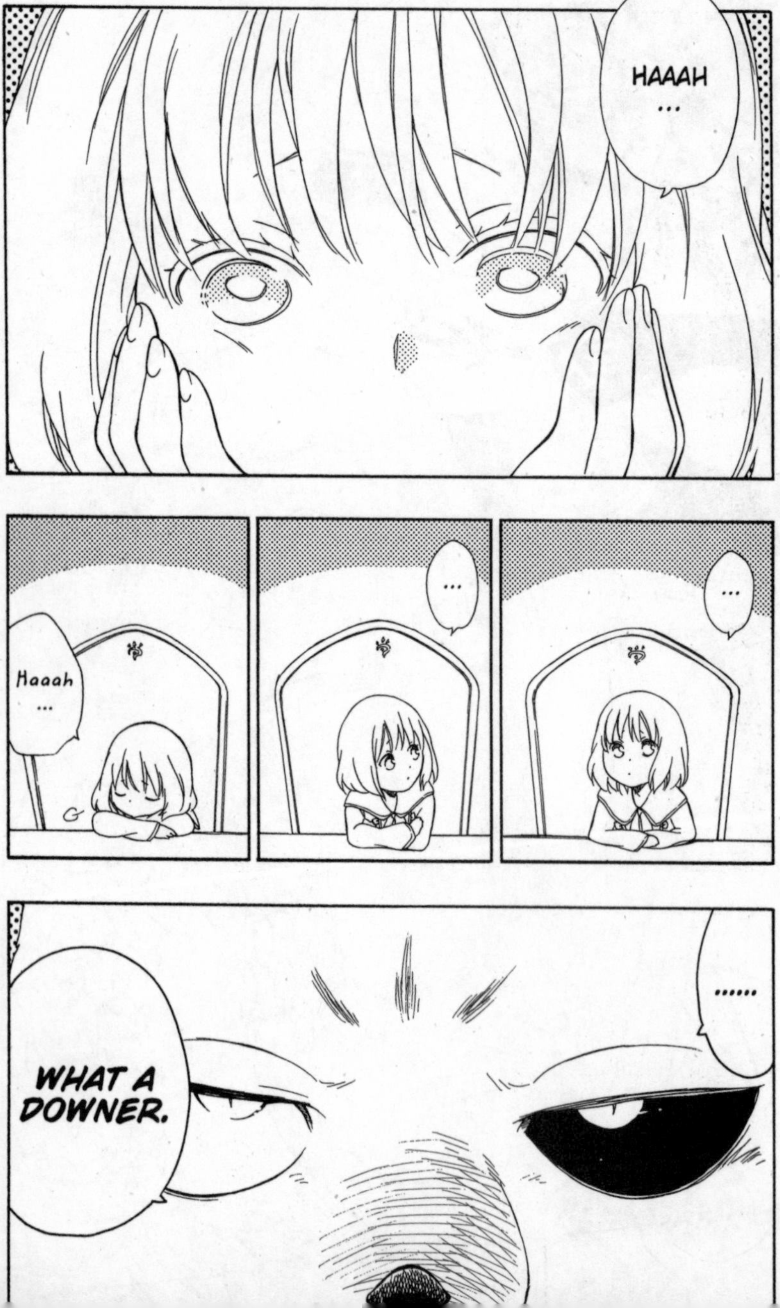
HAAAH ...
...
...
Haaah ...
......
WHAT A DOWNER.

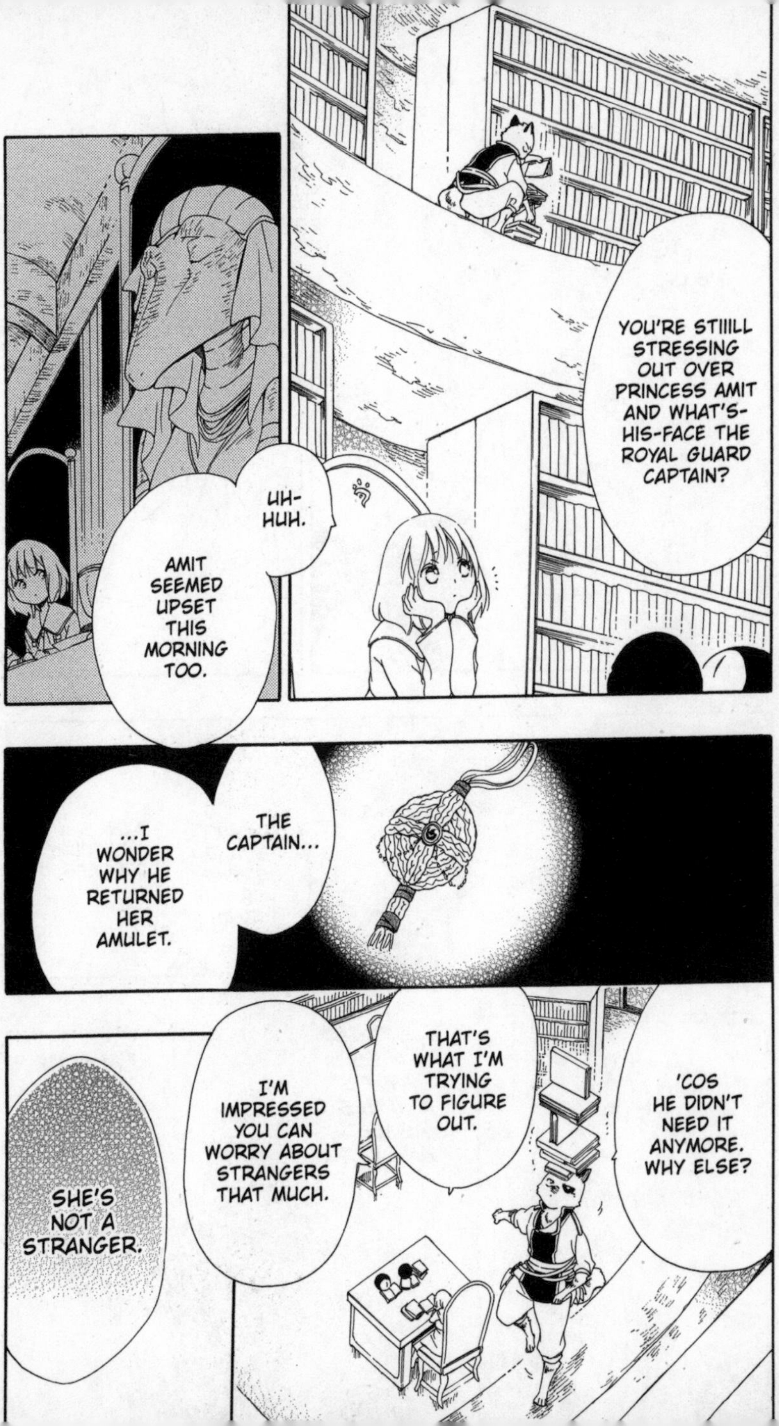
YOU'RE STIIILL STRESSING OUT OVER PRINCESS AMIT AND WHAT'S-HIS-FACE THE ROYAL GUARD CAPTAIN?
UH-HUH.
AMIT SEEMED UPSET THIS MORNING TOO.
THE CAPTAIN...
...I WONDER WHY HE RETURNED HER AMULET.
'COS HE DIDN'T NEED IT ANYMORE. WHY ELSE?
THAT'S WHAT I'M TRYING TO FIGURE OUT.
I'M IMPRESSED YOU CAN WORRY ABOUT STRANGERS THAT MUCH.
SHE'S NOT A STRANGER.

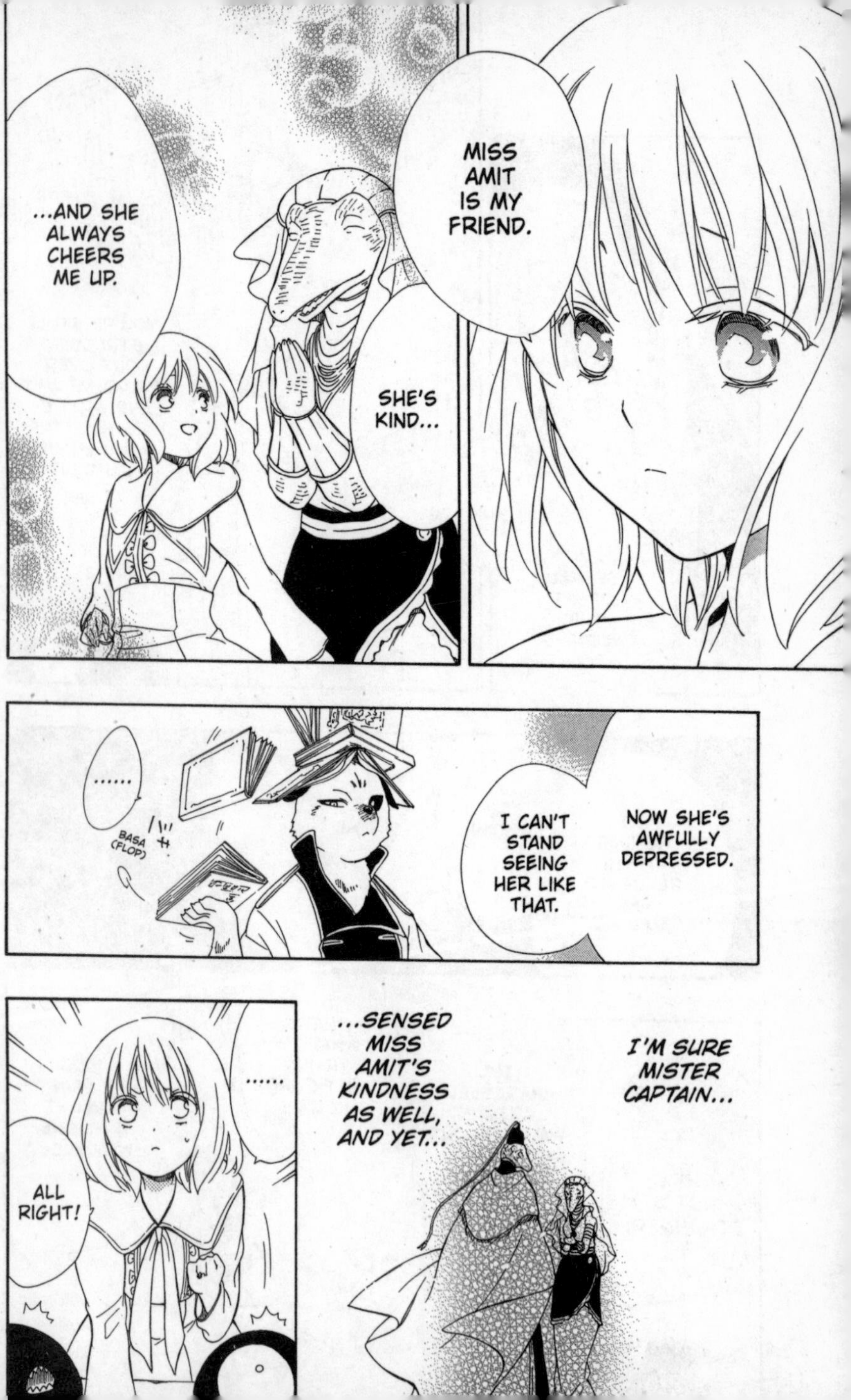
MISS AMIT IS MY FRIEND.
SHE'S KIND...
...AND SHE ALWAYS CHEERS ME UP.
NOW SHE'S AWFULLY DEPRESSED.
I CAN'T STAND SEEING HER LIKE THAT.
......
BASA (FLOP)
I'M SURE MISTER CAPTAIN...
...SENSED MISS AMIT'S KINDNESS AS WELL, AND YET...
......
ALL RIGHT!

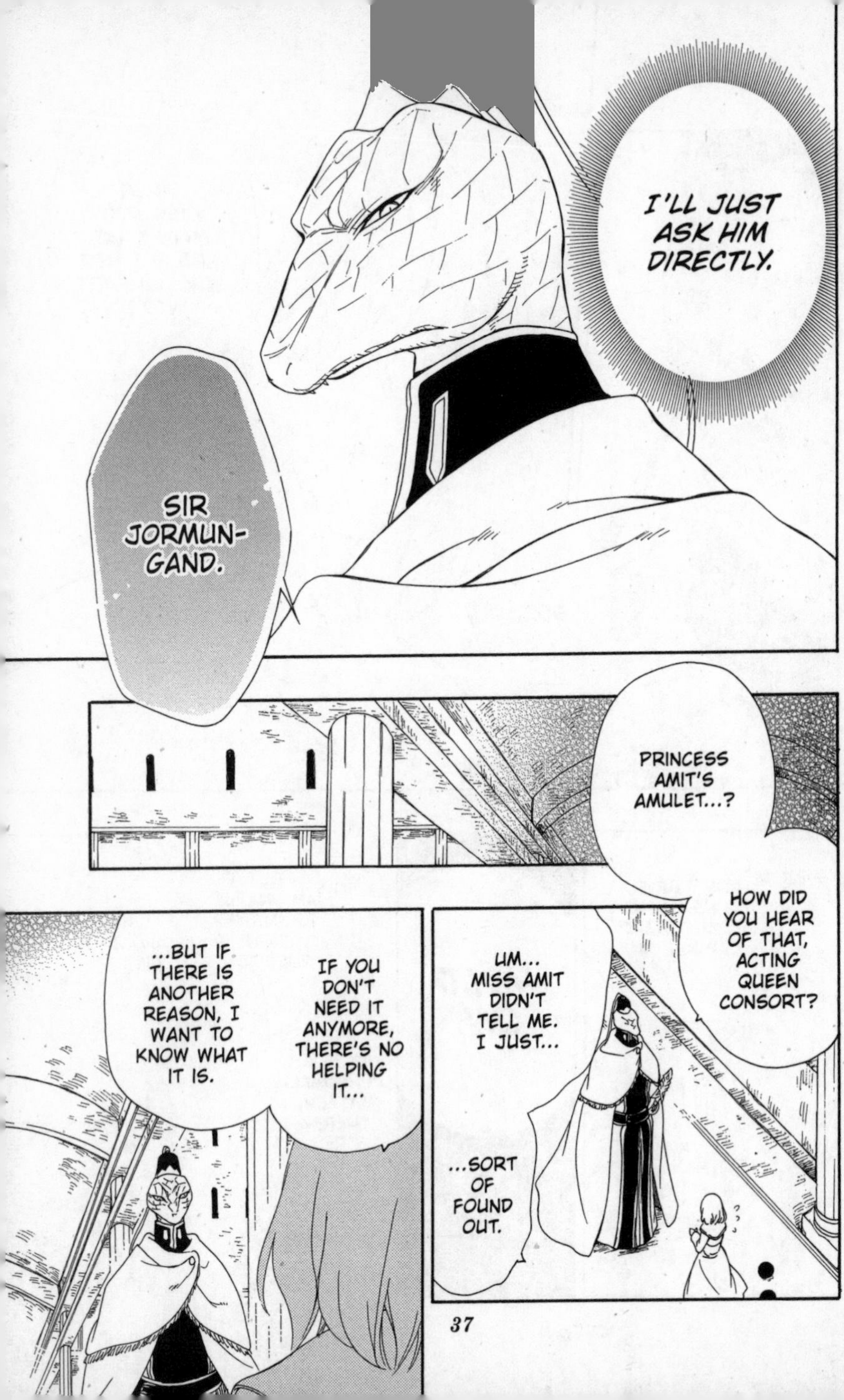
I'LL JUST ASK HIM DIRECTLY.
SIR JORMUN-GAND.
PRINCESS AMIT'S AMULET...?
HOW DID YOU HEAR OF THAT, ACTING QUEEN CONSORT?
UM... MISS AMIT DIDN'T TELL ME. I JUST...
...SORT OF FOUND OUT.
IF YOU DON'T NEED IT ANYMORE, THERE'S NO HELPING IT...
...BUT IF THERE IS ANOTHER REASON, I WANT TO KNOW WHAT IT IS.

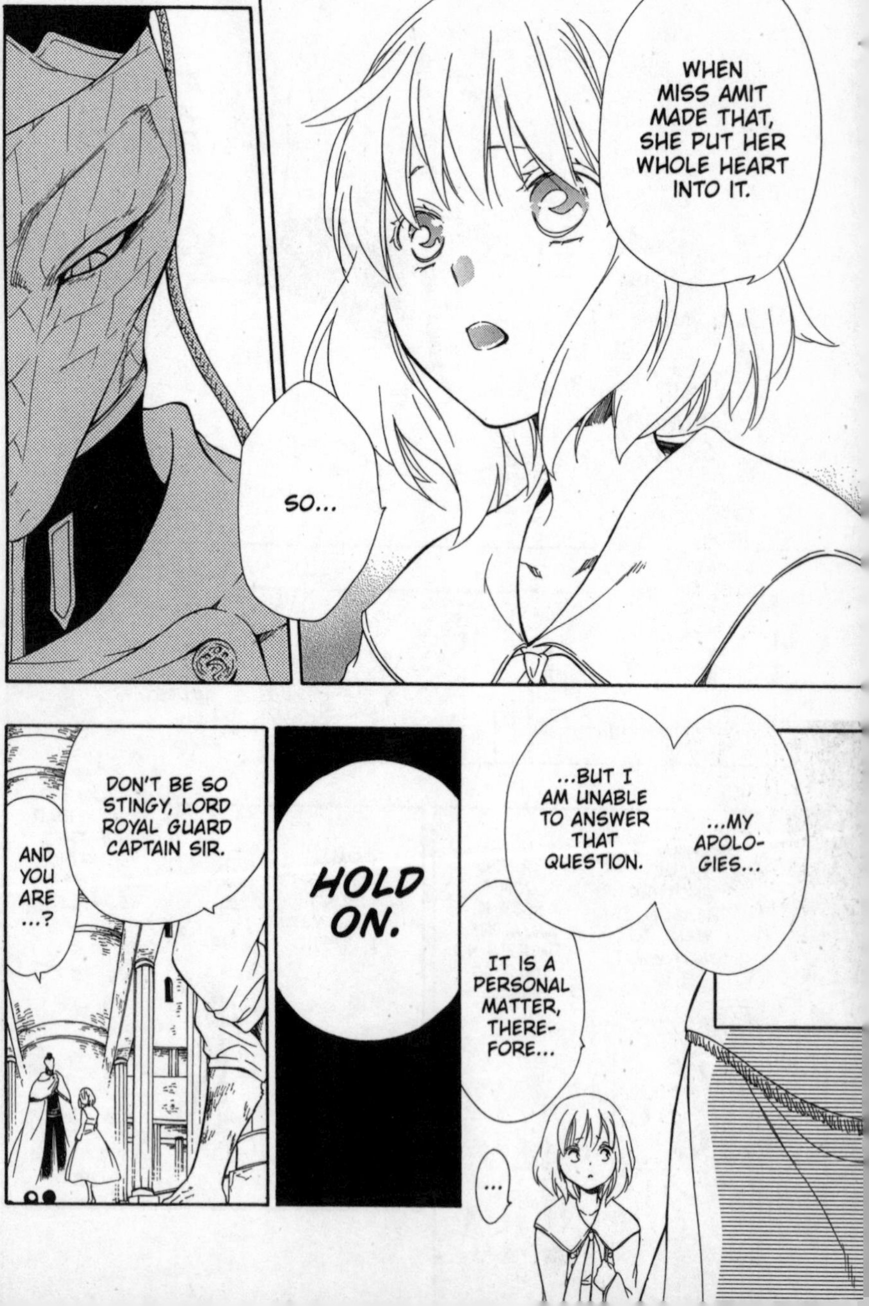
WHEN MISS AMIT MADE THAT, SHE PUT HER WHOLE HEART INTO IT.
SO...
...MY APOLO-GIES...
...BUT I AM UNABLE TO ANSWER THAT QUESTION.
IT IS A PERSONAL MATTER, THERE-FORE...
...
HOLD ON.
DON'T BE SO STINGY, LORD ROYAL GUARD CAPTAIN SIR.
AND YOU ARE ...?

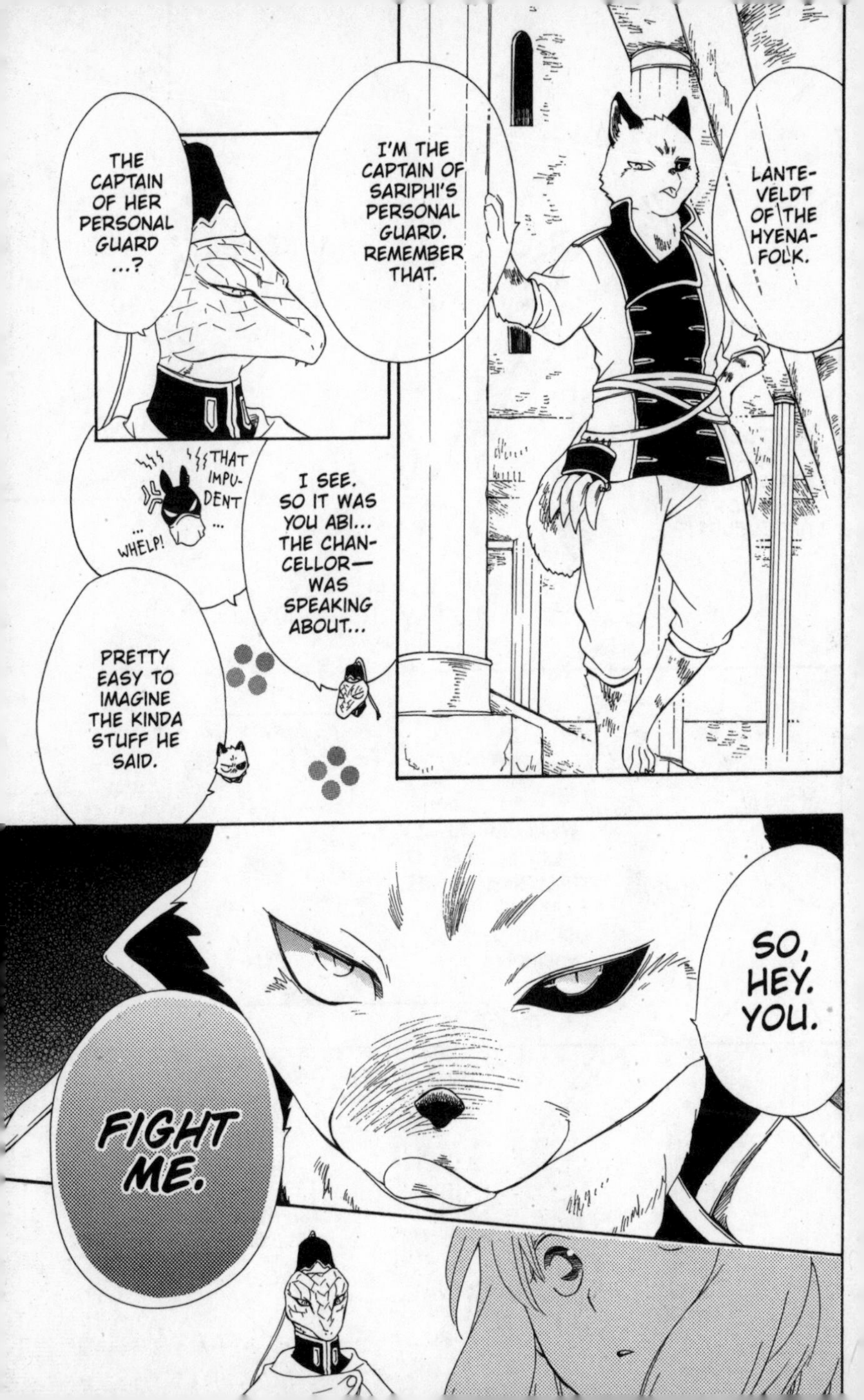
LANTE-VELDT OF THE HYENA-FOLK.
I'M THE CAPTAIN OF SARIPHI'S PERSONAL GUARD. REMEMBER THAT.
THE CAPTAIN OF HER PERSONAL GUARD ...?
I SEE. SO IT WAS YOU ABI... THE CHAN-CELLOR— WAS SPEAKING ABOUT...
THAT IMPU-DENT... ...WHELP!
PRETTY EASY TO IMAGINE THE KINDA STUFF HE SAID.
SO, HEY. YOU.
FIGHT ME.

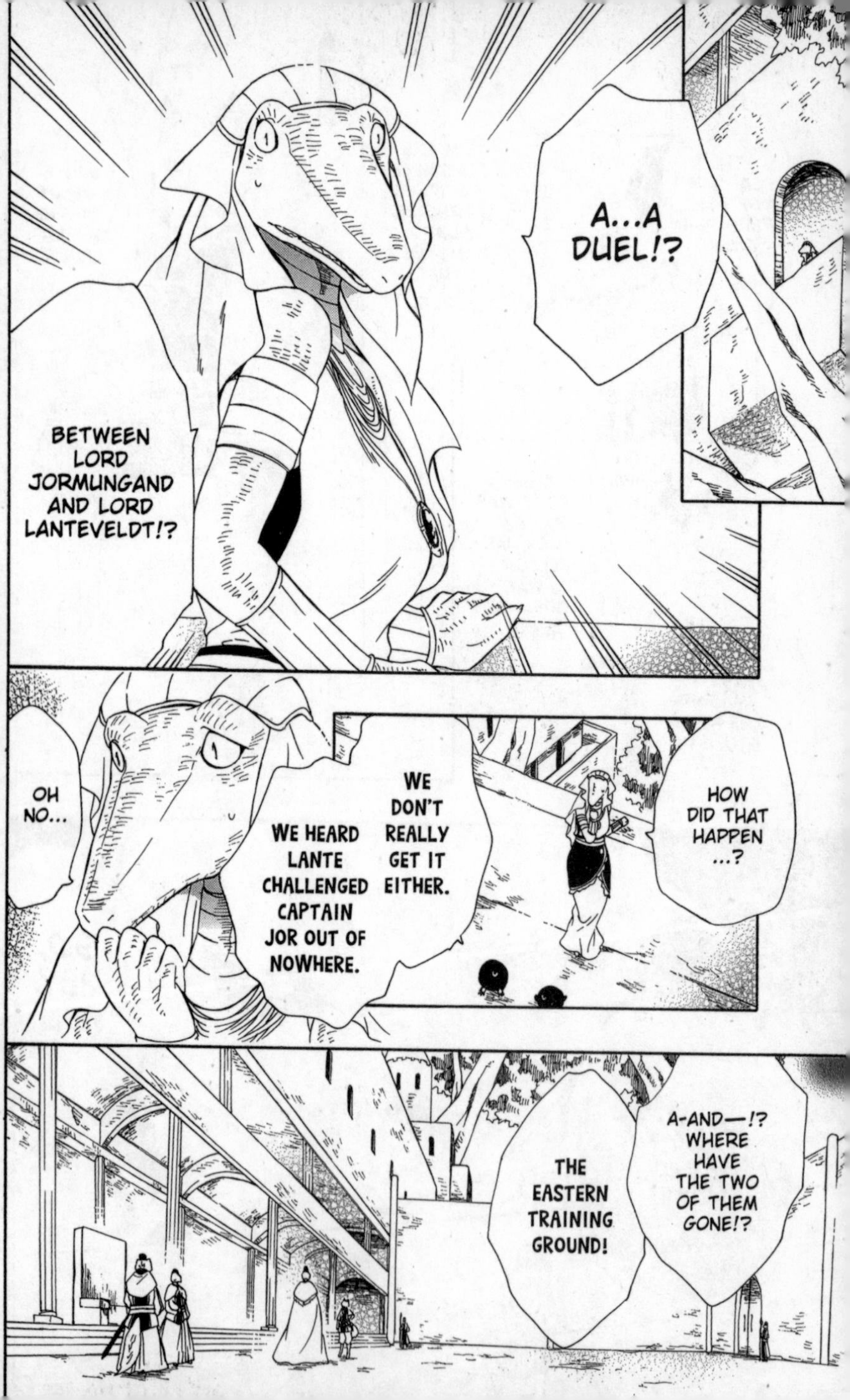
A...A DUEL!?
BETWEEN LORD JORMUNGAND AND LORD LANTEVELDT!?
HOW DID THAT HAPPEN...?
WE DON'T REALLY GET IT EITHER.
WE HEARD LANTE CHALLENGED CAPTAIN JOR OUT OF NOWHERE.
OH NO...
A-AND—!? WHERE HAVE THE TWO OF THEM GONE!?
THE EASTERN TRAINING GROUND!

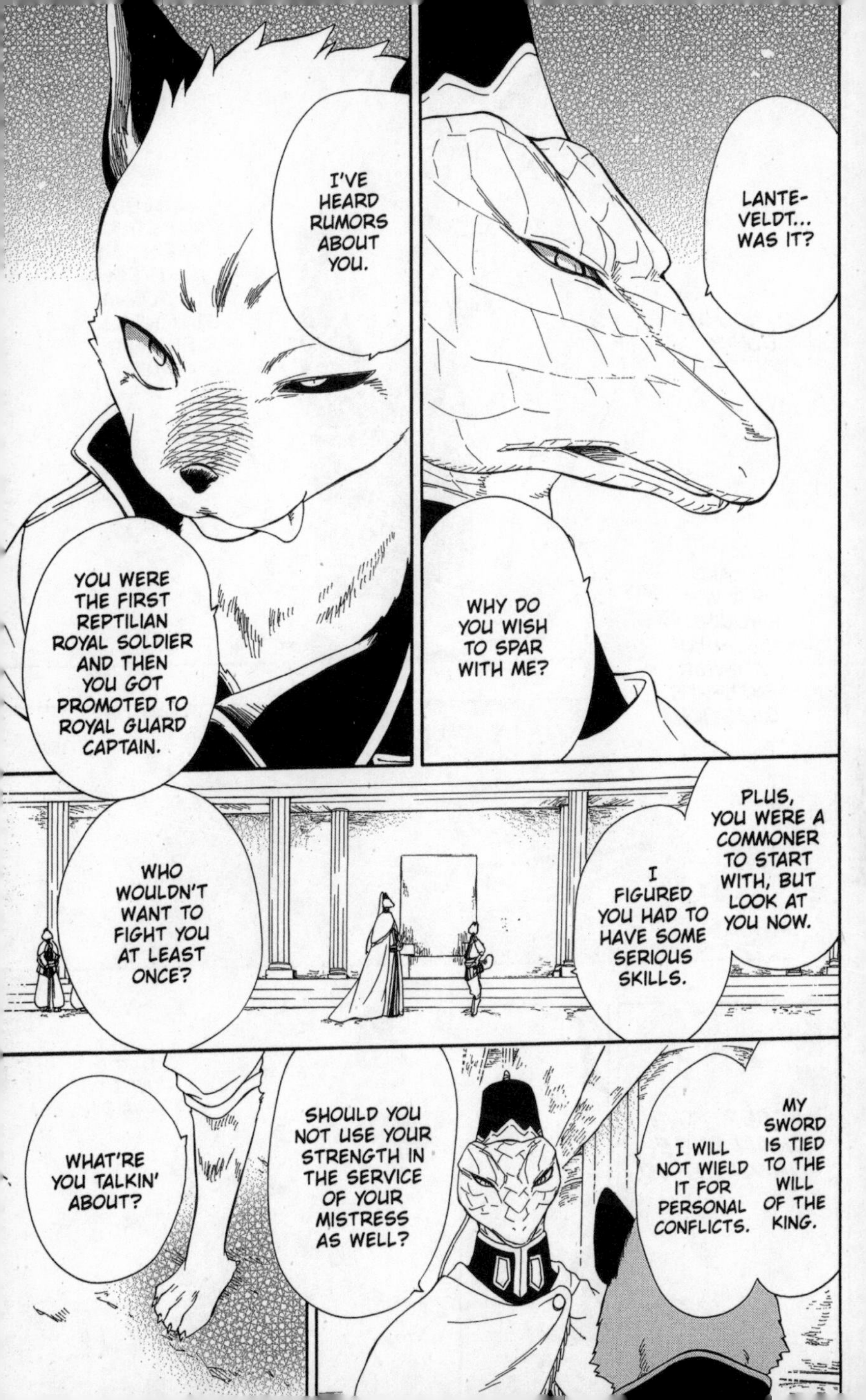
LANTE-VELDT... WAS IT?
WHY DO YOU WISH TO SPAR WITH ME?
I'VE HEARD RUMORS ABOUT YOU.
YOU WERE THE FIRST REPTILIAN ROYAL SOLDIER AND THEN YOU GOT PROMOTED TO ROYAL GUARD CAPTAIN.
PLUS, YOU WERE A COMMONER TO START WITH, BUT LOOK AT YOU NOW.
I FIGURED YOU HAD TO HAVE SOME SERIOUS SKILLS.
WHO WOULDN'T WANT TO FIGHT YOU AT LEAST ONCE?
MY SWORD IS TIED TO THE WILL OF THE KING.
I WILL NOT WIELD IT FOR PERSONAL CONFLICTS.
SHOULD YOU NOT USE YOUR STRENGTH IN THE SERVICE OF YOUR MISTRESS AS WELL?
WHAT'RE YOU TALKIN' ABOUT?

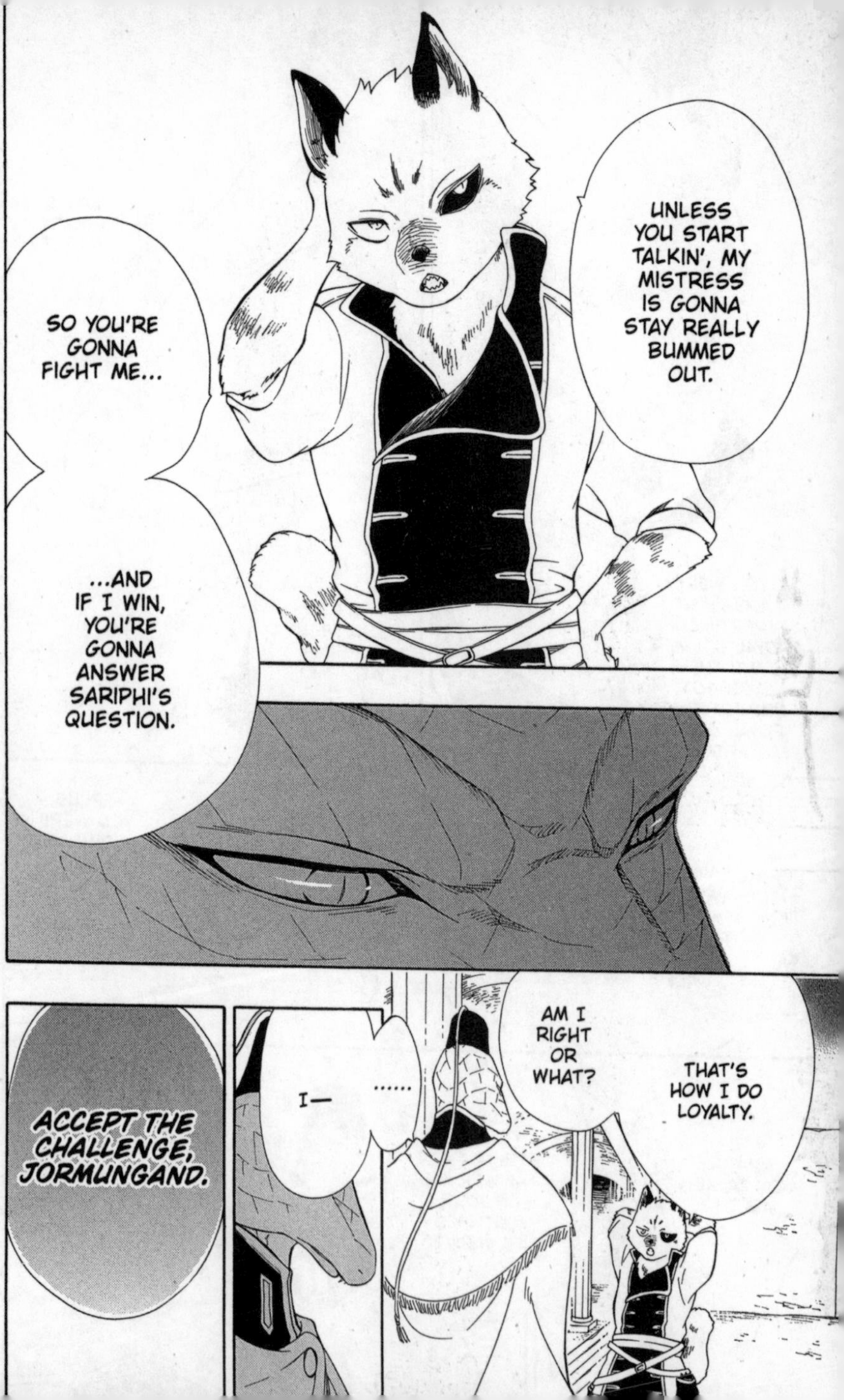
UNLESS YOU START TALKIN', MY MISTRESS IS GONNA STAY REALLY BUMMED OUT.
SO YOU'RE GONNA FIGHT ME...
...AND IF I WIN, YOU'RE GONNA ANSWER SARIPHI'S QUESTION.
THAT'S HOW I DO LOYALTY.
AM I RIGHT OR WHAT?
......
I—
ACCEPT THE CHALLENGE, JORMUNGAND.

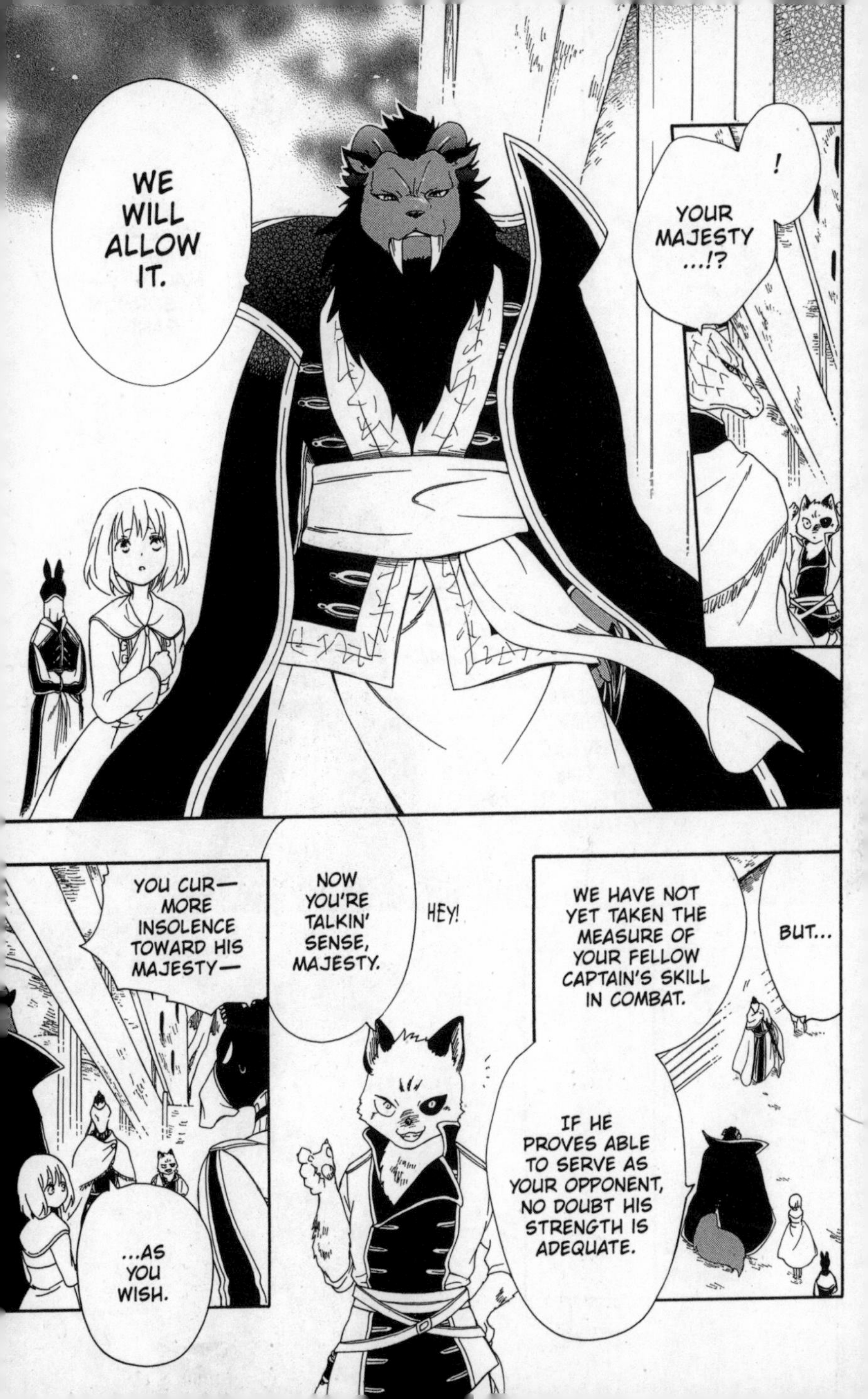
WE WILL ALLOW IT.
!
YOUR MAJESTY ...!?
BUT...
WE HAVE NOT YET TAKEN THE MEASURE OF YOUR FELLOW CAPTAIN'S SKILL IN COMBAT.
IF HE PROVES ABLE TO SERVE AS YOUR OPPONENT, NO DOUBT HIS STRENGTH IS ADEQUATE.
HEY!
NOW YOU'RE TALKIN' SENSE, MAJESTY.
YOU CUR— MORE INSOLENCE TOWARD HIS MAJESTY—
...AS YOU WISH.

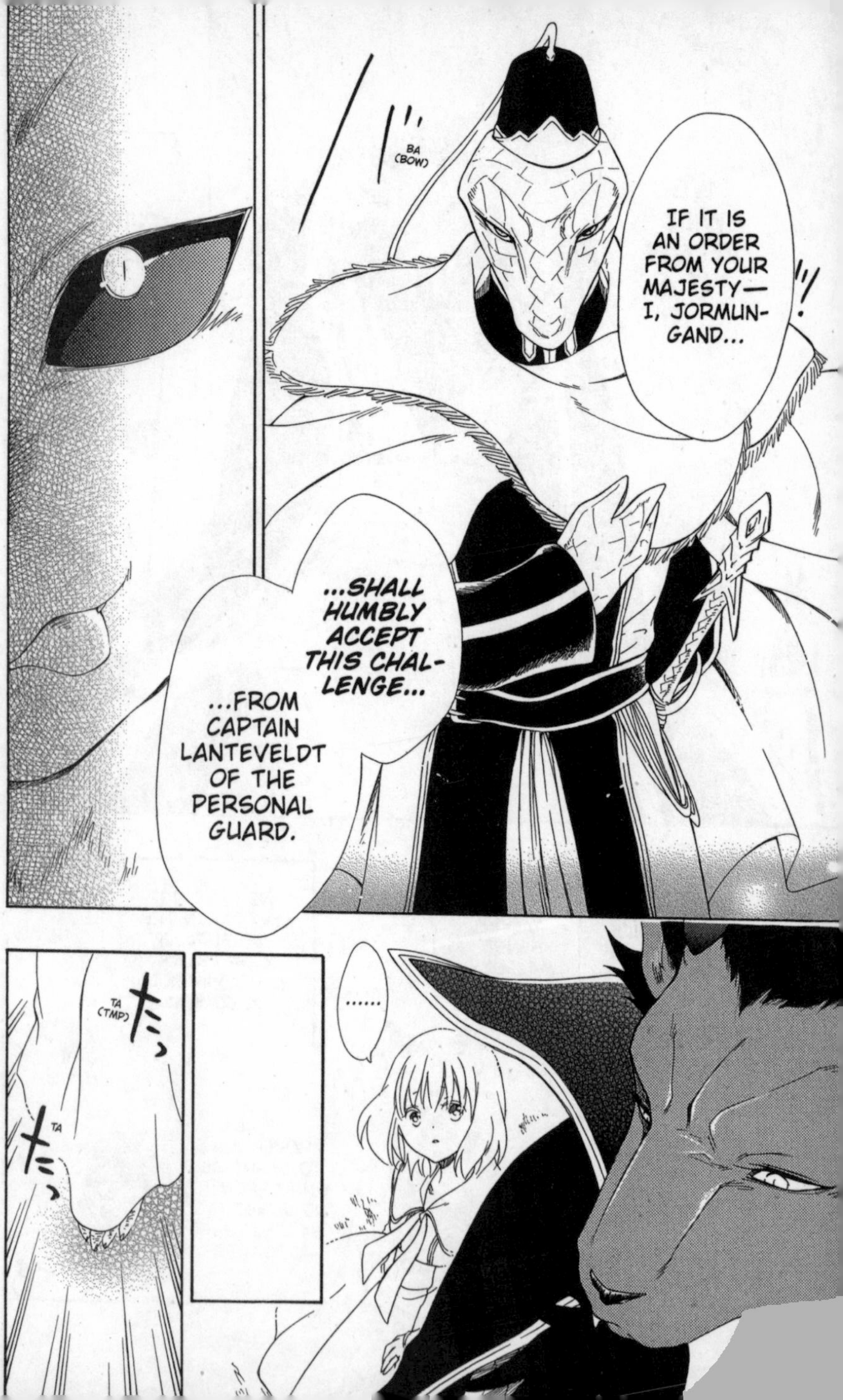
BA (BOW)
IF IT IS AN ORDER FROM YOUR MAJESTY— I, JORMUN-GAND...
...SHALL HUMBLY ACCEPT THIS CHAL-LENGE...
...FROM CAPTAIN LANTEVELDT OF THE PERSONAL GUARD.
......
TA (TMP)
TA

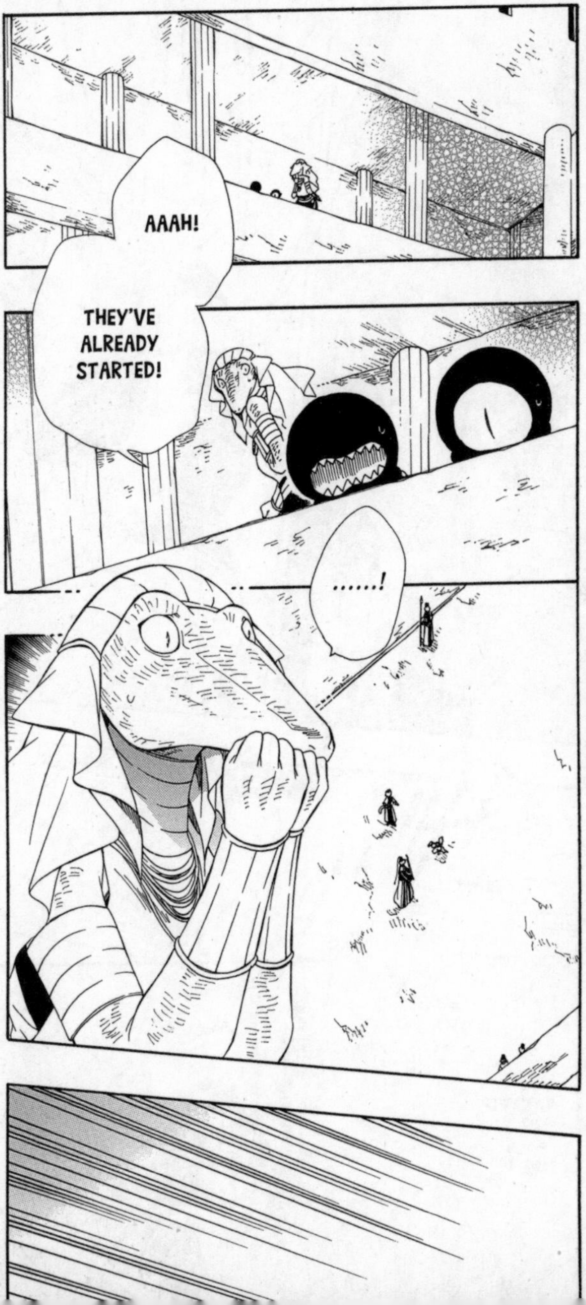
AAAH!
THEY'VE ALREADY STARTED!
......!

HELLO, IT'S TOMOFUJI! *SACRIFICIAL PRINCESS* IS ON VOLUME 9 ALREADY... IT HAPPENED SO FAST. IN THE BEGINNING, I THOUGHT I'D BE THRILLED IF THEY LET ME KEEP GOING FOR THREE VOLUMES OR SO. YET SOMEHOW, BETWEEN THEN AND NOW, THIS IS THE LAST VOLUME OF THE SINGLE DIGITS. WOW... SERIOUSLY, THANK YOU. I'D LIKE TO WORK HARD AND KEEP GOING FOR AS LONG AS I CAN, SO PLEASE ENJOY VOLUME 9!

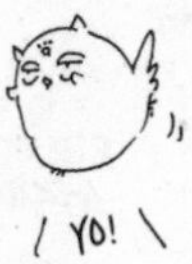
YO!

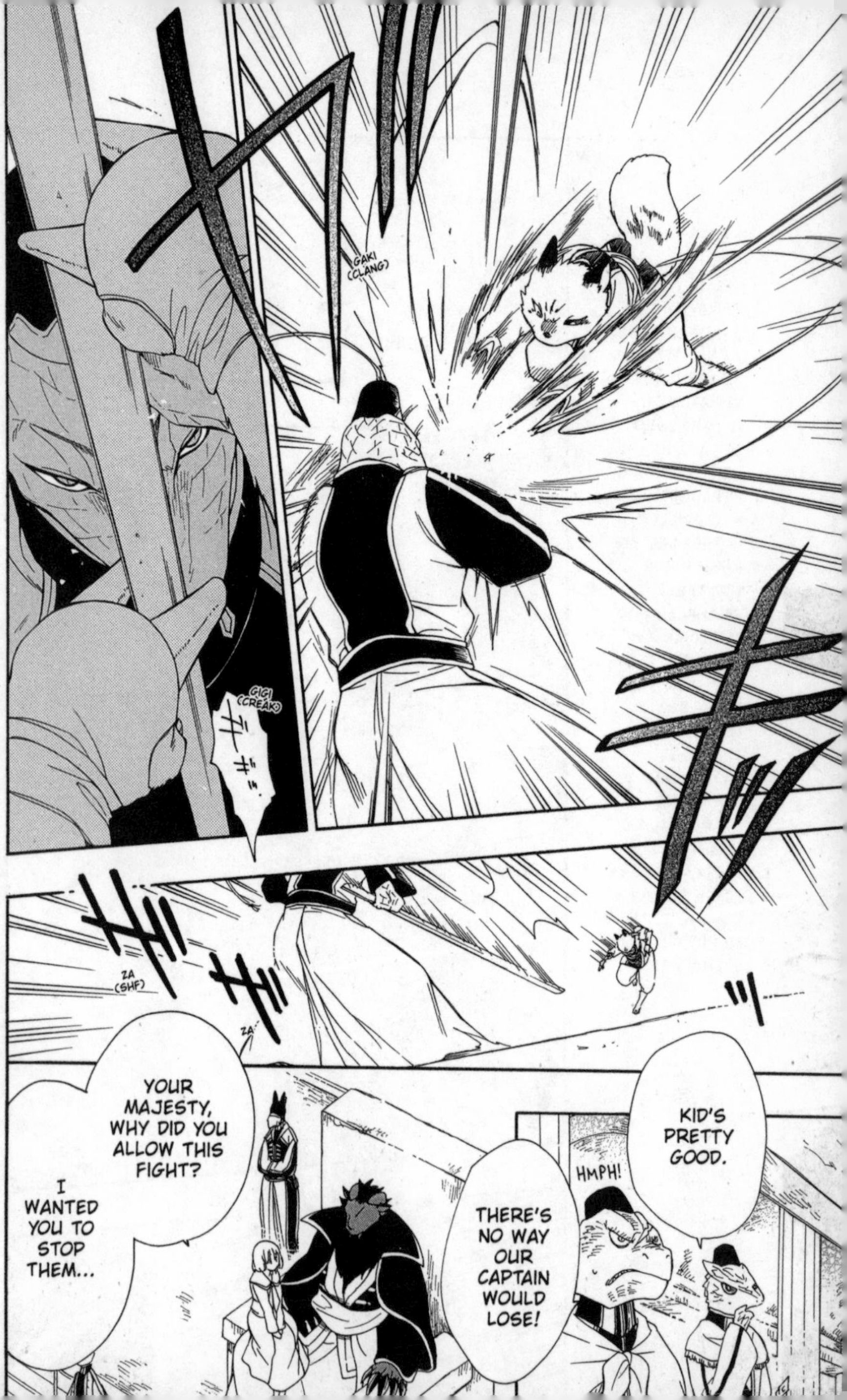
GAKI (CLANG)
GIGI (CREAK)
ZA (SHF)
ZA
KID'S PRETTY GOOD.
HMPH!
THERE'S NO WAY OUR CAPTAIN WOULD LOSE!
YOUR MAJESTY, WHY DID YOU ALLOW THIS FIGHT?
I WANTED YOU TO STOP THEM...

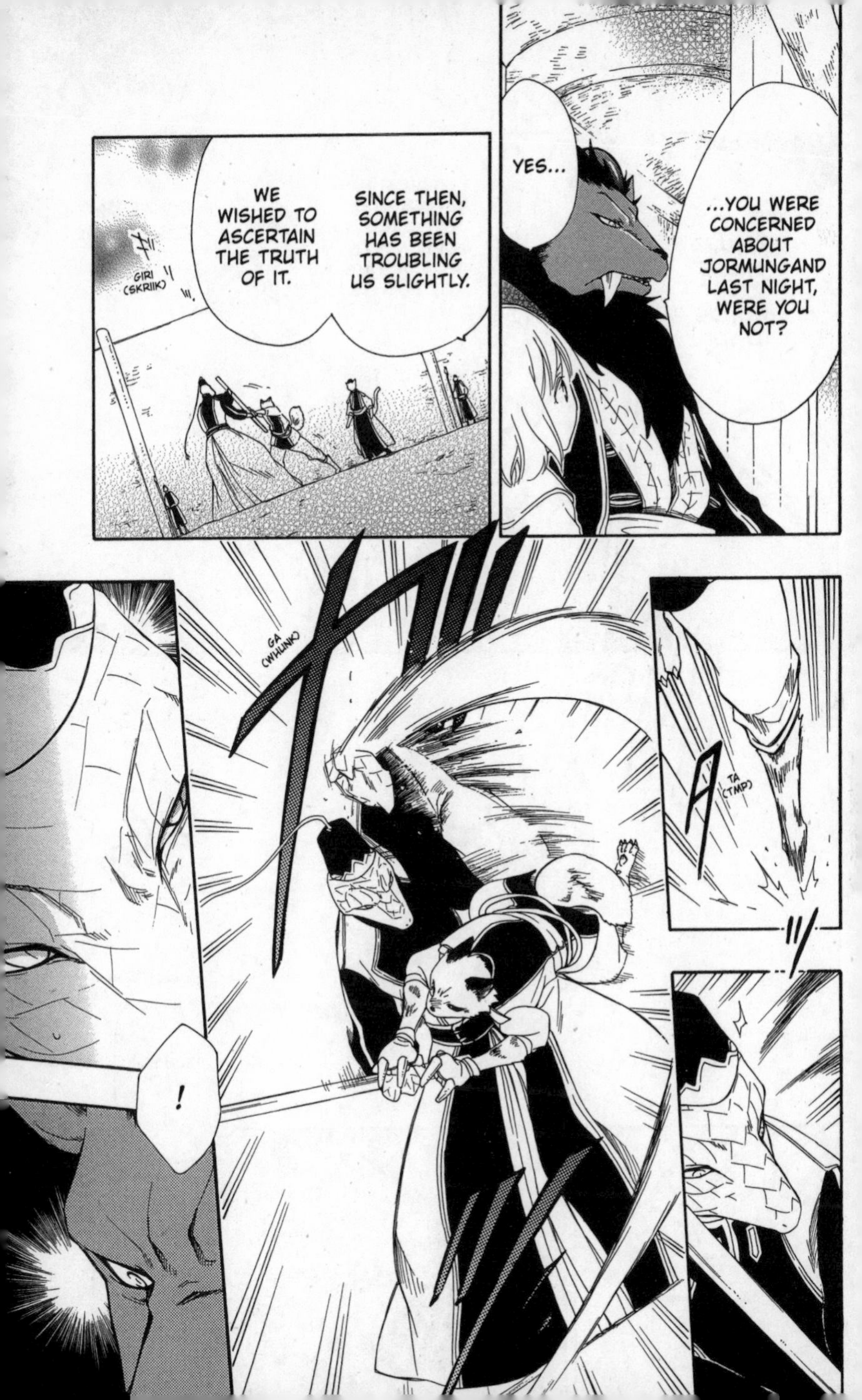

...YOU WERE CONCERNED ABOUT JORMUNGAND LAST NIGHT, WERE YOU NOT?
YES...
SINCE THEN, SOMETHING HAS BEEN TROUBLING US SLIGHTLY.
WE WISHED TO ASCERTAIN THE TRUTH OF IT.
GIRI (SKRIIK)
TA (TMP)
GA (WHUNK)
!

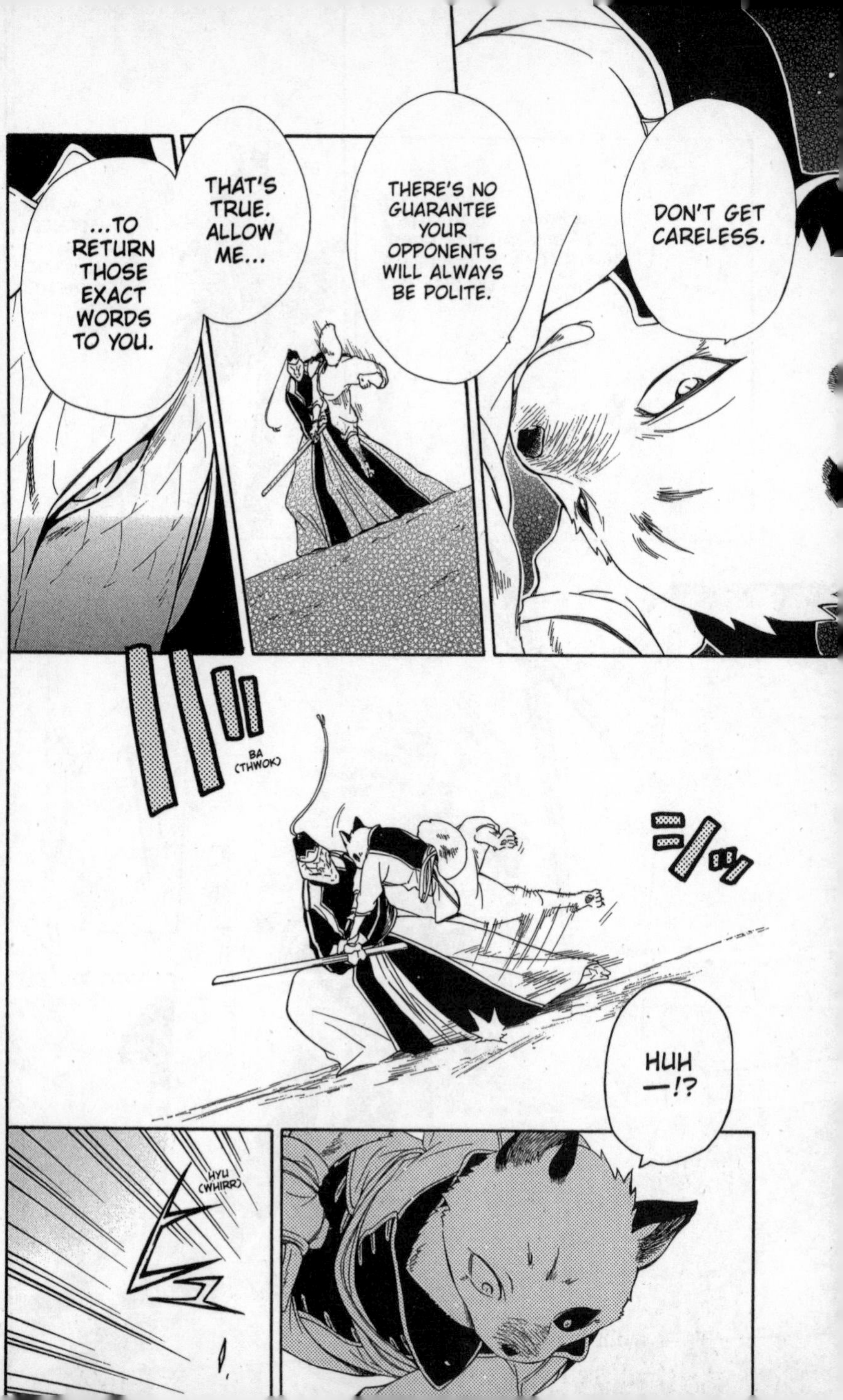
DON'T GET CARELESS.
THERE'S NO GUARANTEE YOUR OPPONENTS WILL ALWAYS BE POLITE.
THAT'S TRUE. ALLOW ME...
...TO RETURN THOSE EXACT WORDS TO YOU.
BA (THWOK)
HUH—!?
HYU (WHIRR)

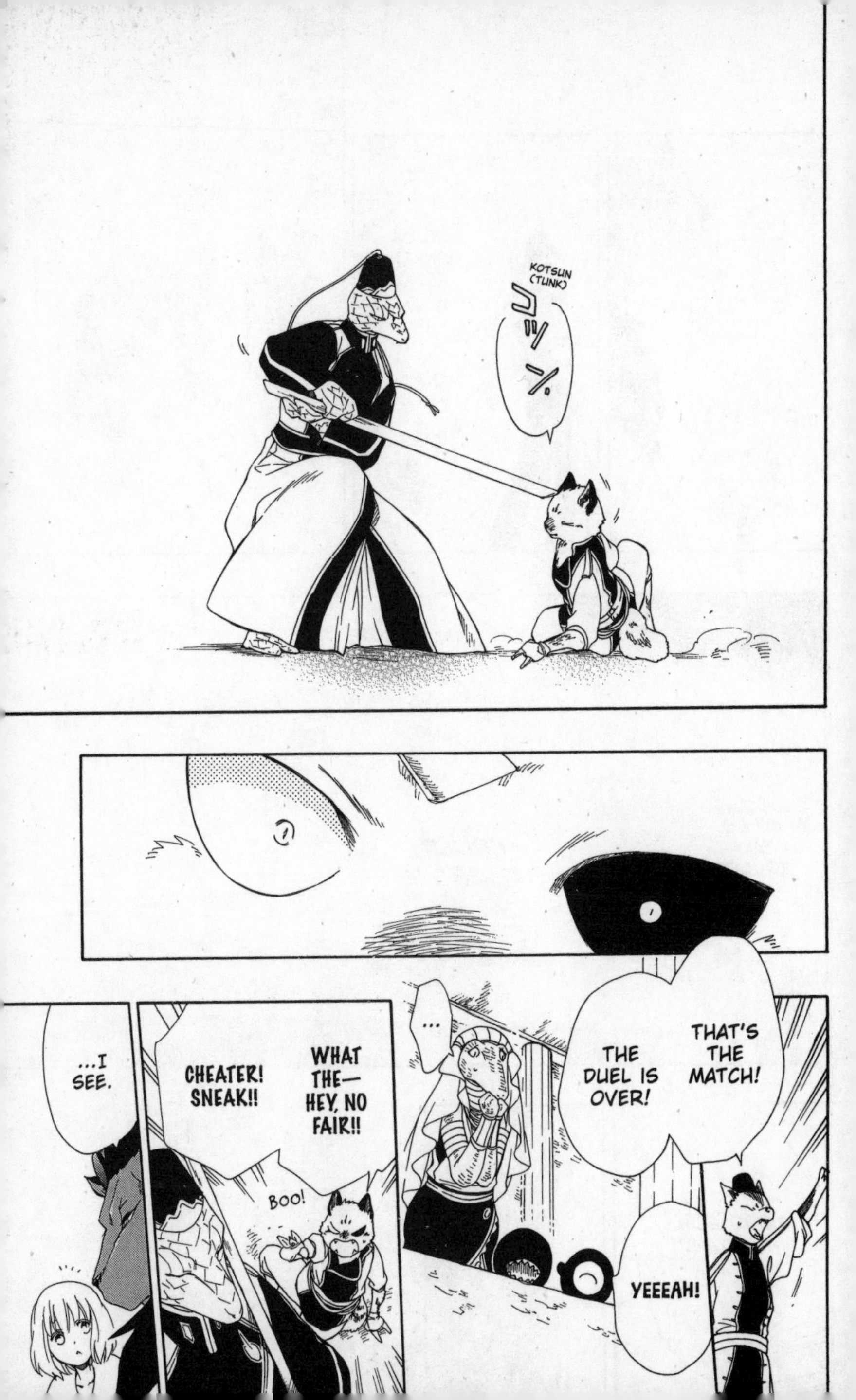
KOTSUN (TUNK)
THAT'S THE MATCH!
THE DUEL IS OVER!
YEEEAH!
...
WHAT THE— HEY, NO FAIR!!
CHEATER! SNEAK!!
BOO!
...I SEE.

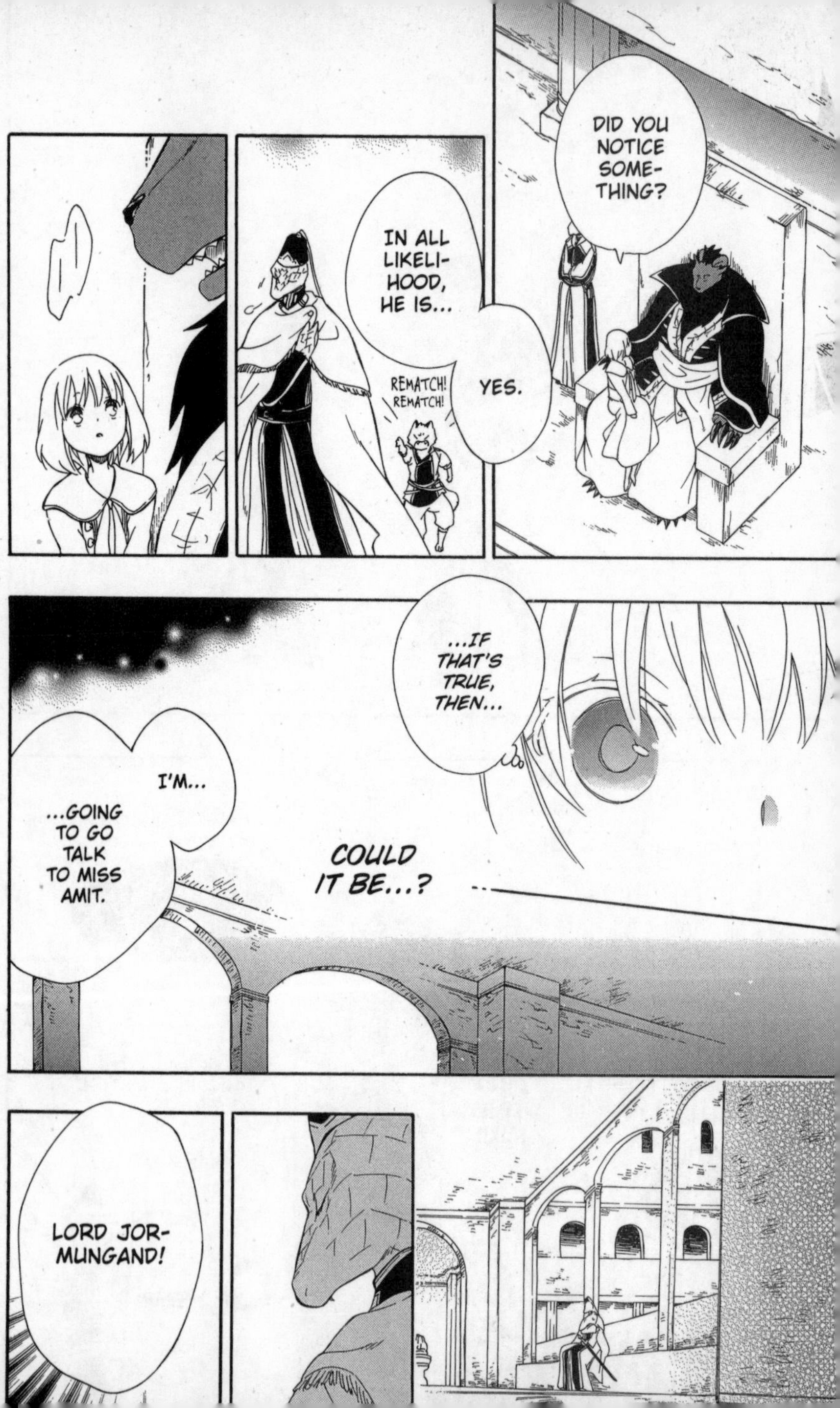
DID YOU NOTICE SOME-THING?
YES.
IN ALL LIKELI-HOOD, HE IS...
REMATCH! REMATCH!
...IF THAT'S TRUE, THEN...
COULD IT BE...?
I'M...
...GOING TO GO TALK TO MISS AMIT.
LORD JOR-MUNGAND!

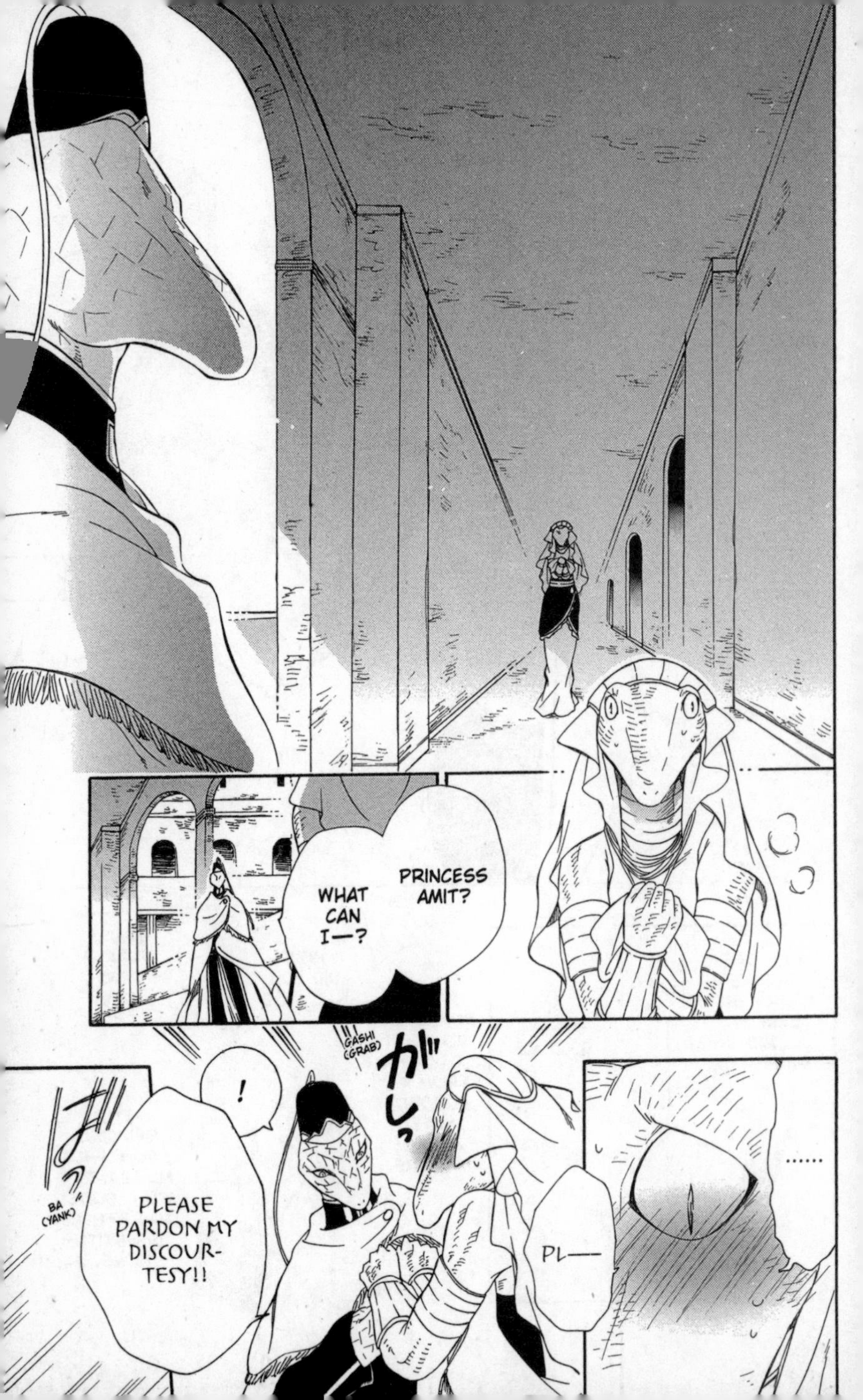
PRINCESS AMIT?
WHAT CAN I—?
......
GASHI (GRAB)
PL—
!
PLEASE PARDON MY DISCOUR-TESY!!
BA (YANK)

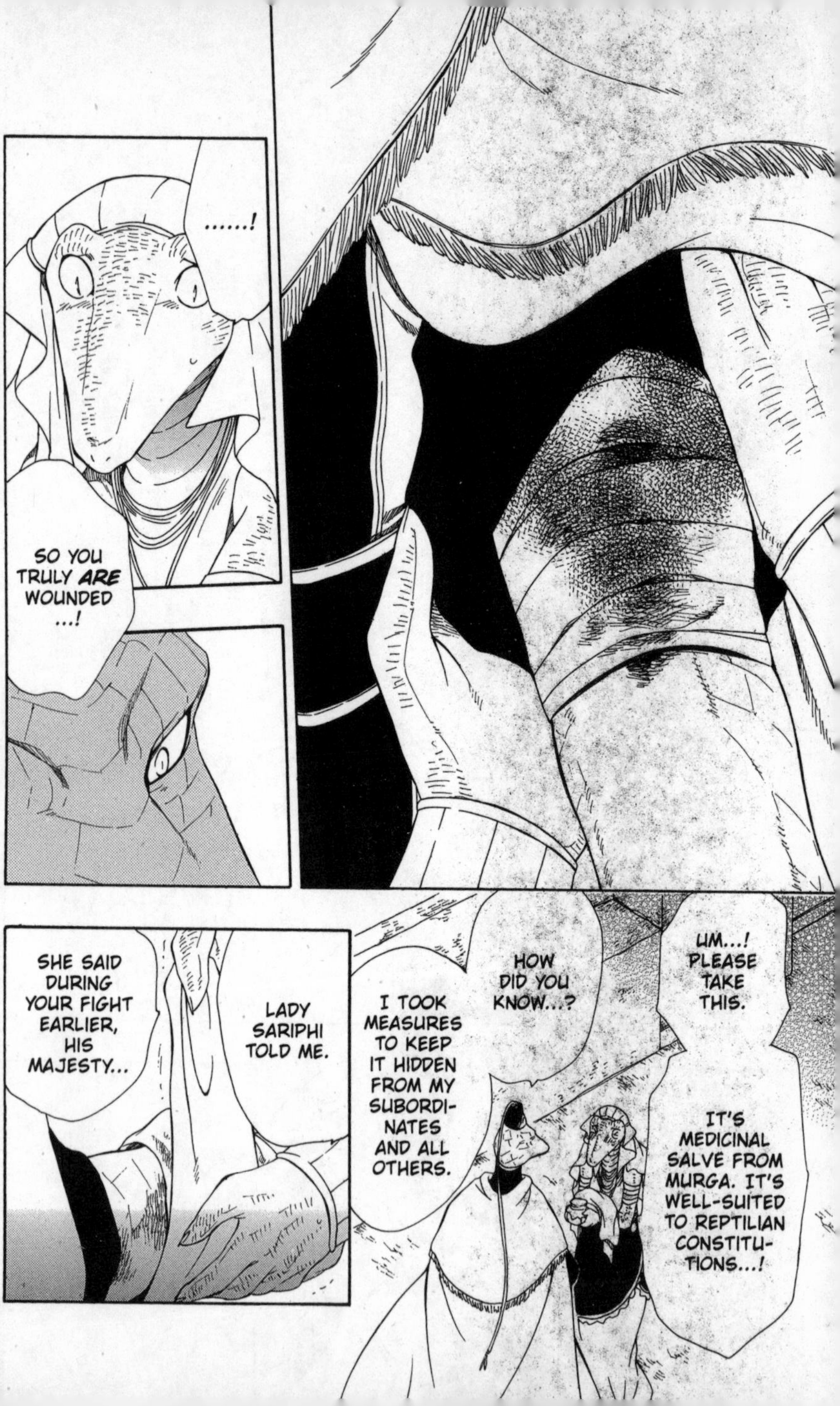
......!
SO YOU TRULY ***ARE*** WOUNDED ...!
UM...! PLEASE TAKE THIS.
IT'S MEDICINAL SALVE FROM MURGA. IT'S WELL-SUITED TO REPTILIAN CONSTITUTIONS...!
HOW DID YOU KNOW...?
I TOOK MEASURES TO KEEP IT HIDDEN FROM MY SUBORDINATES AND ALL OTHERS.
LADY SARIPHI TOLD ME.
SHE SAID DURING YOUR FIGHT EARLIER, HIS MAJESTY...

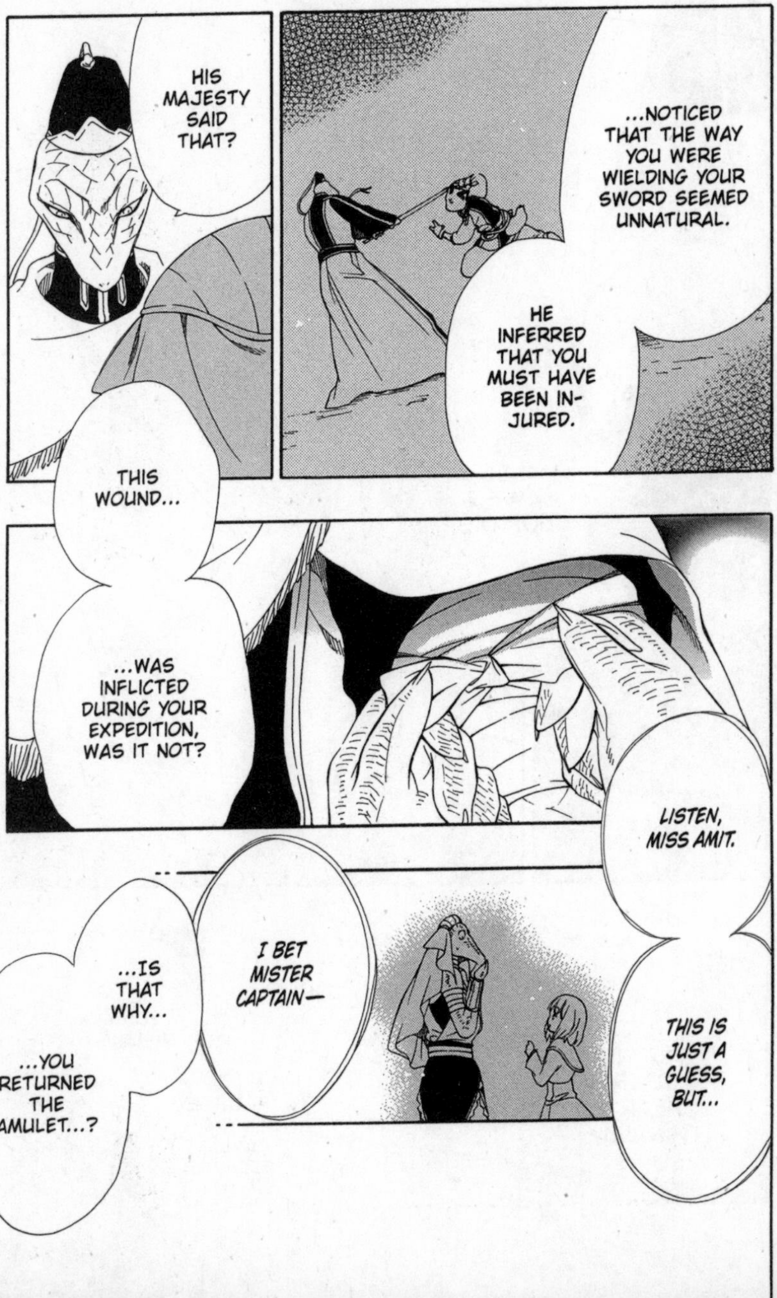
...NOTICED THAT THE WAY YOU WERE WIELDING YOUR SWORD SEEMED UNNATURAL.
HE INFERRED THAT YOU MUST HAVE BEEN IN-JURED.
HIS MAJESTY SAID THAT?
THIS WOUND...
...WAS INFLICTED DURING YOUR EXPEDITION, WAS IT NOT?
LISTEN, MISS AMIT.
THIS IS JUST A GUESS, BUT...
I BET MISTER CAPTAIN—
...IS THAT WHY...
...YOU RETURNED THE AMULET...?

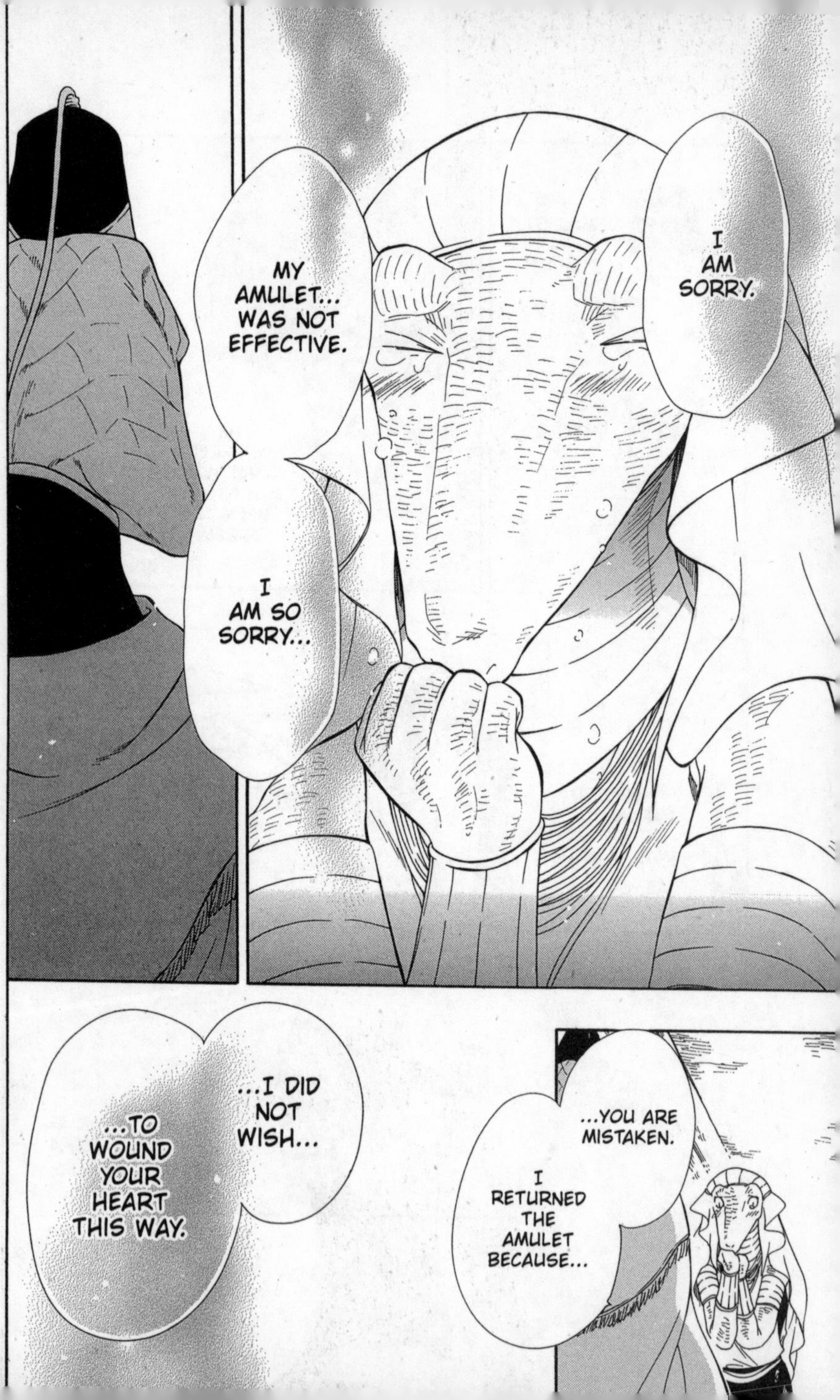
I AM SORRY.
MY AMULET... WAS NOT EFFECTIVE.
I AM SO SORRY...
...YOU ARE MISTAKEN.
I RETURNED THE AMULET BECAUSE...
...I DID NOT WISH...
...TO WOUND YOUR HEART THIS WAY.

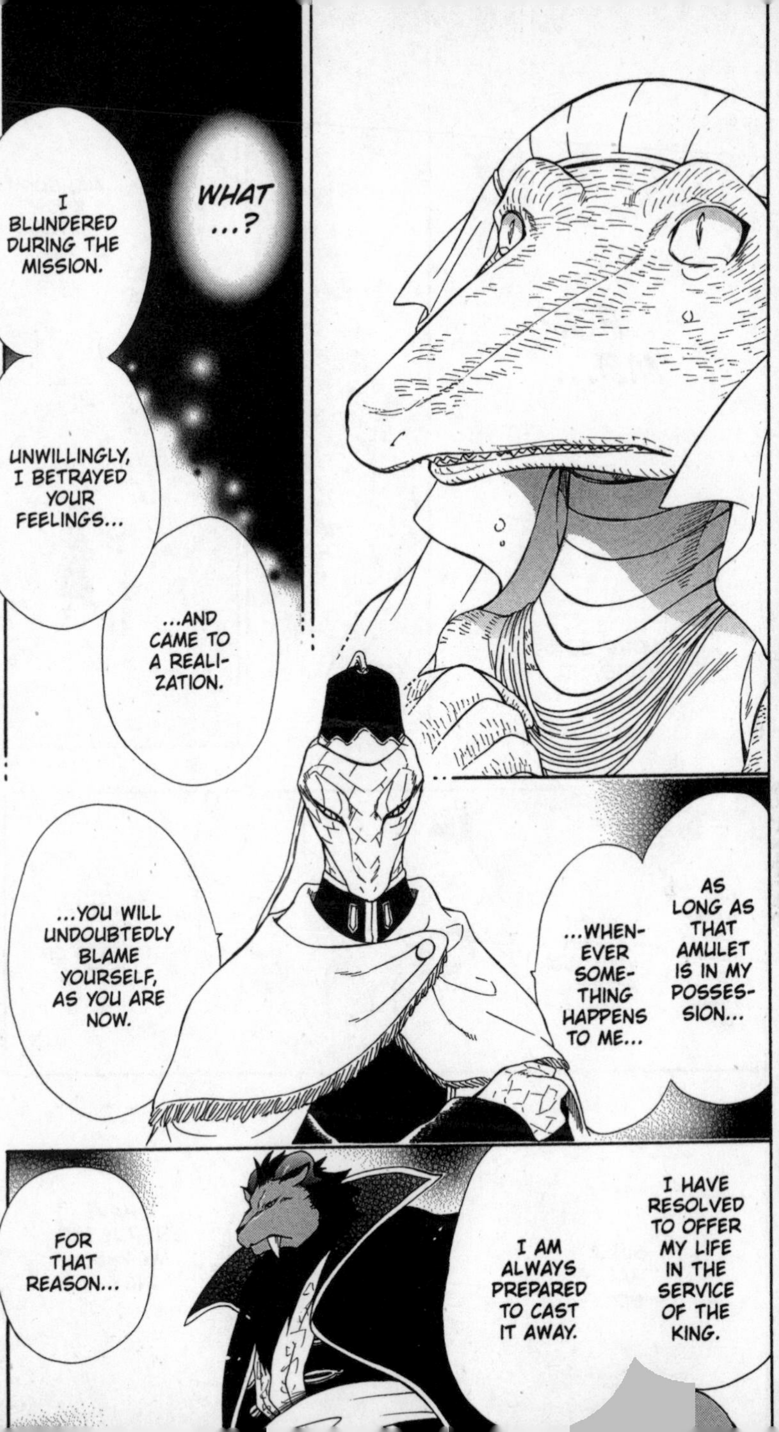
WHAT ...?
I BLUNDERED DURING THE MISSION.
UNWILLINGLY, I BETRAYED YOUR FEELINGS...
...AND CAME TO A REALIZATION.
AS LONG AS THAT AMULET IS IN MY POSSESSION...
...WHENEVER SOMETHING HAPPENS TO ME...
...YOU WILL UNDOUBTEDLY BLAME YOURSELF, AS YOU ARE NOW.
I HAVE RESOLVED TO OFFER MY LIFE IN THE SERVICE OF THE KING.
I AM ALWAYS PREPARED TO CAST IT AWAY.
FOR THAT REASON...

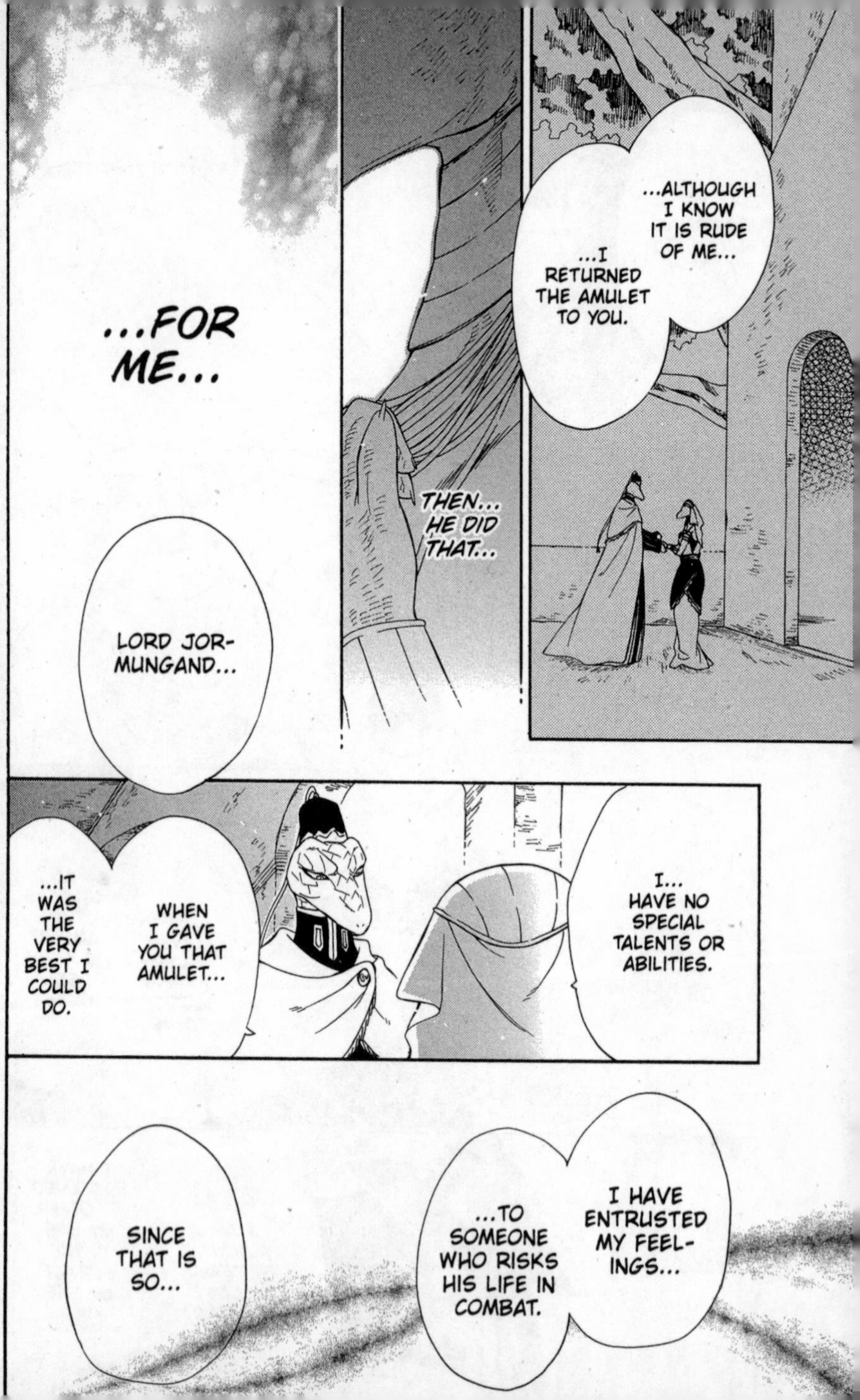
...ALTHOUGH I KNOW IT IS RUDE OF ME...
...I RETURNED THE AMULET TO YOU.
THEN... HE DID THAT...
...FOR ME...
LORD JOR-MUNGAND...
I... HAVE NO SPECIAL TALENTS OR ABILITIES.
WHEN I GAVE YOU THAT AMULET...
...IT WAS THE VERY BEST I COULD DO.
I HAVE ENTRUSTED MY FEEL-INGS...
...TO SOMEONE WHO RISKS HIS LIFE IN COMBAT.
SINCE THAT IS SO...

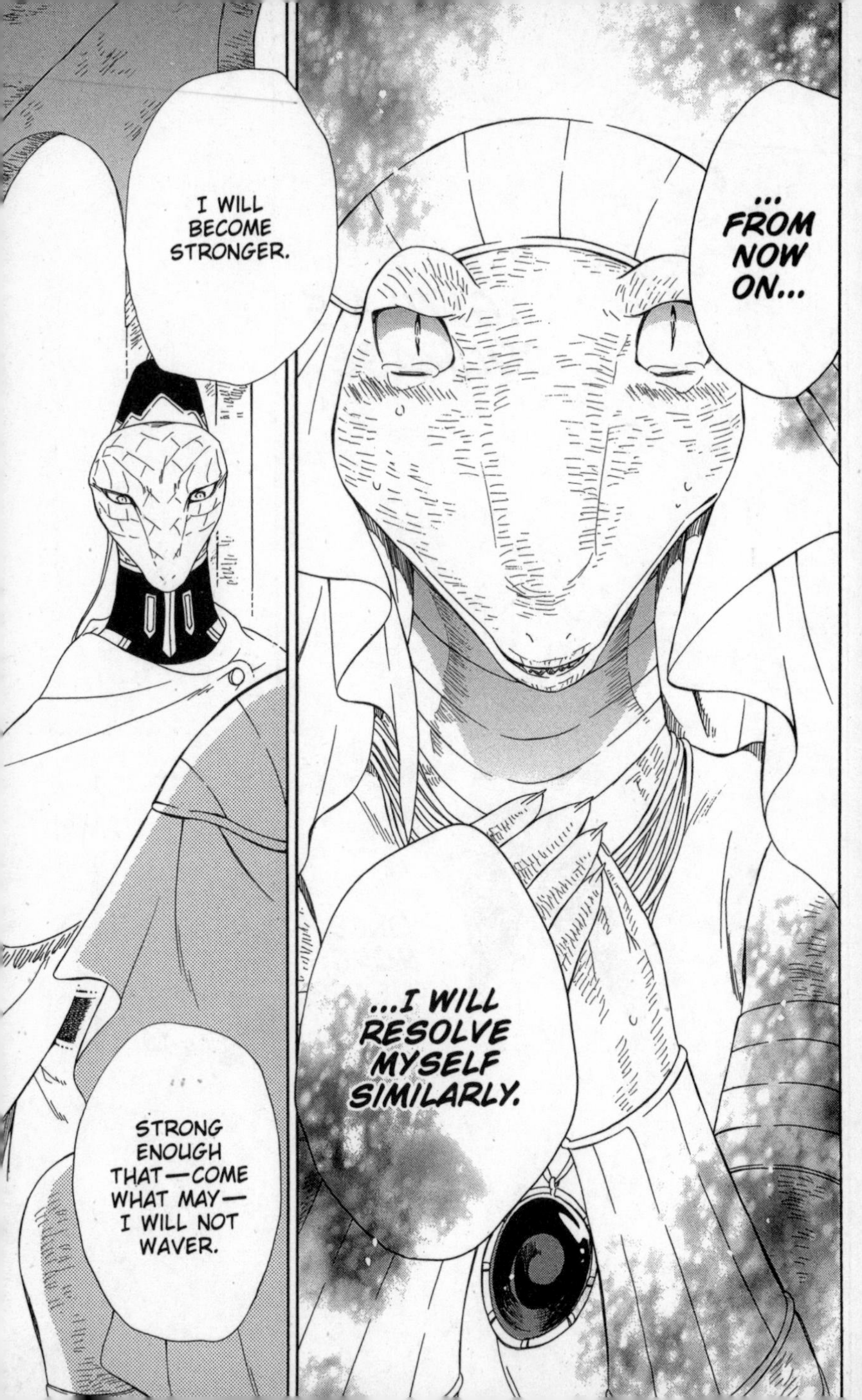
...FROM NOW ON...
...I WILL RESOLVE MYSELF SIMILARLY.
I WILL BECOME STRONGER.
STRONG ENOUGH THAT—COME WHAT MAY—I WILL NOT WAVER.

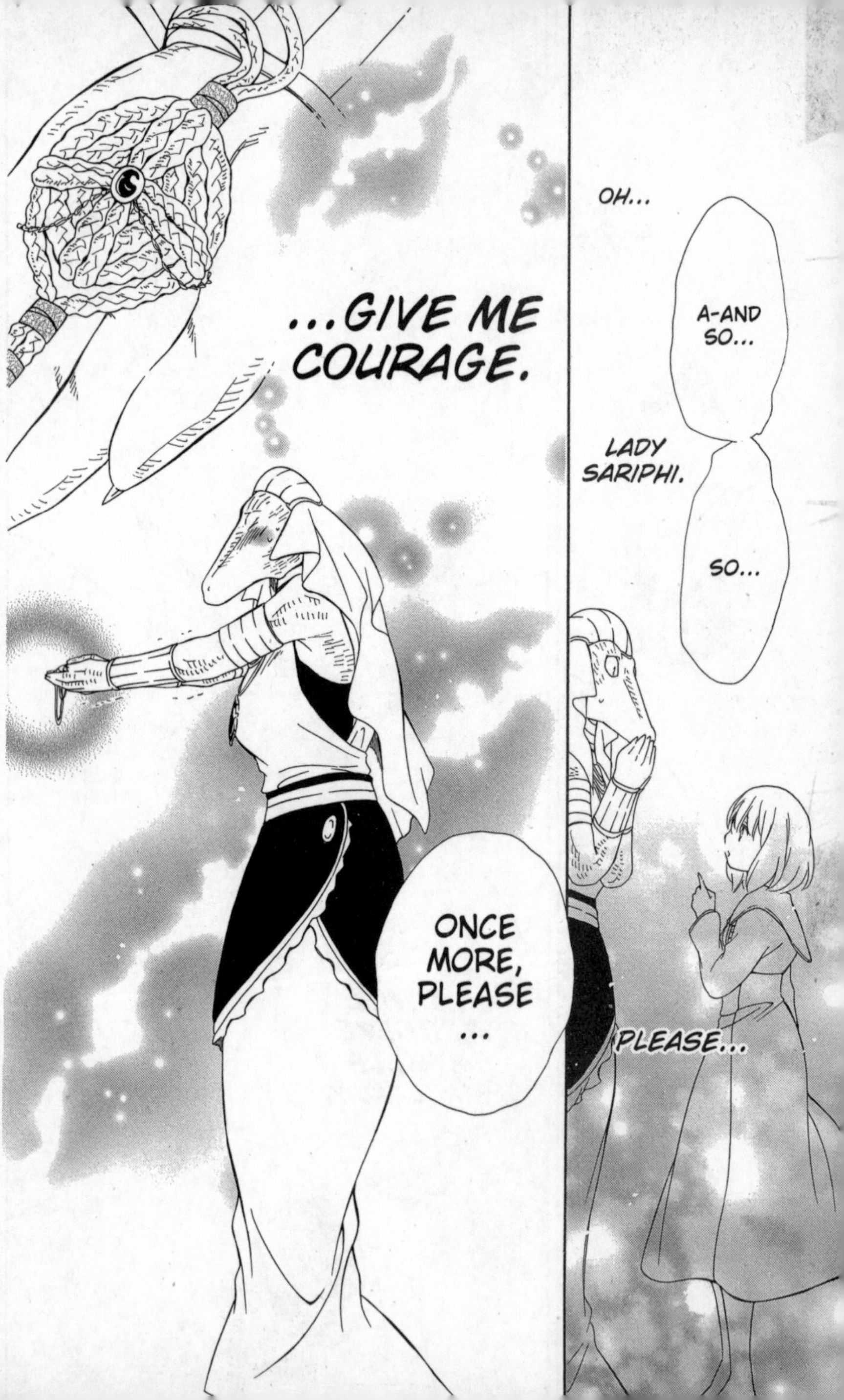
A-AND SO...
SO...
OH...
LADY SARIPHI.
PLEASE...
...GIVE ME COURAGE.
ONCE MORE, PLEASE...

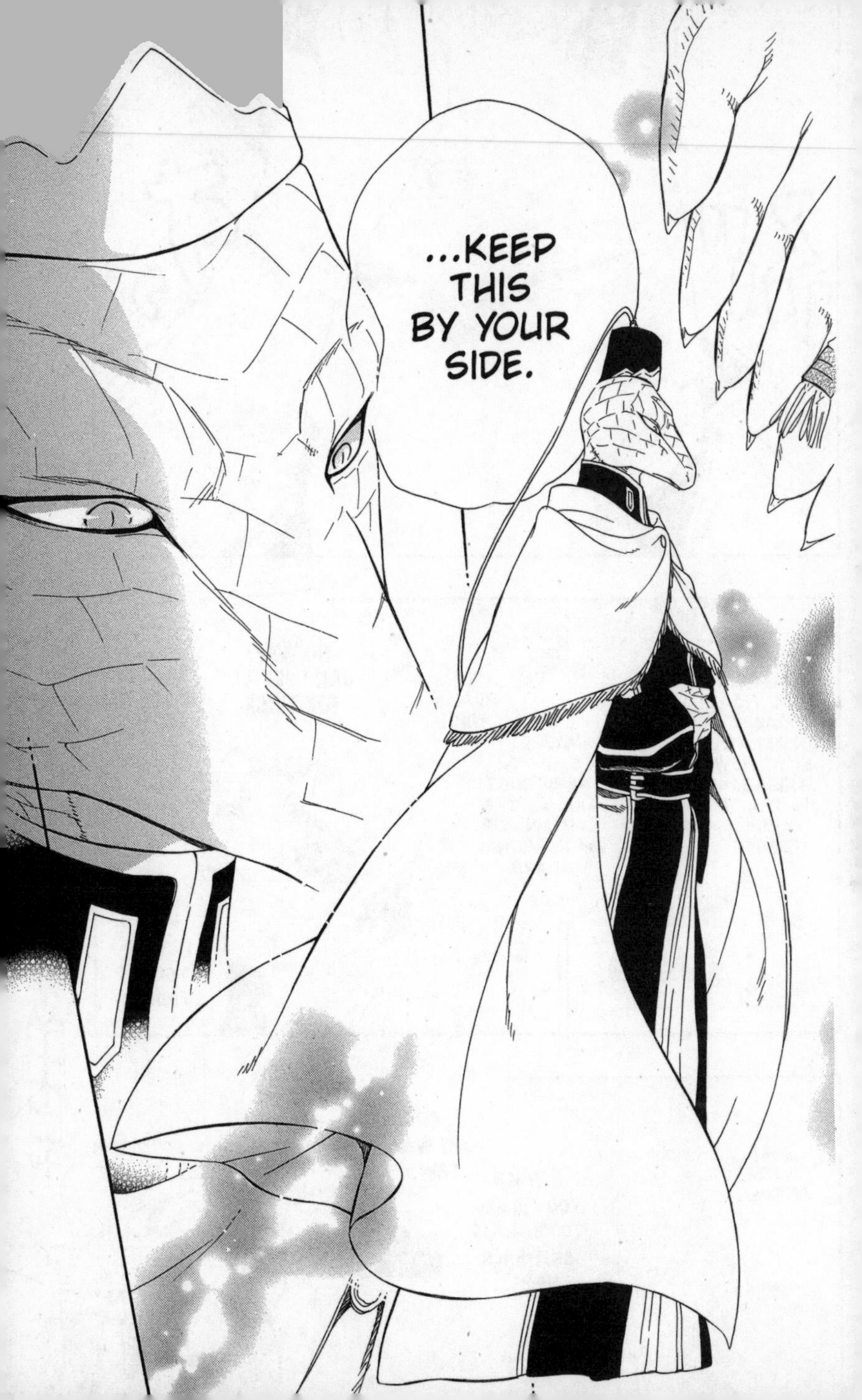
...KEEP THIS BY YOUR SIDE.

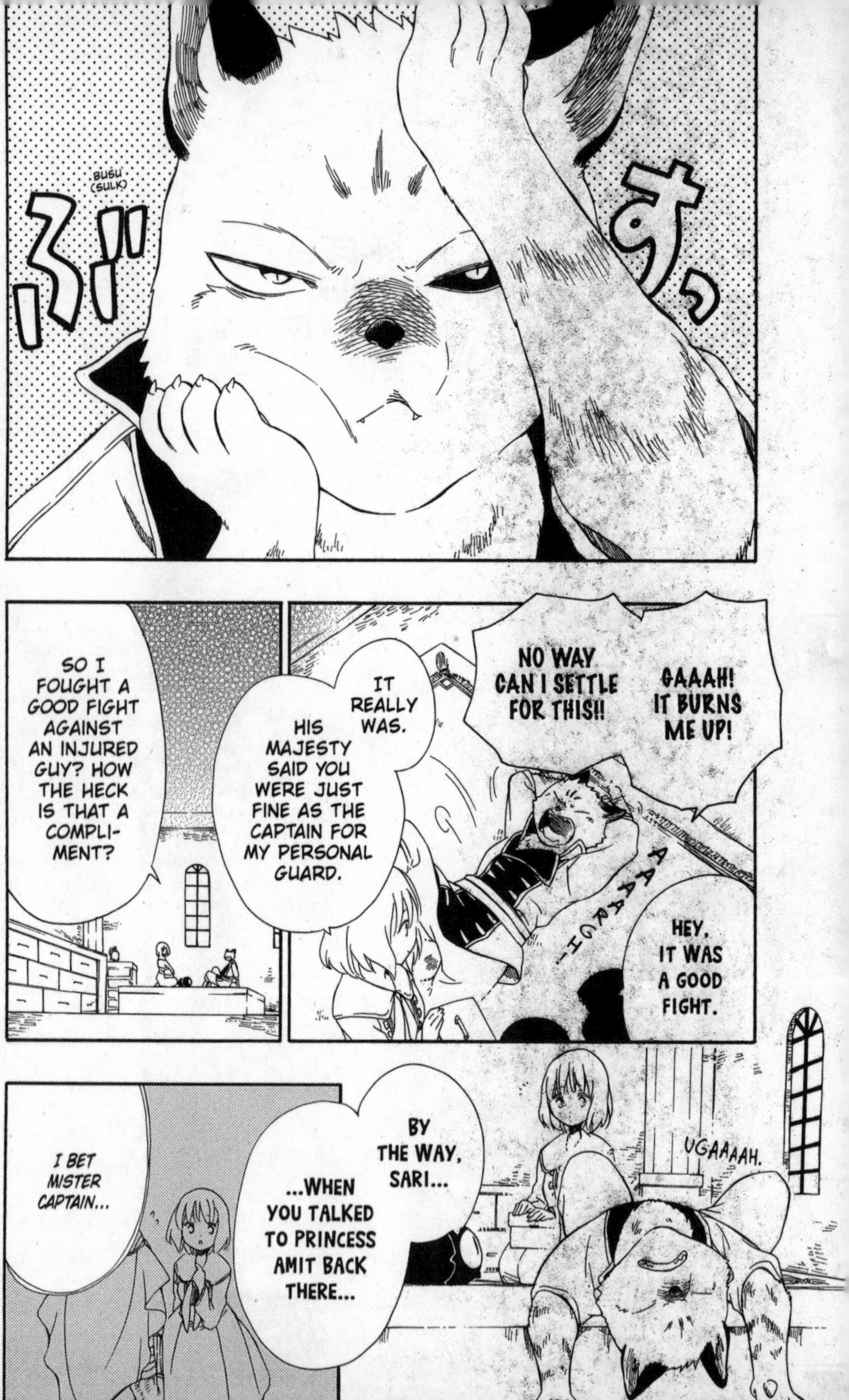
すっ
BUSU (SULK)
ぶ
GAAAH! IT BURNS ME UP!
NO WAY CAN I SETTLE FOR THIS!!
AAAARGH!
HEY, IT WAS A GOOD FIGHT.
IT REALLY WAS.
HIS MAJESTY SAID YOU WERE JUST FINE AS THE CAPTAIN FOR MY PERSONAL GUARD.
SO I FOUGHT A GOOD FIGHT AGAINST AN INJURED GUY? HOW THE HECK IS THAT A COMPLI-MENT?
UGAAAAH.
BY THE WAY, SARI...
...WHEN YOU TALKED TO PRINCESS AMIT BACK THERE...
I BET MISTER CAPTAIN...

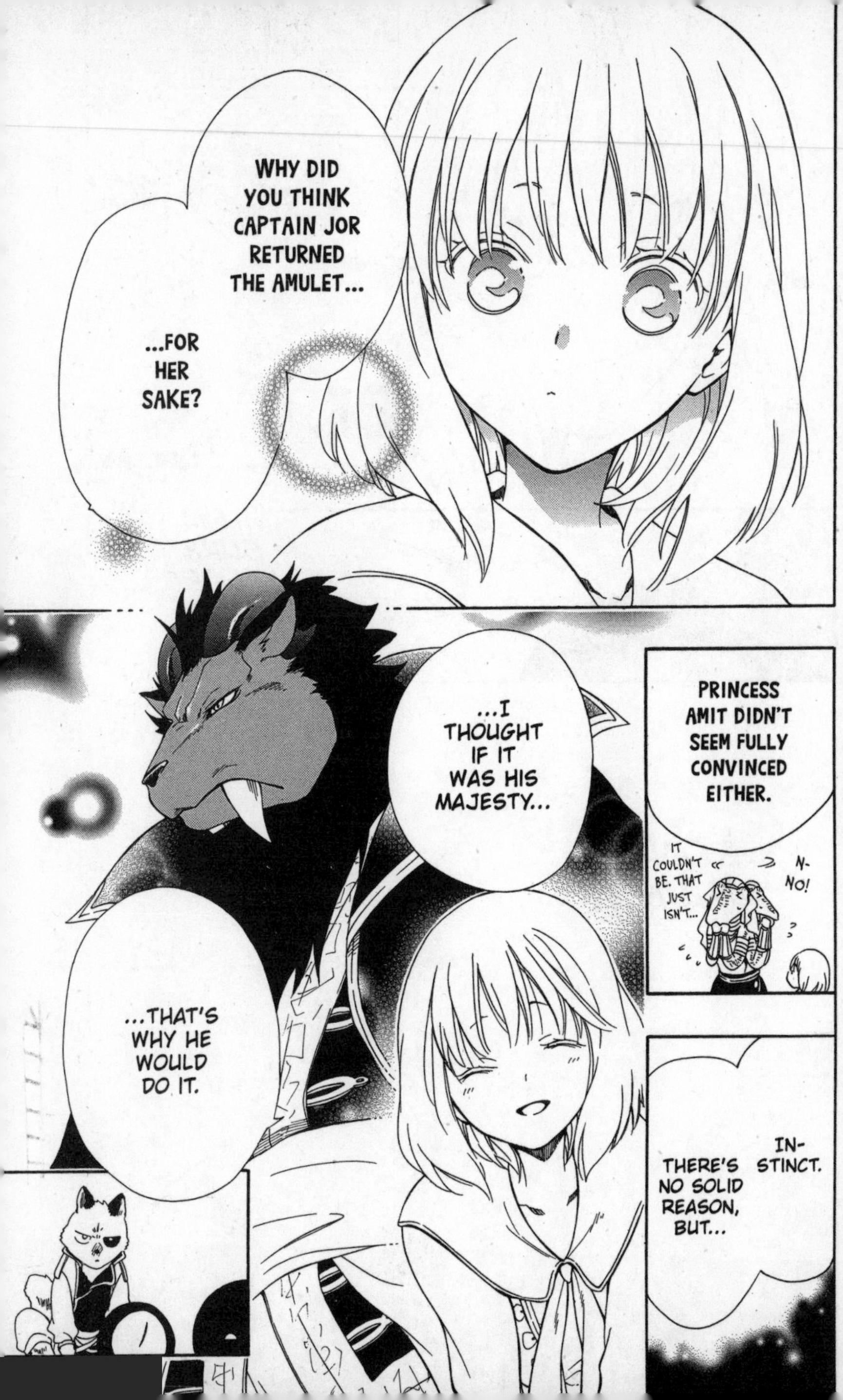
WHY DID YOU THINK CAPTAIN JOR RETURNED THE AMULET...
...FOR HER SAKE?
PRINCESS AMIT DIDN'T SEEM FULLY CONVINCED EITHER.
N-NO!
IT COULDN'T BE. THAT JUST ISN'T...
THERE'S NO SOLID REASON, BUT... IN-STINCT.
...I THOUGHT IF IT WAS HIS MAJESTY...
...THAT'S WHY HE WOULD DO IT.

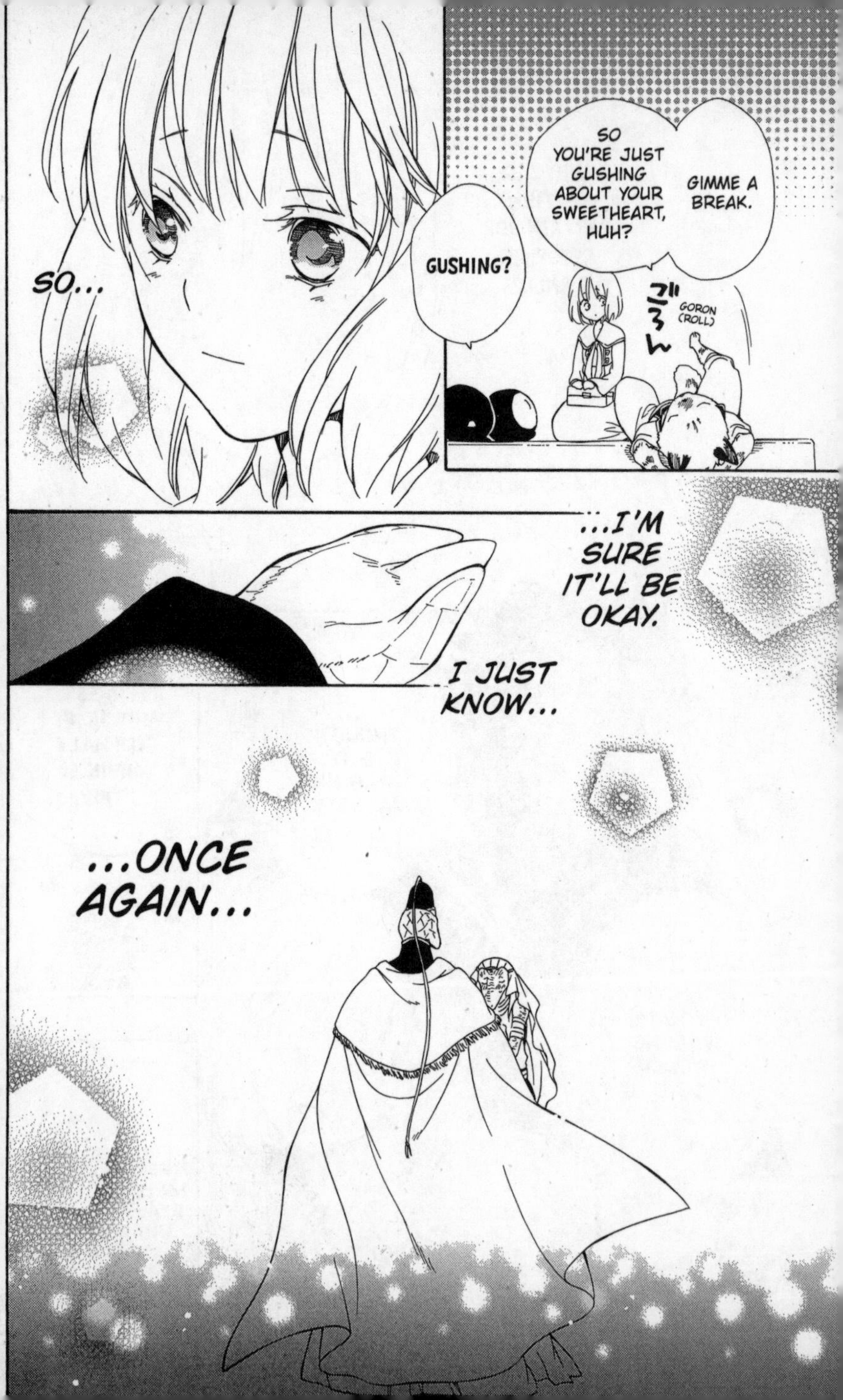

SO YOU'RE JUST GUSHING ABOUT YOUR SWEETHEART, HUH?
GIMME A BREAK.
ごろん
GORON (ROLL)
GUSHING?
SO...
...I'M SURE IT'LL BE OKAY.
I JUST KNOW...
...ONCE AGAIN...

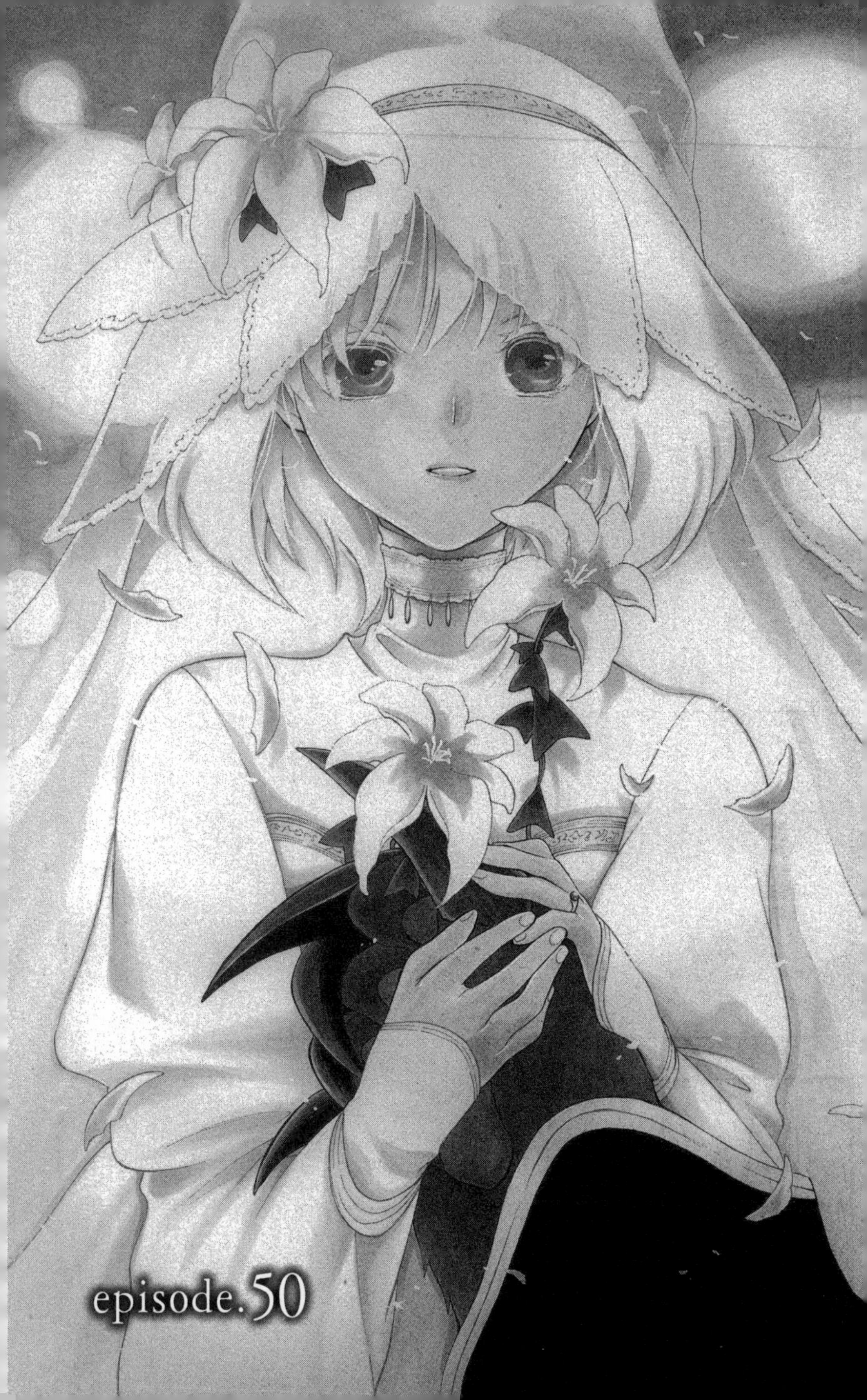
episode.50

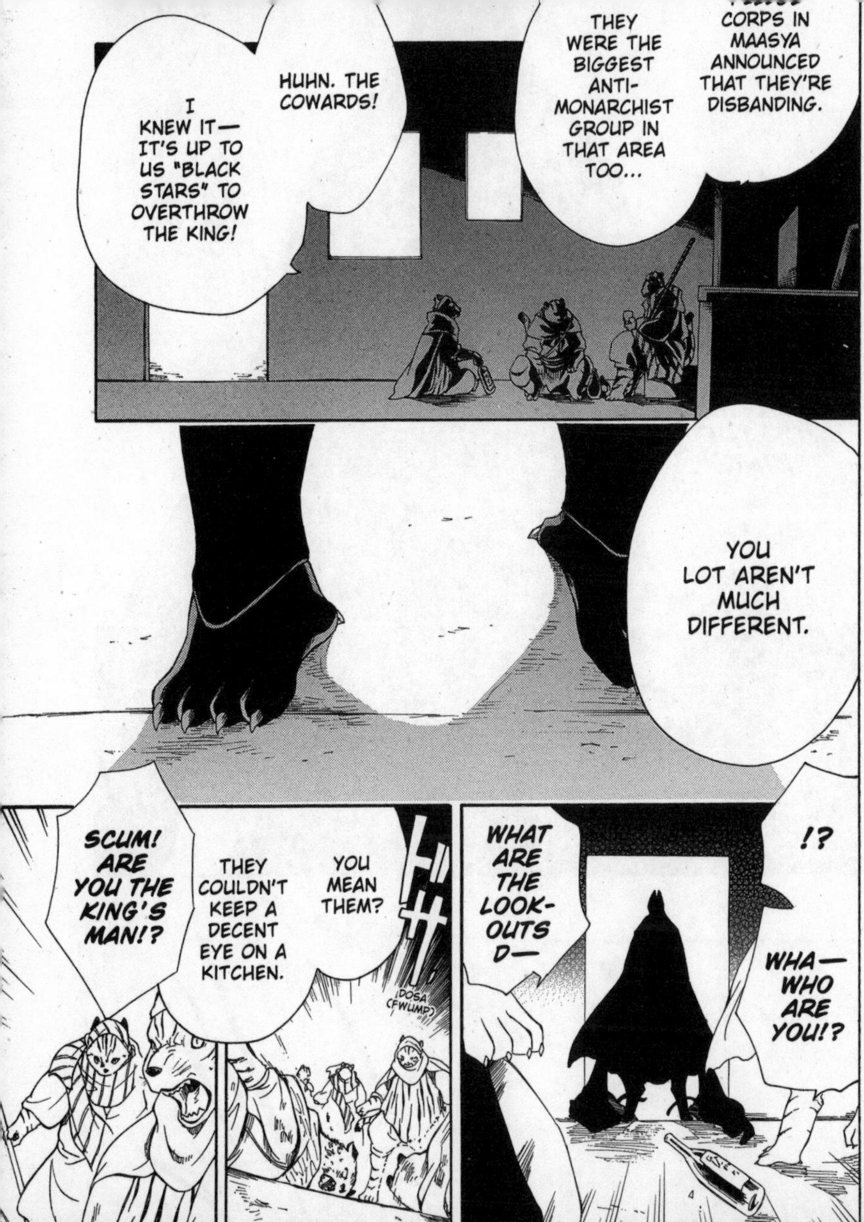
CORPS IN MAASYA ANNOUNCED THAT THEY'RE DISBANDING.
THEY WERE THE BIGGEST ANTI-MONARCHIST GROUP IN THAT AREA TOO...
HUHN. THE COWARDS!
I KNEW IT— IT'S UP TO US "BLACK STARS" TO OVERTHROW THE KING!
YOU LOT AREN'T MUCH DIFFERENT.
!?
WHAT ARE THE LOOK-OUTS D—
WHA— WHO ARE YOU!?
YOU MEAN THEM?
DOSA (FWUMP)
THEY COULDN'T KEEP A DECENT EYE ON A KITCHEN.
SCUM! ARE YOU THE KING'S MAN!?

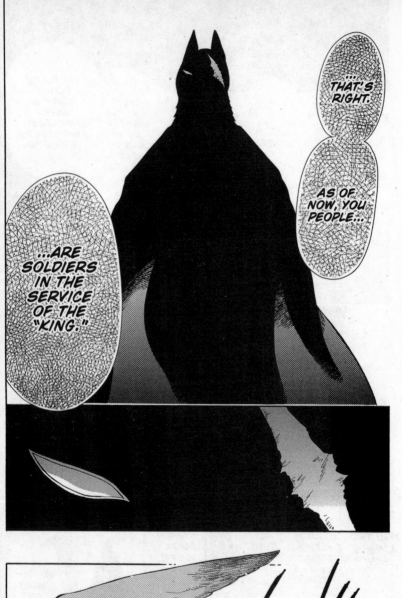

"...THAT'S RIGHT.

AS OF NOW, YOU PEOPLE...

...ARE SOLDIERS IN THE SERVICE OF THE "KING."

BA
(FLAP)

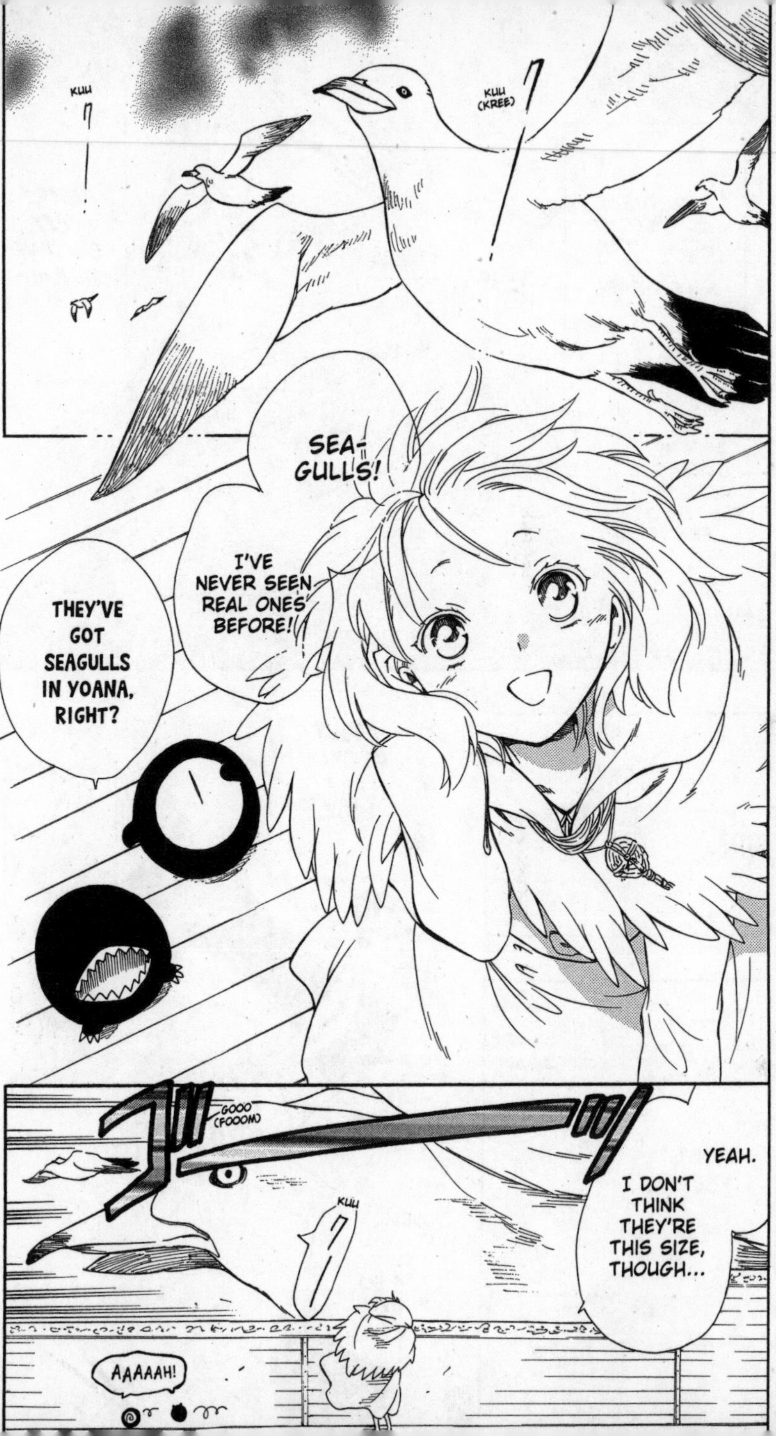
KUU (KREE)
KUU
SEA-GULLS!
I'VE NEVER SEEN REAL ONES BEFORE!
THEY'VE GOT SEAGULLS IN YOANA, RIGHT?
YEAH.
I DON'T THINK THEY'RE THIS SIZE, THOUGH...
GOOO (FOOOM)
KUU
AAAAAH!

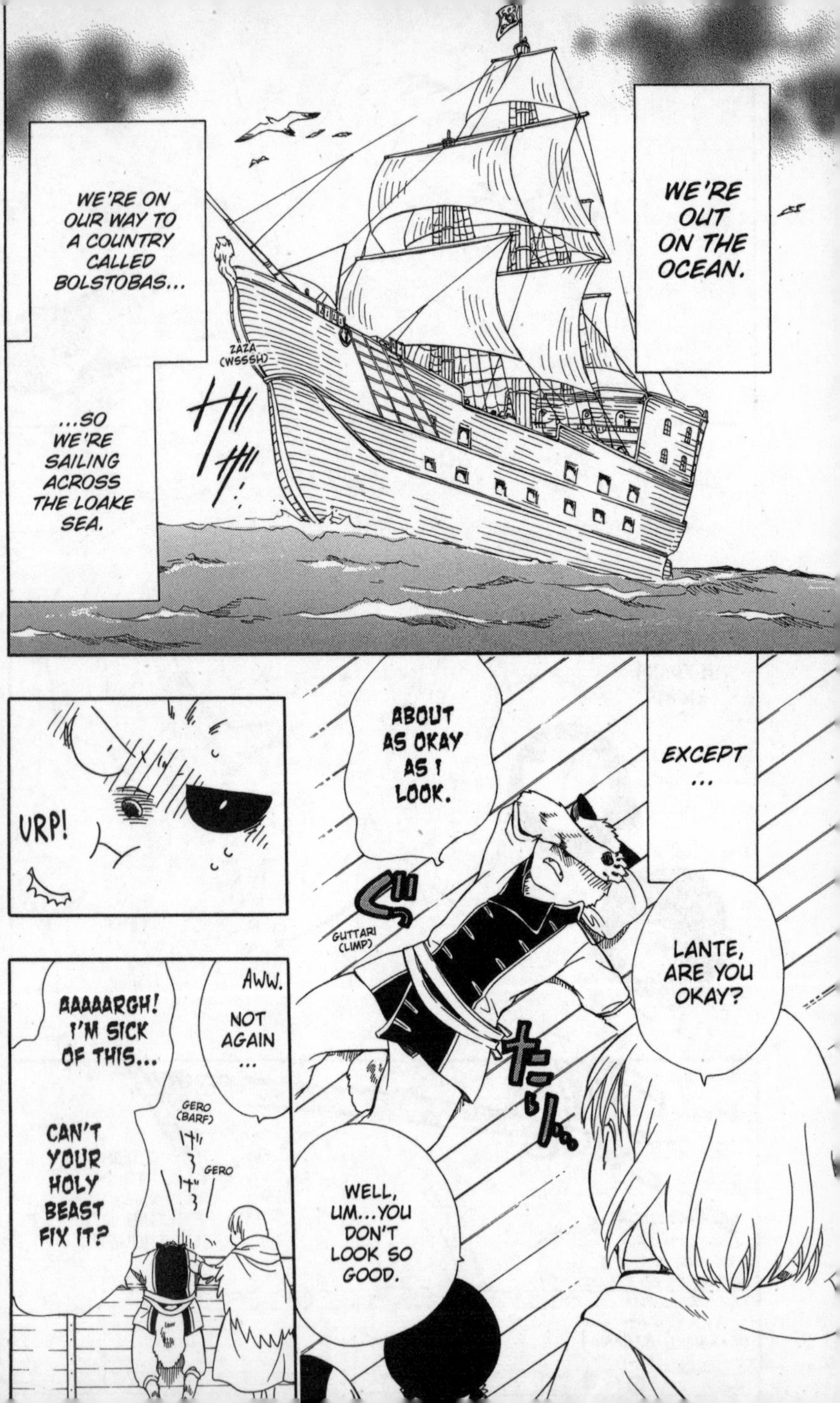
WE'RE OUT ON THE OCEAN.
WE'RE ON OUR WAY TO A COUNTRY CALLED BOLSTOBAS...
...SO WE'RE SAILING ACROSS THE LOAKE SEA.
ZAZA (WSSSH)
EXCEPT...
LANTE, ARE YOU OKAY?
ABOUT AS OKAY AS I LOOK.
GUTTARI (LIMP)
WELL, UM...YOU DON'T LOOK SO GOOD.
URP!
AWW. NOT AGAIN...
AAAAARGH! I'M SICK OF THIS...
GERO (BARF)
GERO
CAN'T YOUR HOLY BEAST FIX IT?

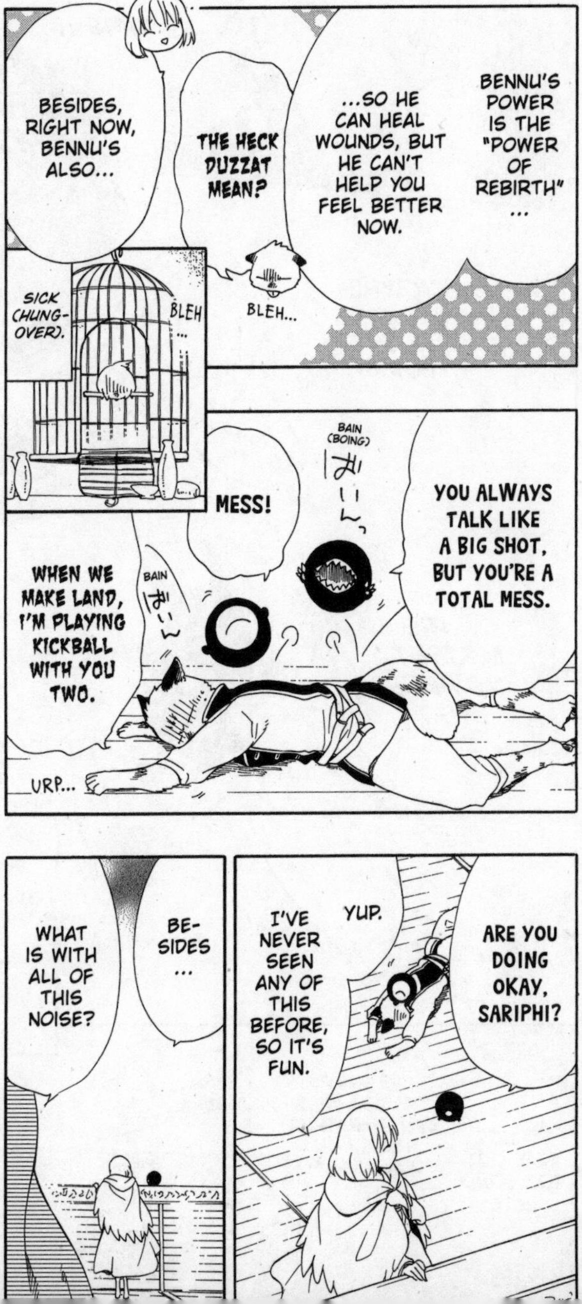
BENNU'S POWER IS THE "POWER OF REBIRTH"...
...SO HE CAN HEAL WOUNDS, BUT HE CAN'T HELP YOU FEEL BETTER NOW.
THE HECK DUZZAT MEAN?
BESIDES, RIGHT NOW, BENNU'S ALSO...
BLEH...
BLEH...
SICK (HUNG-OVER).
YOU ALWAYS TALK LIKE A BIG SHOT, BUT YOU'RE A TOTAL MESS.
BAIN (BOING)
MESS!
BAIN
WHEN WE MAKE LAND, I'M PLAYING KICKBALL WITH YOU TWO.
URP...
ARE YOU DOING OKAY, SARIPHI?
YUP.
I'VE NEVER SEEN ANY OF THIS BEFORE, SO IT'S FUN.
BE-SIDES...
WHAT IS WITH ALL OF THIS NOISE?

SIDE CHARACTERS, COME ON DOWN!

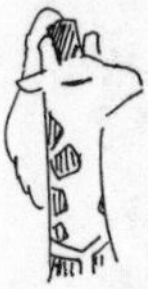

CAPTAIN TEIRYN (VOLS. 7 AND 8)

A GIRAFFE. I VISUALIZED HIM WITH THE FACE OF A COURT NOBLE. HE WAS A WARRIOR TYPE WHO WAS SIMILAR TO JORMUNGAND, SO I MADE HIS FACE MORE NOBLE TO SET THEM APART. EVERY TIME I DREW THIS GUY, HIS NECK GOT LONGER.

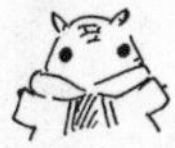

MAALO (VOL. 8)

HE'S AN ARMADILLO, SO "MAALO." ANY BEASTFOLK WHO GOT INVOLVED WITH ILYA HAD TO BE PRETTY STRAIGHT-FORWARD AND NOT HAVE THE SLIGHTEST HINT OF A SHADOW ABOUT THEM OR IT WOULDN'T WORK OUT, SO NATURALLY HE ENDED UP BEING A YOUNG CHILD. HE SEEMS A LOT LIKE A MASCOT CHARACTER. I MODELED HIM AFTER A CERTAIN PO••MON.

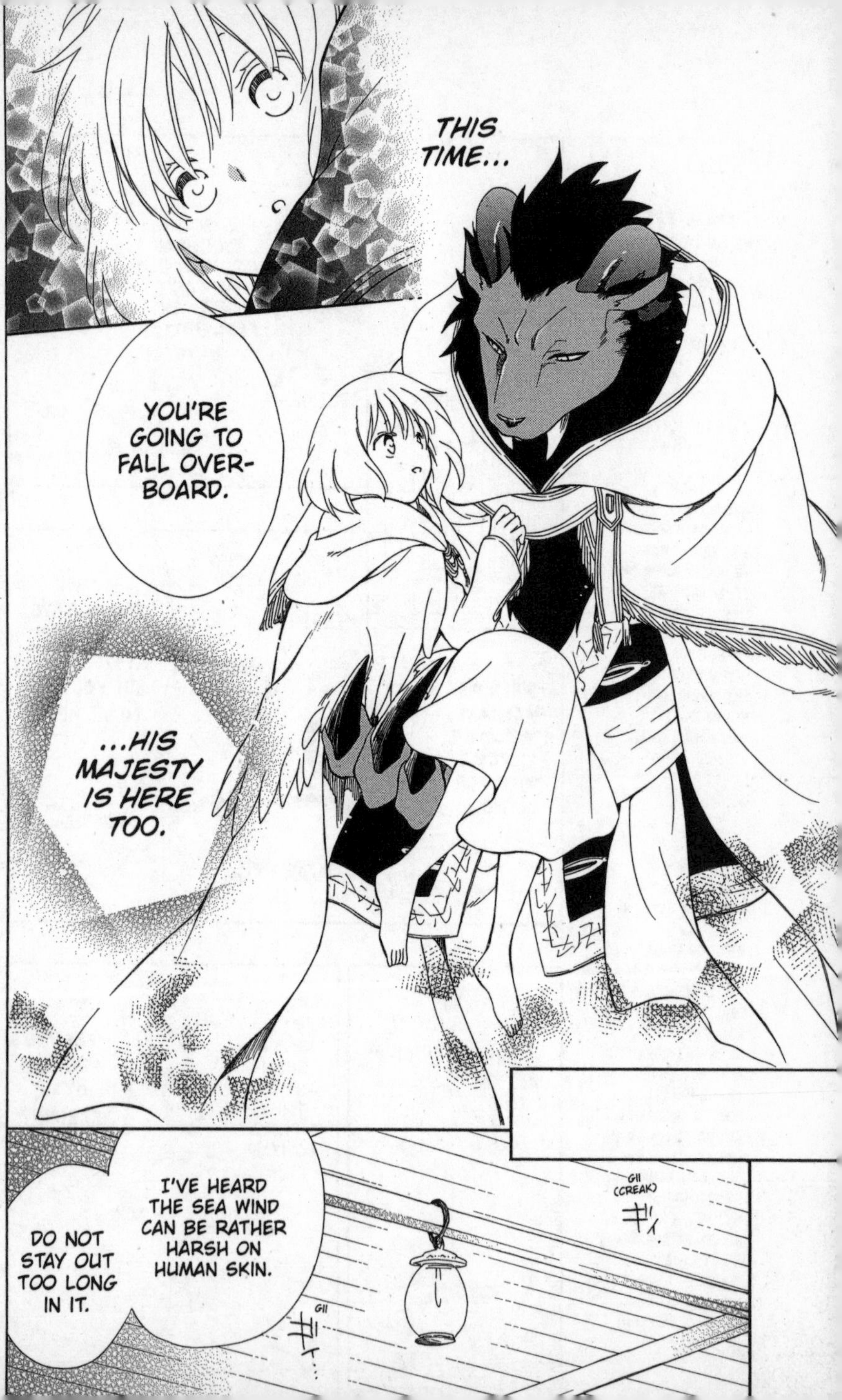
THIS TIME...
...HIS MAJESTY IS HERE TOO.
YOU'RE GOING TO FALL OVER-BOARD.
GII (CREAK)
ギィ
I'VE HEARD THE SEA WIND CAN BE RATHER HARSH ON HUMAN SKIN.
DO NOT STAY OUT TOO LONG IN IT.
GII
ギィ…

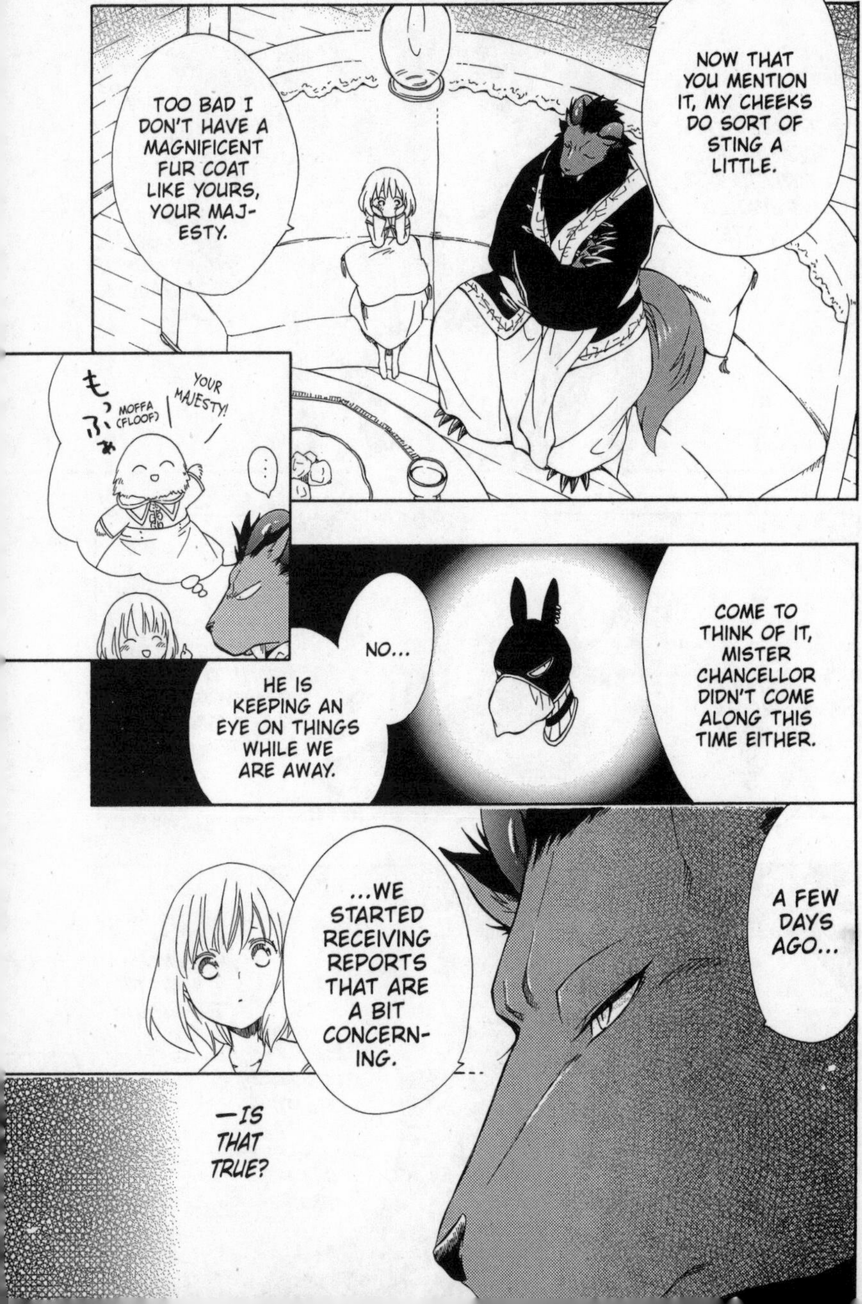
NOW THAT YOU MENTION IT, MY CHEEKS DO SORT OF STING A LITTLE.
TOO BAD I DON'T HAVE A MAGNIFICENT FUR COAT LIKE YOURS, YOUR MAJ-ESTY.
もっふぁ
MOFFA (FLOOF)
YOUR MAJESTY!
...
COME TO THINK OF IT, MISTER CHANCELLOR DIDN'T COME ALONG THIS TIME EITHER.
NO...
HE IS KEEPING AN EYE ON THINGS WHILE WE ARE AWAY.
A FEW DAYS AGO...
...WE STARTED RECEIVING REPORTS THAT ARE A BIT CONCERN-ING.
—IS THAT TRUE?

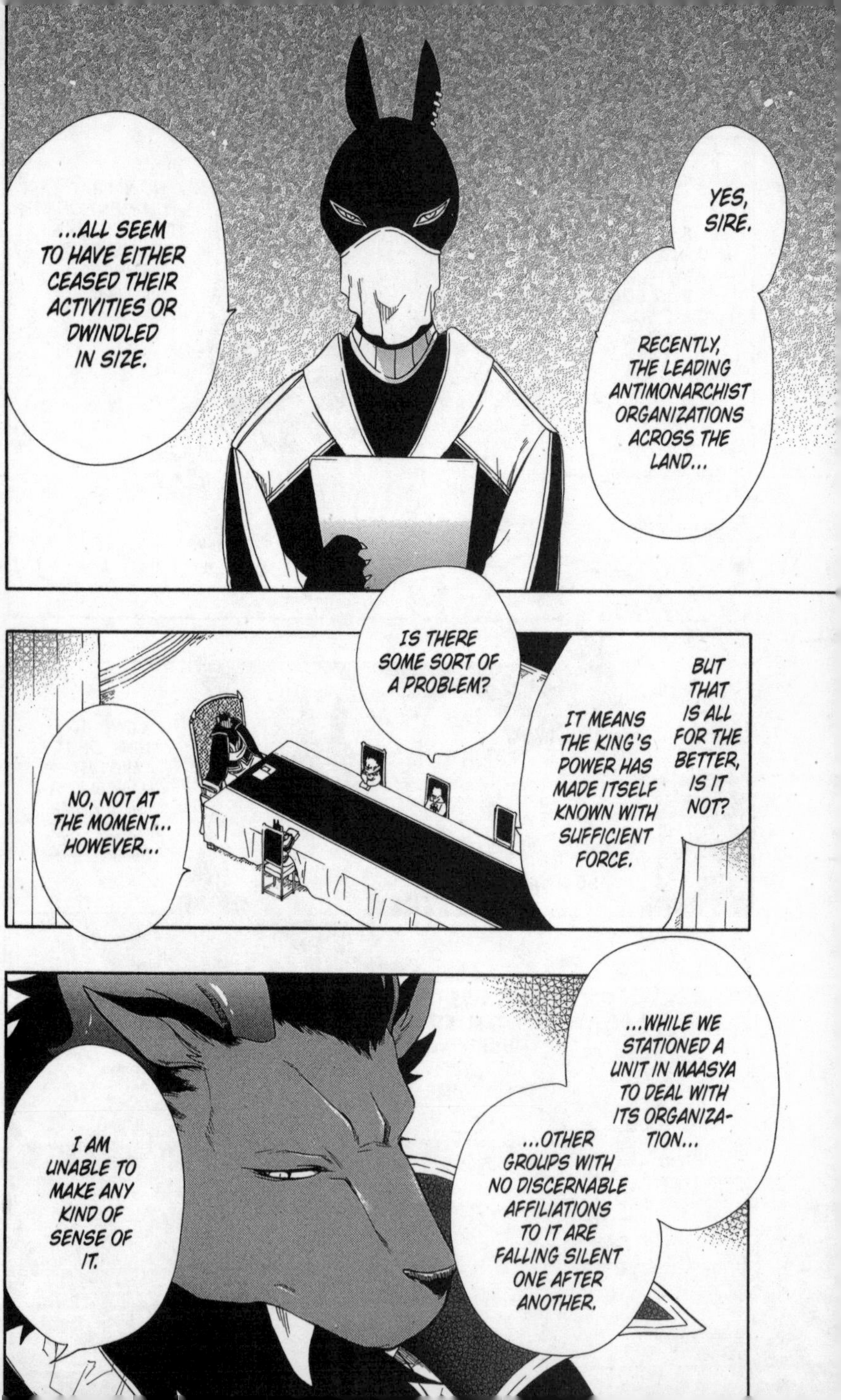
YES, SIRE.
RECENTLY, THE LEADING ANTIMONARCHIST ORGANIZATIONS ACROSS THE LAND...
...ALL SEEM TO HAVE EITHER CEASED THEIR ACTIVITIES OR DWINDLED IN SIZE.
BUT THAT IS ALL FOR THE BETTER, IS IT NOT?
IT MEANS THE KING'S POWER HAS MADE ITSELF KNOWN WITH SUFFICIENT FORCE.
IS THERE SOME SORT OF A PROBLEM?
NO, NOT AT THE MOMENT... HOWEVER...
...WHILE WE STATIONED A UNIT IN MAASYA TO DEAL WITH ITS ORGANIZATION...
...OTHER GROUPS WITH NO DISCERNABLE AFFILIATIONS TO IT ARE FALLING SILENT ONE AFTER ANOTHER.
I AM UNABLE TO MAKE ANY KIND OF SENSE OF IT.

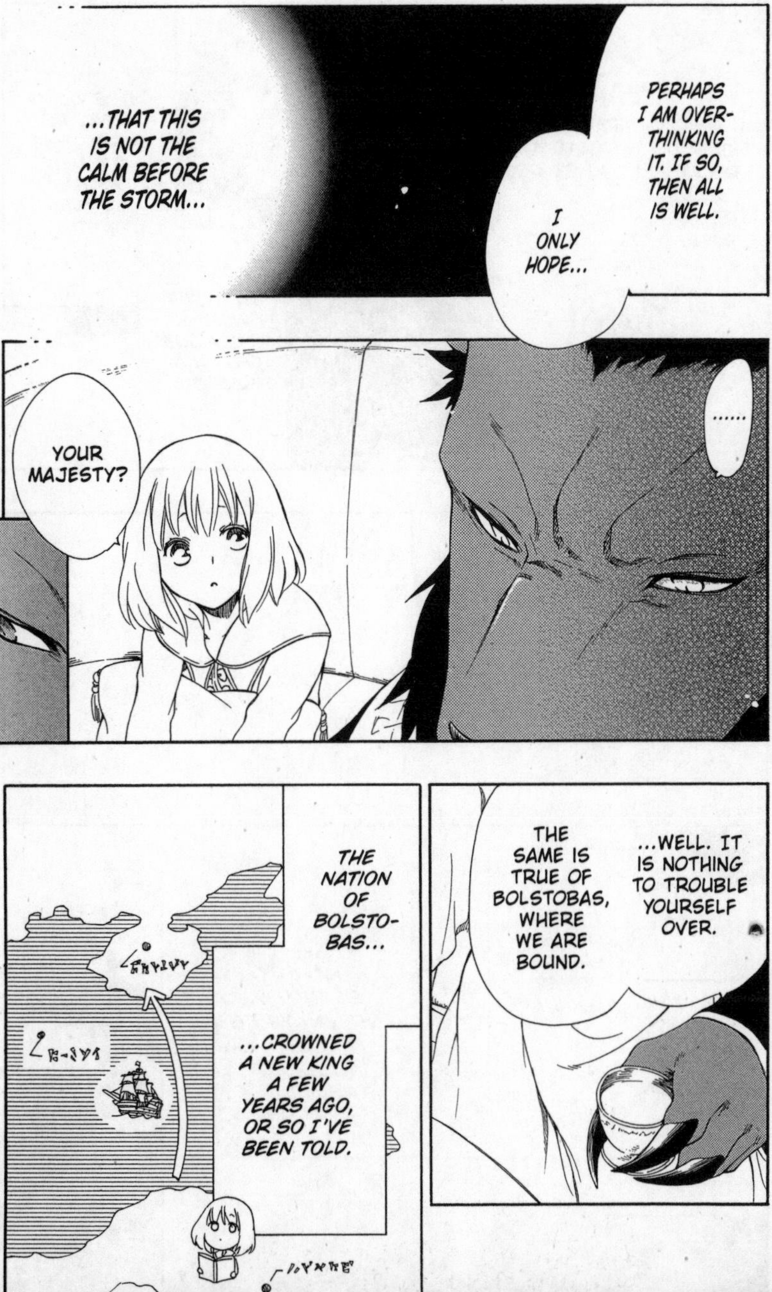
PERHAPS I AM OVER-THINKING IT. IF SO, THEN ALL IS WELL.
I ONLY HOPE...
...THAT THIS IS NOT THE CALM BEFORE THE STORM...
......
YOUR MAJESTY?
...WELL. IT IS NOTHING TO TROUBLE YOURSELF OVER.
THE SAME IS TRUE OF BOLSTOBAS, WHERE WE ARE BOUND.
THE NATION OF BOLSTO-BAS...
...CROWNED A NEW KING A FEW YEARS AGO, OR SO I'VE BEEN TOLD.

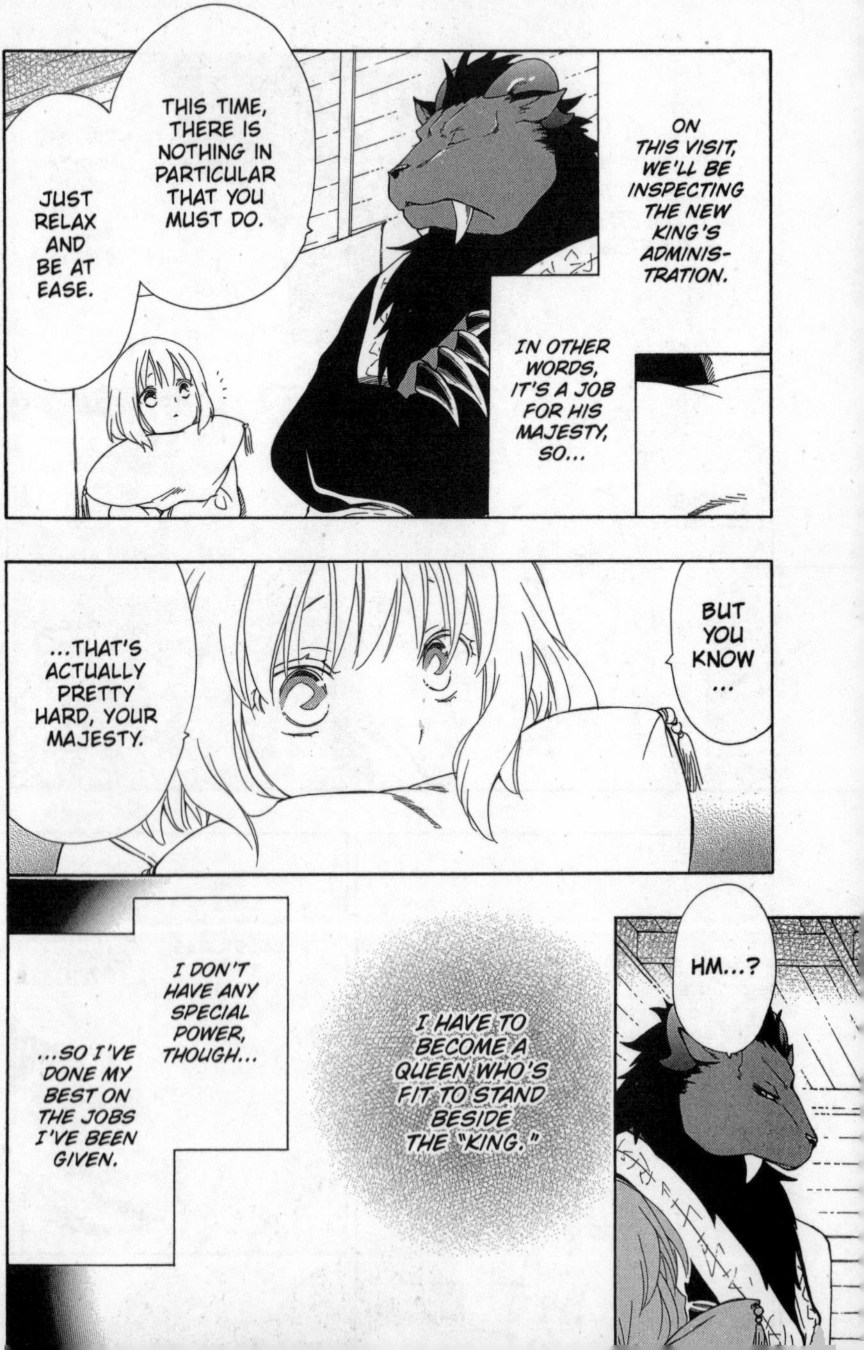
ON THIS VISIT, WE'LL BE INSPECTING THE NEW KING'S ADMINIS-TRATION.
IN OTHER WORDS, IT'S A JOB FOR HIS MAJESTY, SO...
THIS TIME, THERE IS NOTHING IN PARTICULAR THAT YOU MUST DO.
JUST RELAX AND BE AT EASE.
BUT YOU KNOW...
...THAT'S ACTUALLY PRETTY HARD, YOUR MAJESTY.
HM...?
I HAVE TO BECOME A QUEEN WHO'S FIT TO STAND BESIDE THE "KING."
I DON'T HAVE ANY SPECIAL POWER, THOUGH...
...SO I'VE DONE MY BEST ON THE JOBS I'VE BEEN GIVEN.

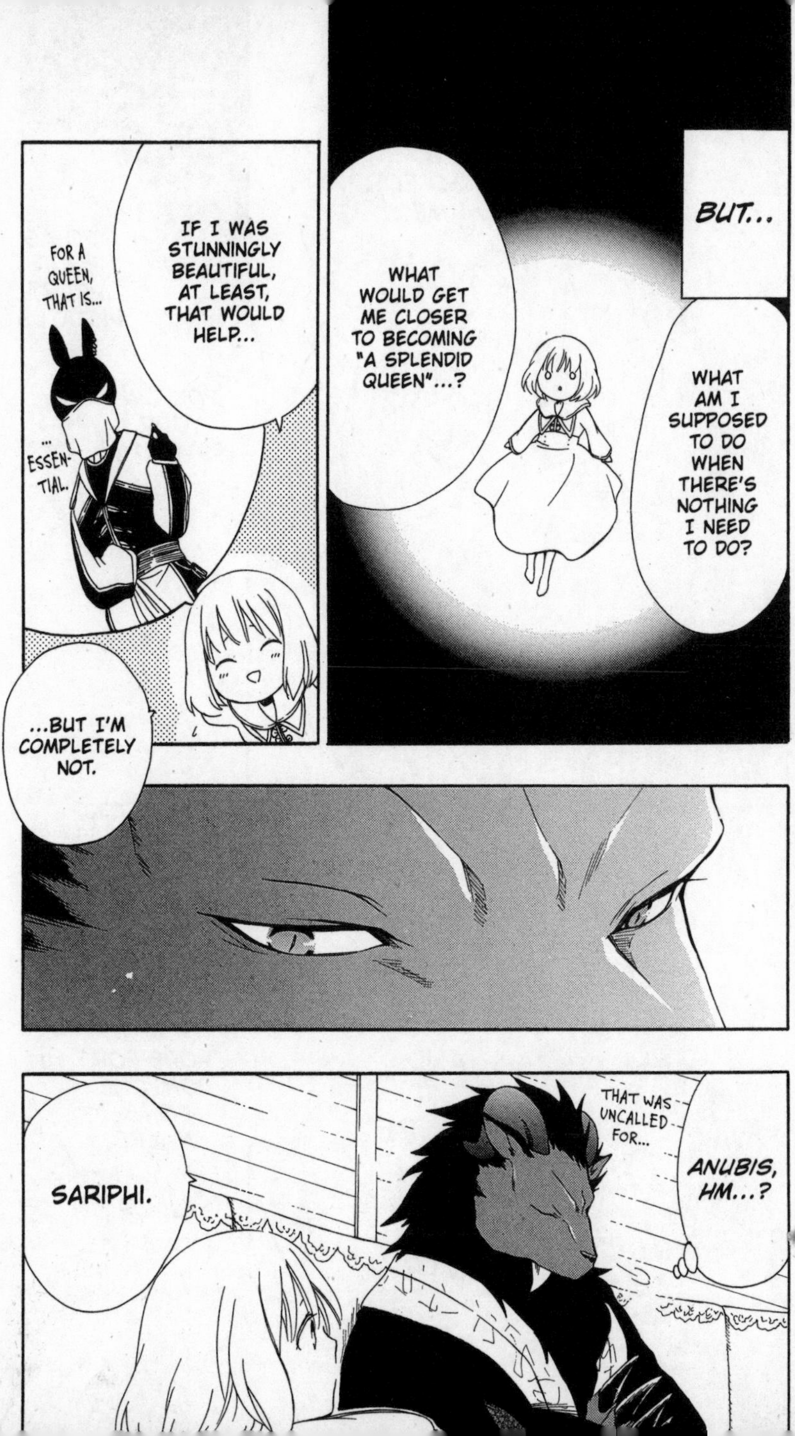
BUT...
WHAT AM I SUPPOSED TO DO WHEN THERE'S NOTHING I NEED TO DO?
WHAT WOULD GET ME CLOSER TO BECOMING "A SPLENDID QUEEN"...?
IF I WAS STUNNINGLY BEAUTIFUL, AT LEAST, THAT WOULD HELP...
FOR A QUEEN, THAT IS...
...ESSEN-TIAL.
...BUT I'M COMPLETELY NOT.
THAT WAS UNCALLED FOR...
ANUBIS, HM...?
SARIPHI.

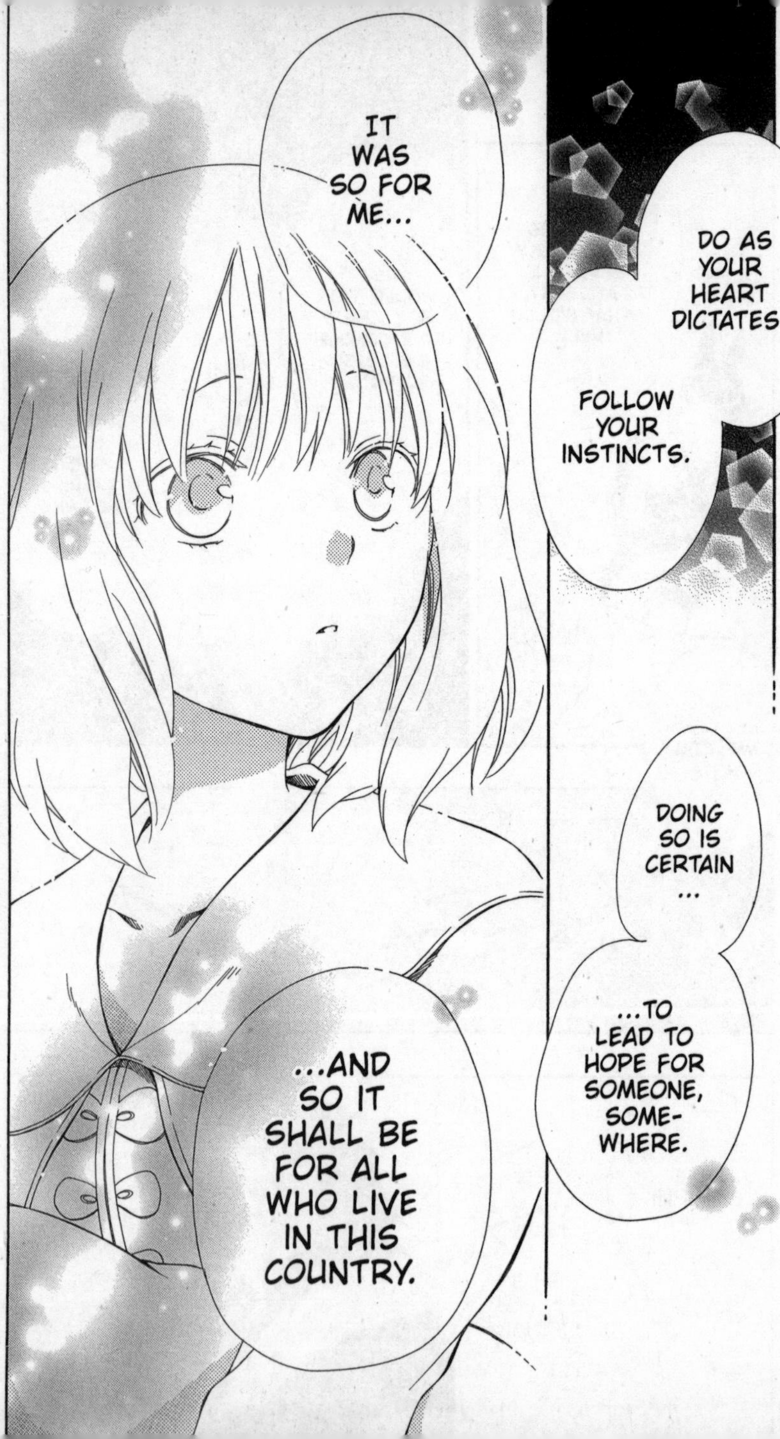
DO AS YOUR HEART DICTATES.
FOLLOW YOUR INSTINCTS.
DOING SO IS CERTAIN ...
...TO LEAD TO HOPE FOR SOMEONE, SOME-WHERE.
IT WAS SO FOR ME...
...AND SO IT SHALL BE FOR ALL WHO LIVE IN THIS COUNTRY.

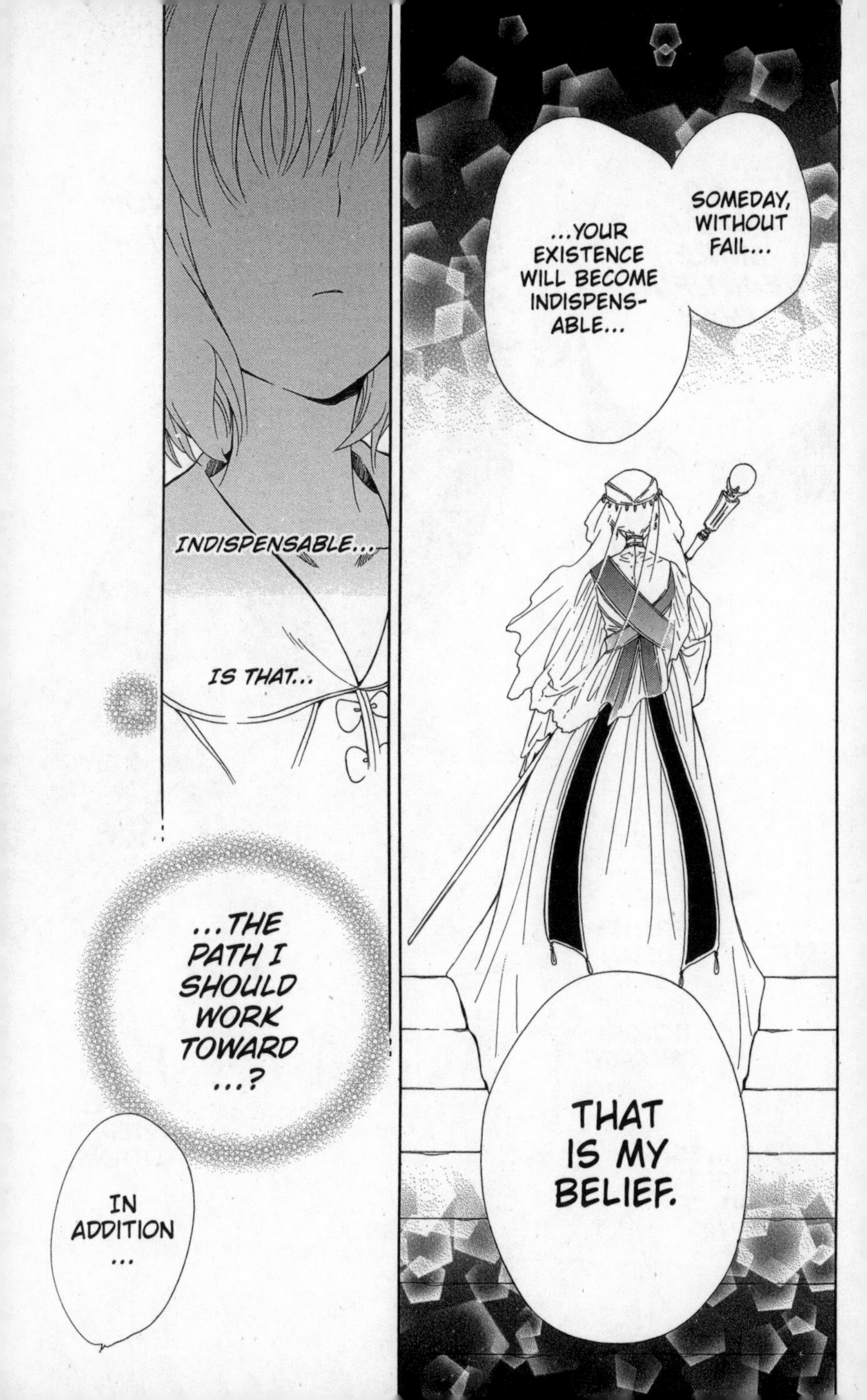
SOMEDAY, WITHOUT FAIL...
...YOUR EXISTENCE WILL BECOME INDISPENS-ABLE...
THAT IS MY BELIEF.
INDISPENSABLE...
IS THAT...
...THE PATH I SHOULD WORK TOWARD ...?
IN ADDITION ...

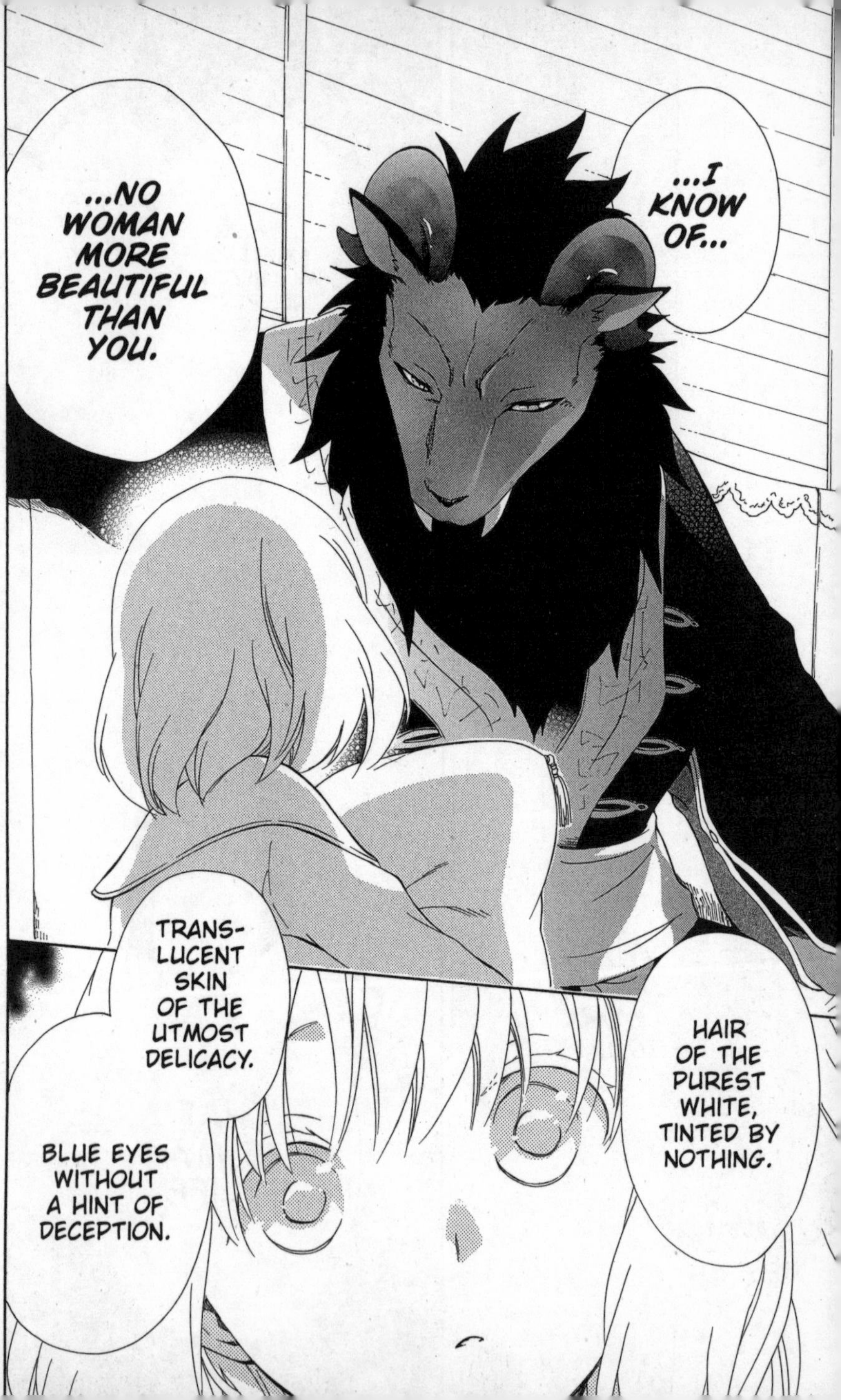
...I KNOW OF...
...NO WOMAN MORE BEAUTIFUL THAN YOU.
HAIR OF THE PUREST WHITE, TINTED BY NOTHING.
TRANS-LUCENT SKIN OF THE UTMOST DELICACY.
BLUE EYES WITHOUT A HINT OF DECEPTION.

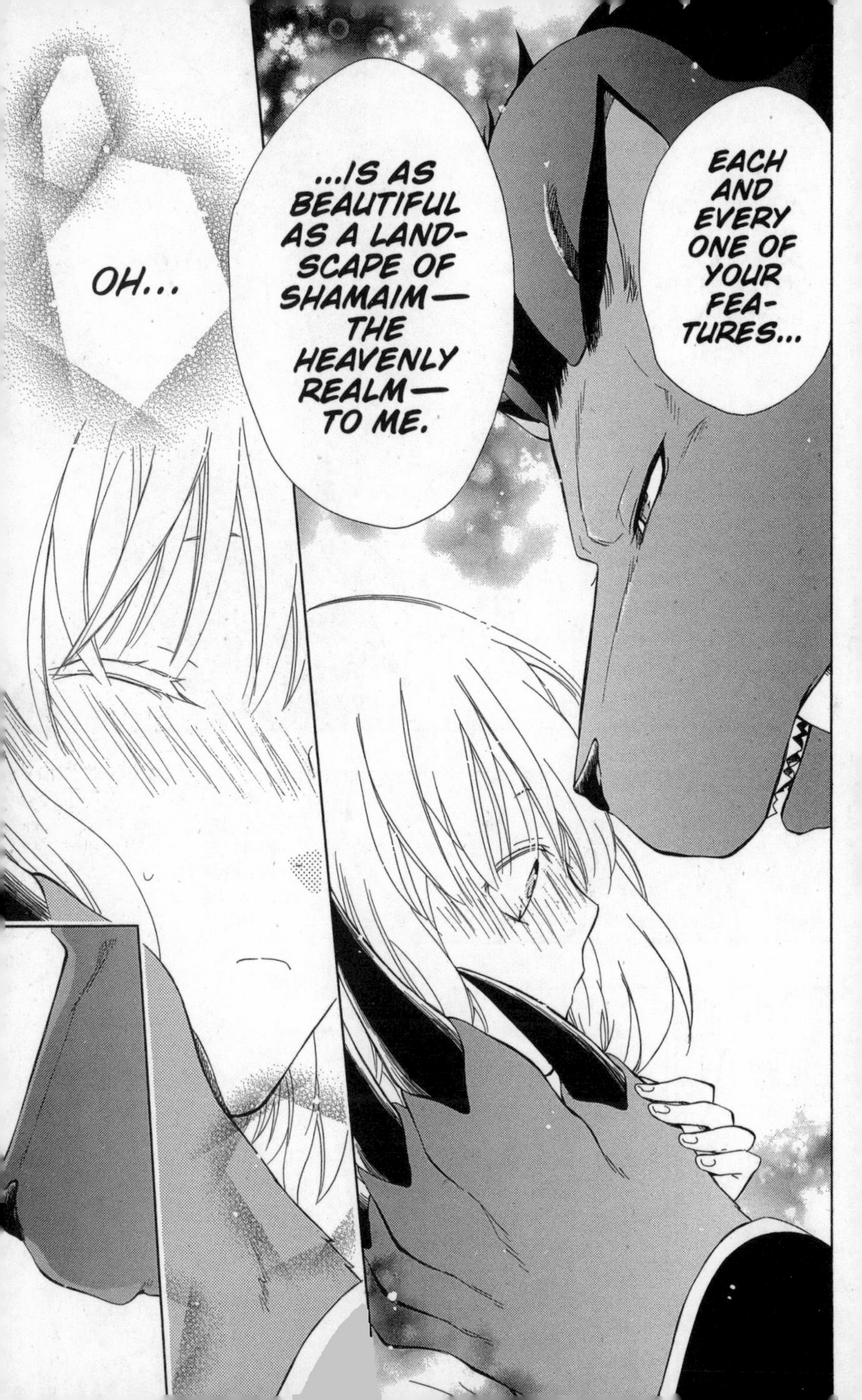
EACH AND EVERY ONE OF YOUR FEA-TURES...
...IS AS BEAUTIFUL AS A LAND-SCAPE OF SHAMAIM—THE HEAVENLY REALM—TO ME.
OH...

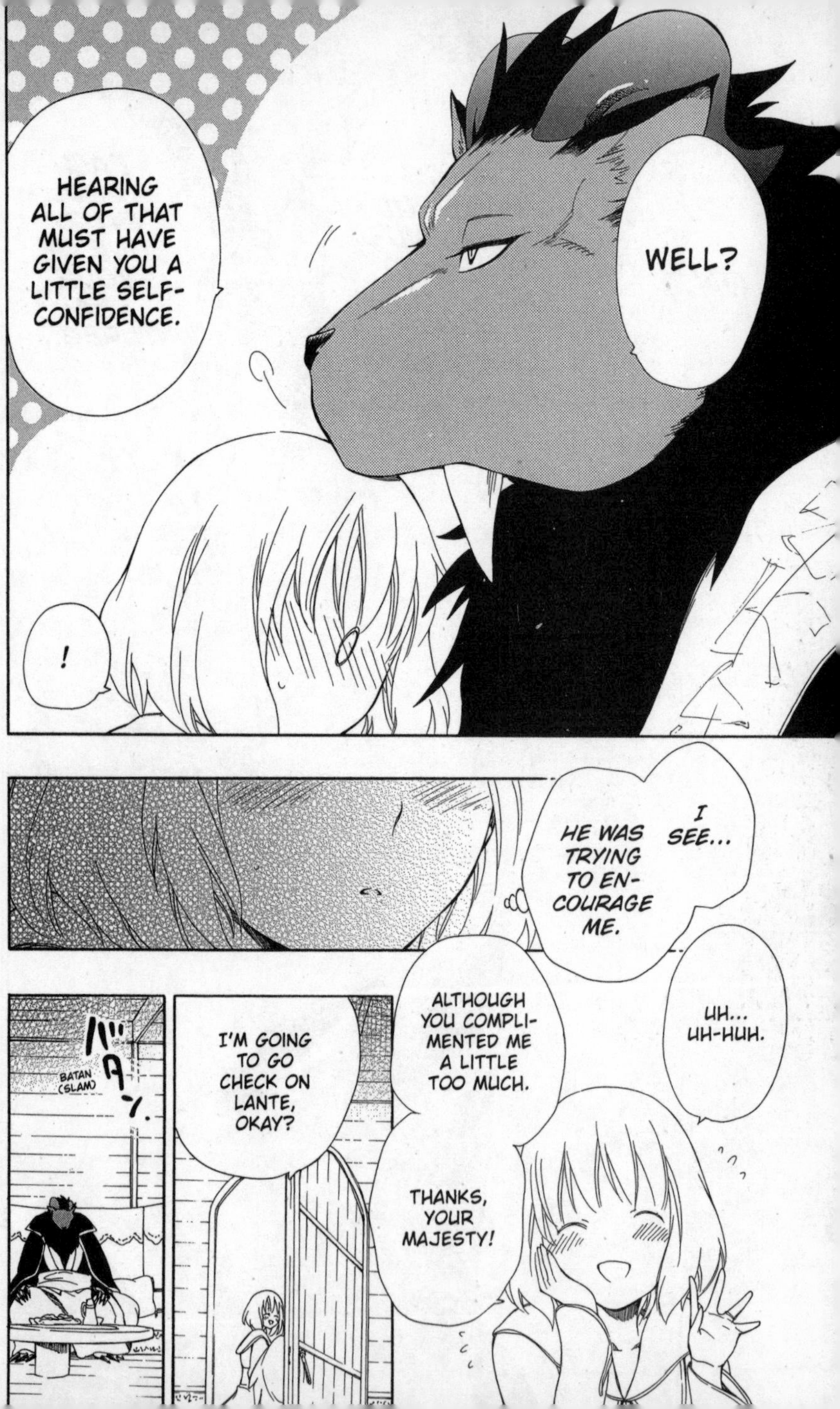
WELL?
HEARING ALL OF THAT MUST HAVE GIVEN YOU A LITTLE SELF-CONFIDENCE.
!
I SEE...
HE WAS TRYING TO EN-COURAGE ME.
UH... UH-HUH.
ALTHOUGH YOU COMPLI-MENTED ME A LITTLE TOO MUCH.
THANKS, YOUR MAJESTY!
I'M GOING TO GO CHECK ON LANTE, OKAY?
バタン
BATAN (SLAM)

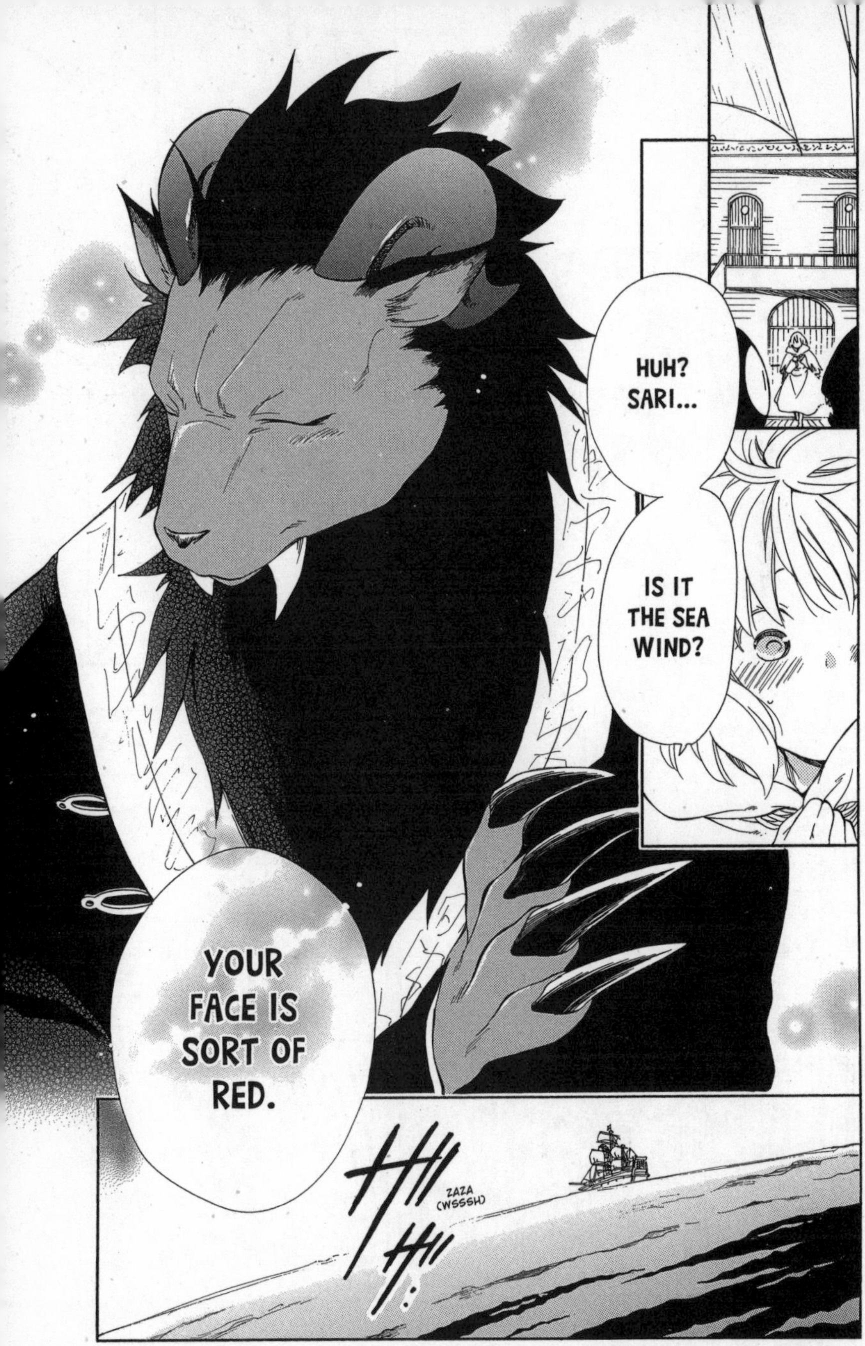
HUH? SARI...
IS IT THE SEA WIND?
YOUR FACE IS SORT OF RED.
ZAZA (WSSSH)

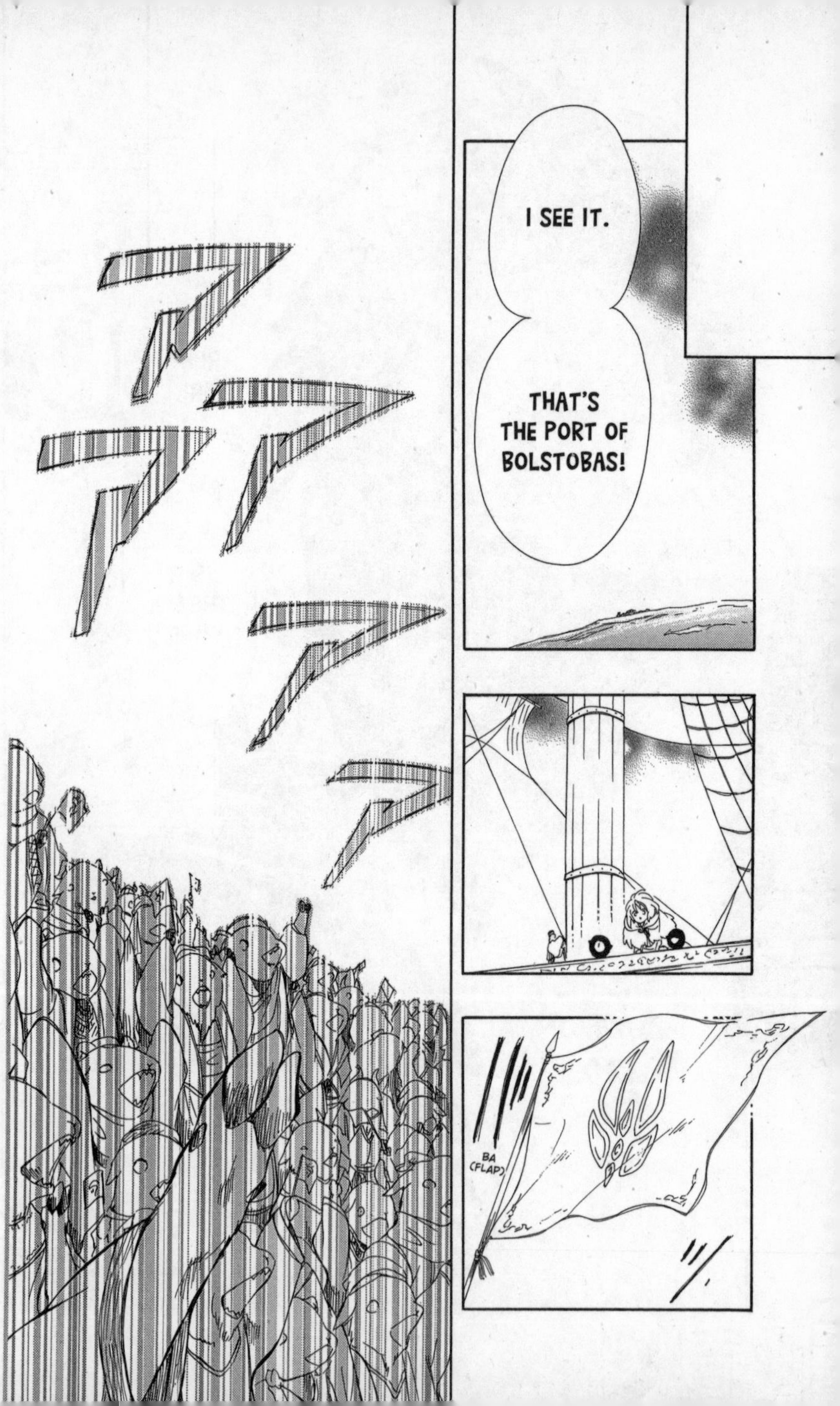
I SEE IT.
THAT'S THE PORT OF BOLSTOBAS!
BA (FLAP)

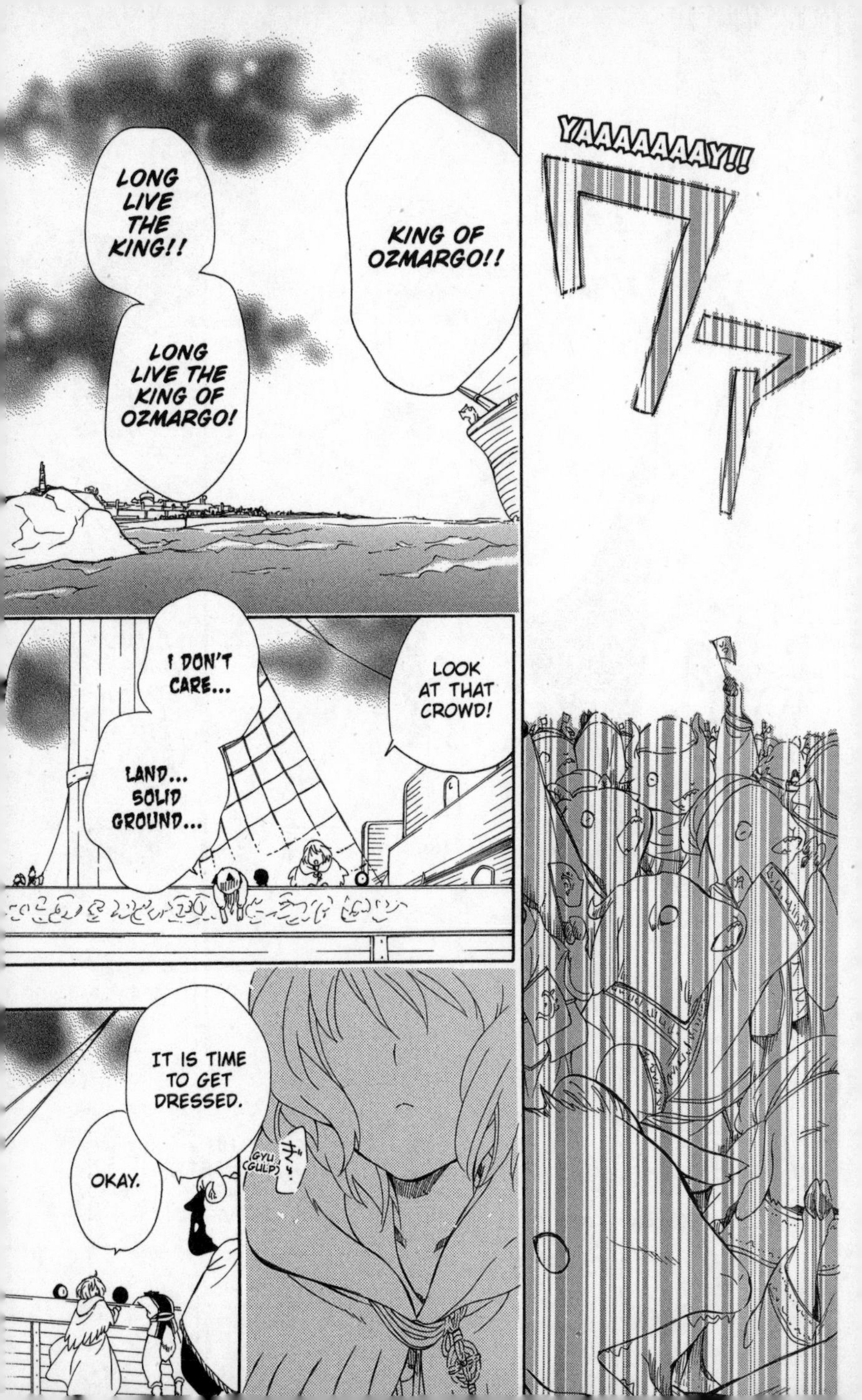
YAAAAAAAY!!
KING OF OZMARGO!!
LONG LIVE THE KING!!
LONG LIVE THE KING OF OZMARGO!
LOOK AT THAT CROWD!
I DON'T CARE...
LAND... SOLID GROUND...
GYU (GULP)
IT IS TIME TO GET DRESSED.
OKAY.

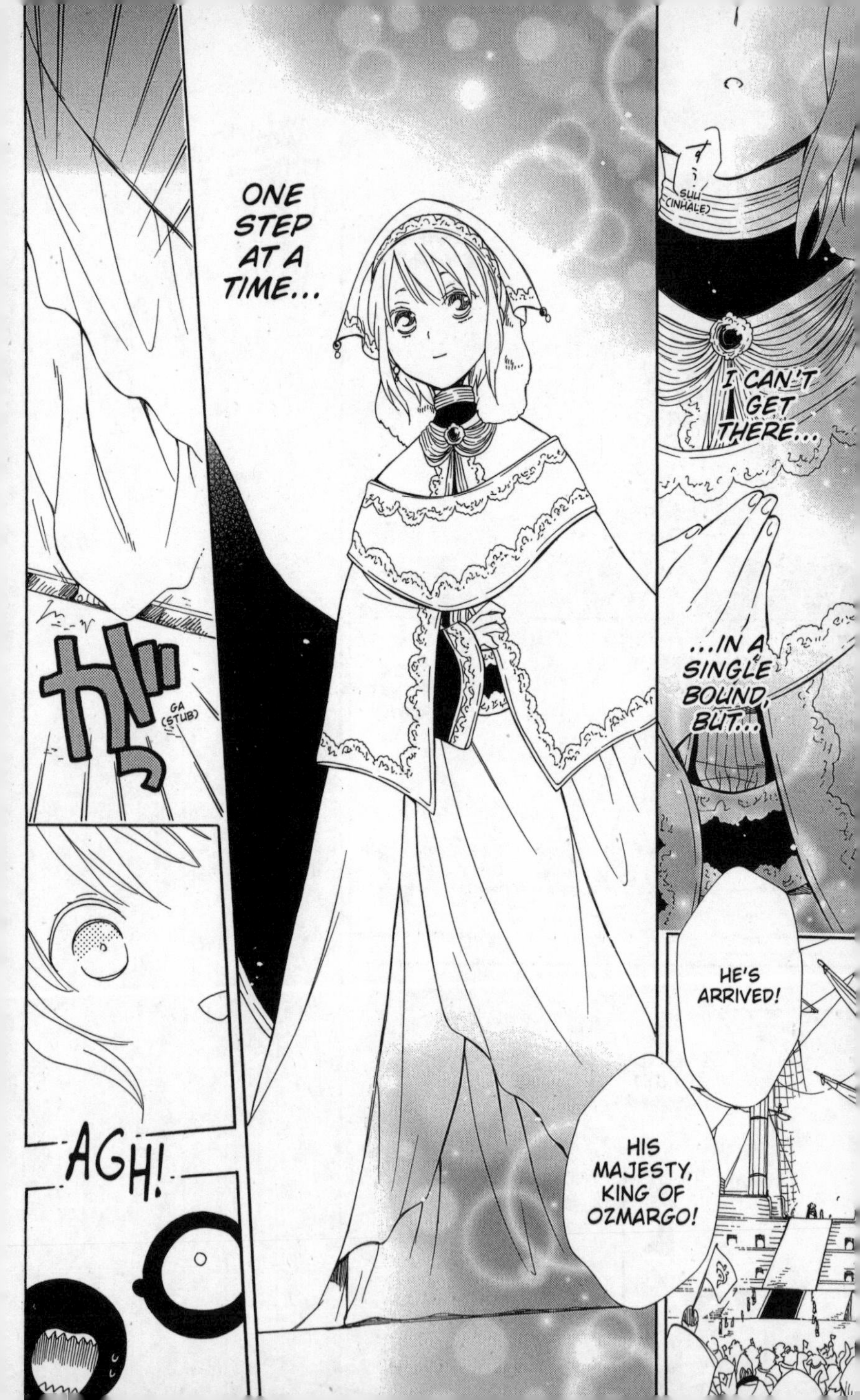
SUU (INHALE)
I CAN'T GET THERE...
...IN A SINGLE BOUND, BUT...
HE'S ARRIVED!
HIS MAJESTY, KING OF OZMARGO!
ONE STEP AT A TIME...
GA (STUB)
AGH!

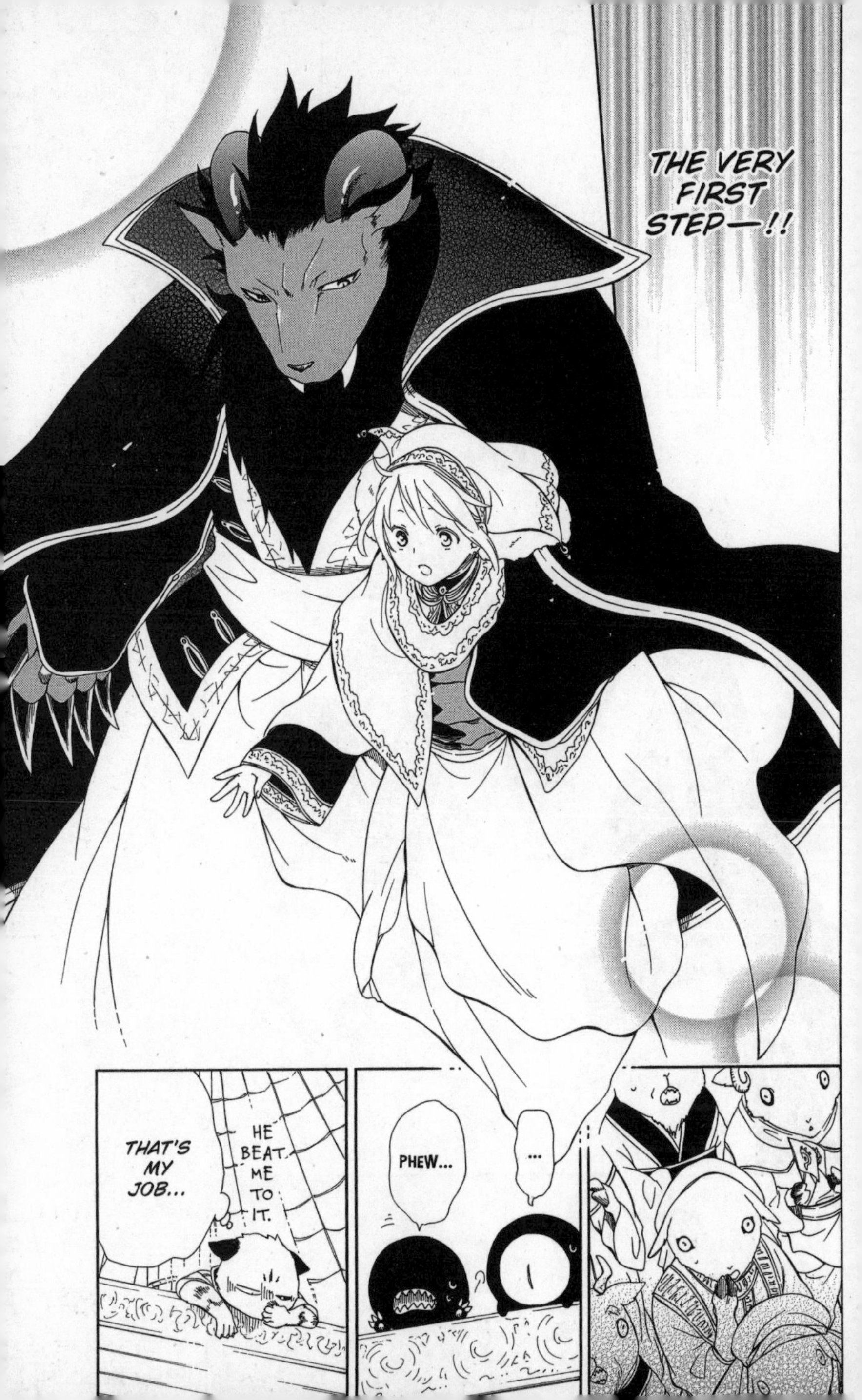
THE VERY FIRST STEP—!!
...
PHEW...
HE BEAT ME TO IT.
THAT'S MY JOB...

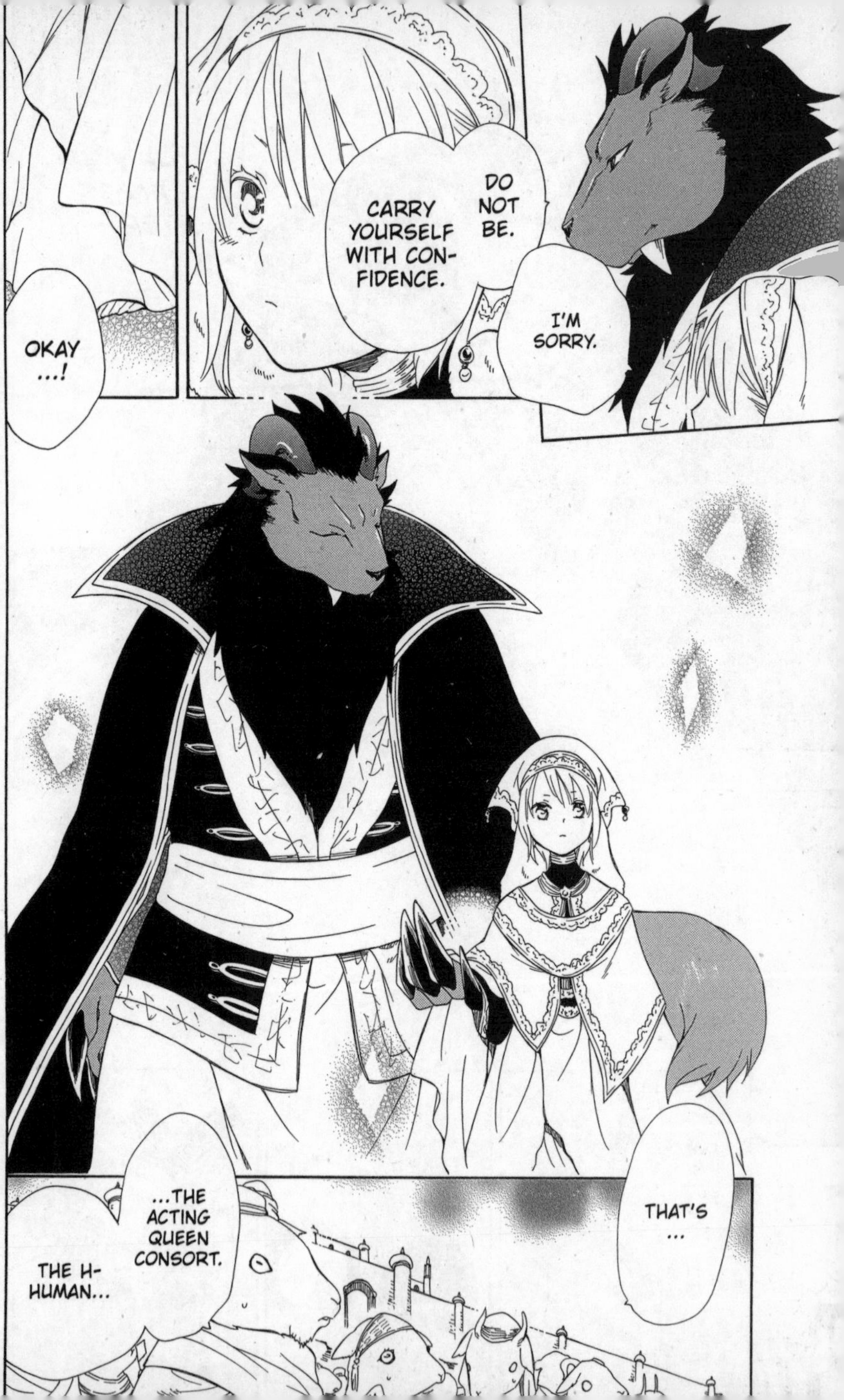
I'M SORRY.
DO NOT BE.
CARRY YOURSELF WITH CON- FIDENCE.
OKAY ...!
THAT'S ...
...THE ACTING QUEEN CONSORT.
THE H- HUMAN...

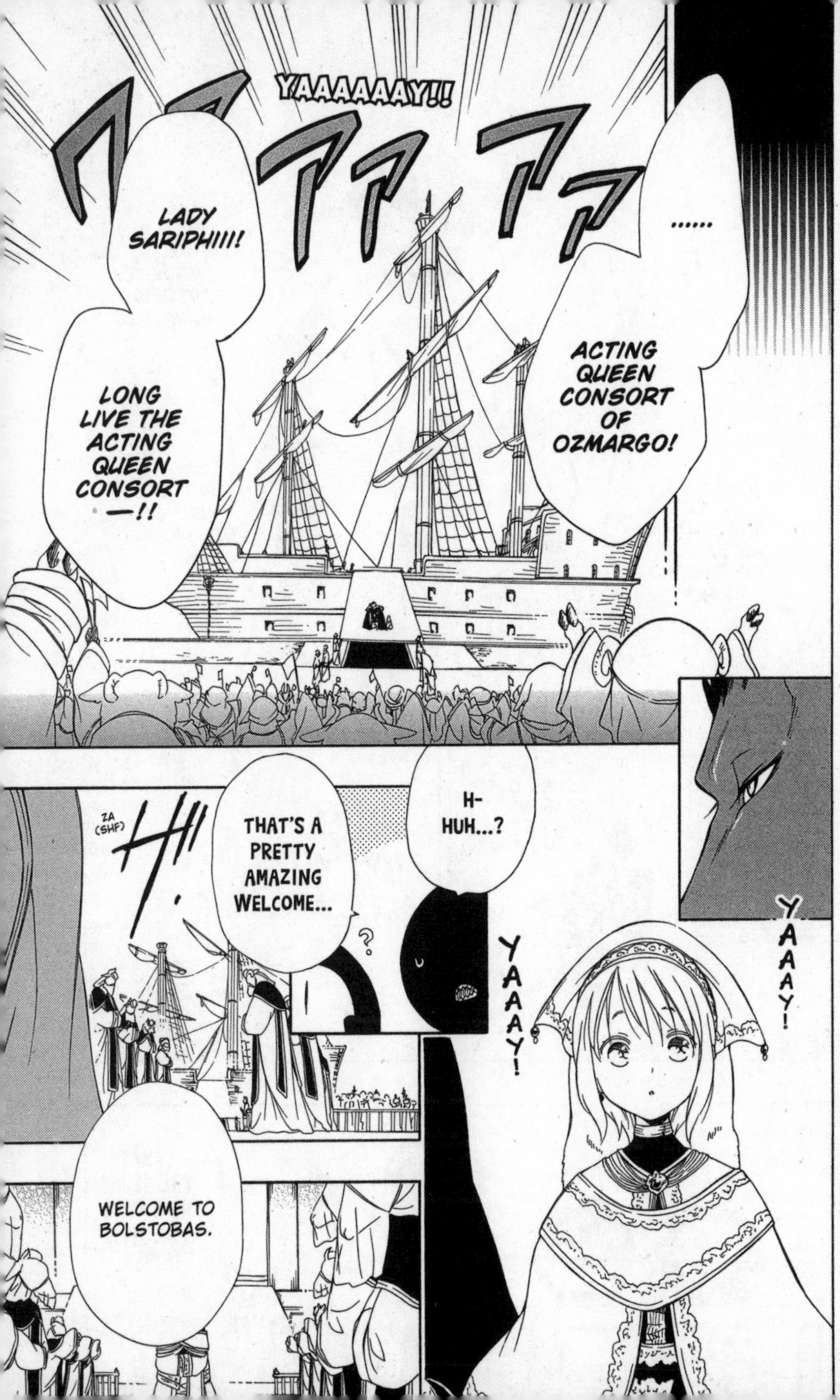
......
YAAAAAAY!!
LADY SARIPHIII!
ACTING QUEEN CONSORT OF OZMARGO!
LONG LIVE THE ACTING QUEEN CONSORT—!!
YAAAY!
YAAAY!
H-HUH...?
THAT'S A PRETTY AMAZING WELCOME...
ZA (SHF)
WELCOME TO BOLSTOBAS.

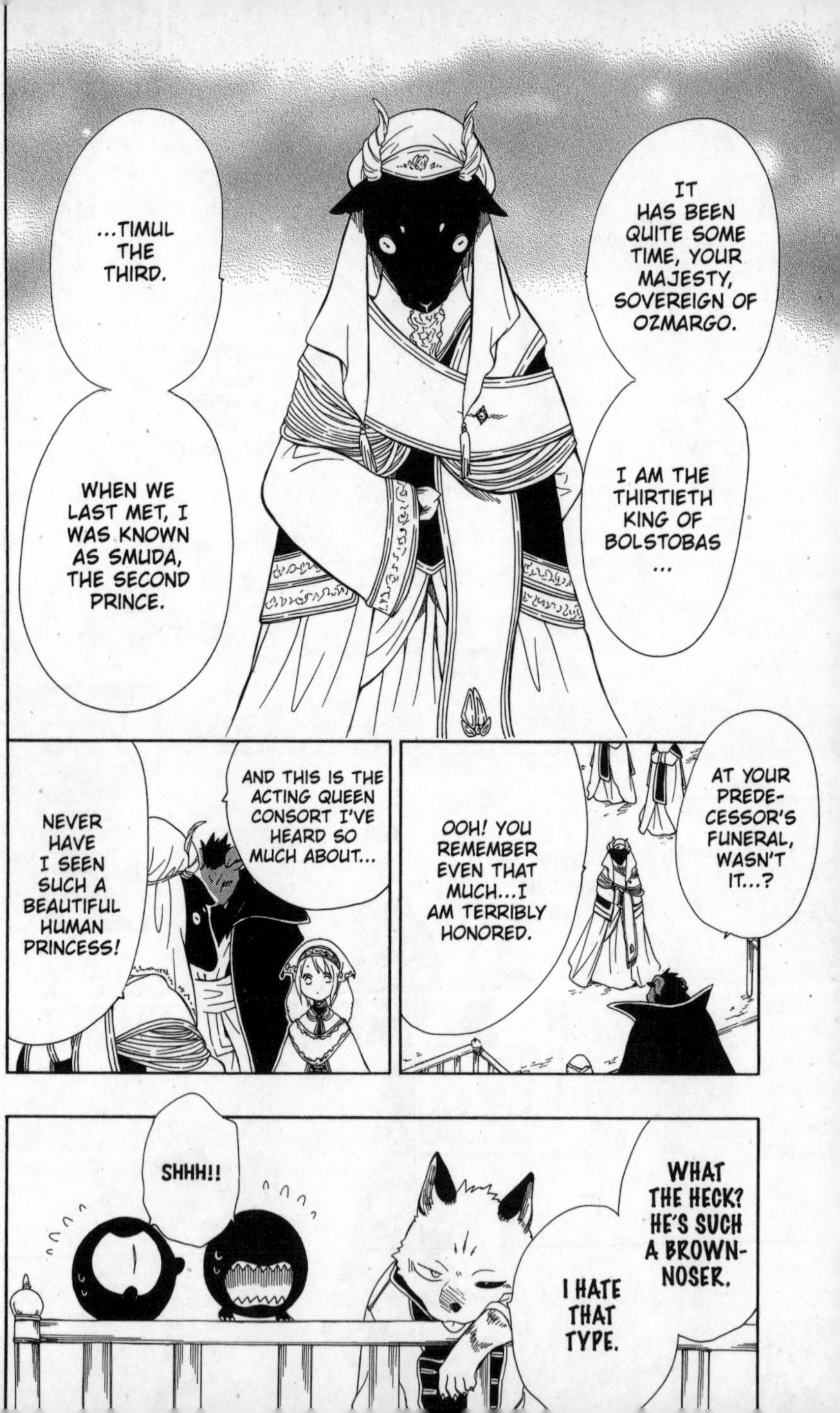
IT HAS BEEN QUITE SOME TIME, YOUR MAJESTY, SOVEREIGN OF OZMARGO.
I AM THE THIRTIETH KING OF BOLSTOBAS...
...TIMUL THE THIRD.
WHEN WE LAST MET, I WAS KNOWN AS SMUDA, THE SECOND PRINCE.
AT YOUR PREDECESSOR'S FUNERAL, WASN'T IT...?
OOH! YOU REMEMBER EVEN THAT MUCH...I AM TERRIBLY HONORED.
AND THIS IS THE ACTING QUEEN CONSORT I'VE HEARD SO MUCH ABOUT...
NEVER HAVE I SEEN SUCH A BEAUTIFUL HUMAN PRINCESS!
WHAT THE HECK? HE'S SUCH A BROWN-NOSER.
I HATE THAT TYPE.
SHHH!!

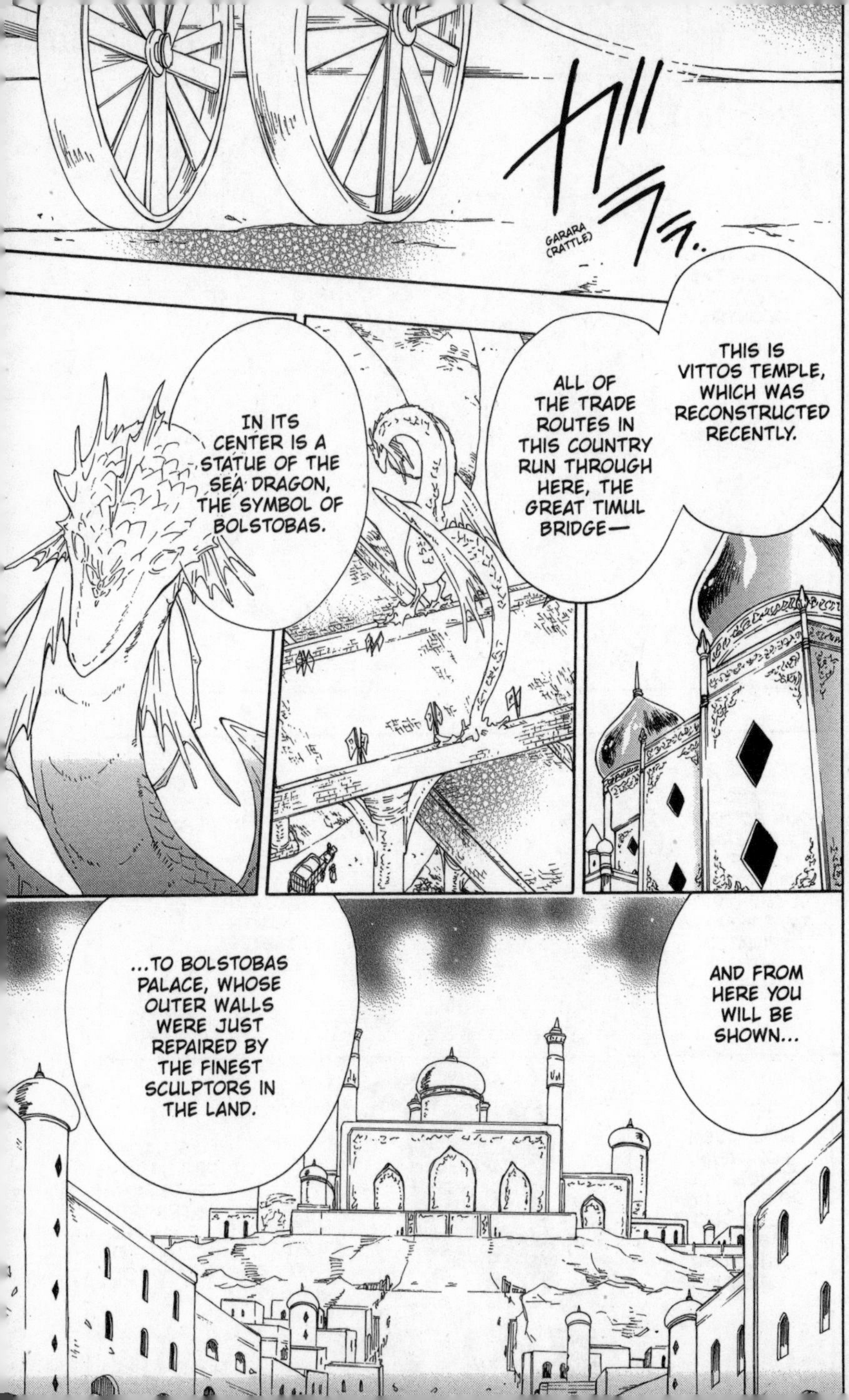
GARARA (RATTLE)
THIS IS VITTOS TEMPLE, WHICH WAS RECONSTRUCTED RECENTLY.
ALL OF THE TRADE ROUTES IN THIS COUNTRY RUN THROUGH HERE, THE GREAT TIMUL BRIDGE—
IN ITS CENTER IS A STATUE OF THE SEA DRAGON, THE SYMBOL OF BOLSTOBAS.
AND FROM HERE YOU WILL BE SHOWN...
...TO BOLSTOBAS PALACE, WHOSE OUTER WALLS WERE JUST REPAIRED BY THE FINEST SCULPTORS IN THE LAND.

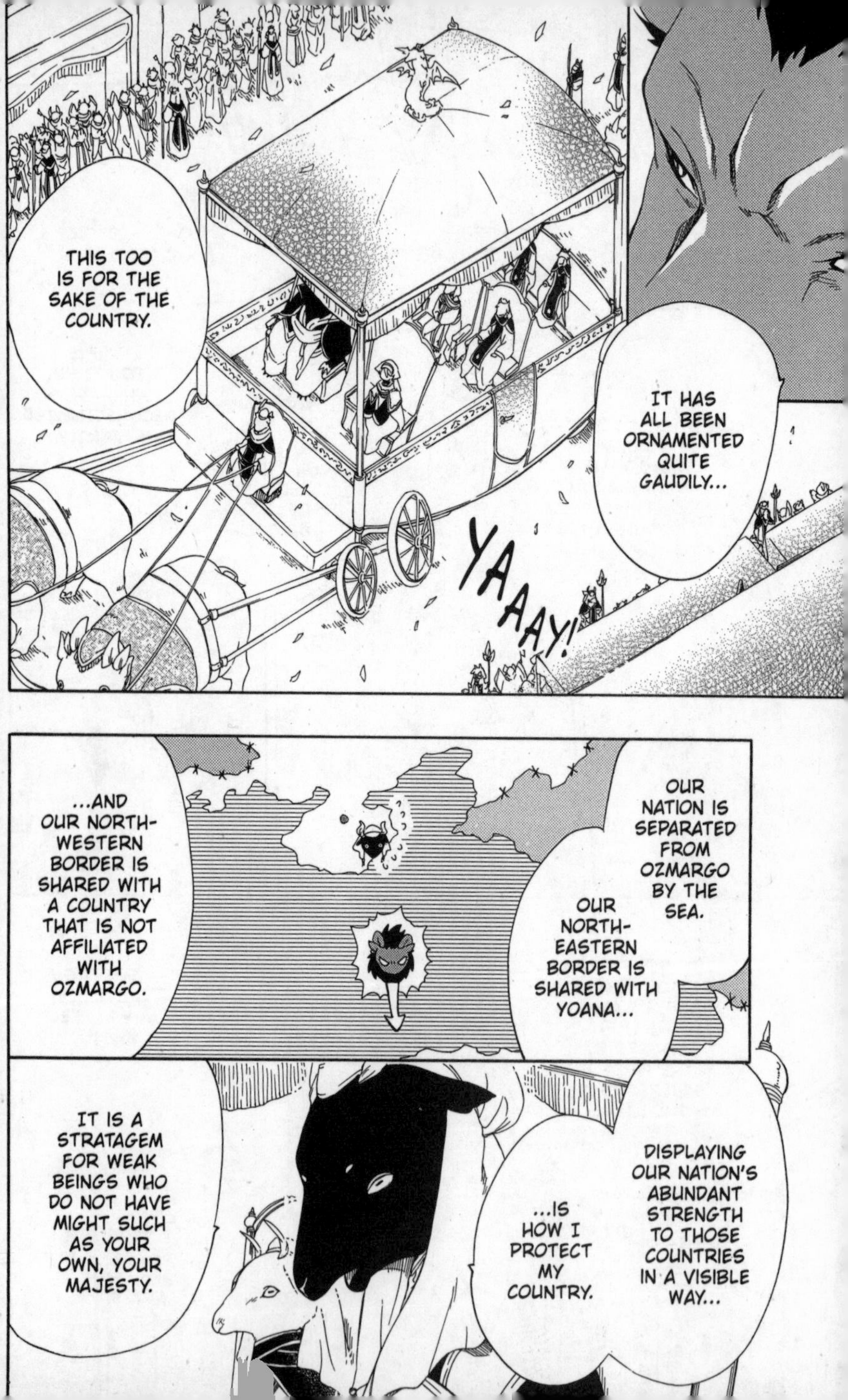
IT HAS ALL BEEN ORNAMENTED QUITE GAUDILY...
THIS TOO IS FOR THE SAKE OF THE COUNTRY.
YAAAAY!
OUR NATION IS SEPARATED FROM OZMARGO BY THE SEA.
OUR NORTH-EASTERN BORDER IS SHARED WITH YOANA...
...AND OUR NORTH-WESTERN BORDER IS SHARED WITH A COUNTRY THAT IS NOT AFFILIATED WITH OZMARGO.
DISPLAYING OUR NATION'S ABUNDANT STRENGTH TO THOSE COUNTRIES IN A VISIBLE WAY...
...IS HOW I PROTECT MY COUNTRY.
IT IS A STRATAGEM FOR WEAK BEINGS WHO DO NOT HAVE MIGHT SUCH AS YOUR OWN, YOUR MAJESTY.

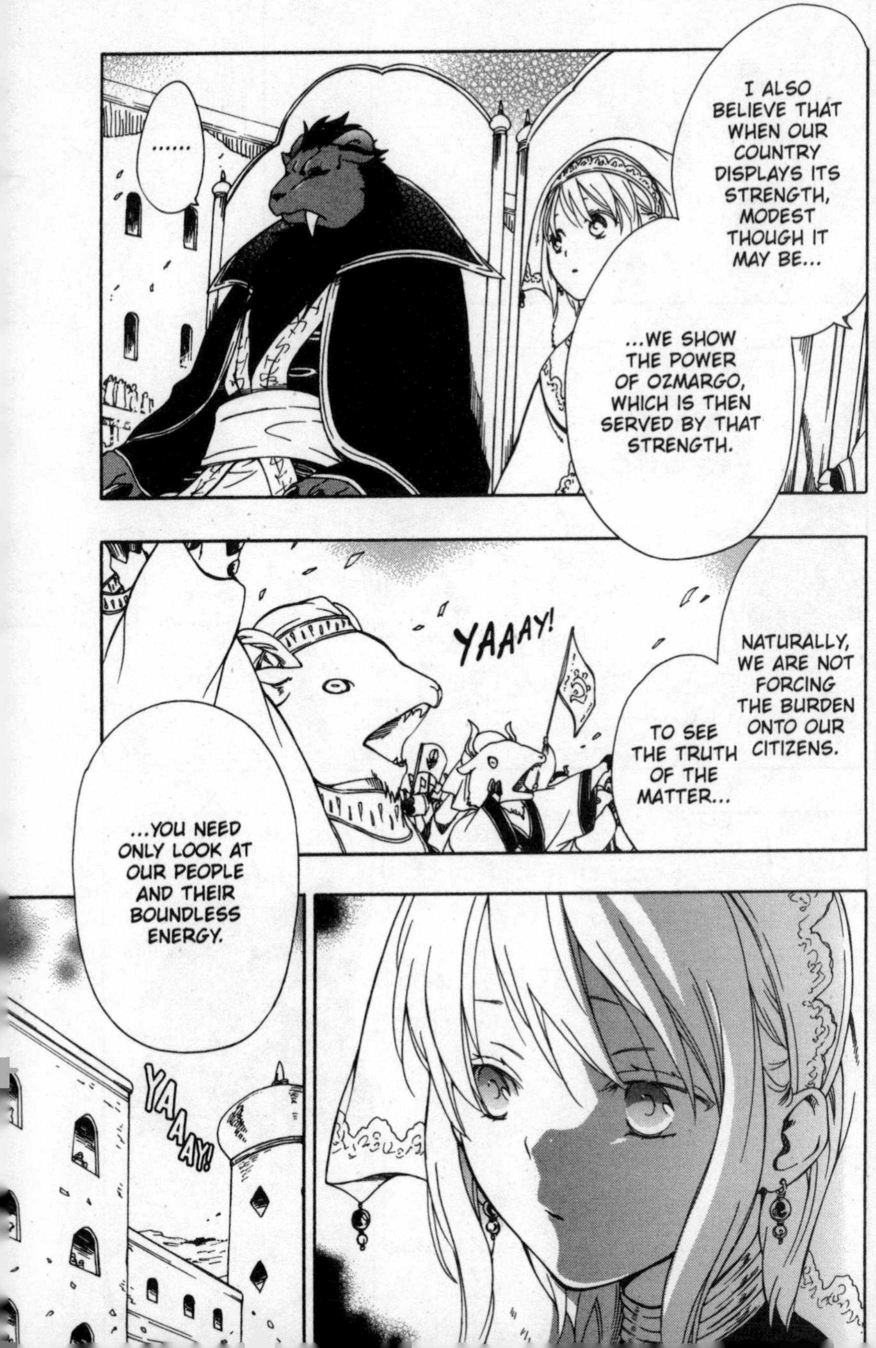
I ALSO BELIEVE THAT WHEN OUR COUNTRY DISPLAYS ITS STRENGTH, MODEST THOUGH IT MAY BE...
...WE SHOW THE POWER OF OZMARGO, WHICH IS THEN SERVED BY THAT STRENGTH.
......
NATURALLY, WE ARE NOT FORCING THE BURDEN ONTO OUR CITIZENS.
TO SEE THE TRUTH OF THE MATTER...
YAAAY!
...YOU NEED ONLY LOOK AT OUR PEOPLE AND THEIR BOUNDLESS ENERGY.
YAAAAY!

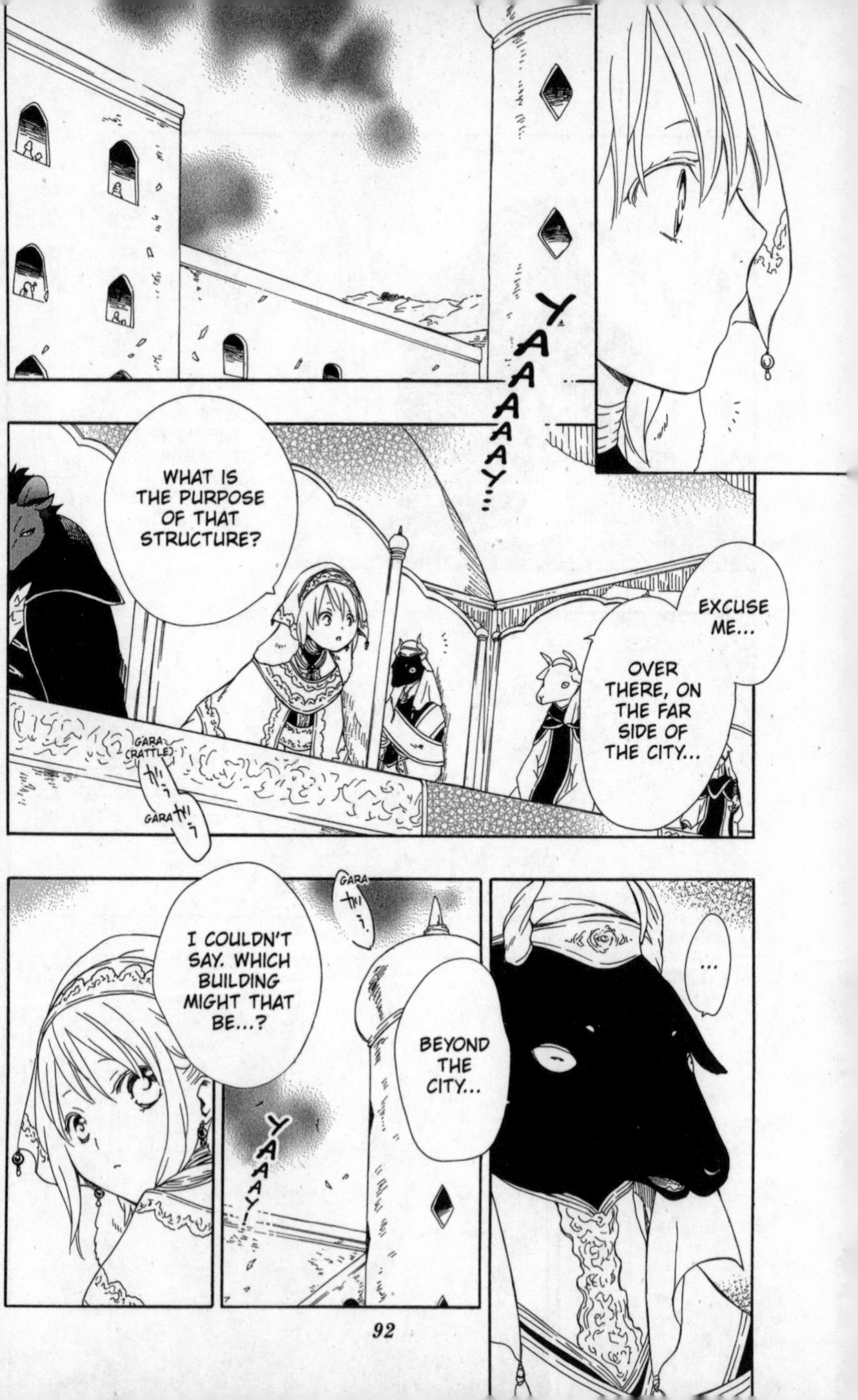
YAAAAAY...
EXCUSE ME...
OVER THERE, ON THE FAR SIDE OF THE CITY...
WHAT IS THE PURPOSE OF THAT STRUCTURE?
GARA (RATTLE)
GARA
...
BEYOND THE CITY...
GARA
I COULDN'T SAY. WHICH BUILDING MIGHT THAT BE...?
YAAAAY!

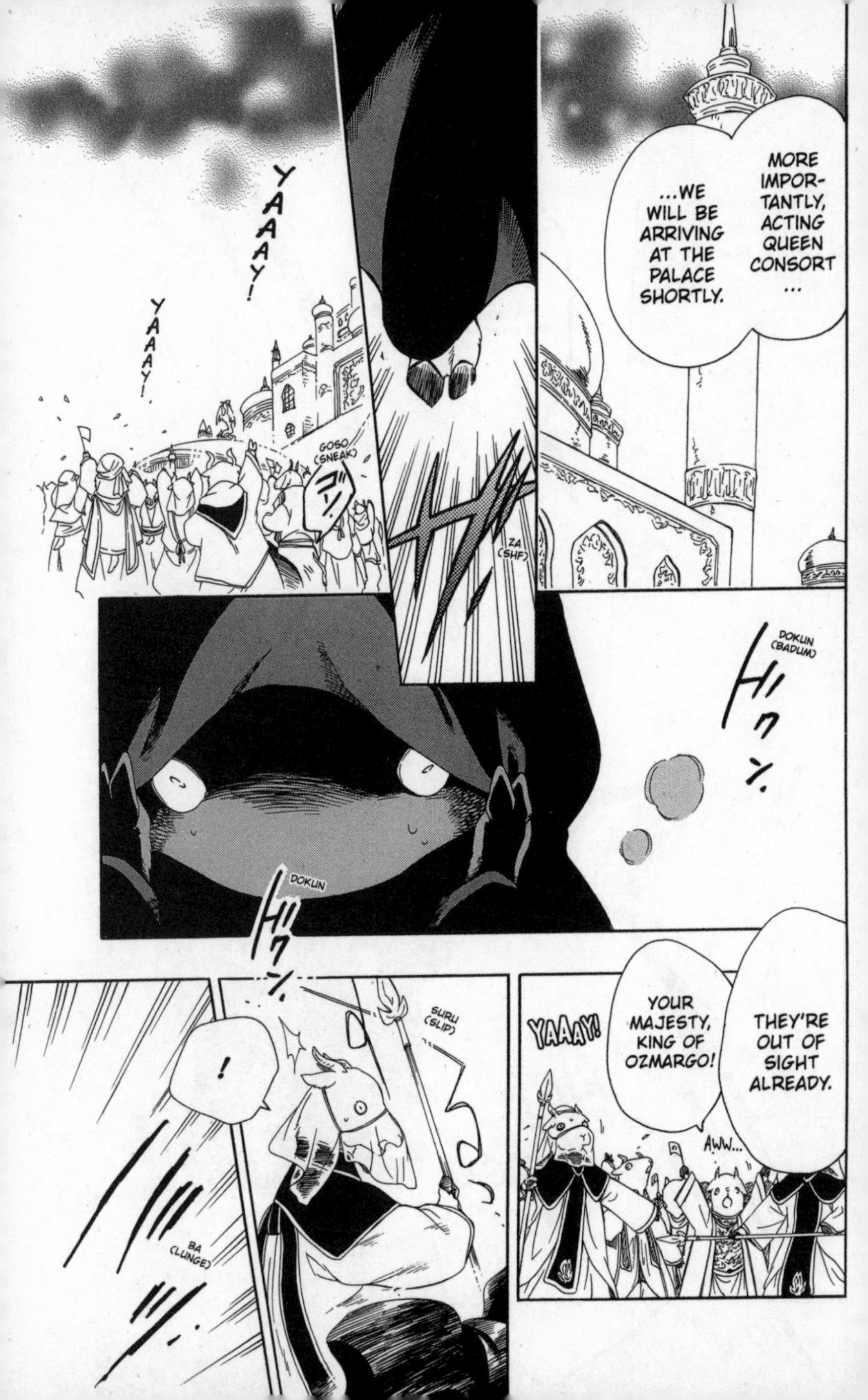
MORE IMPORTANTLY, ACTING QUEEN CONSORT...
...WE WILL BE ARRIVING AT THE PALACE SHORTLY.
ZA (SHF)
YAAAAY!
YAAAY!
GOSO (SNEAK)
DOKUN (BADUM)
DOKUN
THEY'RE OUT OF SIGHT ALREADY.
YOUR MAJESTY, KING OF OZMARGO!
YAAAY!
AWW...
SURU (SLIP)
!
BA (LUNGE)

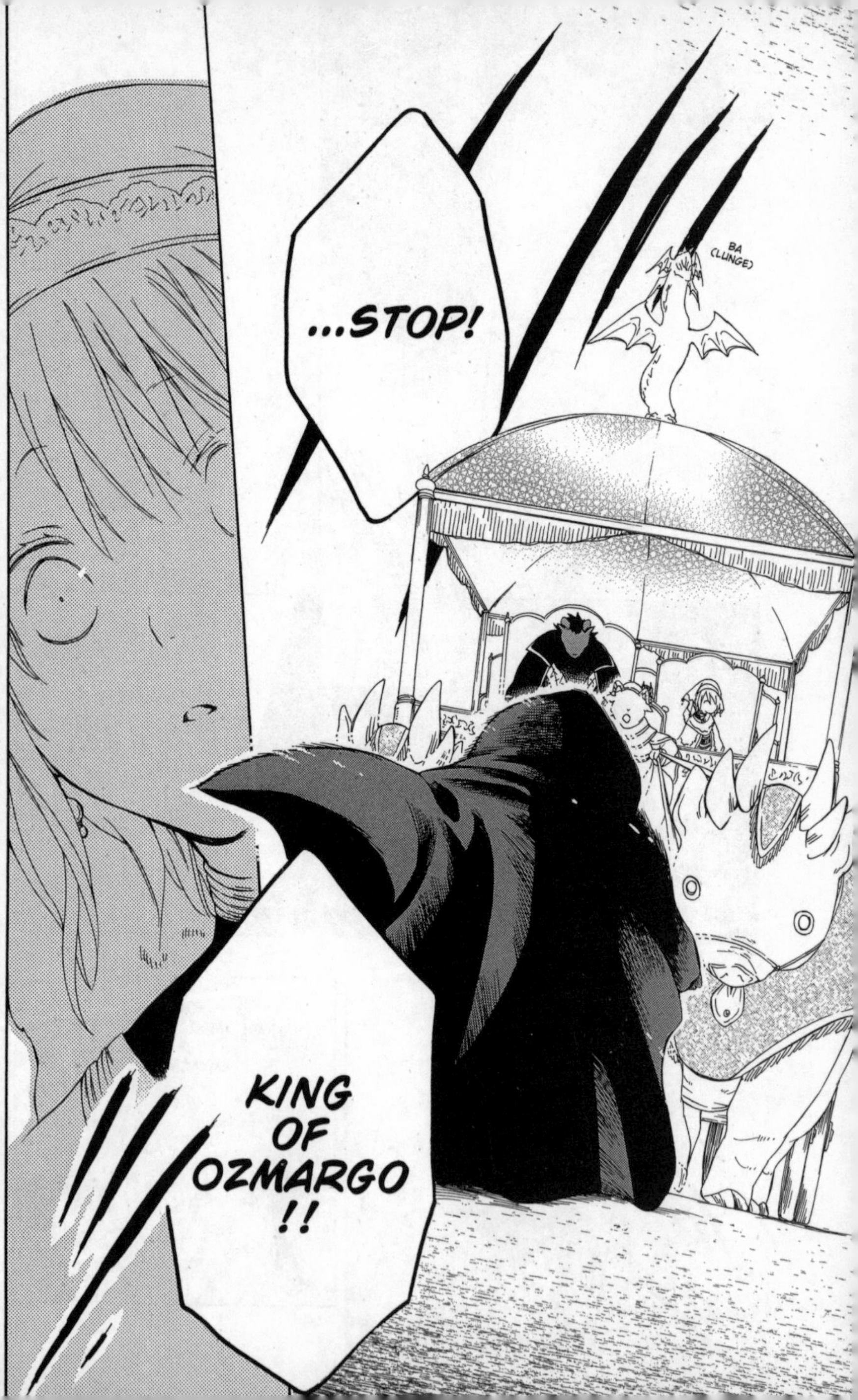
BA (LUNGE)
...STOP!
KING OF OZMARGO !!

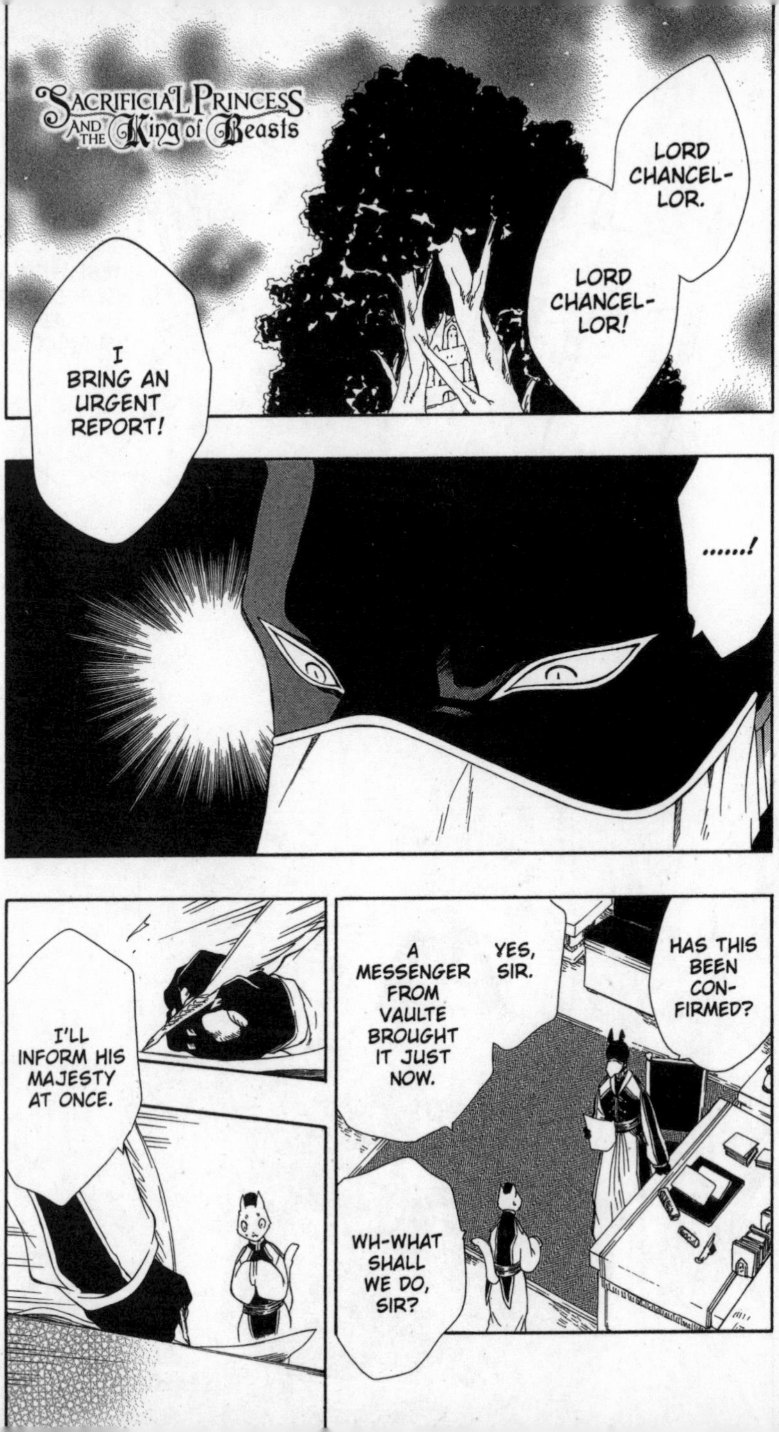
SACRIFICIAL PRINCESS AND THE King of Beasts
LORD CHANCEL-LOR.
LORD CHANCEL-LOR!
I BRING AN URGENT REPORT!
......!
HAS THIS BEEN CON-FIRMED?
YES, SIR.
A MESSENGER FROM VAULTE BROUGHT IT JUST NOW.
WH-WHAT SHALL WE DO, SIR?
I'LL INFORM HIS MAJESTY AT ONCE.

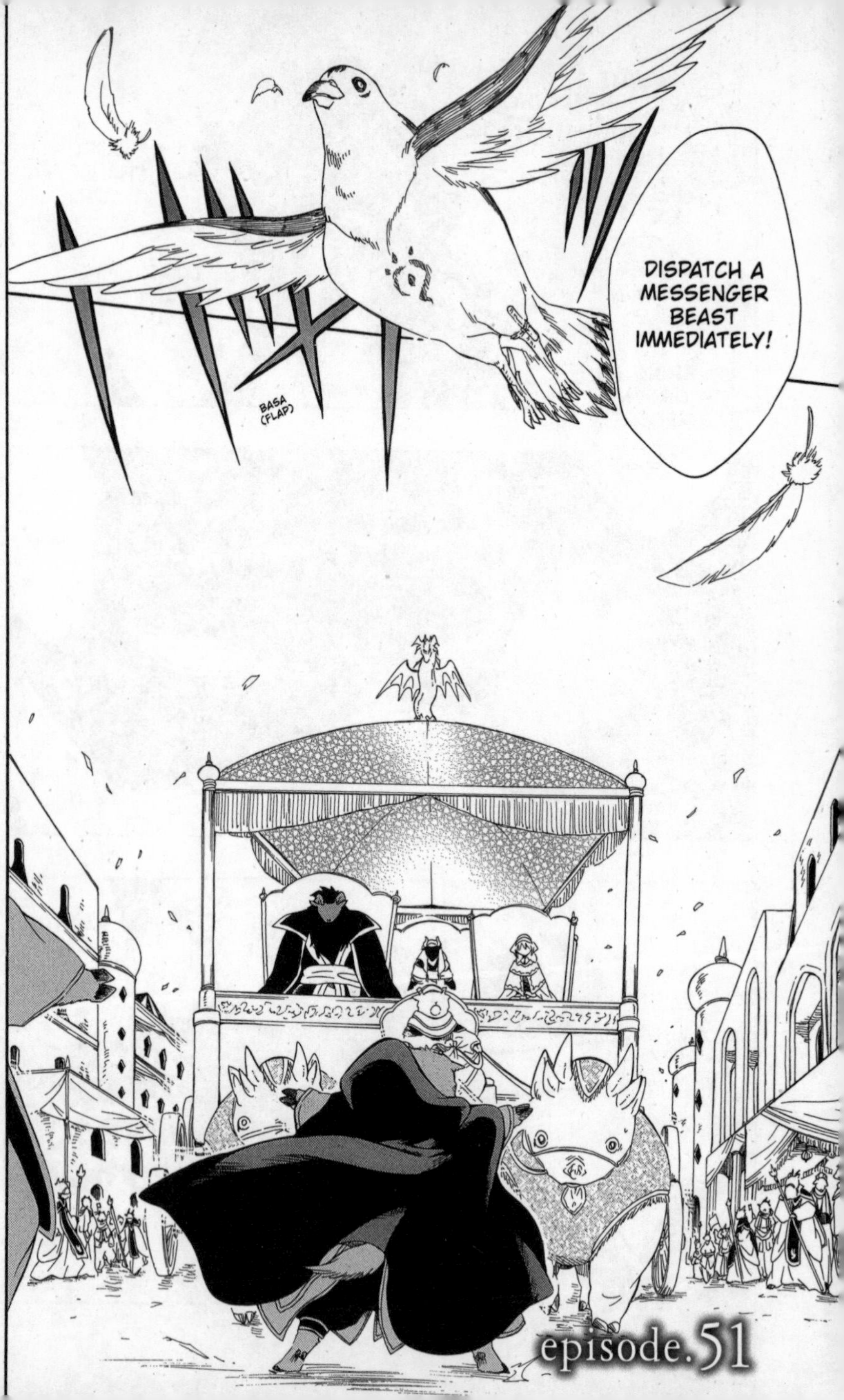
DISPATCH A MESSENGER BEAST IMMEDIATELY!
BASA (FLAP)
episode. 51

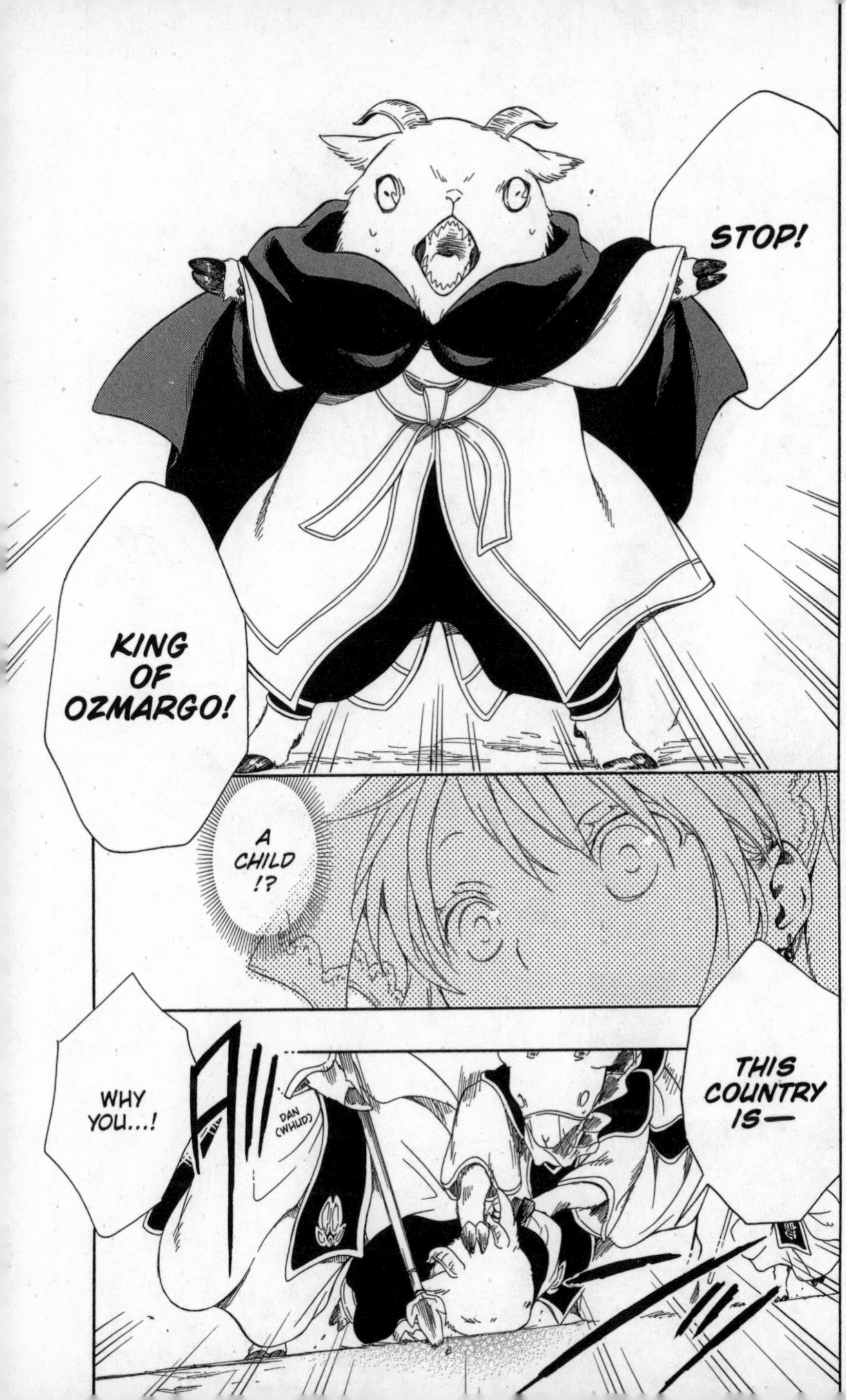
STOP!
KING OF OZMARGO!
A CHILD!?
THIS COUNTRY IS—
DAN (WHUD)
WHY YOU...!

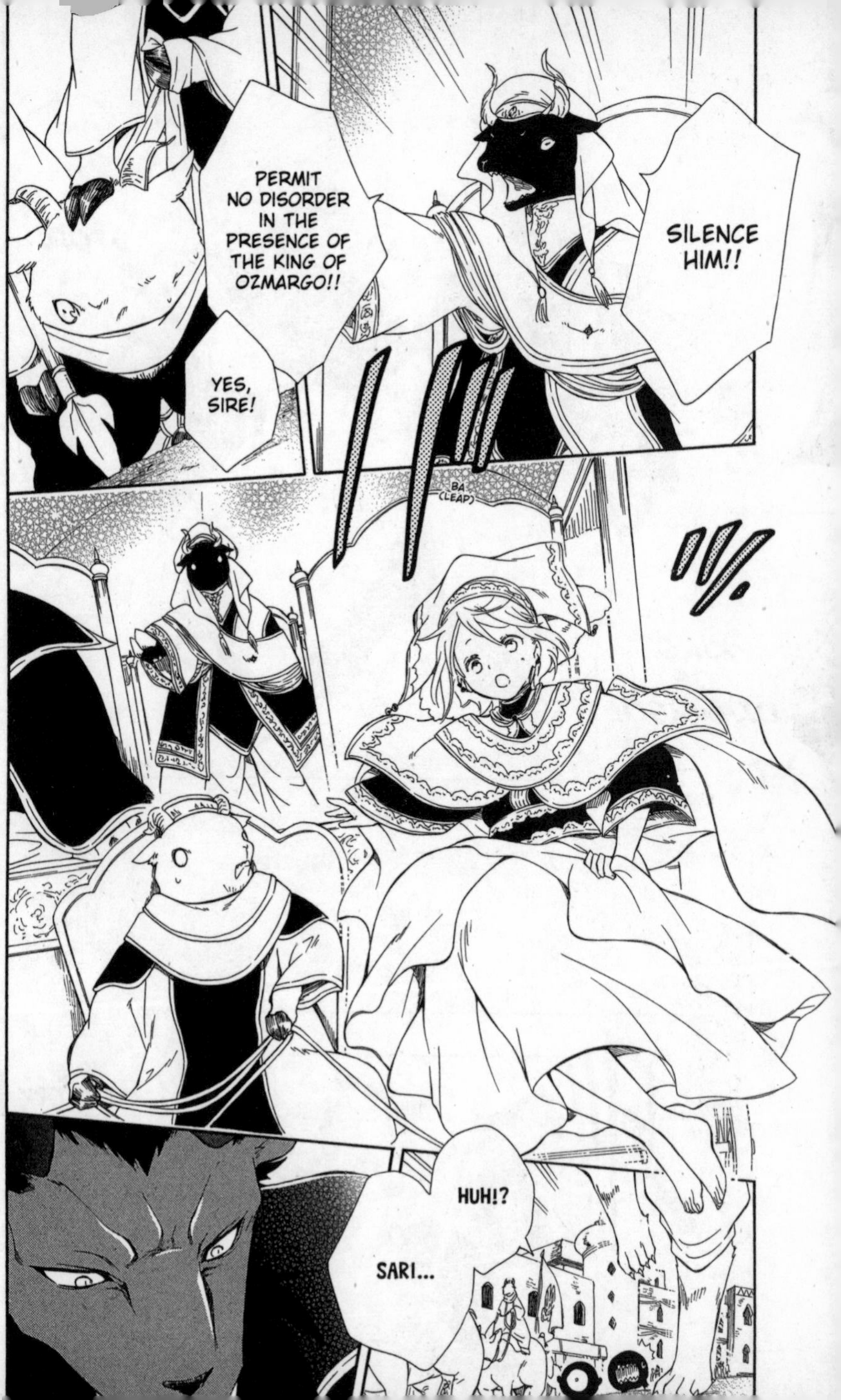
SILENCE HIM!!
PERMIT NO DISORDER IN THE PRESENCE OF THE KING OF OZMARGO!!
YES, SIRE!
BA (LEAP)
HUH!?
SARI...

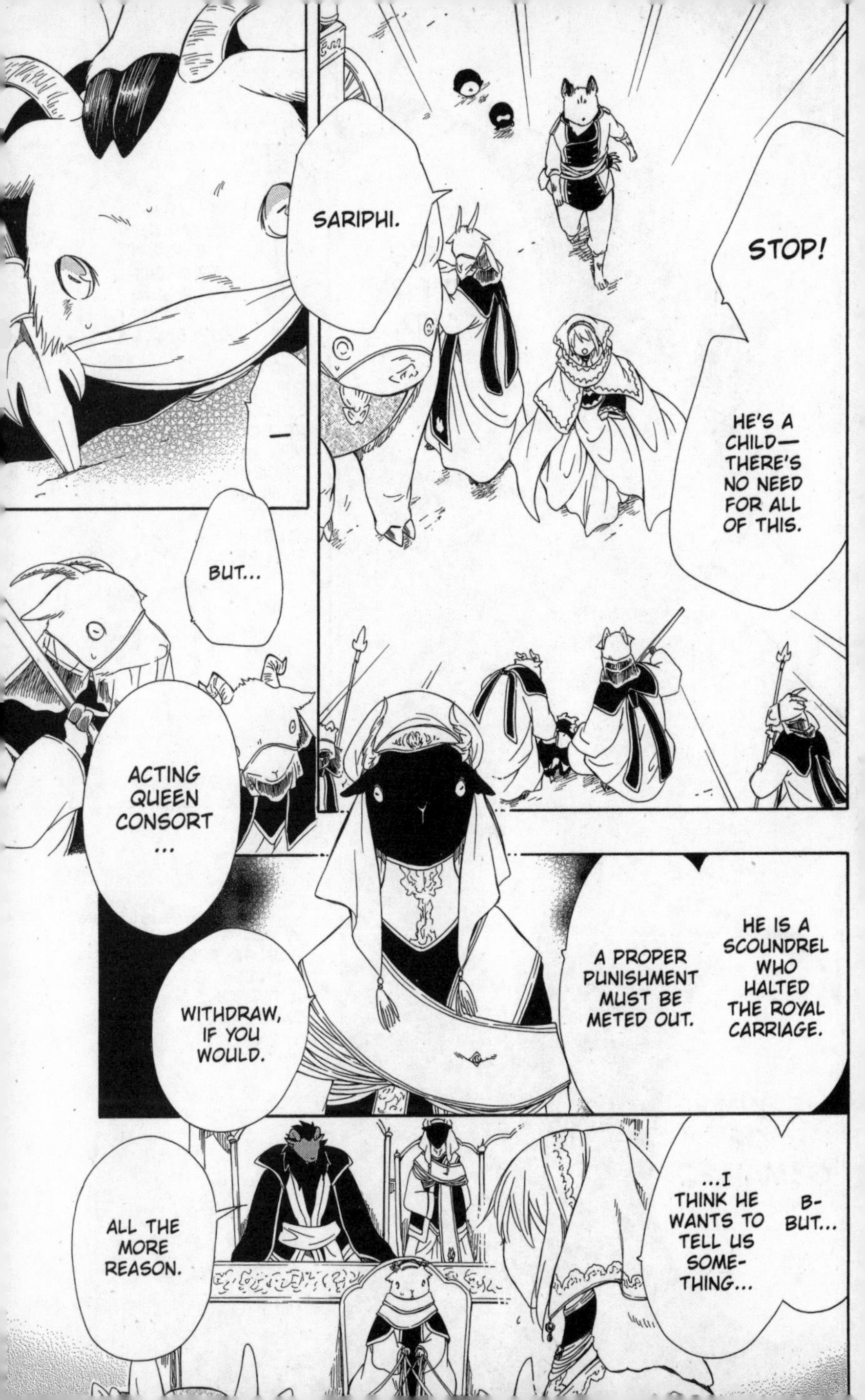
STOP!
HE'S A CHILD—THERE'S NO NEED FOR ALL OF THIS.
SARIPHI.
—
BUT...
ACTING QUEEN CONSORT ...
HE IS A SCOUNDREL WHO HALTED THE ROYAL CARRIAGE.
A PROPER PUNISHMENT MUST BE METED OUT.
WITHDRAW, IF YOU WOULD.
B-BUT...
...I THINK HE WANTS TO TELL US SOME-THING...
ALL THE MORE REASON.

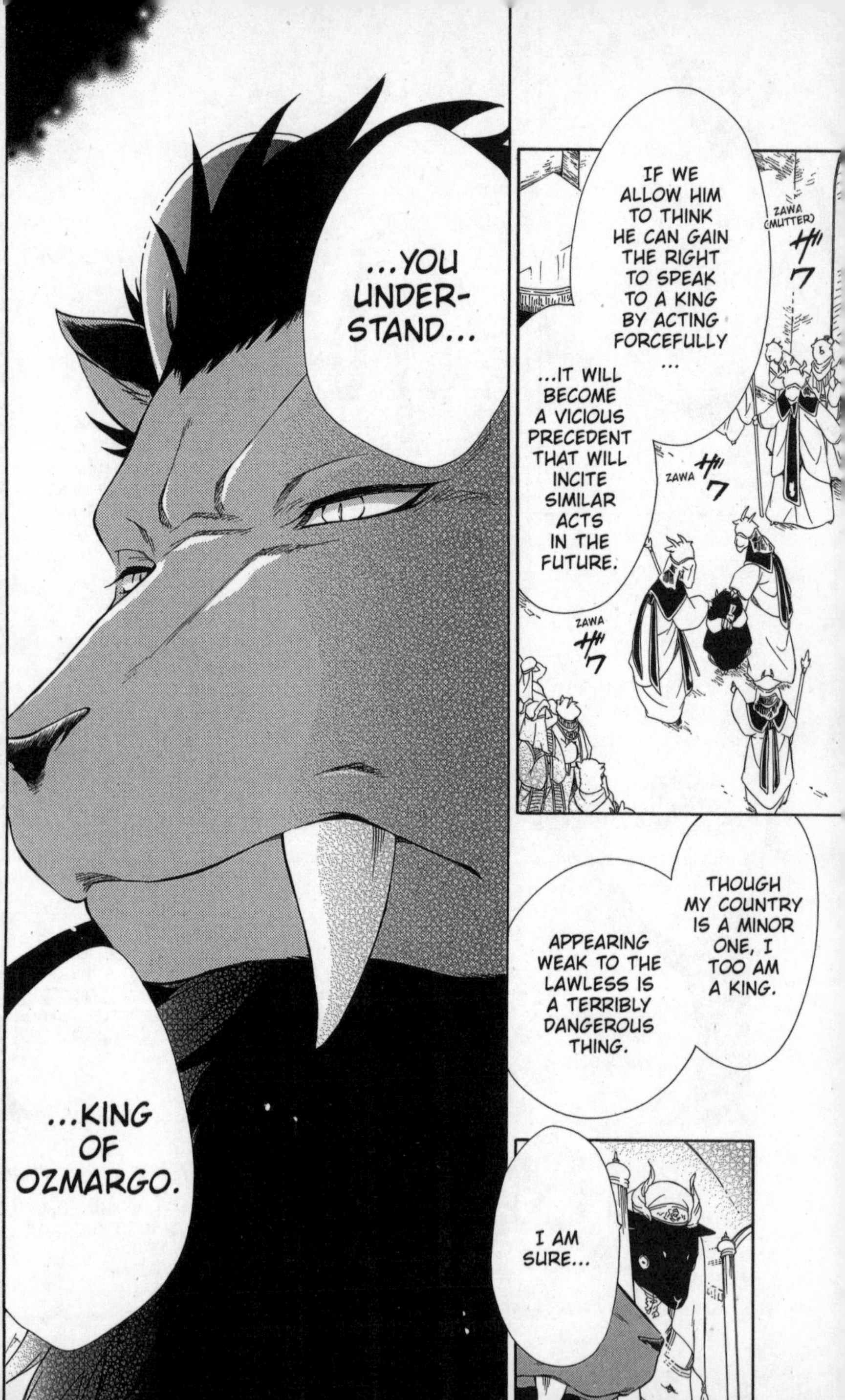
IF WE ALLOW HIM TO THINK HE CAN GAIN THE RIGHT TO SPEAK TO A KING BY ACTING FORCEFULLY...
ZAWA (MUTTER)
...IT WILL BECOME A VICIOUS PRECEDENT THAT WILL INCITE SIMILAR ACTS IN THE FUTURE.
ZAWA
ZAWA
THOUGH MY COUNTRY IS A MINOR ONE, I TOO AM A KING.
APPEARING WEAK TO THE LAWLESS IS A TERRIBLY DANGEROUS THING.
I AM SURE...
...YOU UNDER-STAND...
...KING OF OZMARGO.

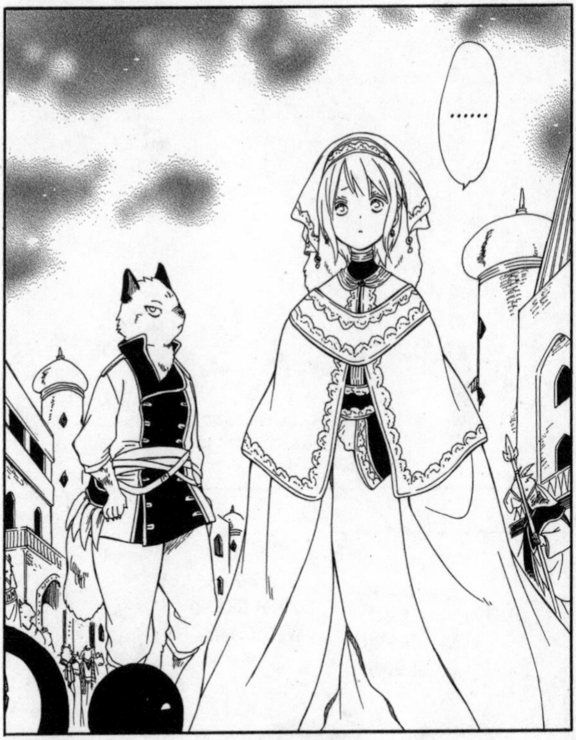
......

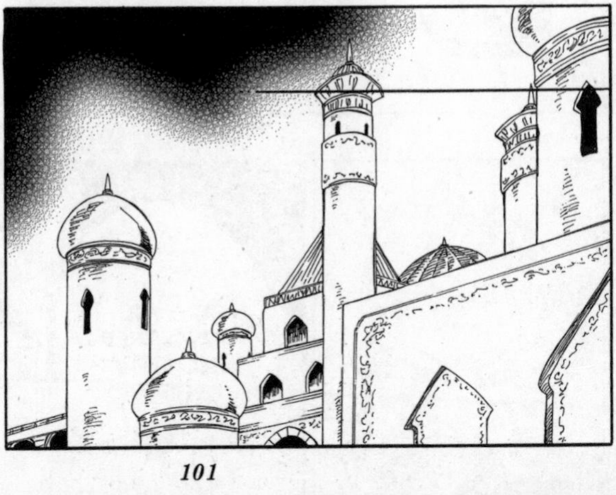

THE "LET'S TALK ABOUT SCRAPPED IDEAS!" CORNER

WAY BACK IN THE BEGINNING, I THOUGHT I'D USE THE IDEA THAT THE MALES OF SPECIES WITH PAW PADS WERE EMBARRASSED TO SHOW THEM INDISCREETLY. IN OTHER WORDS, THE SCENE IN VOLUME 1 WHERE SARIPHI SQUISHES HIS MAJESTY'S PAW PADS IS TERRIBLY EMBARRASSING FOR HIM. THE FACT THAT ANUBIS DOES THIS → 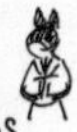 WITH HIS HANDS IS A VESTIGE OF THAT IDEA. BUT IN THE END, I DECIDED TO LIVE TRUE TO MY DESIRE TO DRAW PAW PADS EVERY CHANCE I GOT, AND SO THE IDEA WAS SCRAPPED.

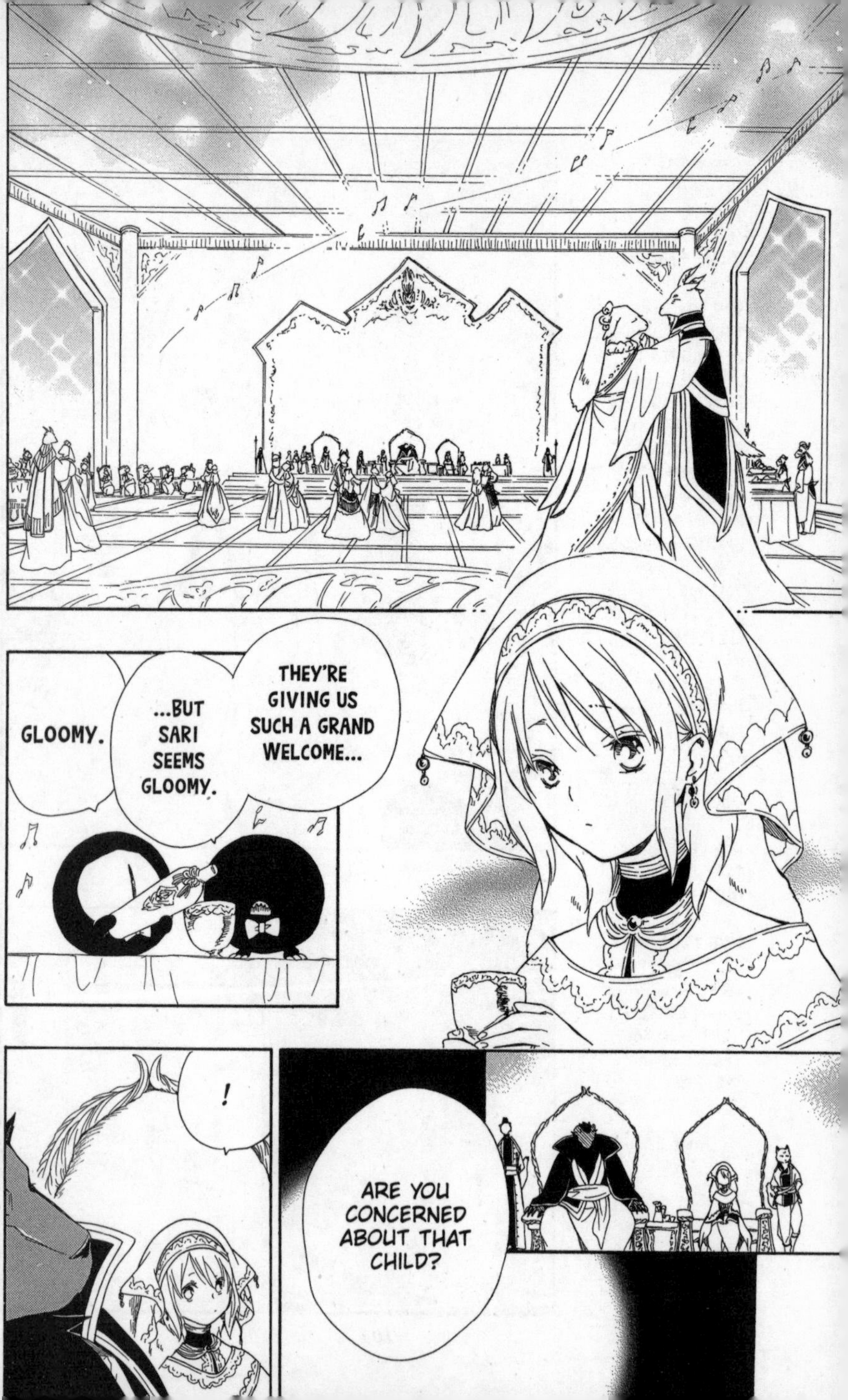
THEY'RE GIVING US SUCH A GRAND WELCOME...
...BUT SARI SEEMS GLOOMY.
GLOOMY.
ARE YOU CONCERNED ABOUT THAT CHILD?
!

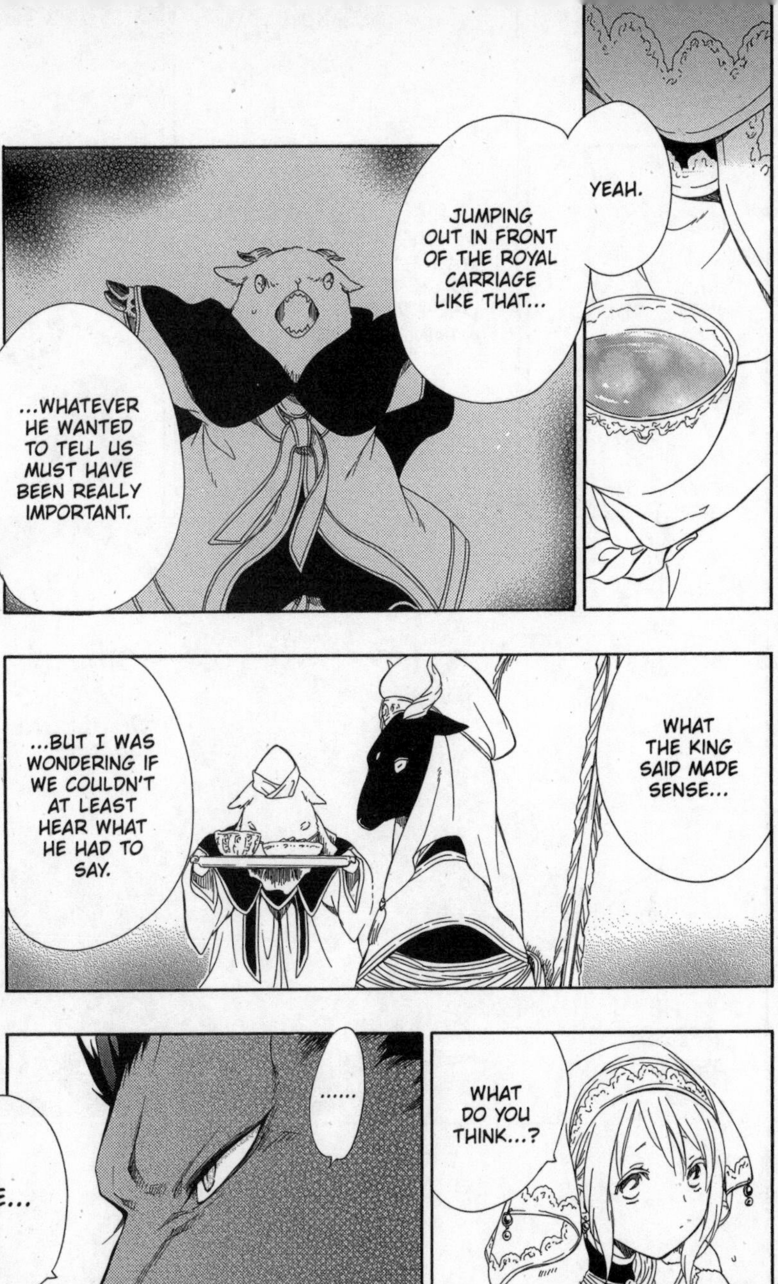
YEAH.
JUMPING OUT IN FRONT OF THE ROYAL CARRIAGE LIKE THAT...
...WHATEVER HE WANTED TO TELL US MUST HAVE BEEN REALLY IMPORTANT.
WHAT THE KING SAID MADE SENSE...
...BUT I WAS WONDERING IF WE COULDN'T AT LEAST HEAR WHAT HE HAD TO SAY.
WHAT DO YOU THINK...?
......
WE...

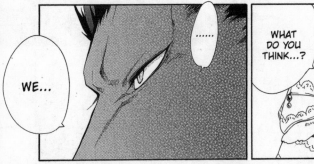

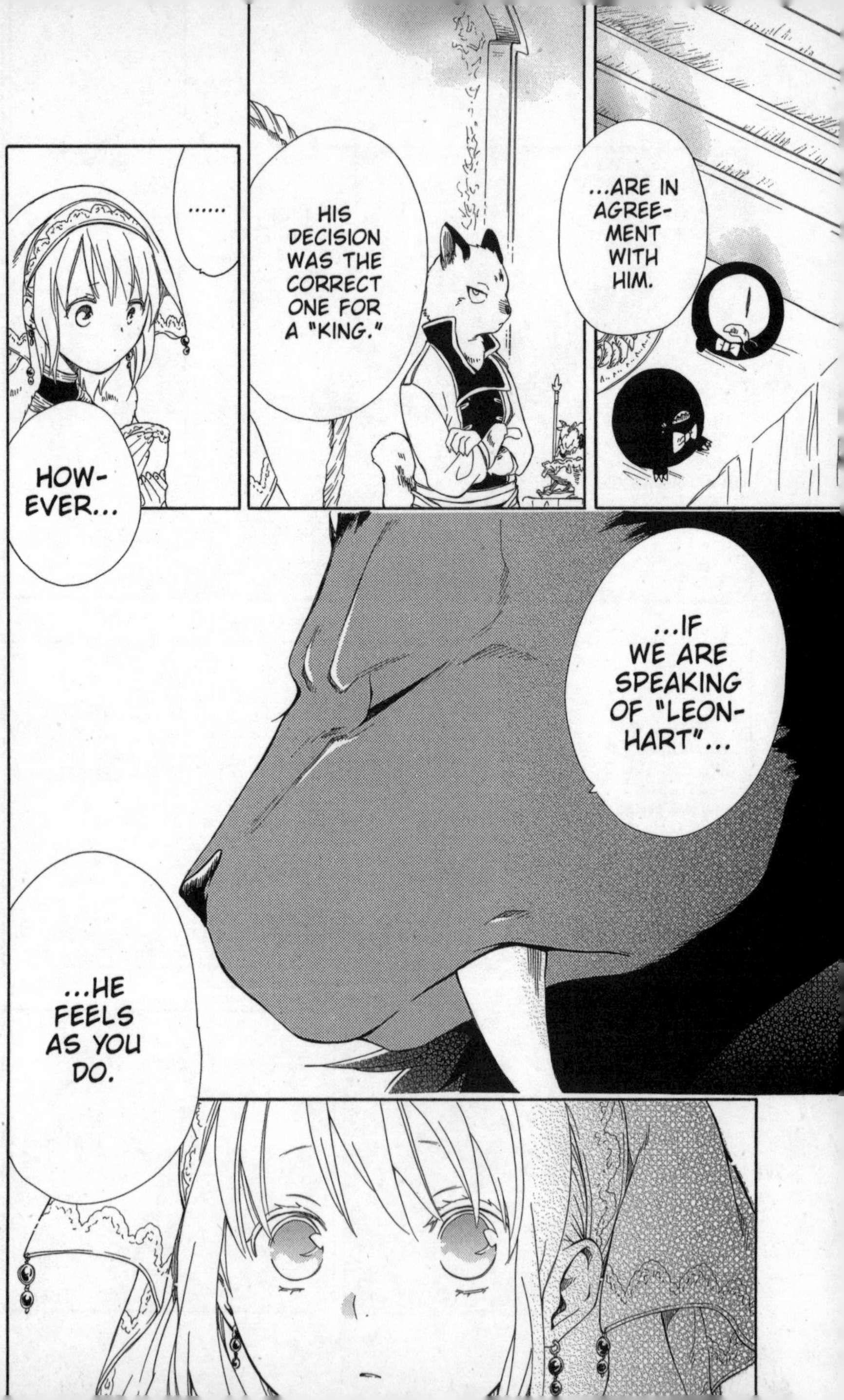
...ARE IN AGREEMENT WITH HIM.
HIS DECISION WAS THE CORRECT ONE FOR A "KING."
......
HOWEVER...
...IF WE ARE SPEAKING OF "LEONHART"...
...HE FEELS AS YOU DO.

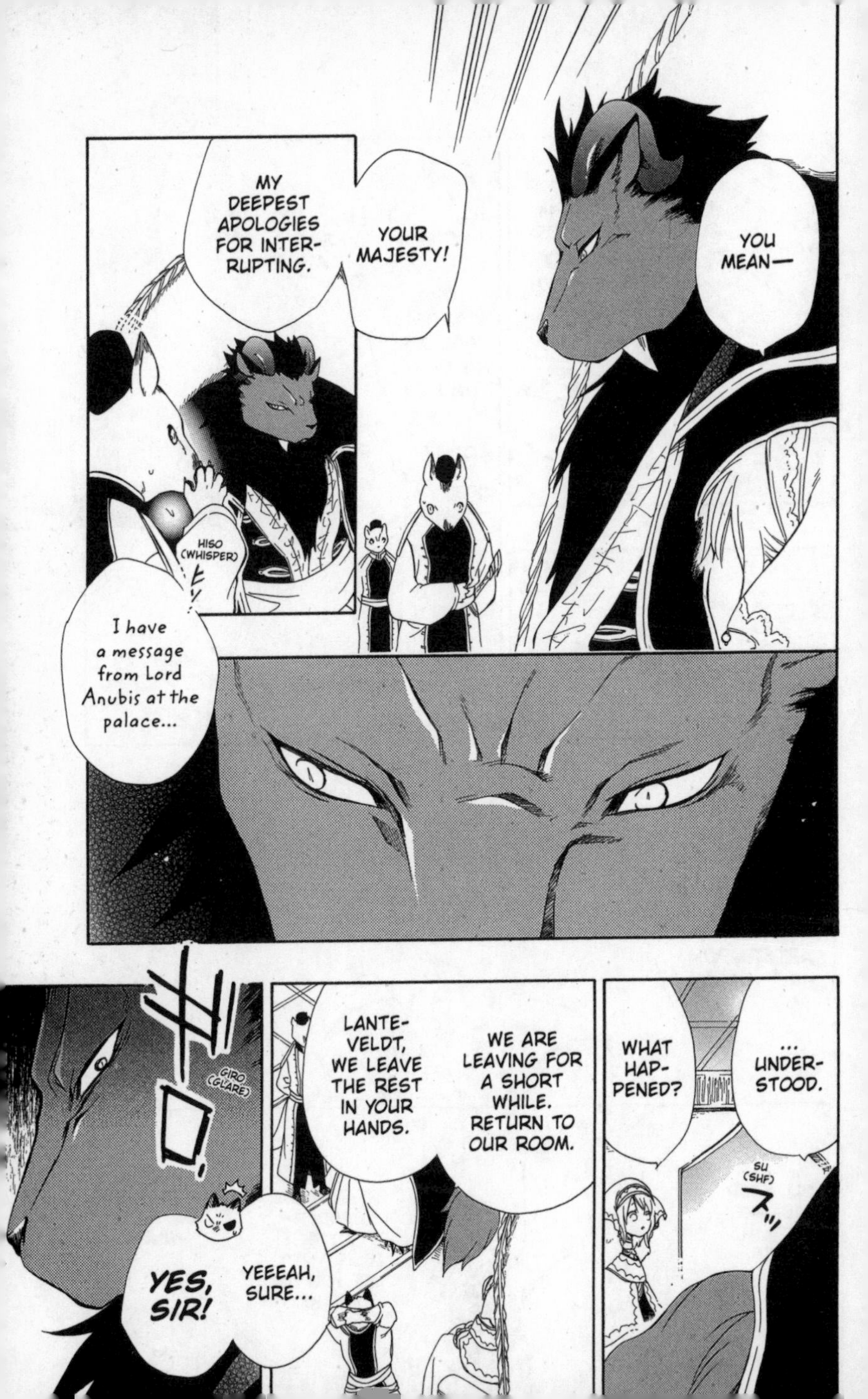
YOU MEAN—
YOUR MAJESTY!
MY DEEPEST APOLOGIES FOR INTER-RUPTING.
HISO (WHISPER)
I have a message from Lord Anubis at the palace...
...UNDER-STOOD.
WHAT HAP-PENED?
SU (SHF)
WE ARE LEAVING FOR A SHORT WHILE. RETURN TO OUR ROOM.
LANTE-VELDT, WE LEAVE THE REST IN YOUR HANDS.
GIRO (GLARE)
YEEEAH, SURE...
YES, SIR!

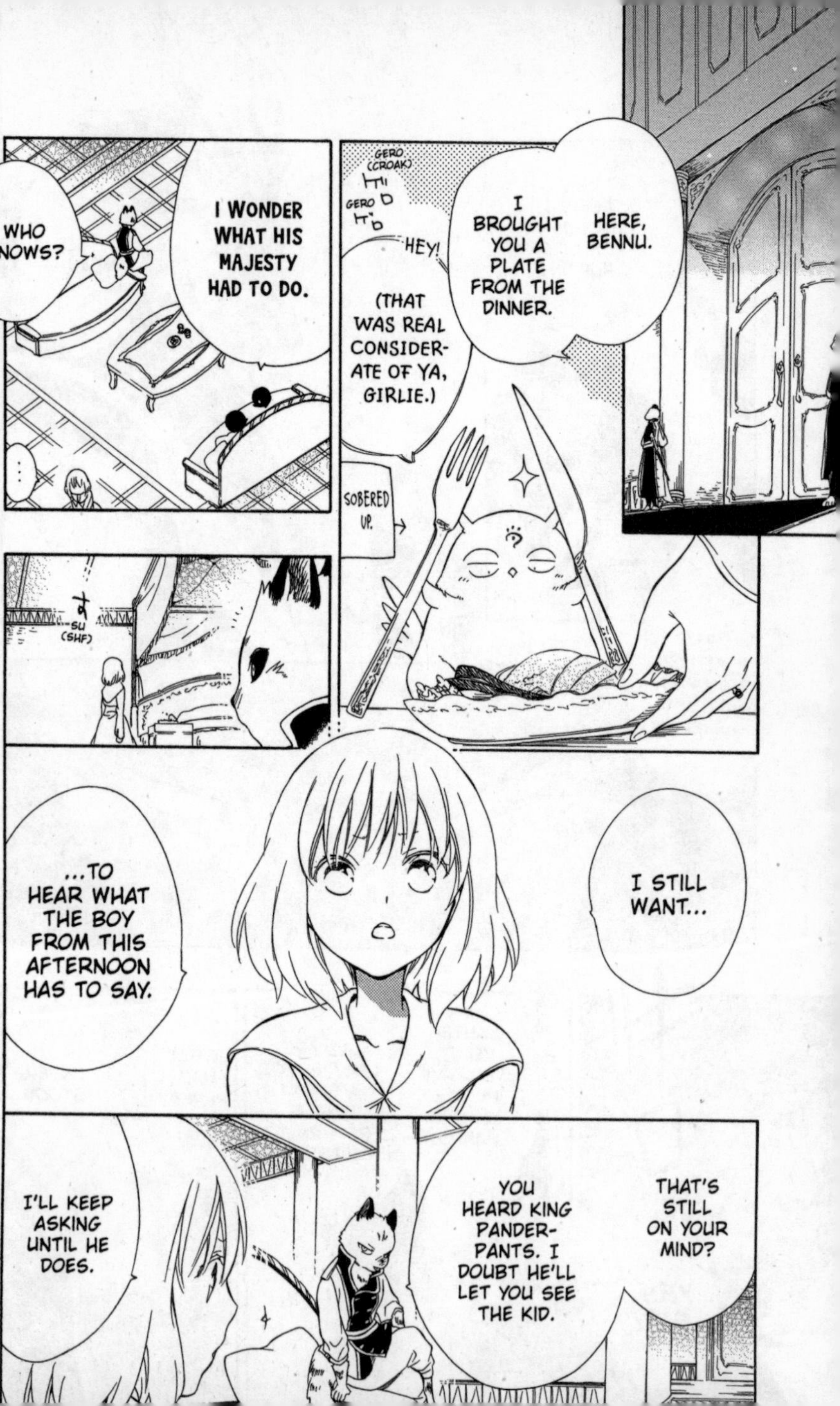
HERE, BENNU.
I BROUGHT YOU A PLATE FROM THE DINNER.
GERO (CROAK)
GERO
HEY!
(THAT WAS REAL CONSIDER-ATE OF YA, GIRLIE.)
SOBERED UP.
I WONDER WHAT HIS MAJESTY HAD TO DO.
WHO KNOWS?
...
SU (SHF)
I STILL WANT...
...TO HEAR WHAT THE BOY FROM THIS AFTERNOON HAS TO SAY.
THAT'S STILL ON YOUR MIND?
YOU HEARD KING PANDER-PANTS. I DOUBT HE'LL LET YOU SEE THE KID.
I'LL KEEP ASKING UNTIL HE DOES.

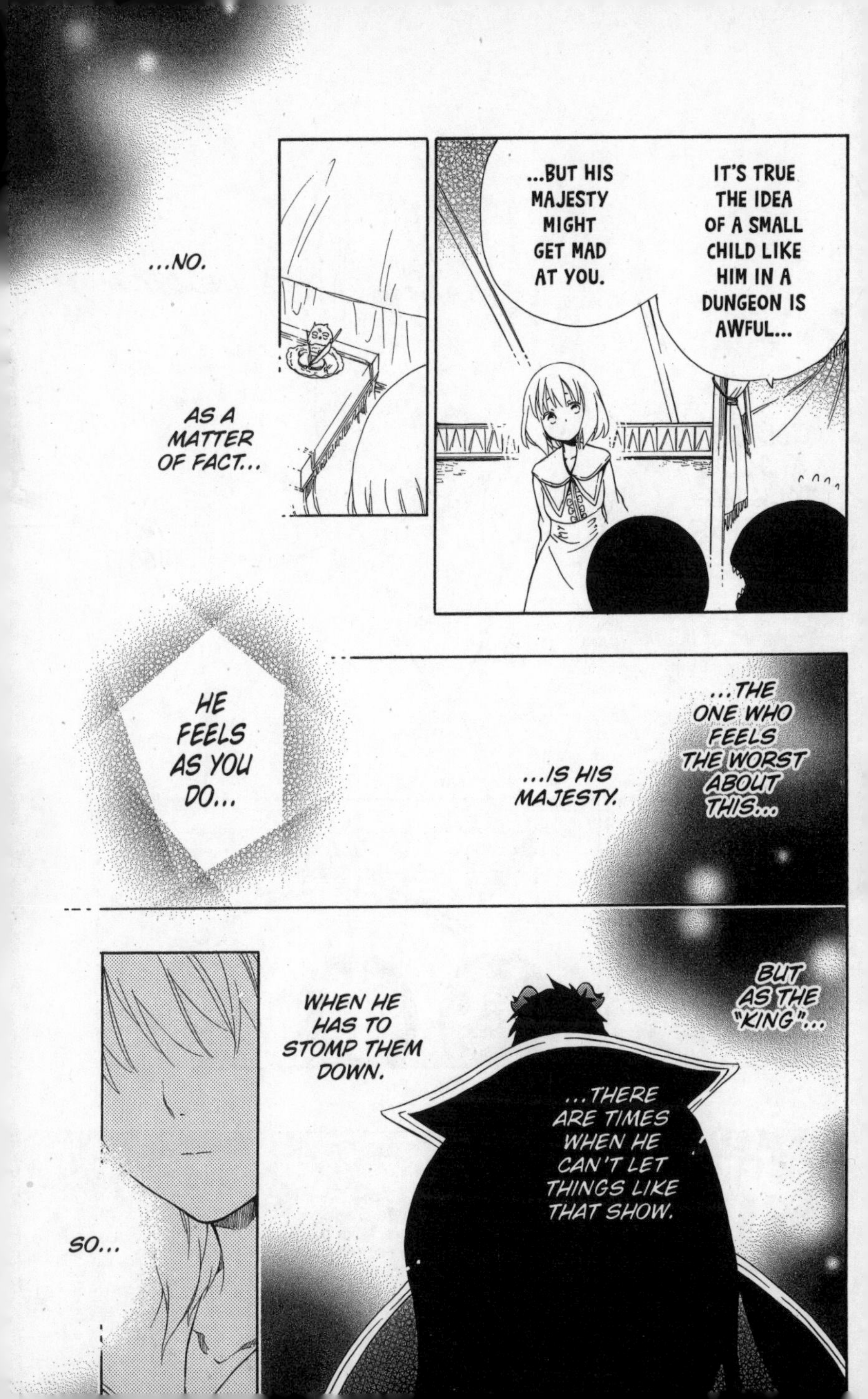
IT'S TRUE THE IDEA OF A SMALL CHILD LIKE HIM IN A DUNGEON IS AWFUL...
...BUT HIS MAJESTY MIGHT GET MAD AT YOU.
...NO.
AS A MATTER OF FACT...
...THE ONE WHO FEELS THE WORST ABOUT THIS...
...IS HIS MAJESTY.
HE FEELS AS YOU DO...
BUT AS THE "KING"...
...THERE ARE TIMES WHEN HE CAN'T LET THINGS LIKE THAT SHOW.
WHEN HE HAS TO STOMP THEM DOWN.
SO...

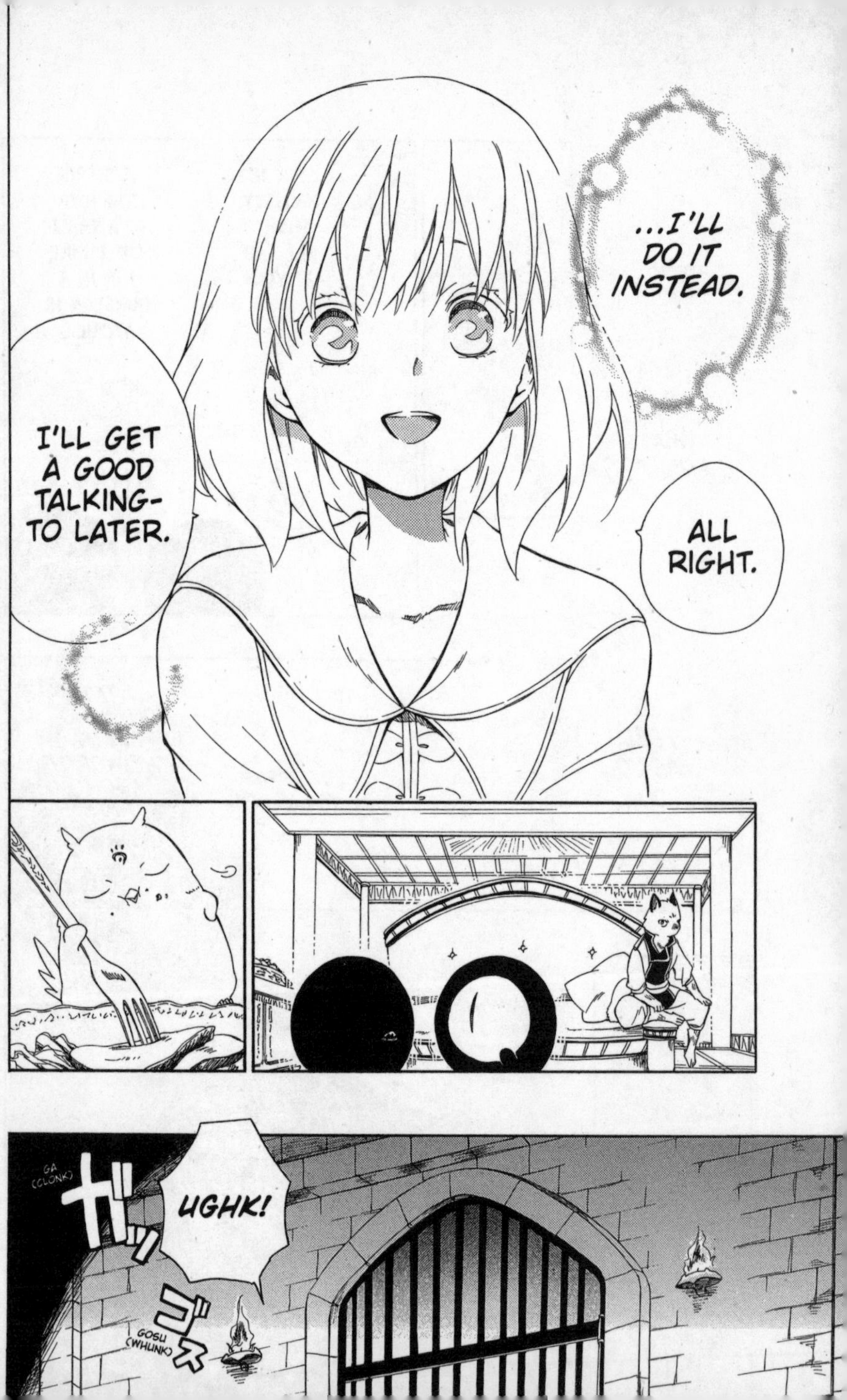
...I'LL DO IT INSTEAD.
ALL RIGHT.
I'LL GET A GOOD TALKING-TO LATER.
UGHK!
GA (CLONK)
GOSU (WHUNK)

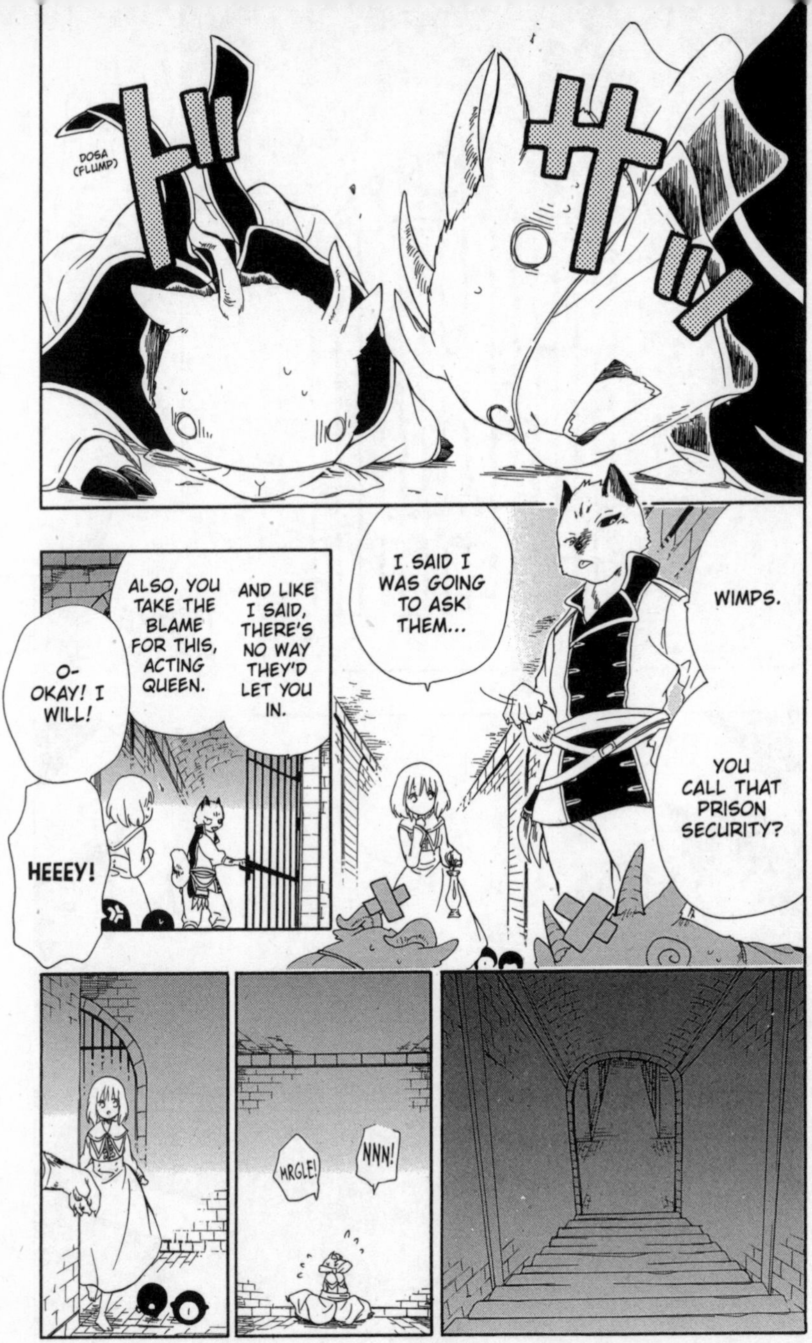

ドサッ
DOSA (FLUMP)
WIMPS.
YOU CALL THAT PRISON SECURITY?
I SAID I WAS GOING TO ASK THEM...
AND LIKE I SAID, THERE'S NO WAY THEY'D LET YOU IN.
ALSO, YOU TAKE THE BLAME FOR THIS, ACTING QUEEN.
O-OKAY! I WILL!
HEEEY!
NNN!
MRGLE!

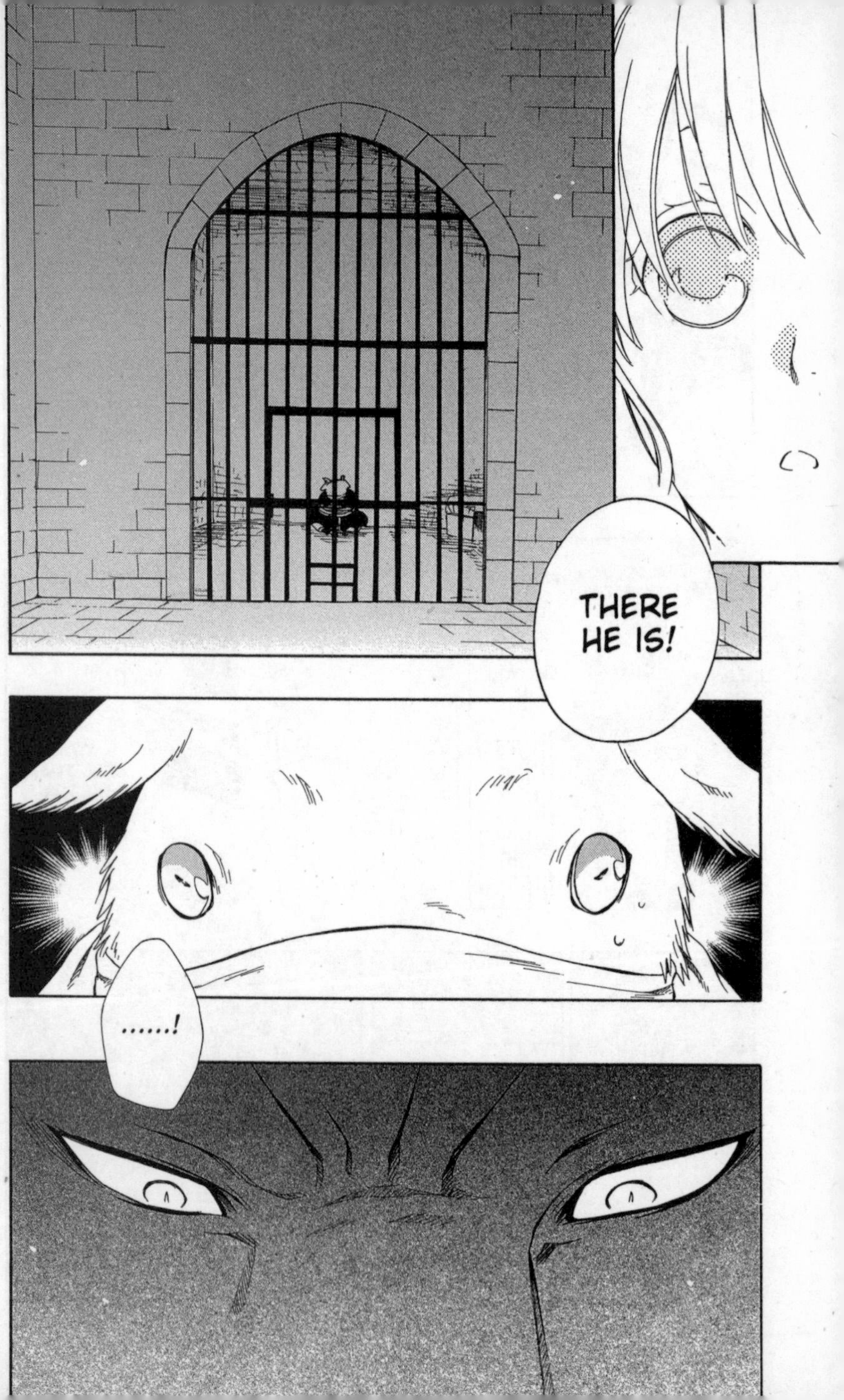
THERE HE IS!
......!

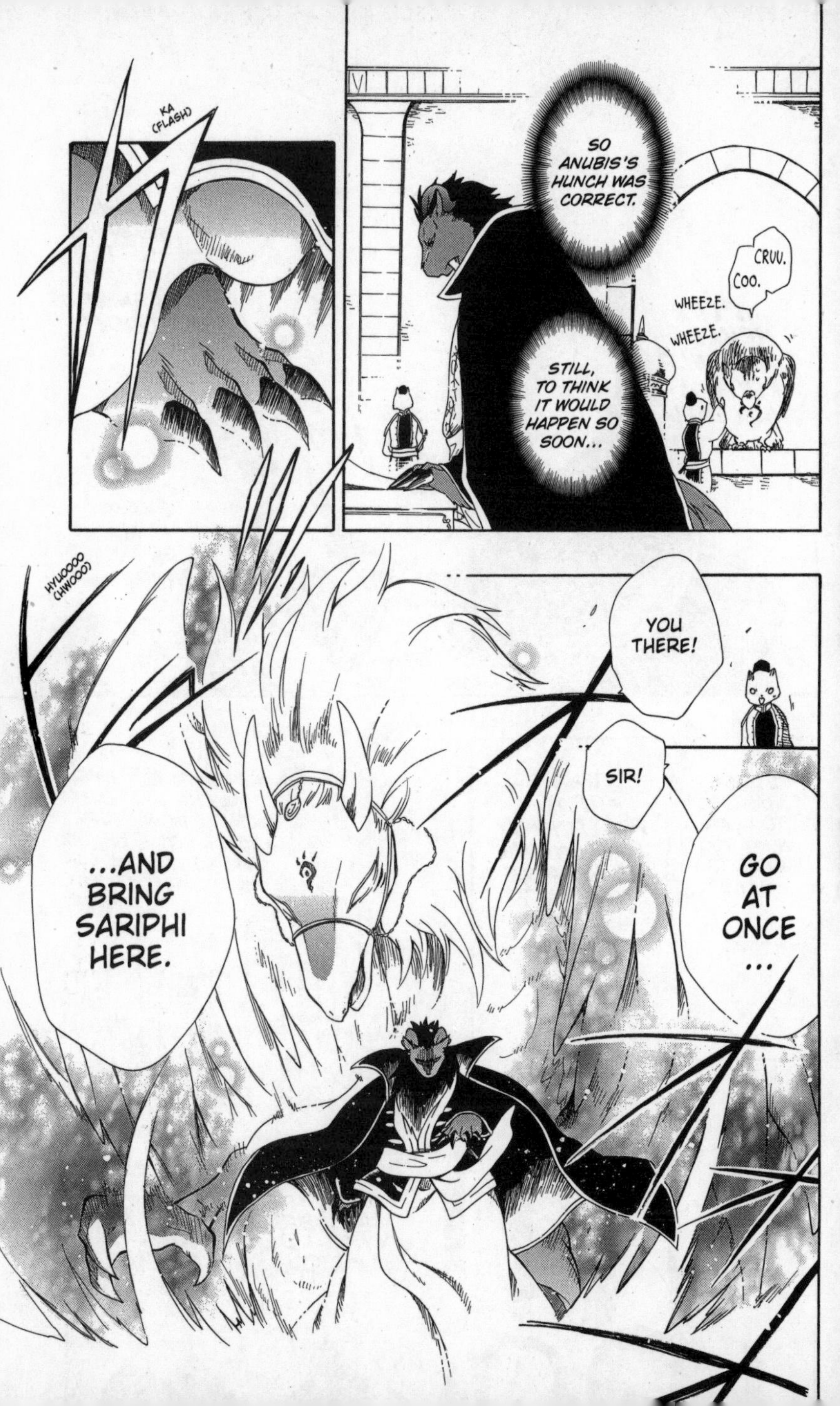
SO ANUBIS'S HUNCH WAS CORRECT.
CRUU. COO.
WHEEZE. WHEEZE.
STILL, TO THINK IT WOULD HAPPEN SO SOON...
KA (FLASH)
YOU THERE!
SIR!
GO AT ONCE...
...AND BRING SARIPHI HERE.
HYUOOOO (AWOOO)

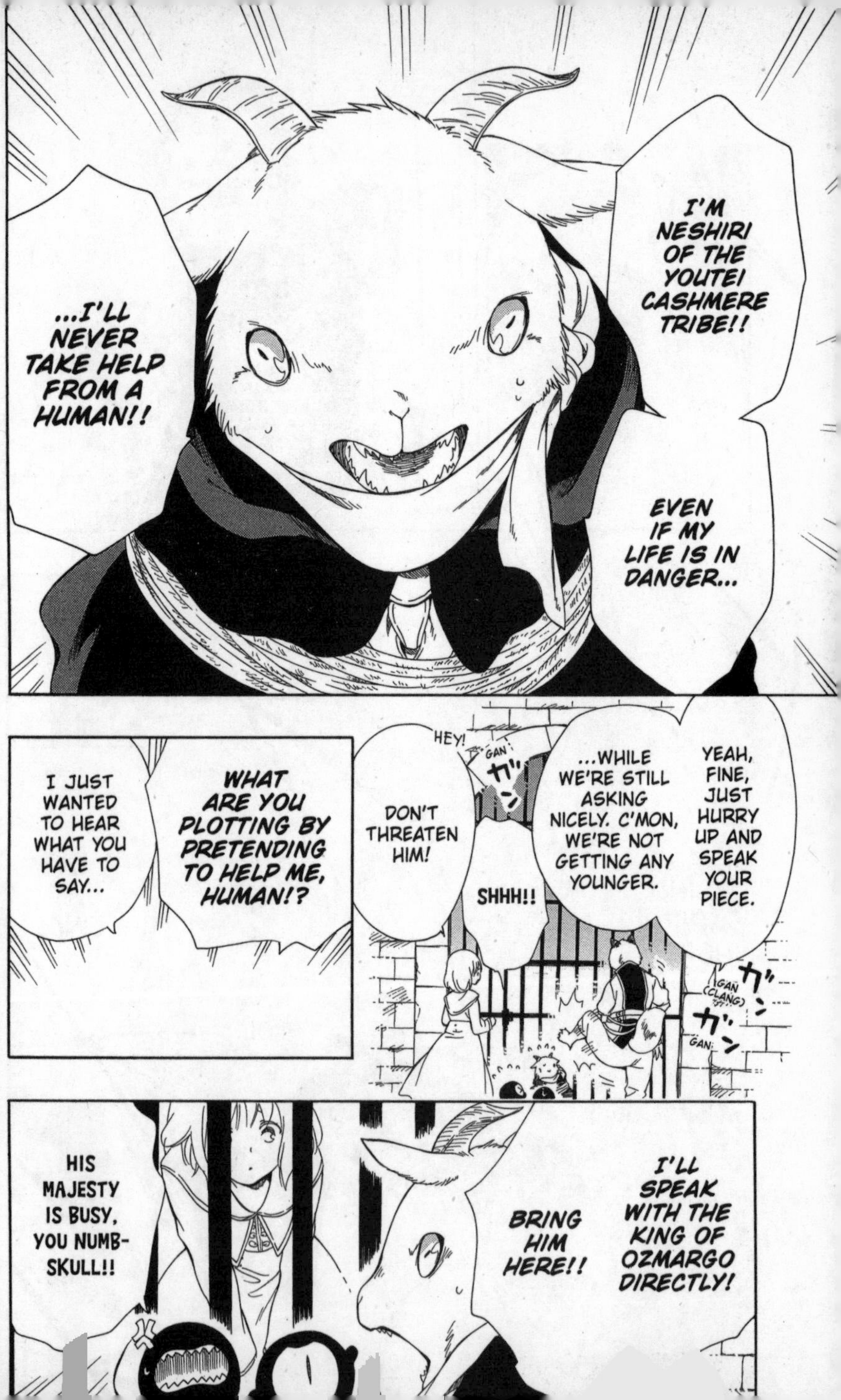
I'M NESHIRI OF THE YOUTEI CASHMERE TRIBE!!
EVEN IF MY LIFE IS IN DANGER...
...I'LL NEVER TAKE HELP FROM A HUMAN!!
YEAH, FINE, JUST HURRY UP AND SPEAK YOUR PIECE.
...WHILE WE'RE STILL ASKING NICELY. C'MON, WE'RE NOT GETTING ANY YOUNGER.
GAN (CLANG)
GAN
GAN
HEY!
DON'T THREATEN HIM!
SHHH!!
WHAT ARE YOU PLOTTING BY PRETENDING TO HELP ME, HUMAN!?
I JUST WANTED TO HEAR WHAT YOU HAVE TO SAY...
I'LL SPEAK WITH THE KING OF OZMARGO DIRECTLY!
BRING HIM HERE!!
HIS MAJESTY IS BUSY, YOU NUMBSKULL!!

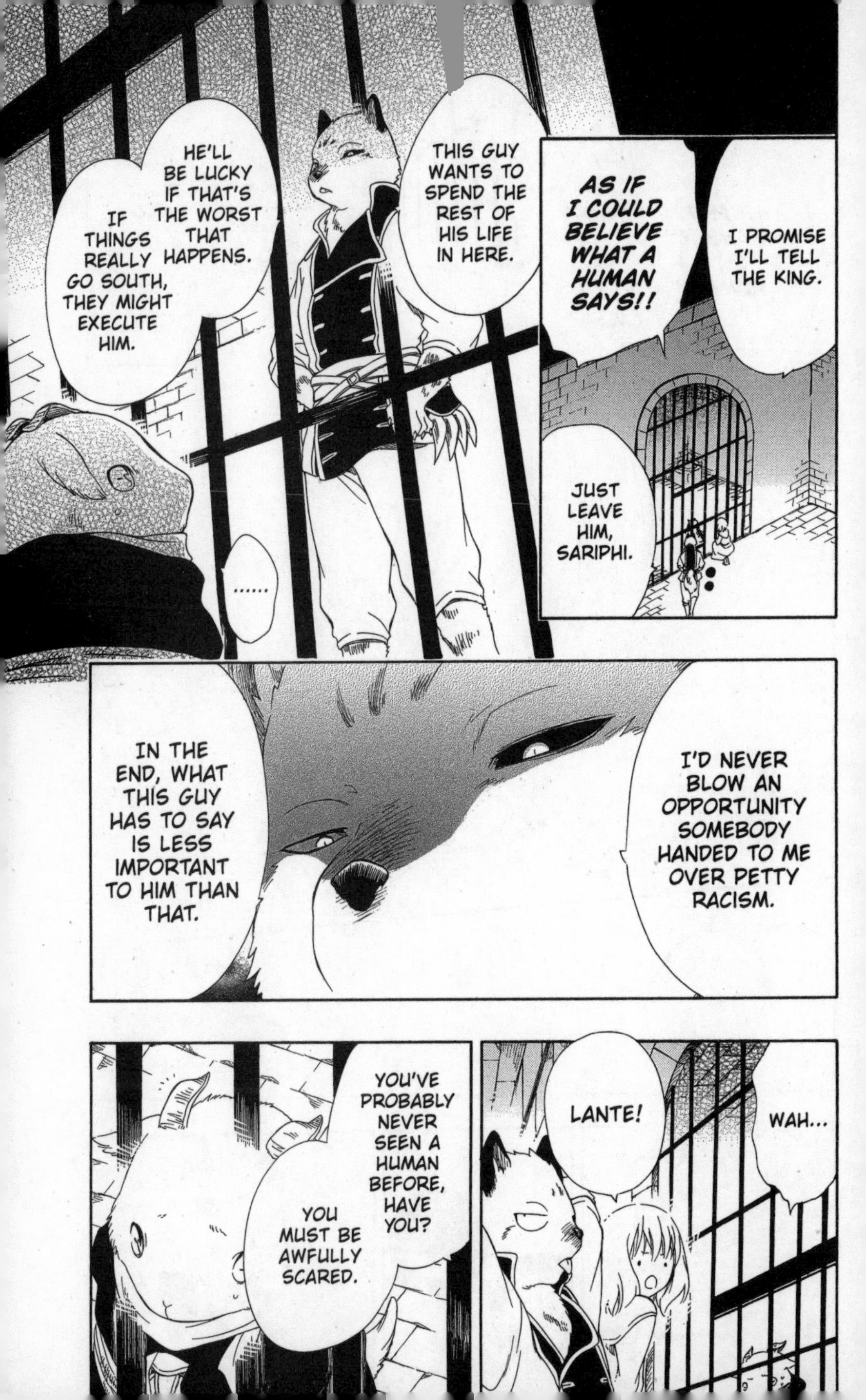
I PROMISE I'LL TELL THE KING.
AS IF I COULD BELIEVE WHAT A HUMAN SAYS!!
JUST LEAVE HIM, SARIPHI.
THIS GUY WANTS TO SPEND THE REST OF HIS LIFE IN HERE.
HE'LL BE LUCKY IF THAT'S THE WORST THAT HAPPENS.
IF THINGS REALLY GO SOUTH, THEY MIGHT EXECUTE HIM.
......
I'D NEVER BLOW AN OPPORTUNITY SOMEBODY HANDED TO ME OVER PETTY RACISM.
IN THE END, WHAT THIS GUY HAS TO SAY IS LESS IMPORTANT TO HIM THAN THAT.
WAH...
LANTE!
YOU'VE PROBABLY NEVER SEEN A HUMAN BEFORE, HAVE YOU?
YOU MUST BE AWFULLY SCARED.

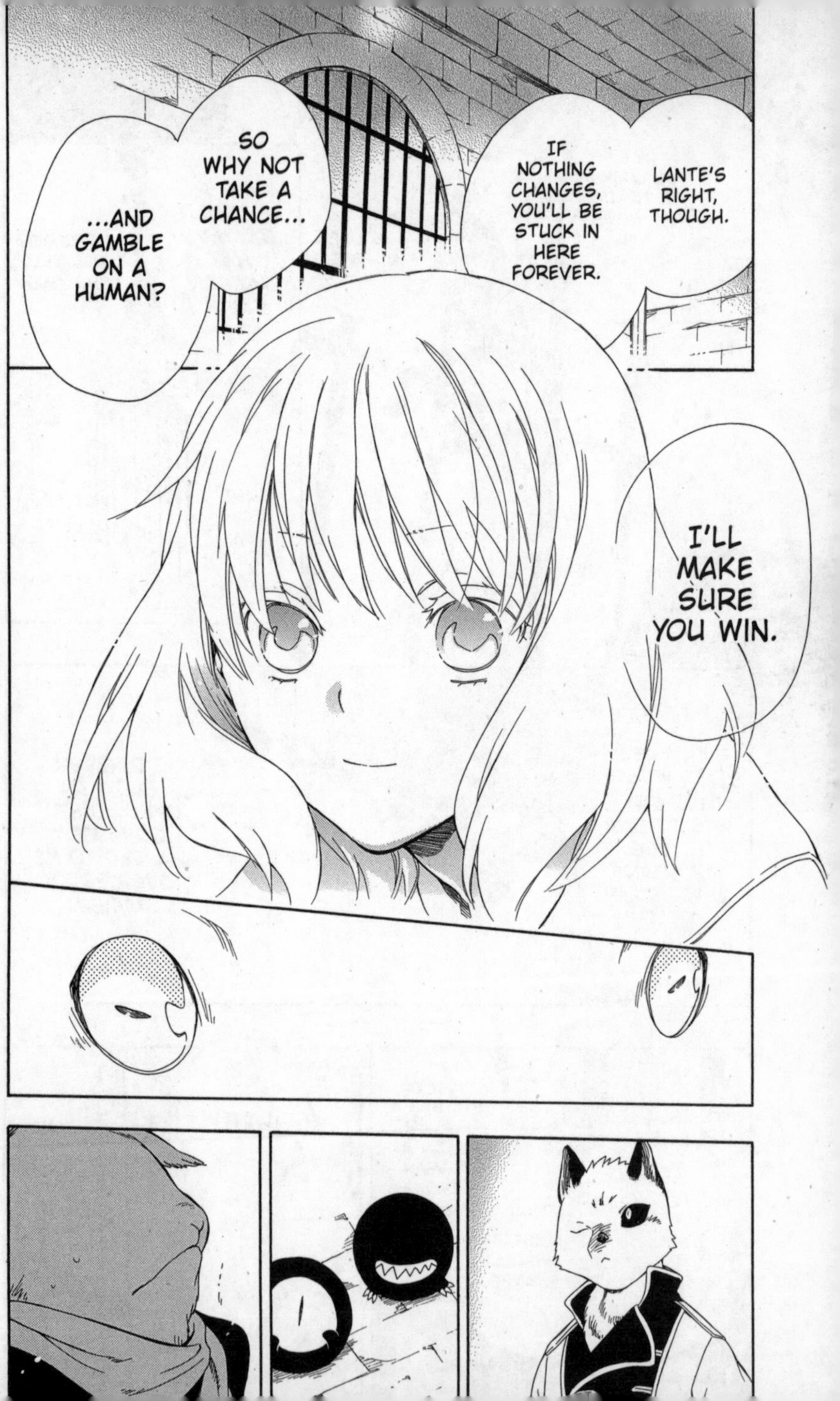
LANTE'S RIGHT, THOUGH.
IF NOTHING CHANGES, YOU'LL BE STUCK IN HERE FOREVER.
SO WHY NOT TAKE A CHANCE...
...AND GAMBLE ON A HUMAN?
I'LL MAKE SURE YOU WIN.

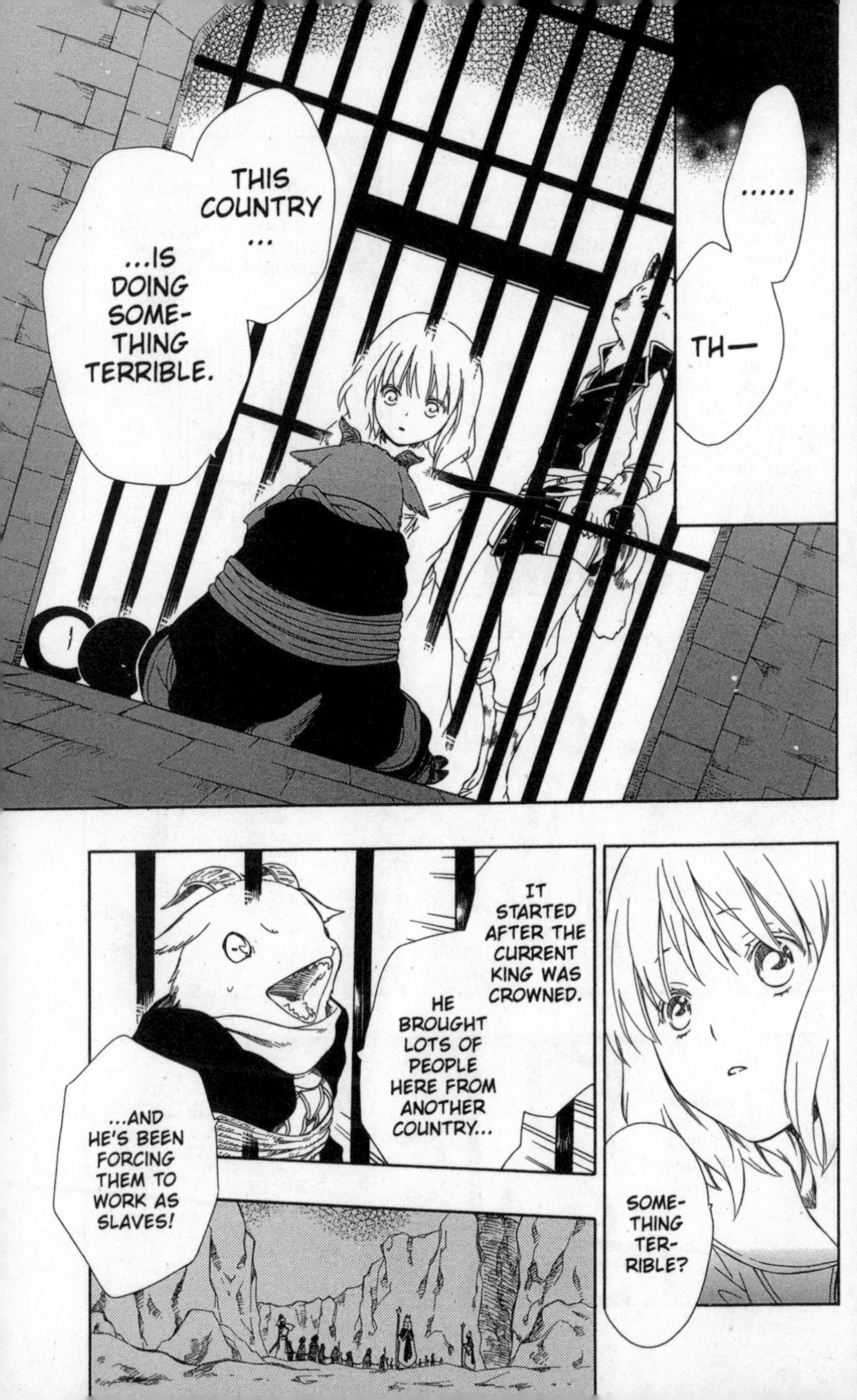
......
TH—
THIS COUNTRY ...
...IS DOING SOME-THING TERRIBLE.
SOME-THING TER-RIBLE?
IT STARTED AFTER THE CURRENT KING WAS CROWNED.
HE BROUGHT LOTS OF PEOPLE HERE FROM ANOTHER COUNTRY...
...AND HE'S BEEN FORCING THEM TO WORK AS SLAVES!

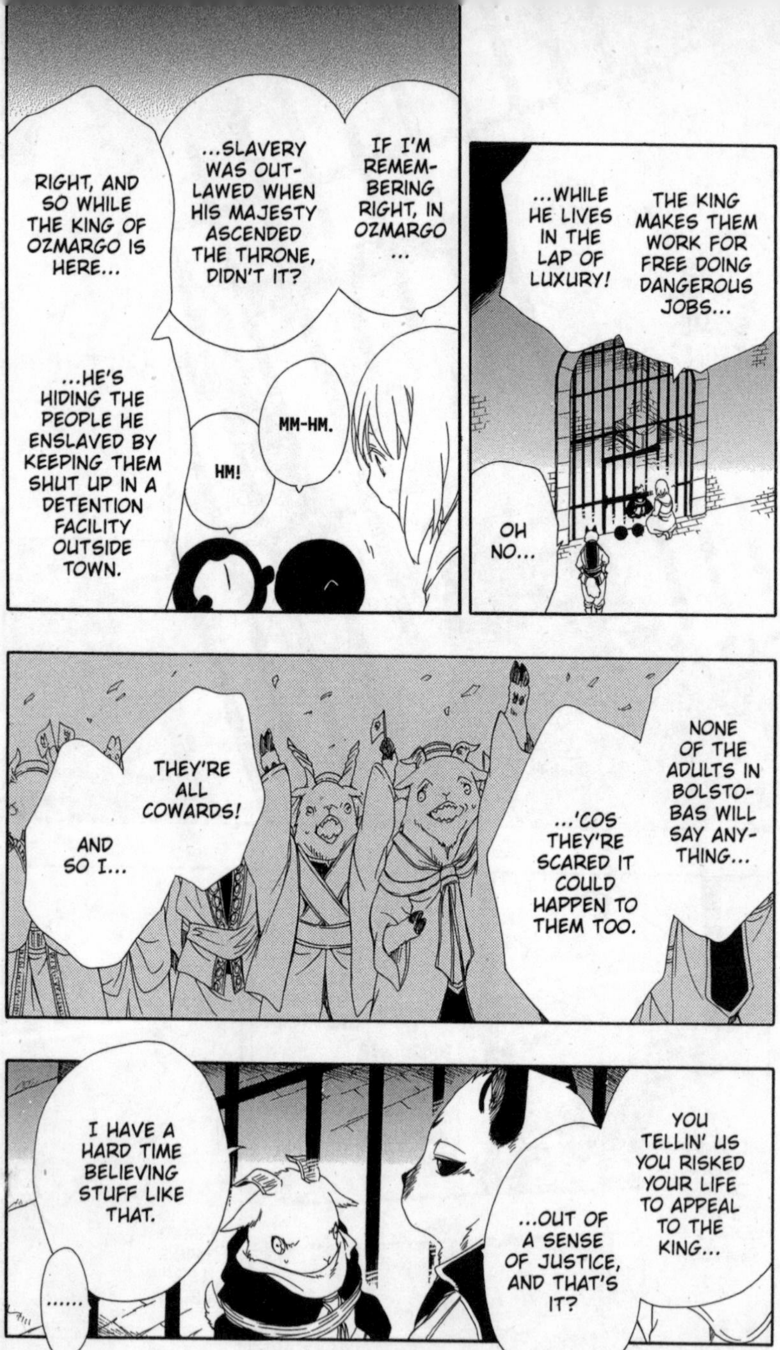
THE KING MAKES THEM WORK FOR FREE DOING DANGEROUS JOBS...
...WHILE HE LIVES IN THE LAP OF LUXURY!
OH NO...
IF I'M REMEM-BERING RIGHT, IN OZMARGO...
...SLAVERY WAS OUT-LAWED WHEN HIS MAJESTY ASCENDED THE THRONE, DIDN'T IT?
RIGHT, AND SO WHILE THE KING OF OZMARGO IS HERE...
MM-HM.
HM!
...HE'S HIDING THE PEOPLE HE ENSLAVED BY KEEPING THEM SHUT UP IN A DETENTION FACILITY OUTSIDE TOWN.
NONE OF THE ADULTS IN BOLSTO-BAS WILL SAY ANY-THING...
...'COS THEY'RE SCARED IT COULD HAPPEN TO THEM TOO.
THEY'RE ALL COWARDS!
AND SO I...
YOU TELLIN' US YOU RISKED YOUR LIFE TO APPEAL TO THE KING...
...OUT OF A SENSE OF JUSTICE, AND THAT'S IT?
I HAVE A HARD TIME BELIEVING STUFF LIKE THAT.
......

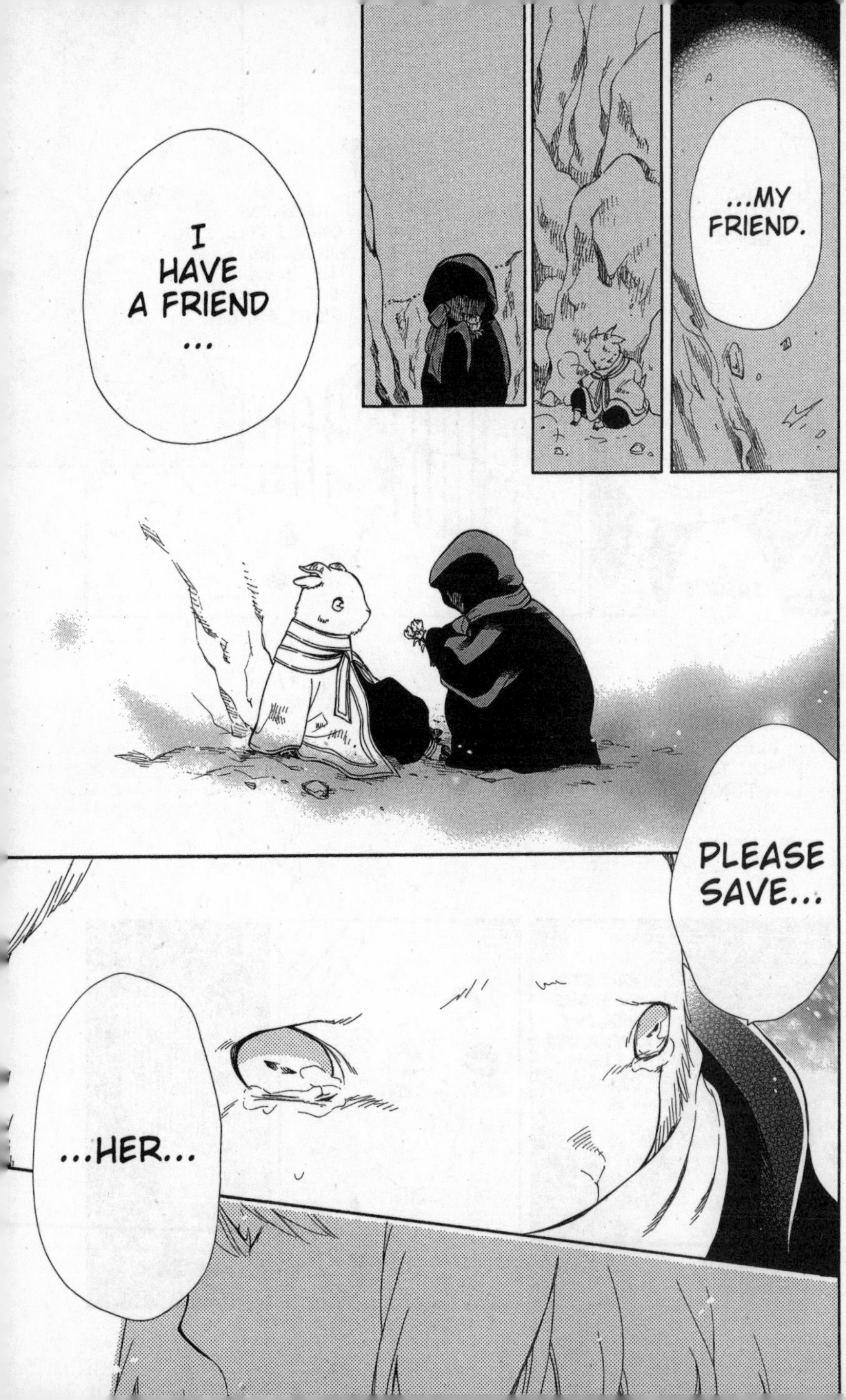
...MY FRIEND.
I HAVE A FRIEND ...
PLEASE SAVE...
...HER...

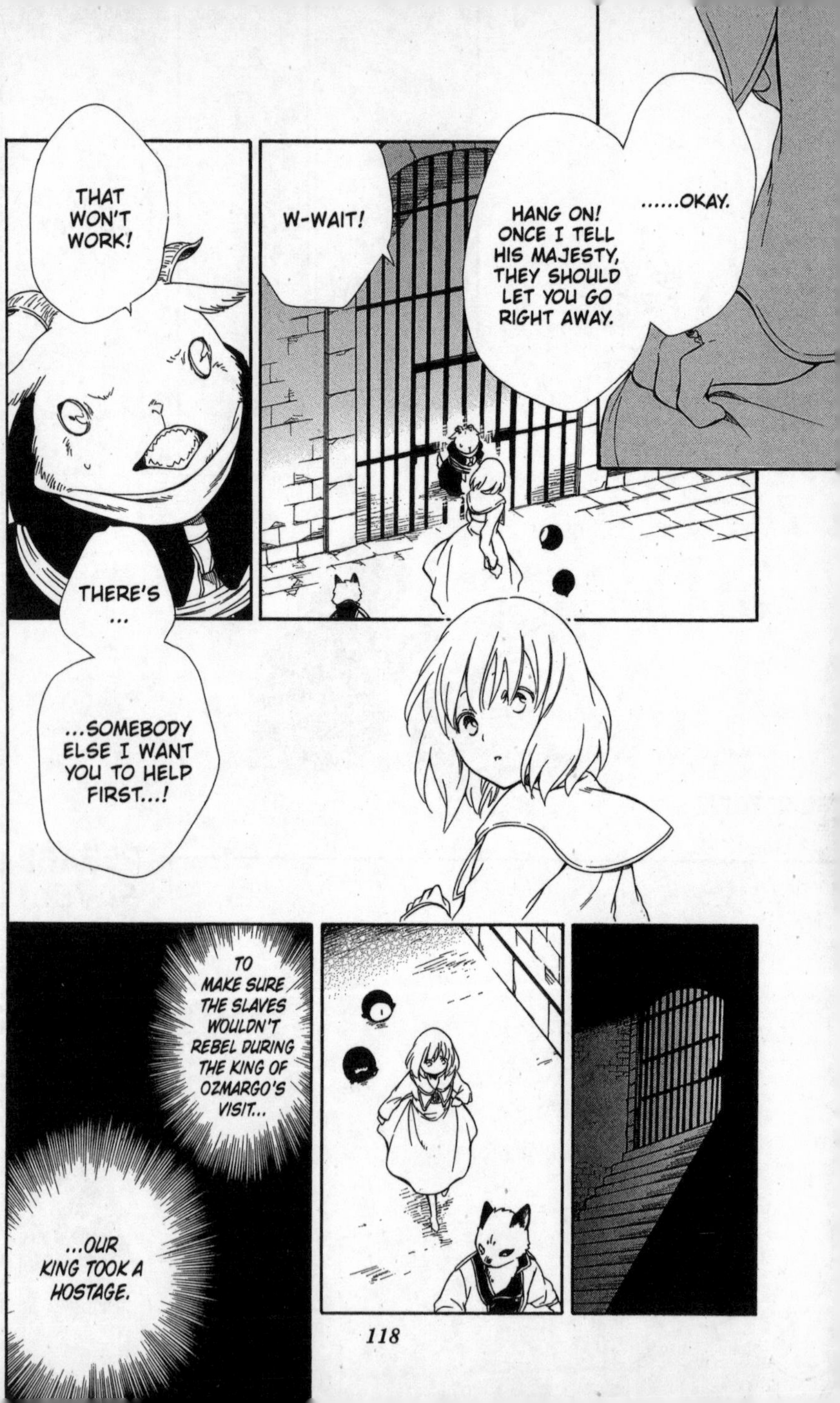
......OKAY.
HANG ON! ONCE I TELL HIS MAJESTY, THEY SHOULD LET YOU GO RIGHT AWAY.
W-WAIT!
THAT WON'T WORK!
THERE'S ...
...SOMEBODY ELSE I WANT YOU TO HELP FIRST...!
TO MAKE SURE THE SLAVES WOULDN'T REBEL DURING THE KING OF OZMARGO'S VISIT...
...OUR KING TOOK A HOSTAGE.

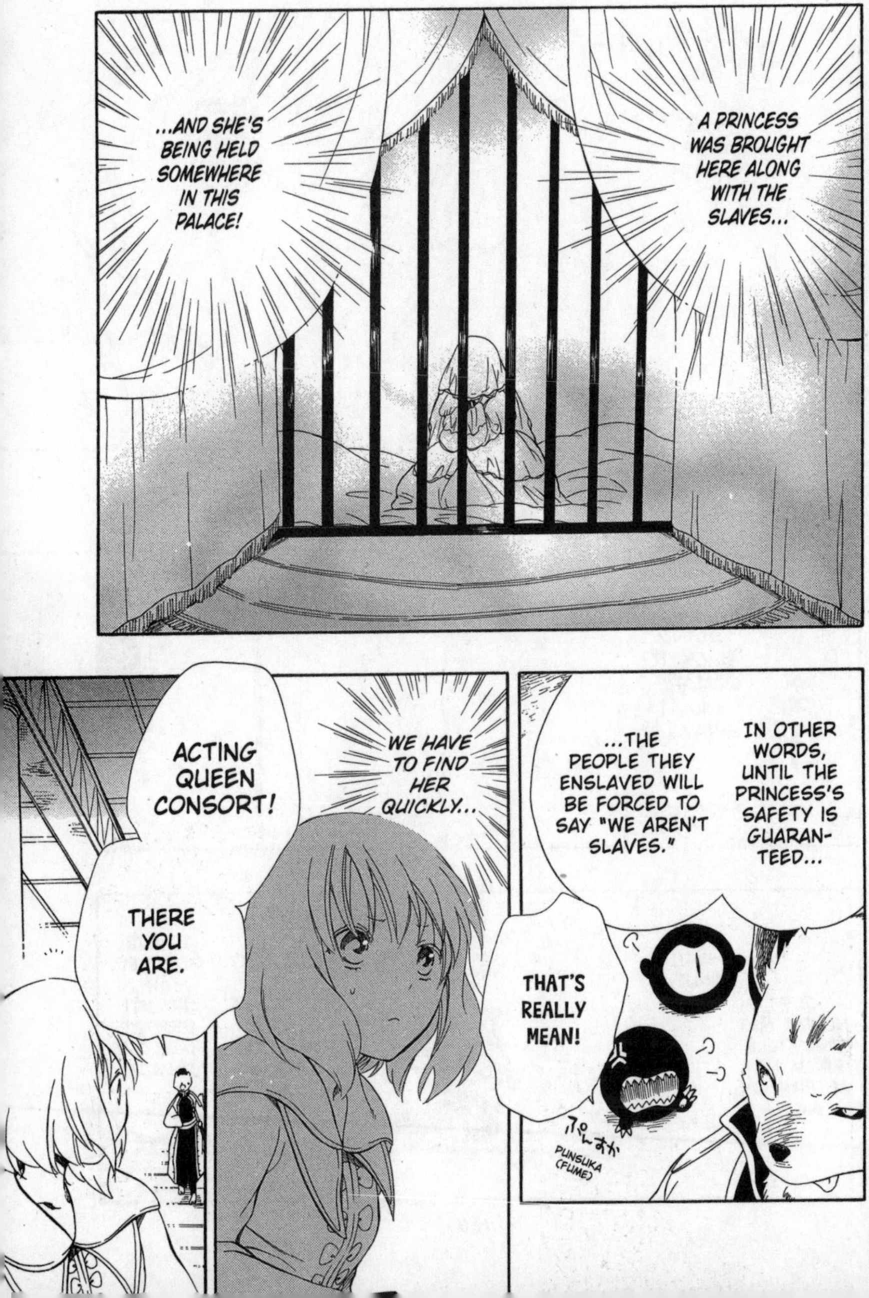
A PRINCESS WAS BROUGHT HERE ALONG WITH THE SLAVES...
...AND SHE'S BEING HELD SOMEWHERE IN THIS PALACE!
IN OTHER WORDS, UNTIL THE PRINCESS'S SAFETY IS GUARAN-TEED...
...THE PEOPLE THEY ENSLAVED WILL BE FORCED TO SAY "WE AREN'T SLAVES."
THAT'S REALLY MEAN!
ぷんすか
PUNSUKA (FUME)
WE HAVE TO FIND HER QUICKLY...
ACTING QUEEN CONSORT!
THERE YOU ARE.

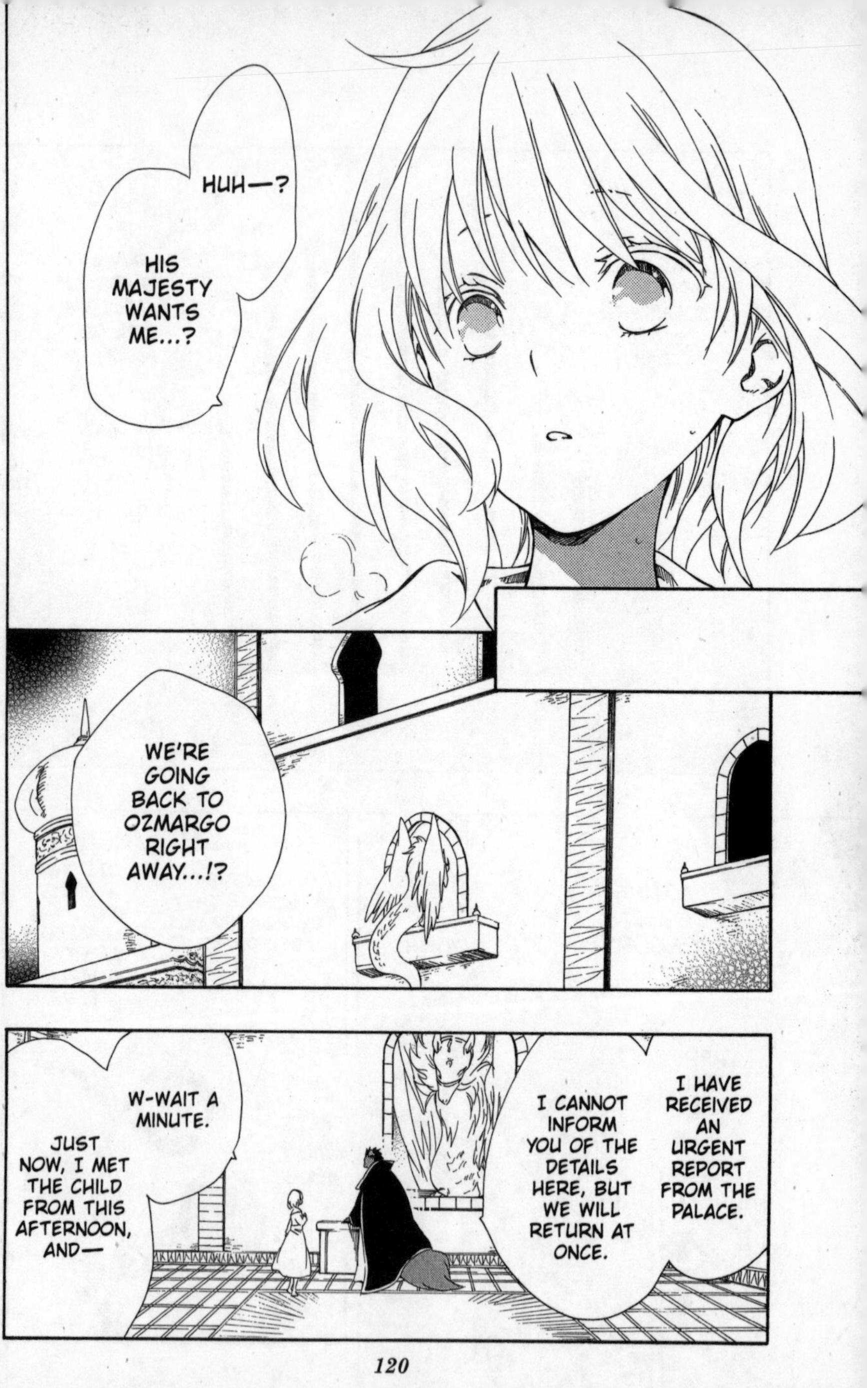
HUH—?
HIS MAJESTY WANTS ME...?
WE'RE GOING BACK TO OZMARGO RIGHT AWAY...!?
I HAVE RECEIVED AN URGENT REPORT FROM THE PALACE.
I CANNOT INFORM YOU OF THE DETAILS HERE, BUT WE WILL RETURN AT ONCE.
W-WAIT A MINUTE.
JUST NOW, I MET THE CHILD FROM THIS AFTERNOON, AND—

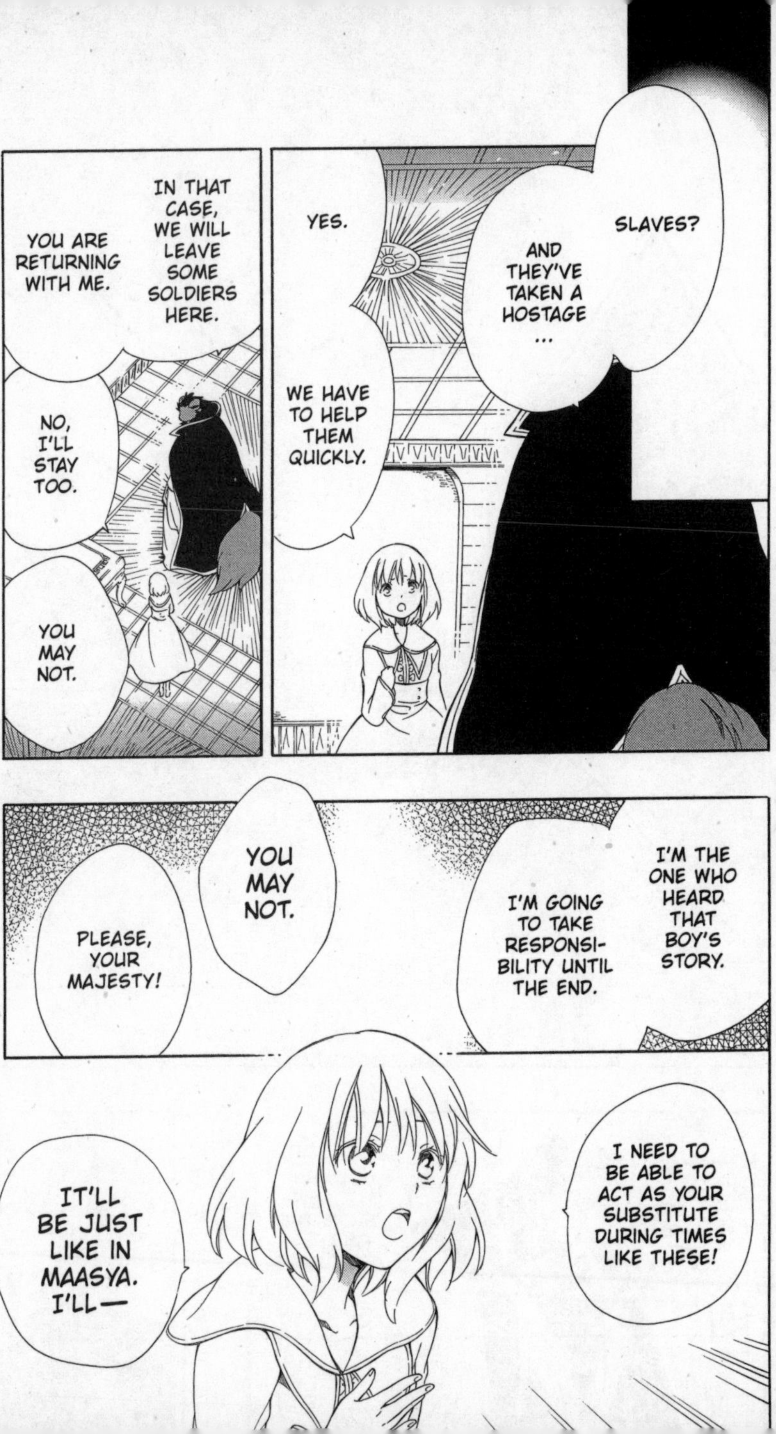
SLAVES?
AND THEY'VE TAKEN A HOSTAGE ...
YES.
WE HAVE TO HELP THEM QUICKLY.
IN THAT CASE, WE WILL LEAVE SOME SOLDIERS HERE.
YOU ARE RETURNING WITH ME.
NO, I'LL STAY TOO.
YOU MAY NOT.
I'M THE ONE WHO HEARD THAT BOY'S STORY.
I'M GOING TO TAKE RESPONSI-BILITY UNTIL THE END.
YOU MAY NOT.
PLEASE, YOUR MAJESTY!
I NEED TO BE ABLE TO ACT AS YOUR SUBSTITUTE DURING TIMES LIKE THESE!
IT'LL BE JUST LIKE IN MAASYA. I'LL—

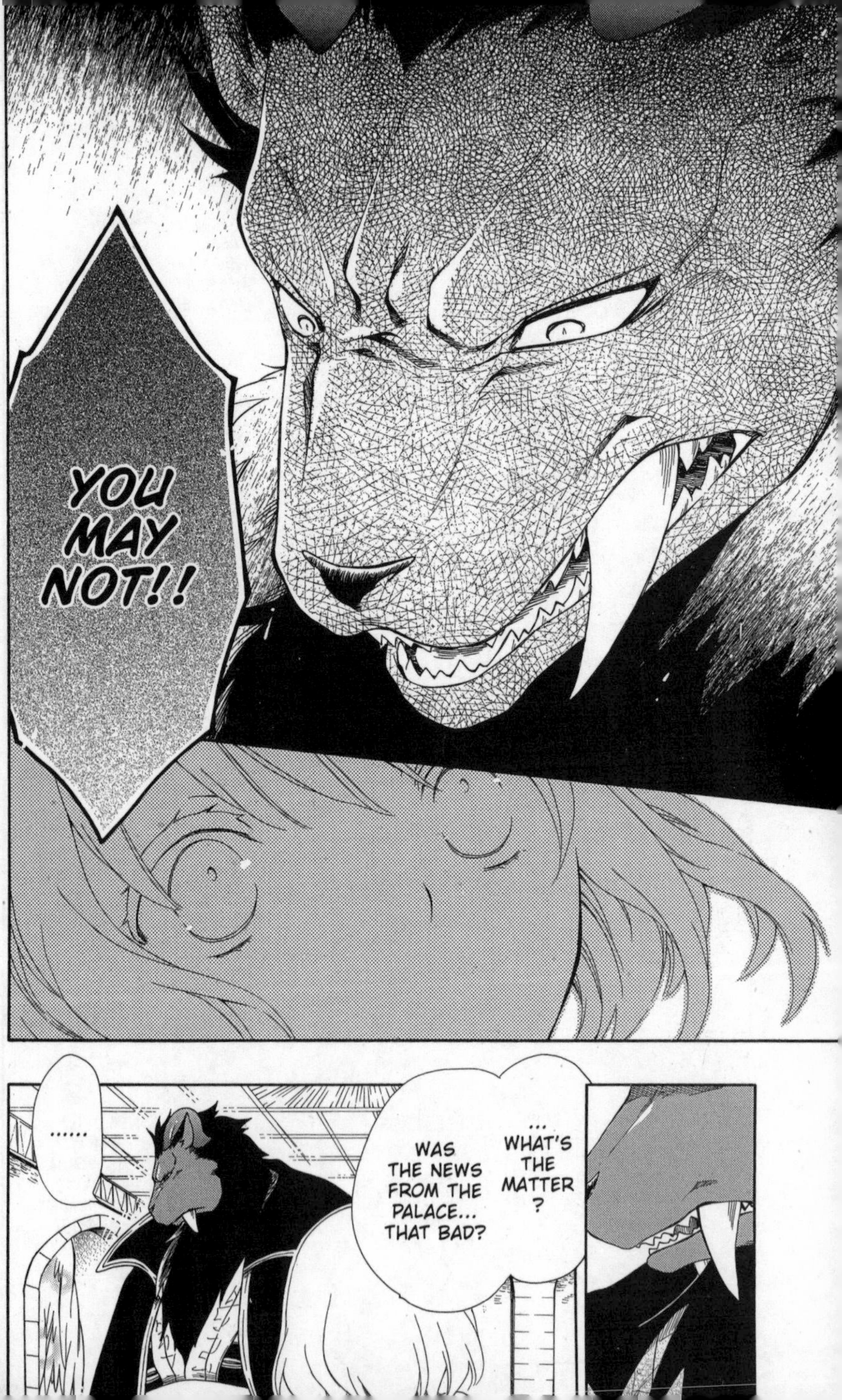
YOU MAY NOT!!
... WHAT'S THE MATTER ?
WAS THE NEWS FROM THE PALACE... THAT BAD?
......

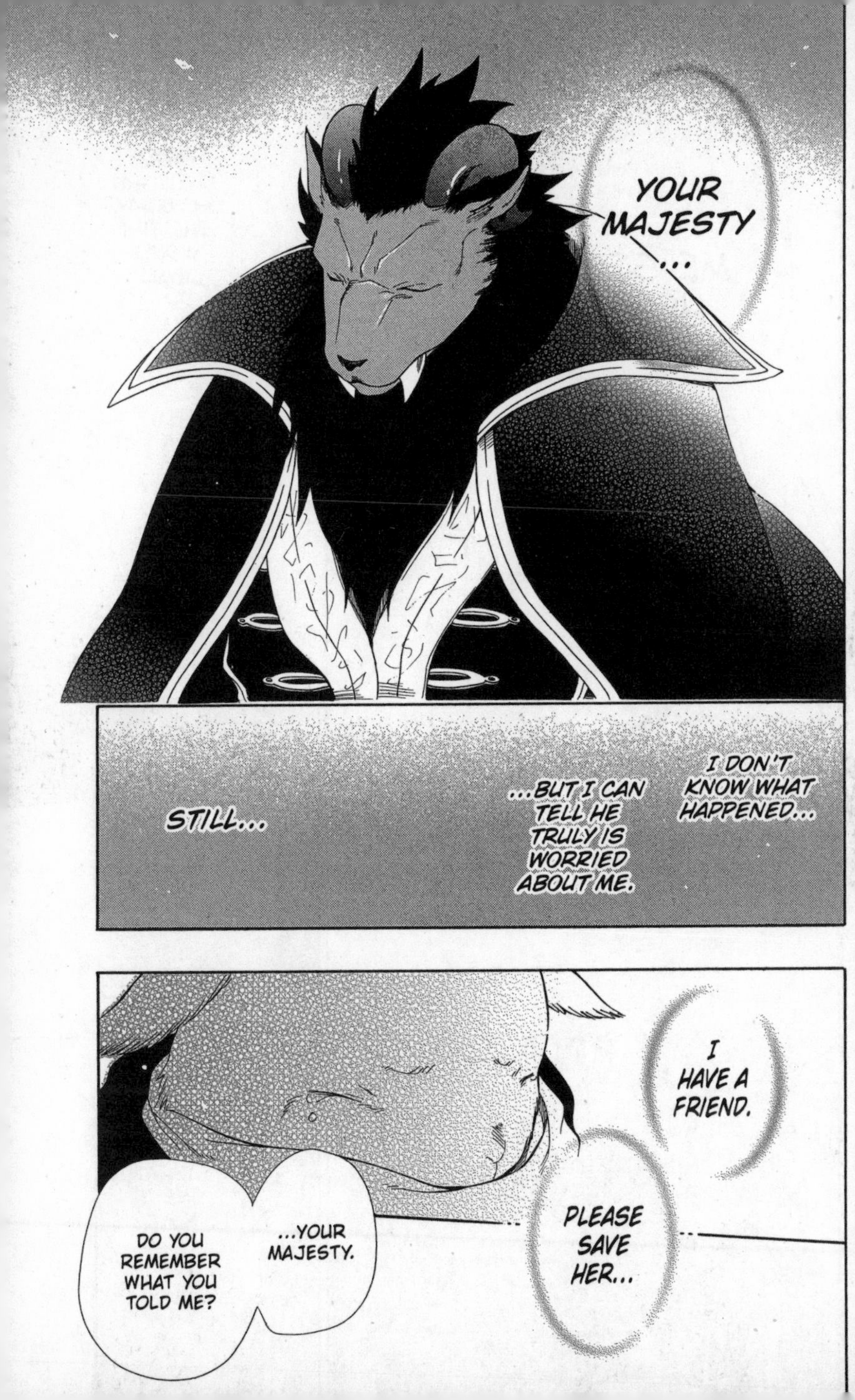
YOUR MAJESTY...
I DON'T KNOW WHAT HAPPENED...
...BUT I CAN TELL HE TRULY IS WORRIED ABOUT ME.
STILL...
I HAVE A FRIEND.
PLEASE SAVE HER...
...YOUR MAJESTY.
DO YOU REMEMBER WHAT YOU TOLD ME?

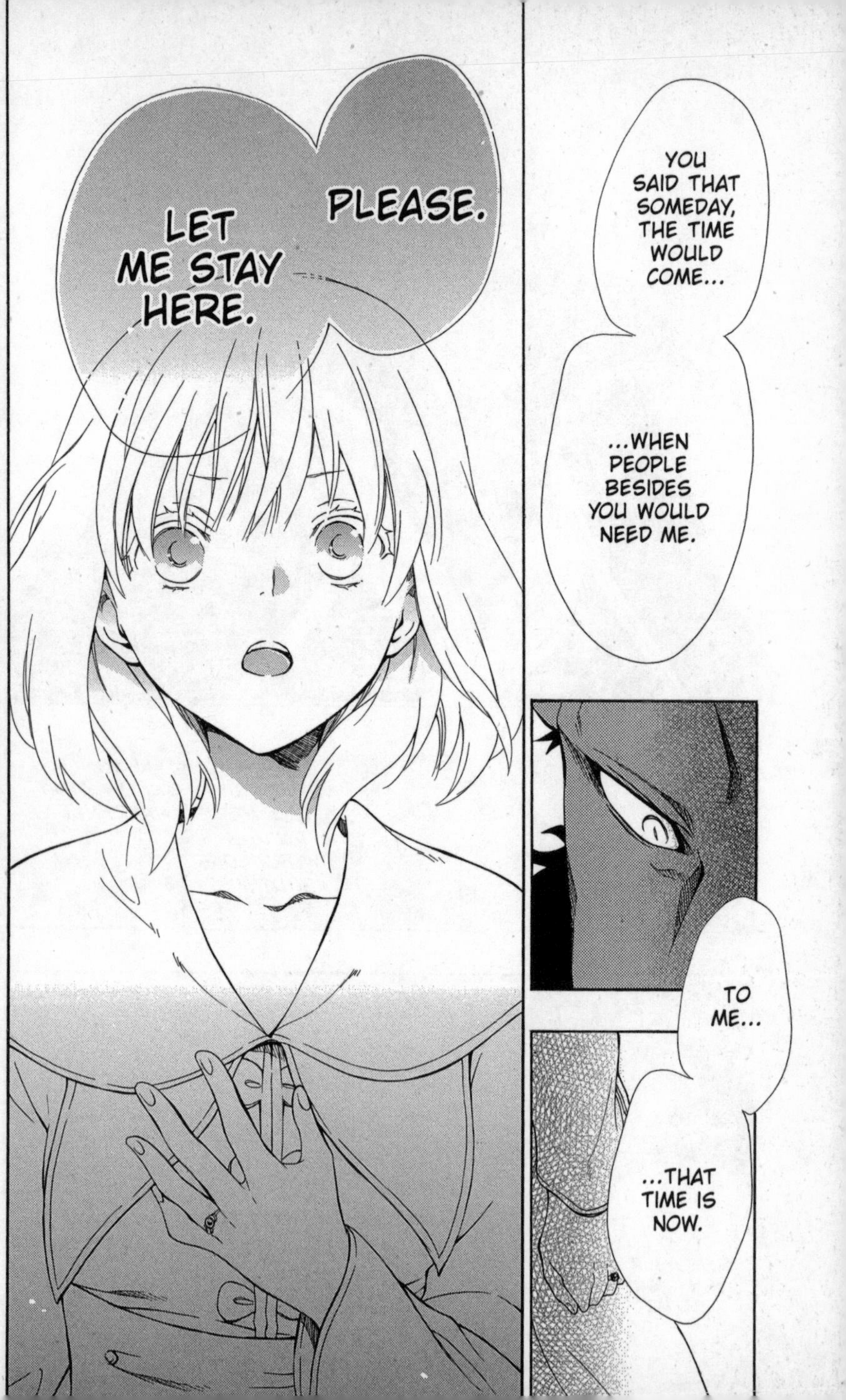
YOU SAID THAT SOMEDAY, THE TIME WOULD COME...
...WHEN PEOPLE BESIDES YOU WOULD NEED ME.
TO ME...
...THAT TIME IS NOW.
PLEASE.
LET ME STAY HERE.

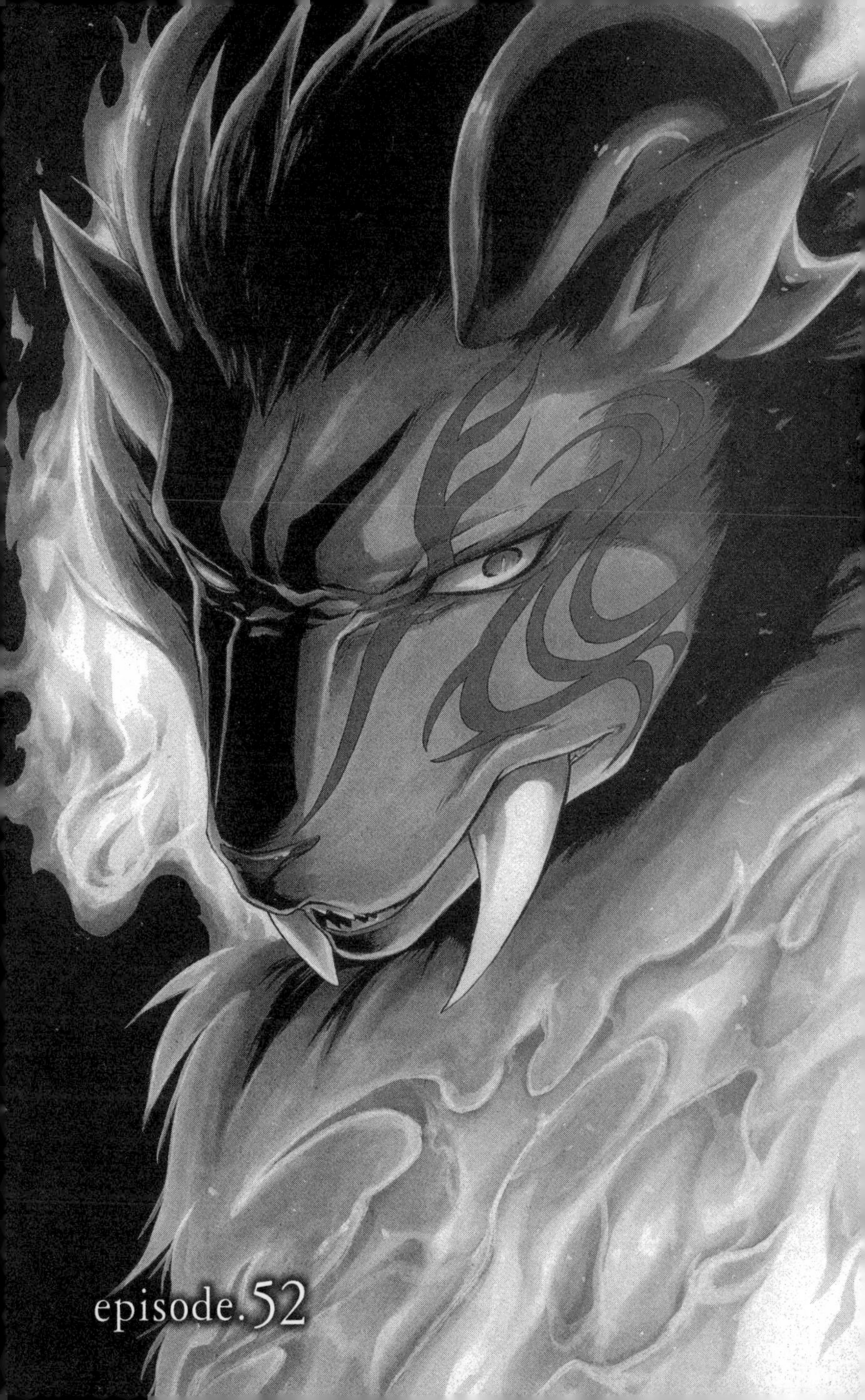
episode.52

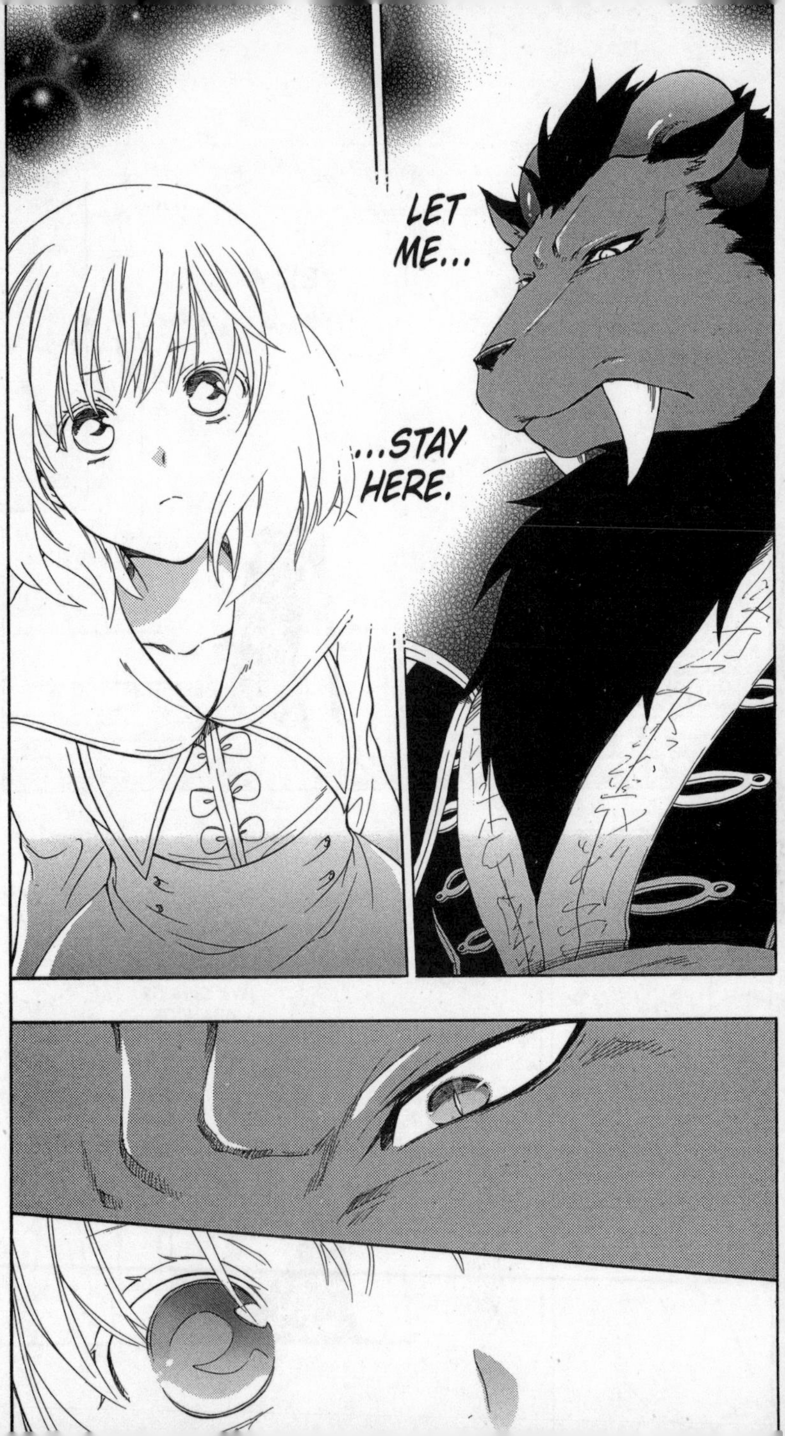
LET ME...
...STAY HERE.

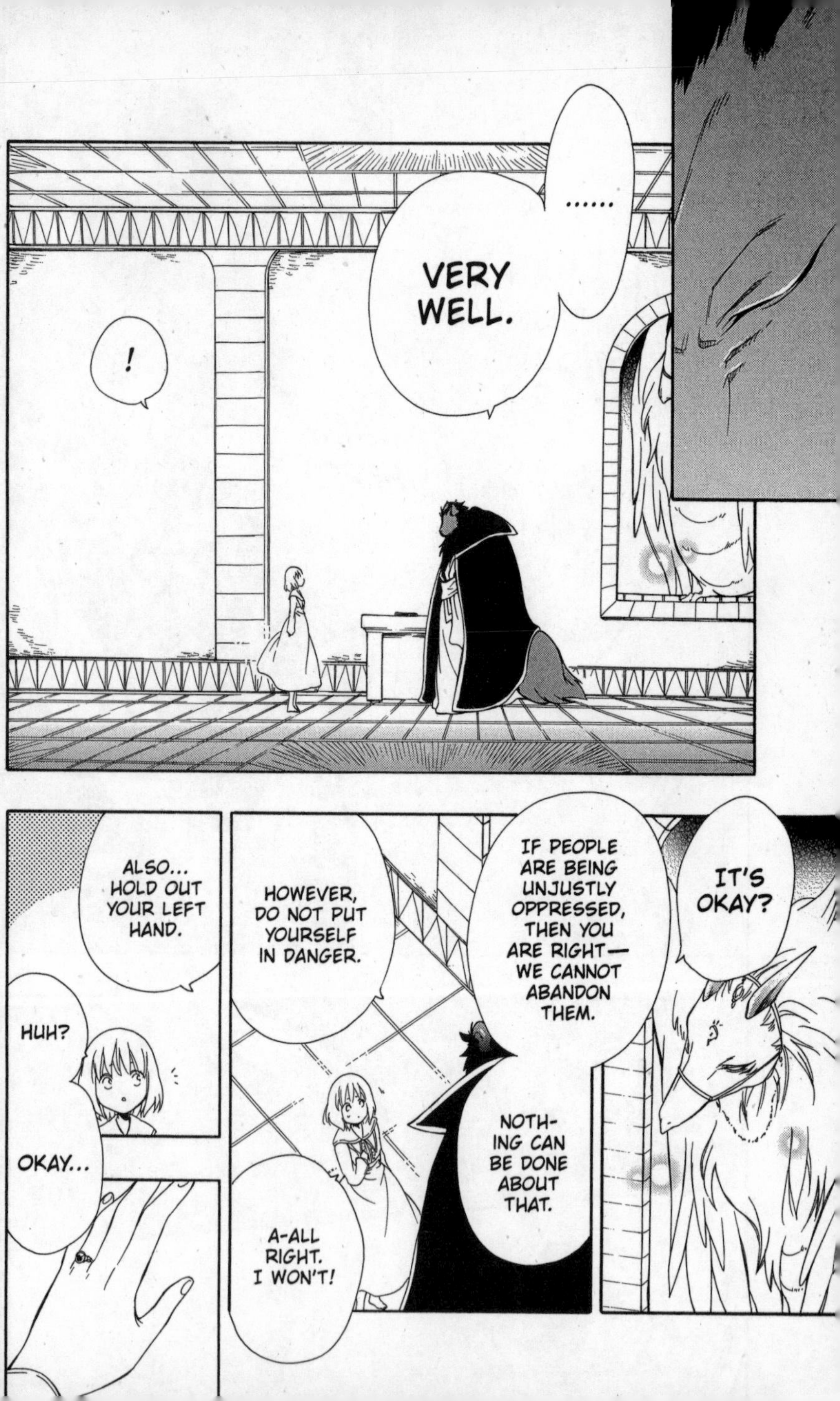
......
VERY WELL.
!
IT'S OKAY?
IF PEOPLE ARE BEING UNJUSTLY OPPRESSED, THEN YOU ARE RIGHT— WE CANNOT ABANDON THEM.
NOTH-ING CAN BE DONE ABOUT THAT.
HOWEVER, DO NOT PUT YOURSELF IN DANGER.
A-ALL RIGHT. I WON'T!
ALSO... HOLD OUT YOUR LEFT HAND.
HUH?
OKAY...

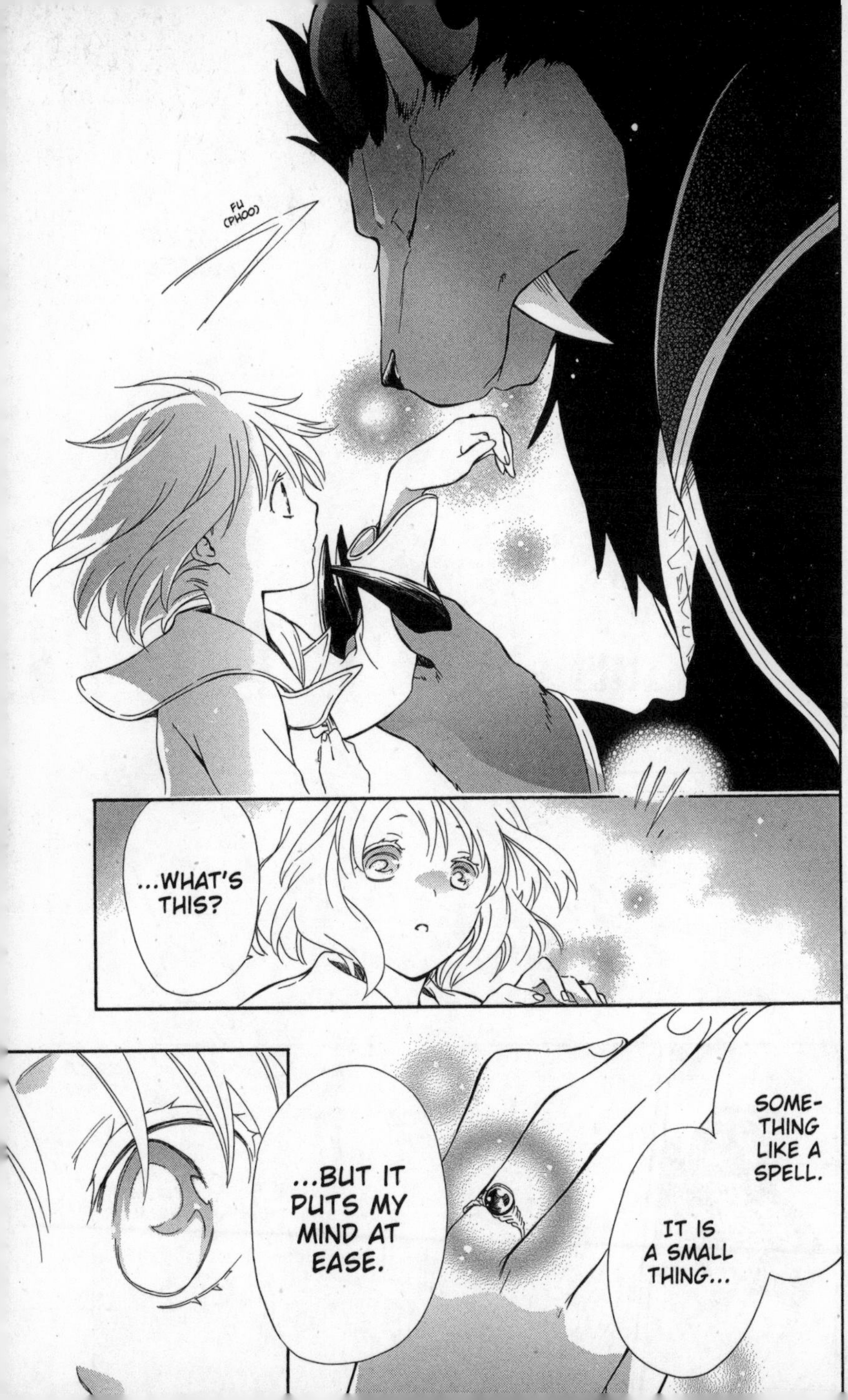
FU (PHOO)
...WHAT'S THIS?
SOME-THING LIKE A SPELL.
IT IS A SMALL THING...
...BUT IT PUTS MY MIND AT EASE.

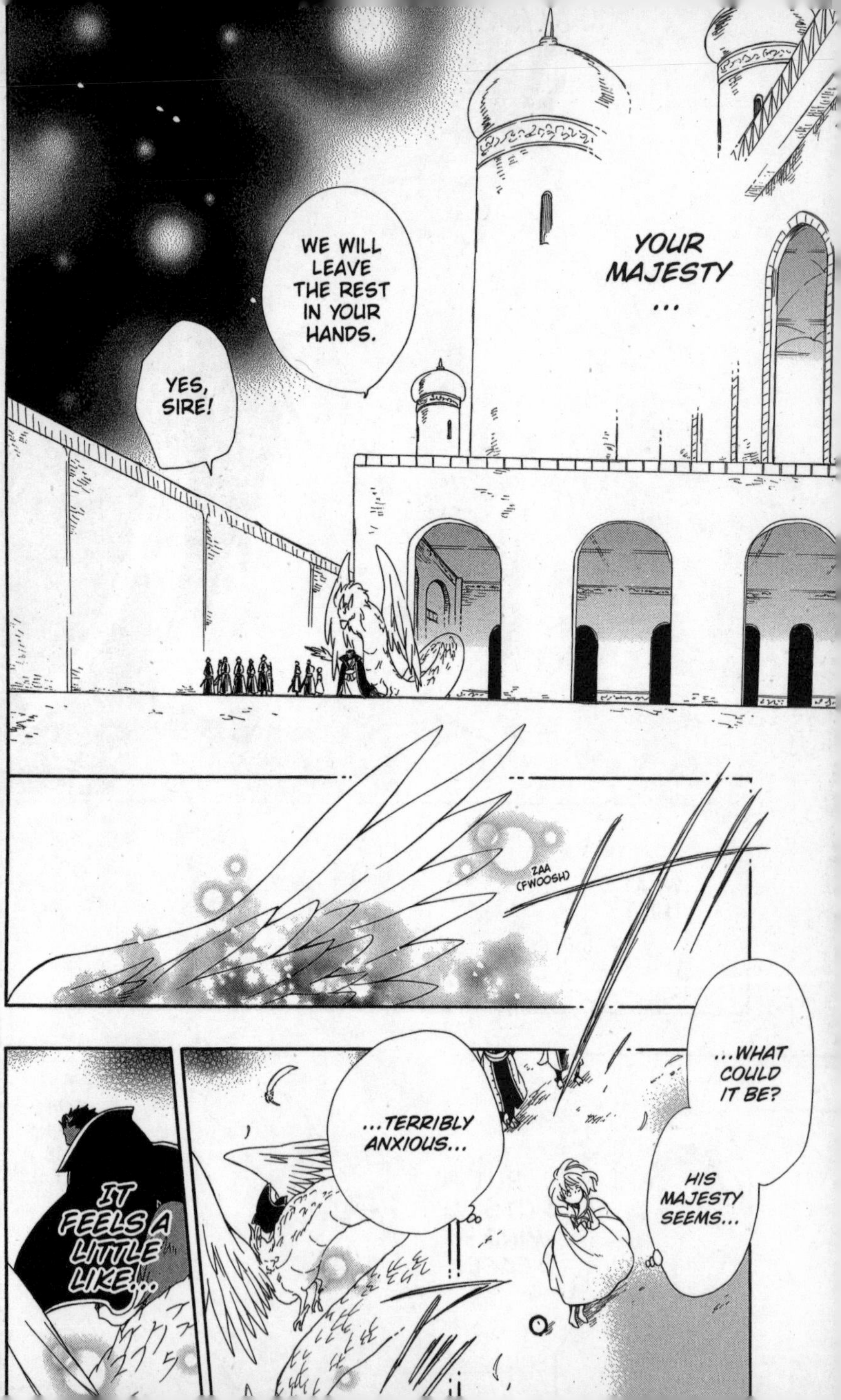
YOUR MAJESTY ...
WE WILL LEAVE THE REST IN YOUR HANDS.
YES, SIRE!
ZAA (FWOOSH)
HIS MAJESTY SEEMS...
...TERRIBLY ANXIOUS...
...WHAT COULD IT BE?
IT FEELS A LITTLE LIKE...

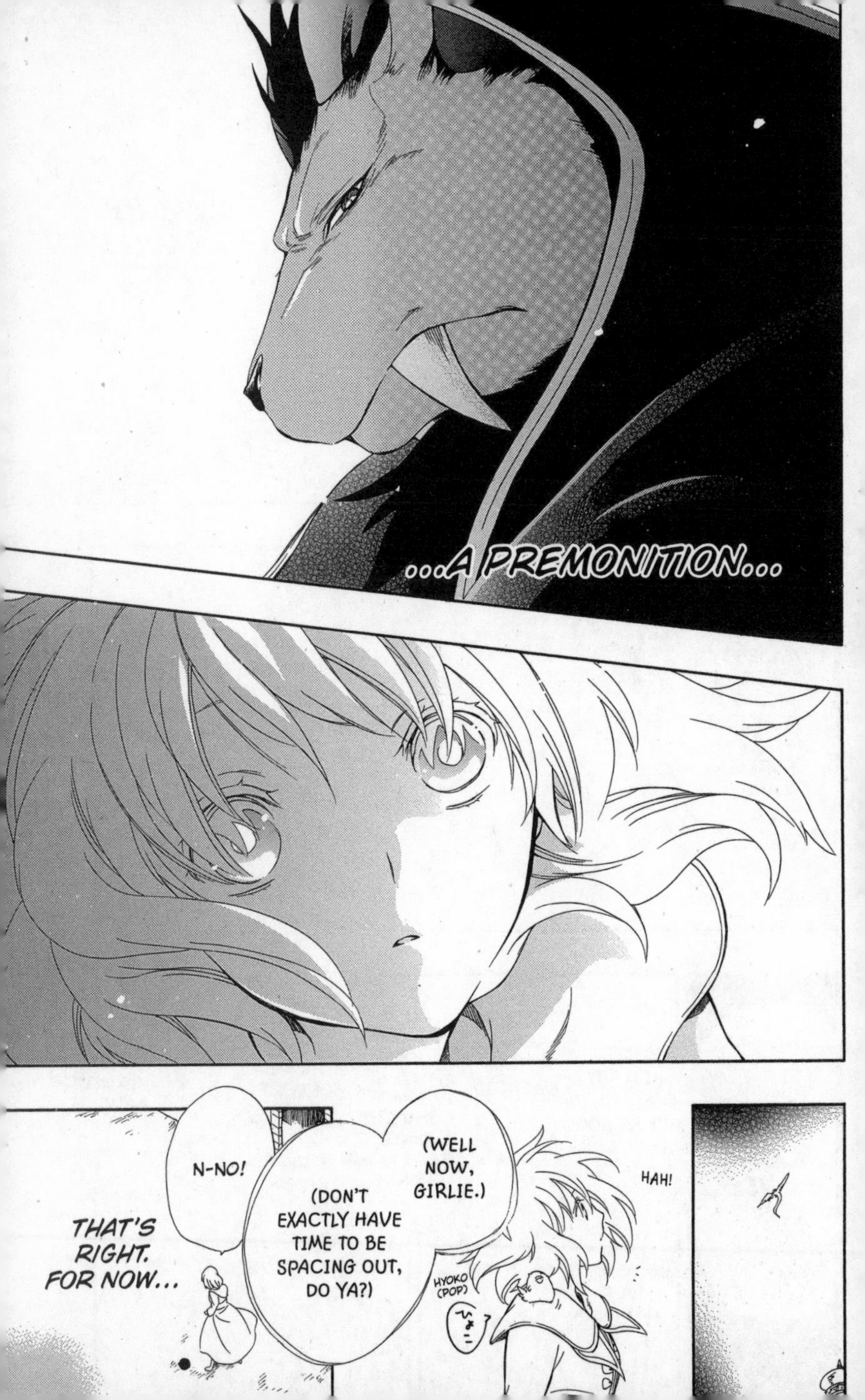
...A PREMONITION...
HAH!
HYOKO (POP)
(WELL NOW, GIRLIE.)
(DON'T EXACTLY HAVE TIME TO BE SPACING OUT, DO YA?)
N-NO!
THAT'S RIGHT. FOR NOW...

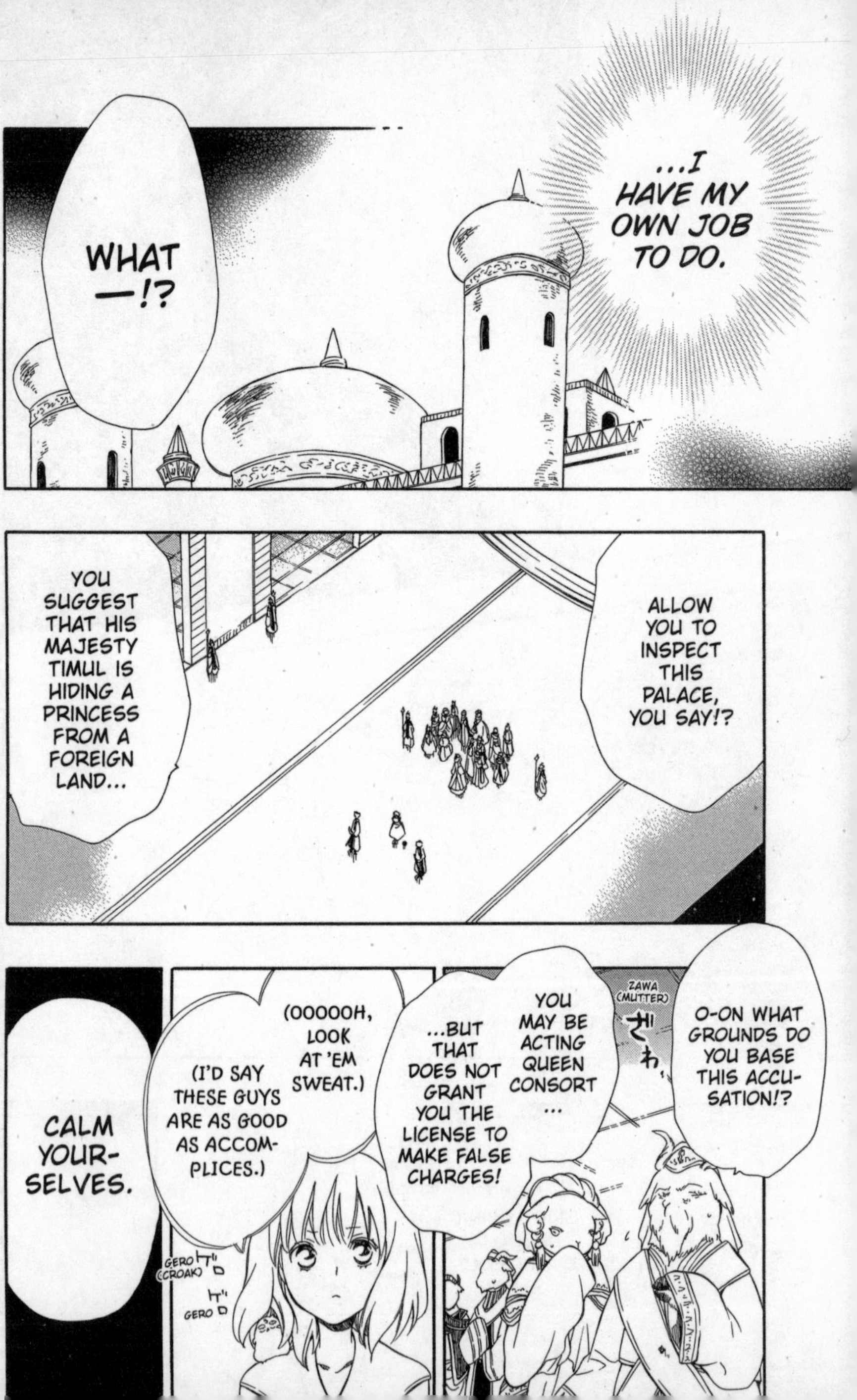
...I HAVE MY OWN JOB TO DO.
WHAT—!?
ALLOW YOU TO INSPECT THIS PALACE, YOU SAY!?
YOU SUGGEST THAT HIS MAJESTY TIMUL IS HIDING A PRINCESS FROM A FOREIGN LAND...
O-ON WHAT GROUNDS DO YOU BASE THIS ACCUSATION!?
ZAWA (MUTTER)
YOU MAY BE ACTING QUEEN CONSORT...
...BUT THAT DOES NOT GRANT YOU THE LICENSE TO MAKE FALSE CHARGES!
(OOOOOH, LOOK AT 'EM SWEAT.)
(I'D SAY THESE GUYS ARE AS GOOD AS ACCOMPLICES.)
GERO (CROAK)
GERO
CALM YOURSELVES.

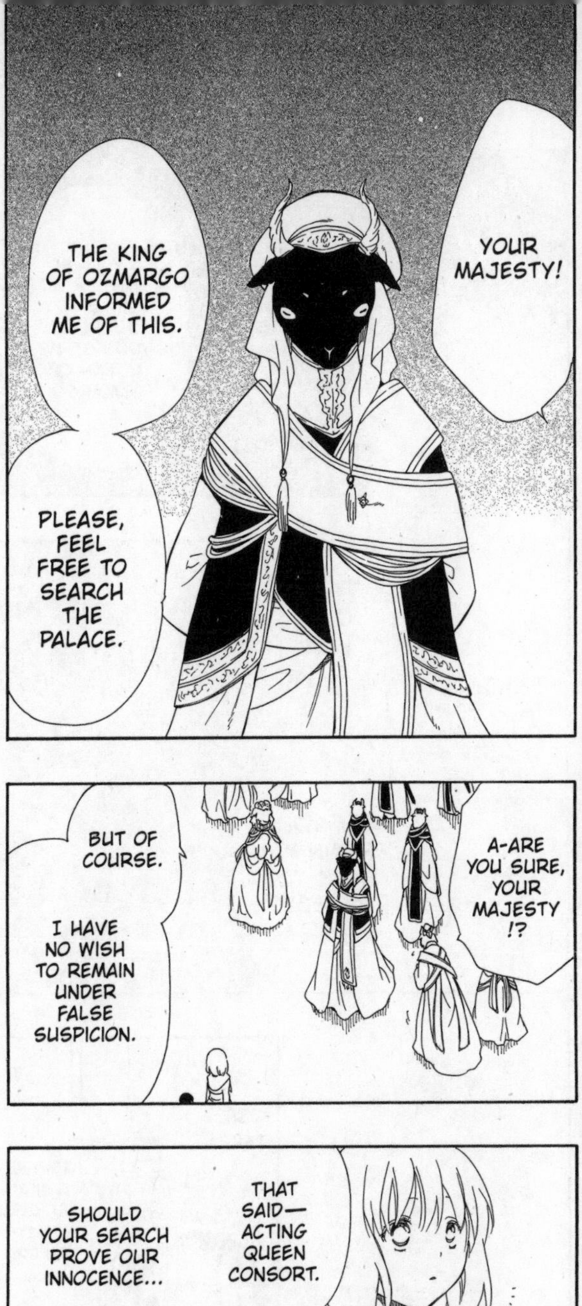
YOUR MAJESTY!
THE KING OF OZMARGO INFORMED ME OF THIS.
PLEASE, FEEL FREE TO SEARCH THE PALACE.
A-ARE YOU SURE, YOUR MAJESTY !?
BUT OF COURSE.
I HAVE NO WISH TO REMAIN UNDER FALSE SUSPICION.
THAT SAID— ACTING QUEEN CONSORT.
SHOULD YOUR SEARCH PROVE OUR INNOCENCE...

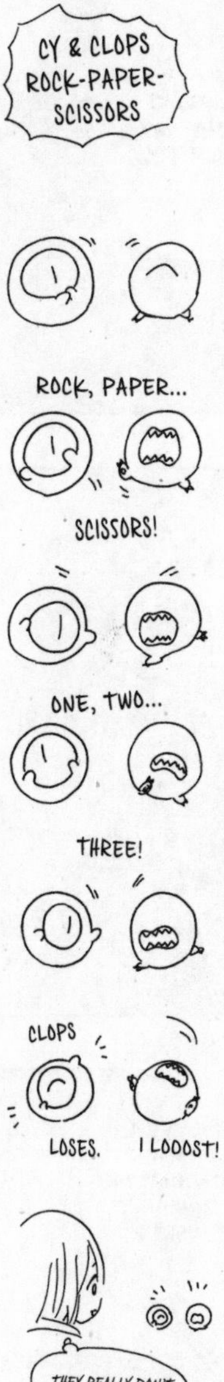
CY & CLOPS ROCK-PAPER-SCISSORS
ROCK, PAPER...
SCISSORS!
ONE, TWO...
THREE!
CLOPS
LOSES.
I LOOOST!
THEY REALLY DON'T KNOW THE RULES...

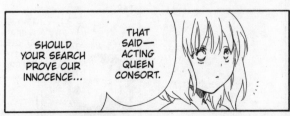

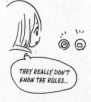

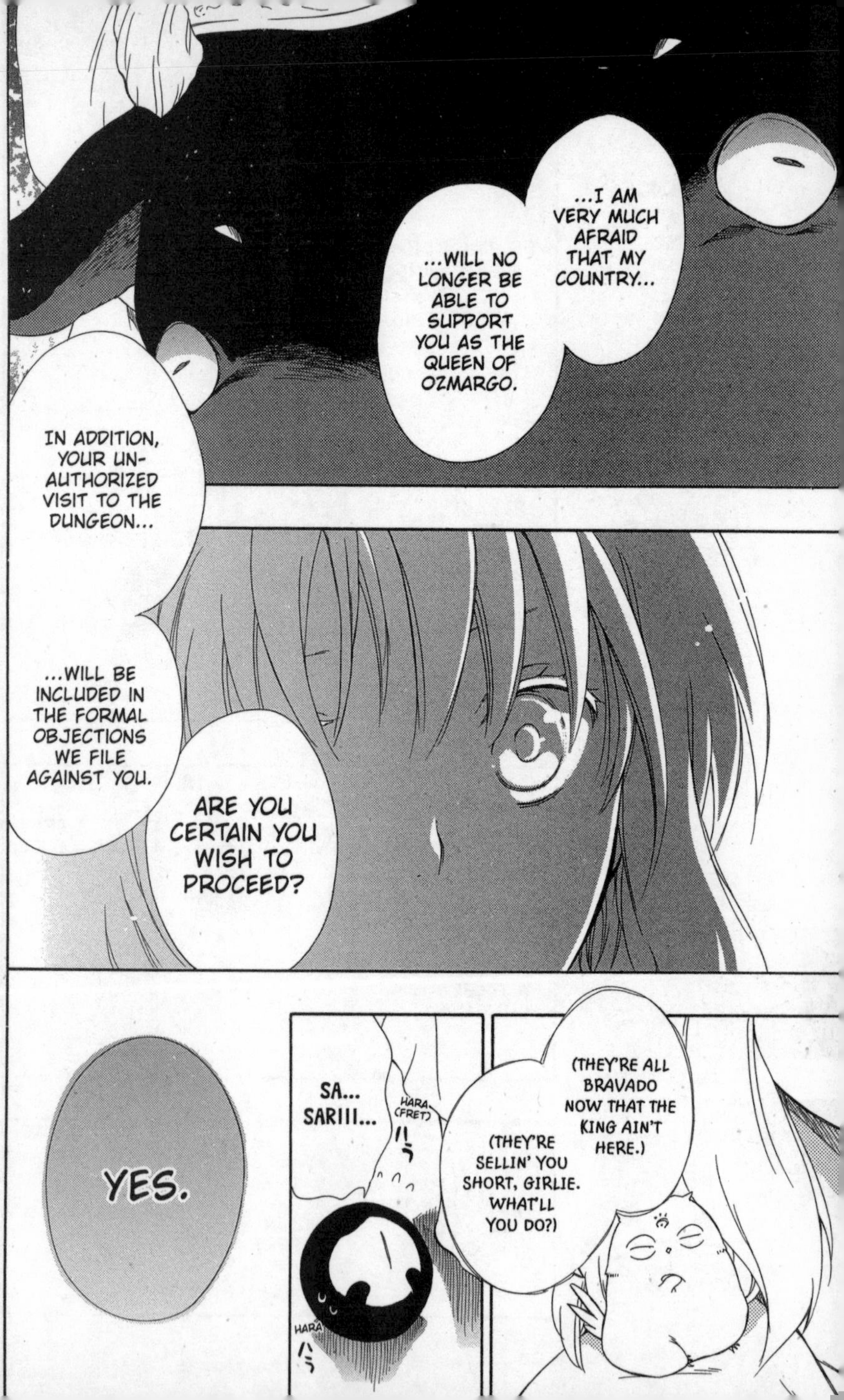
...I AM VERY MUCH AFRAID THAT MY COUNTRY...
...WILL NO LONGER BE ABLE TO SUPPORT YOU AS THE QUEEN OF OZMARGO.
IN ADDITION, YOUR UN-AUTHORIZED VISIT TO THE DUNGEON...
...WILL BE INCLUDED IN THE FORMAL OBJECTIONS WE FILE AGAINST YOU.
ARE YOU CERTAIN YOU WISH TO PROCEED?
(THEY'RE ALL BRAVADO NOW THAT THE KING AIN'T HERE.)
(THEY'RE SELLIN' YOU SHORT, GIRLIE. WHAT'LL YOU DO?)
HARA (FRET)
SA... SARIII...
HARA
YES.

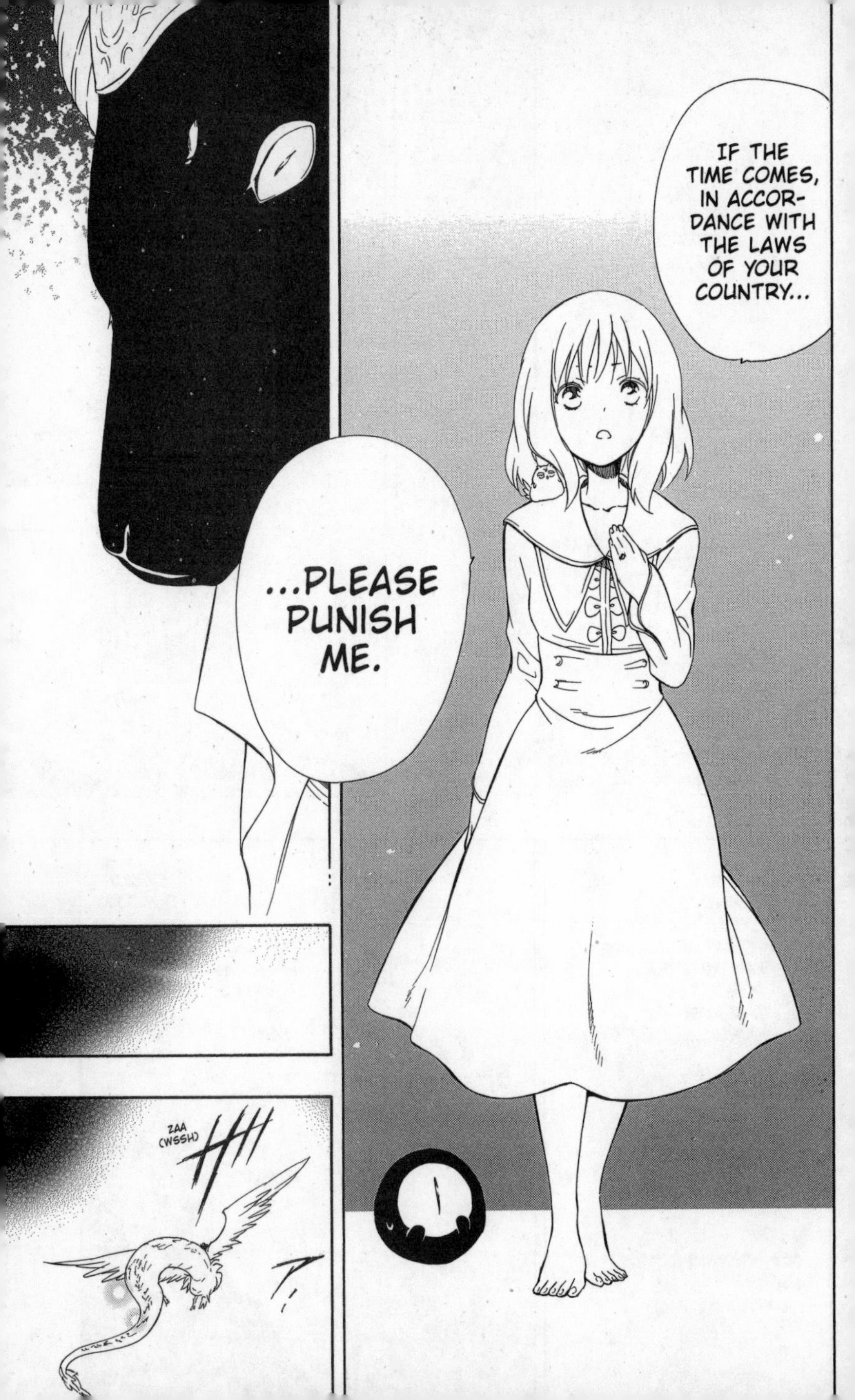
IF THE TIME COMES, IN ACCORDANCE WITH THE LAWS OF YOUR COUNTRY...
...PLEASE PUNISH ME.
ZAA (WSSH)

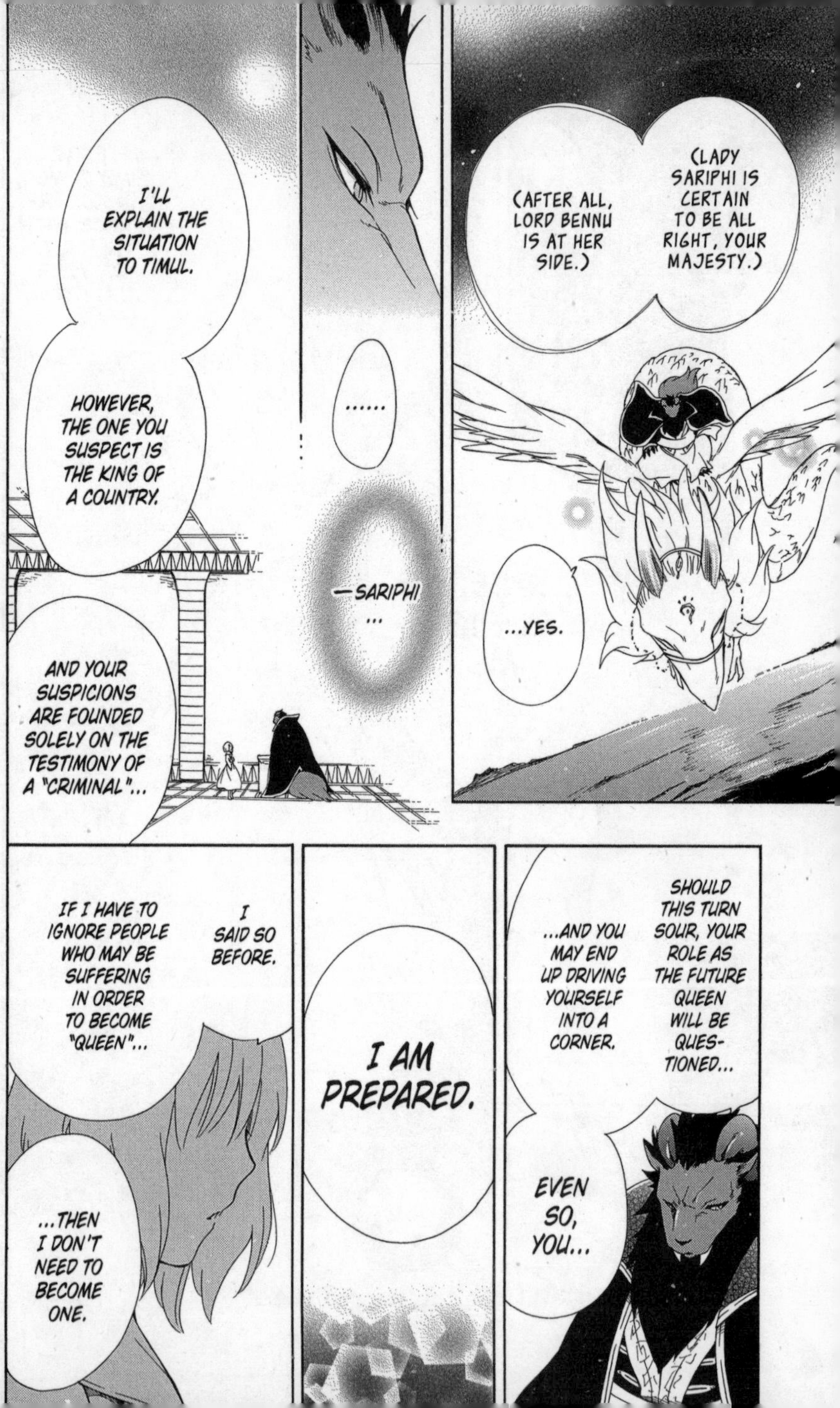
(LADY SARIPHI IS CERTAIN TO BE ALL RIGHT, YOUR MAJESTY.)
(AFTER ALL, LORD BENNU IS AT HER SIDE.)
...YES.
......
—SARIPHI ...
I'LL EXPLAIN THE SITUATION TO TIMUL.
HOWEVER, THE ONE YOU SUSPECT IS THE KING OF A COUNTRY.
AND YOUR SUSPICIONS ARE FOUNDED SOLELY ON THE TESTIMONY OF A "CRIMINAL"...
SHOULD THIS TURN SOUR, YOUR ROLE AS THE FUTURE QUEEN WILL BE QUES-TIONED...
...AND YOU MAY END UP DRIVING YOURSELF INTO A CORNER.
EVEN SO, YOU...
I AM PREPARED.
I SAID SO BEFORE.
IF I HAVE TO IGNORE PEOPLE WHO MAY BE SUFFERING IN ORDER TO BECOME "QUEEN"...
...THEN I DON'T NEED TO BECOME ONE.

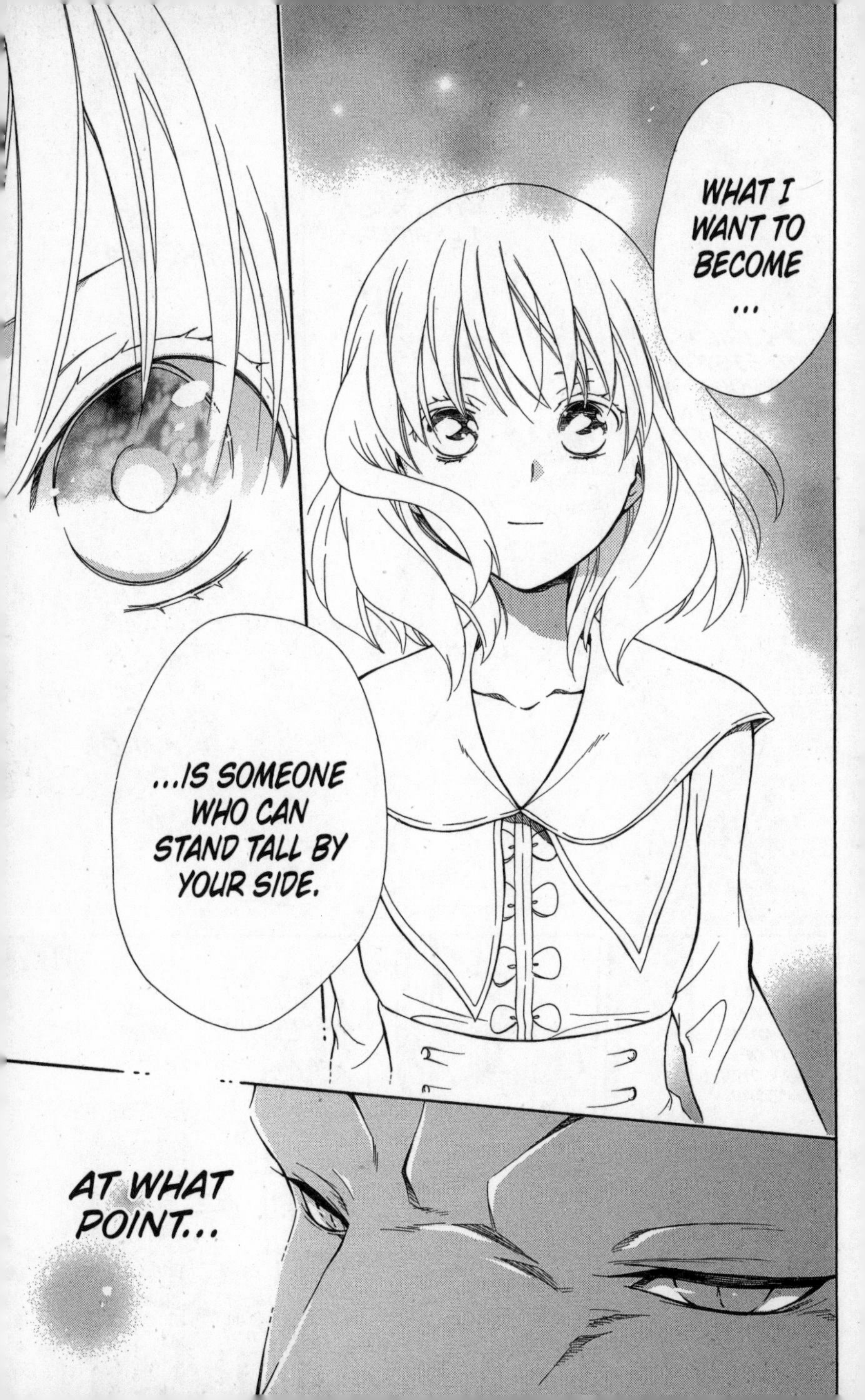
WHAT I WANT TO BECOME ...
...IS SOMEONE WHO CAN STAND TALL BY YOUR SIDE.
AT WHAT POINT...

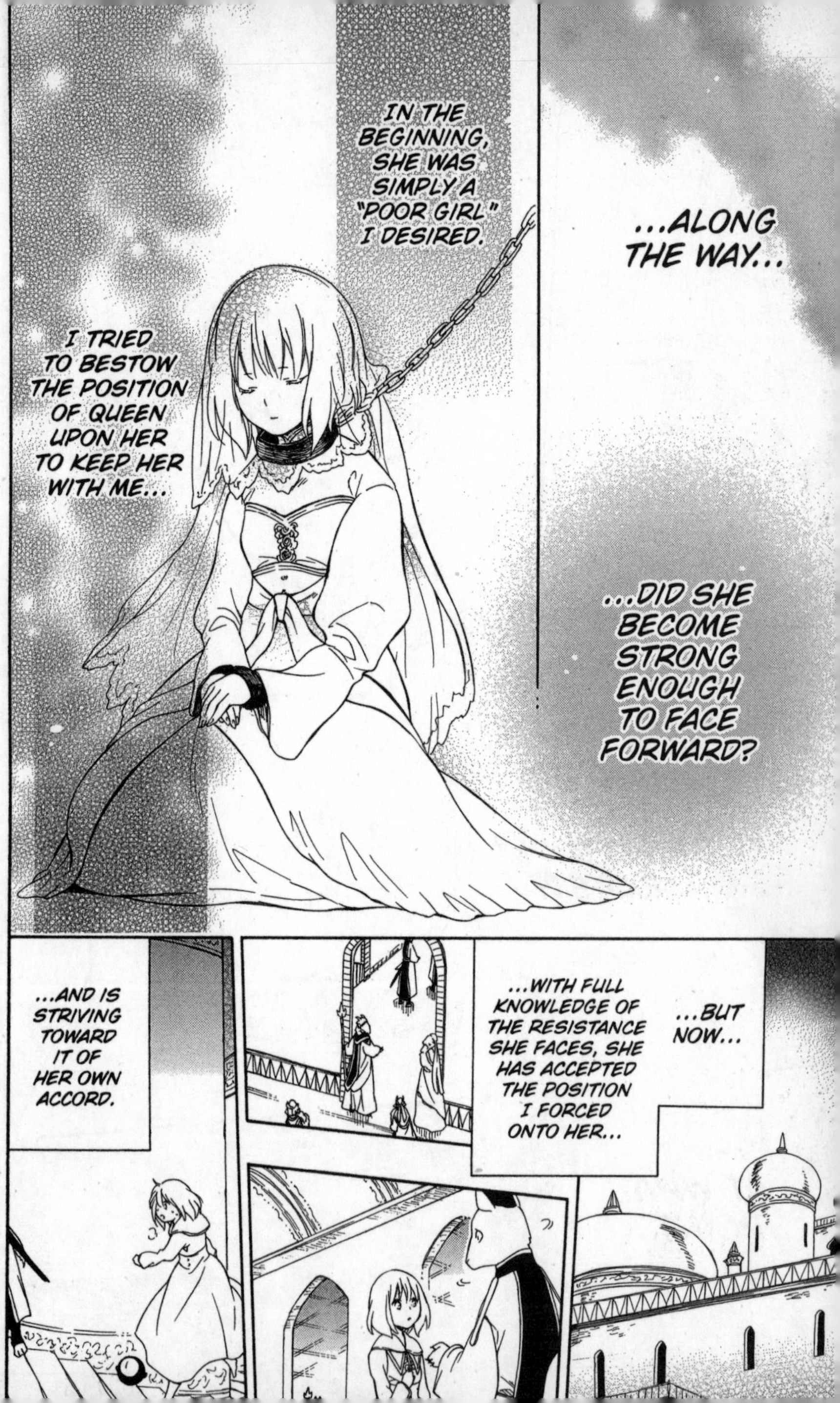
IN THE BEGINNING, SHE WAS SIMPLY A "POOR GIRL" I DESIRED.
I TRIED TO BESTOW THE POSITION OF QUEEN UPON HER TO KEEP HER WITH ME...
...ALONG THE WAY...
...DID SHE BECOME STRONG ENOUGH TO FACE FORWARD?
...BUT NOW...
...WITH FULL KNOWLEDGE OF THE RESISTANCE SHE FACES, SHE HAS ACCEPTED THE POSITION I FORCED ONTO HER...
...AND IS STRIVING TOWARD IT OF HER OWN ACCORD.

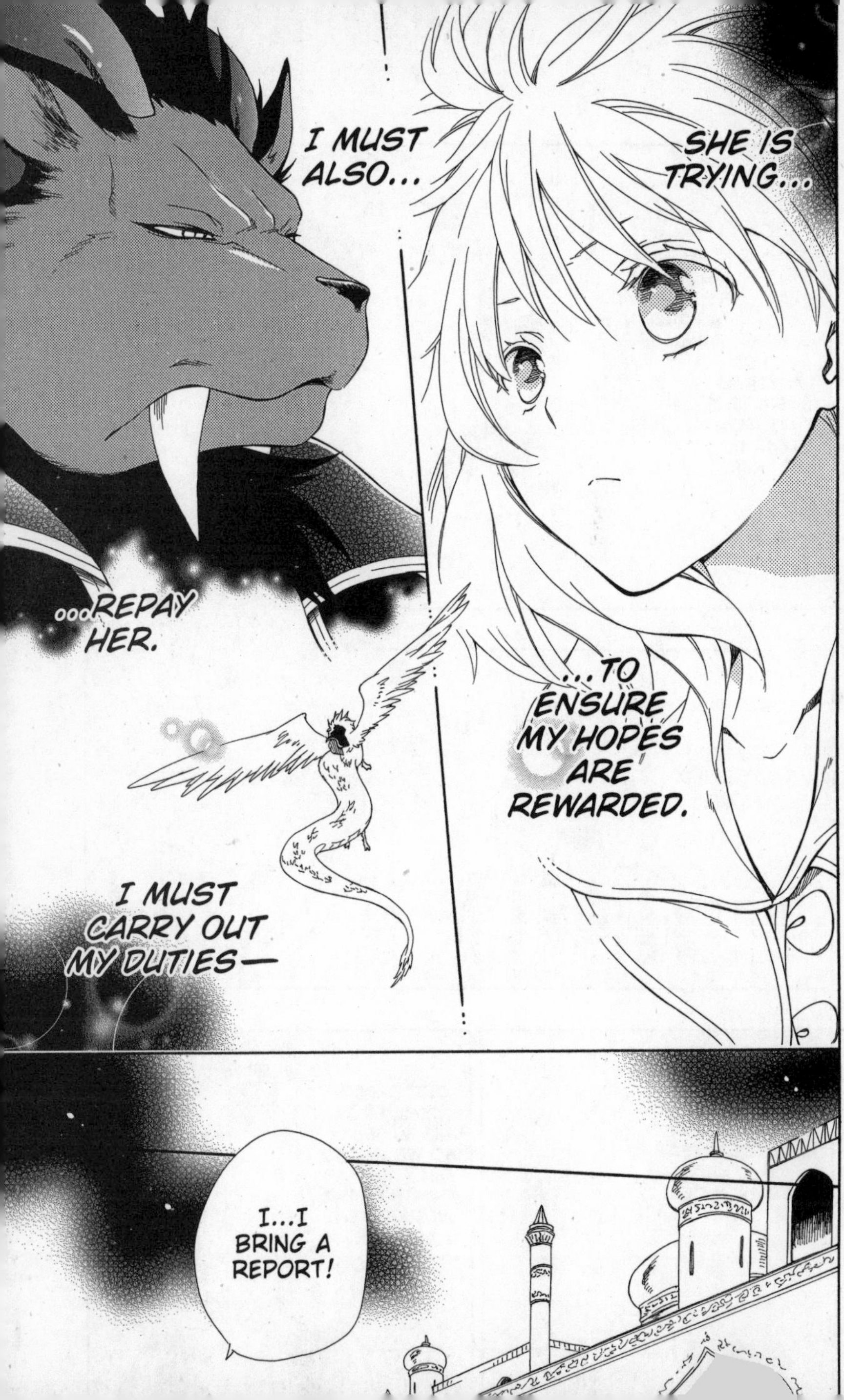
SHE IS TRYING...
...TO ENSURE MY HOPES ARE REWARDED.
I MUST ALSO...
...REPAY HER.
I MUST CARRY OUT MY DUTIES—
I...I BRING A REPORT!

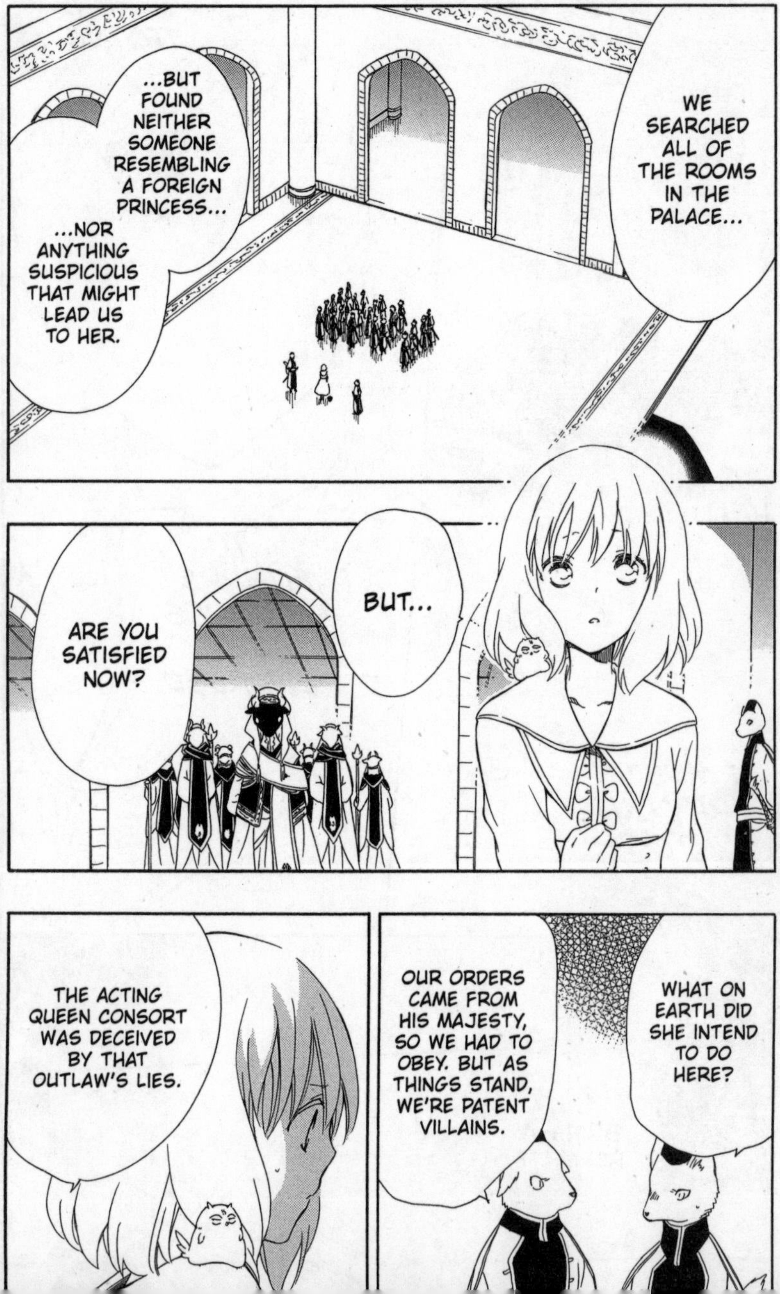
WE SEARCHED ALL OF THE ROOMS IN THE PALACE...
...BUT FOUND NEITHER SOMEONE RESEMBLING A FOREIGN PRINCESS...
...NOR ANYTHING SUSPICIOUS THAT MIGHT LEAD US TO HER.
BUT...
ARE YOU SATISFIED NOW?
WHAT ON EARTH DID SHE INTEND TO DO HERE?
OUR ORDERS CAME FROM HIS MAJESTY, SO WE HAD TO OBEY. BUT AS THINGS STAND, WE'RE PATENT VILLAINS.
THE ACTING QUEEN CONSORT WAS DECEIVED BY THAT OUTLAW'S LIES.

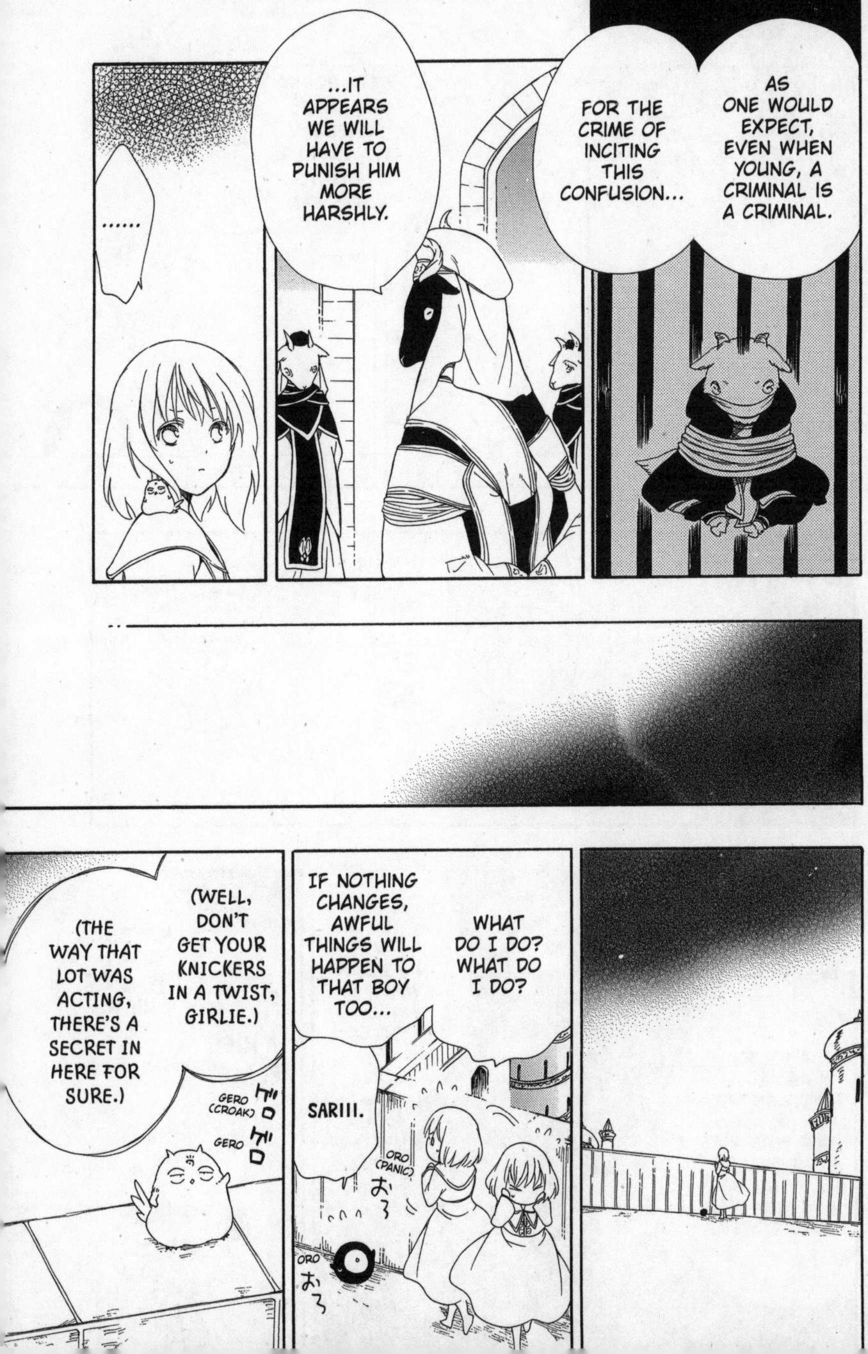
AS ONE WOULD EXPECT, EVEN WHEN YOUNG, A CRIMINAL IS A CRIMINAL.
FOR THE CRIME OF INCITING THIS CONFUSION...
...IT APPEARS WE WILL HAVE TO PUNISH HIM MORE HARSHLY.
......
WHAT DO I DO? WHAT DO I DO?
IF NOTHING CHANGES, AWFUL THINGS WILL HAPPEN TO THAT BOY TOO...
SARIII.
おろ ORO (PANIC)
おろ ORO
(WELL, DON'T GET YOUR KNICKERS IN A TWIST, GIRLIE.)
(THE WAY THAT LOT WAS ACTING, THERE'S A SECRET IN HERE FOR SURE.)
ゲロ GERO (CROAK)
ゲロ GERO

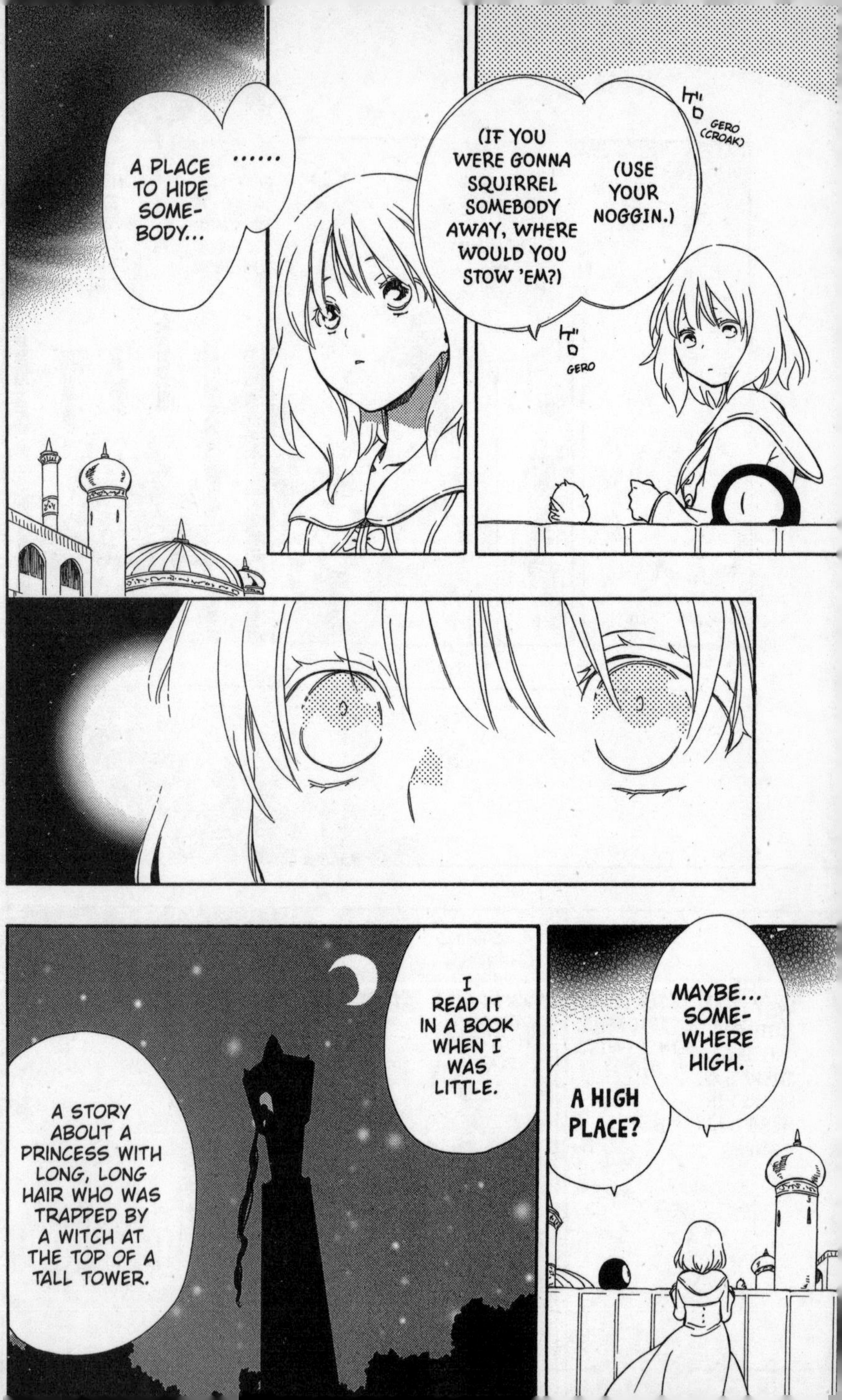
ゲロ
GERO (CROAK)
(IF YOU WERE GONNA SQUIRREL SOMEBODY AWAY, WHERE WOULD YOU STOW 'EM?)
(USE YOUR NOGGIN.)
ゲロ
GERO
......
A PLACE TO HIDE SOME-BODY...
MAYBE... SOME-WHERE HIGH.
A HIGH PLACE?
I READ IT IN A BOOK WHEN I WAS LITTLE.
A STORY ABOUT A PRINCESS WITH LONG, LONG HAIR WHO WAS TRAPPED BY A WITCH AT THE TOP OF A TALL TOWER.

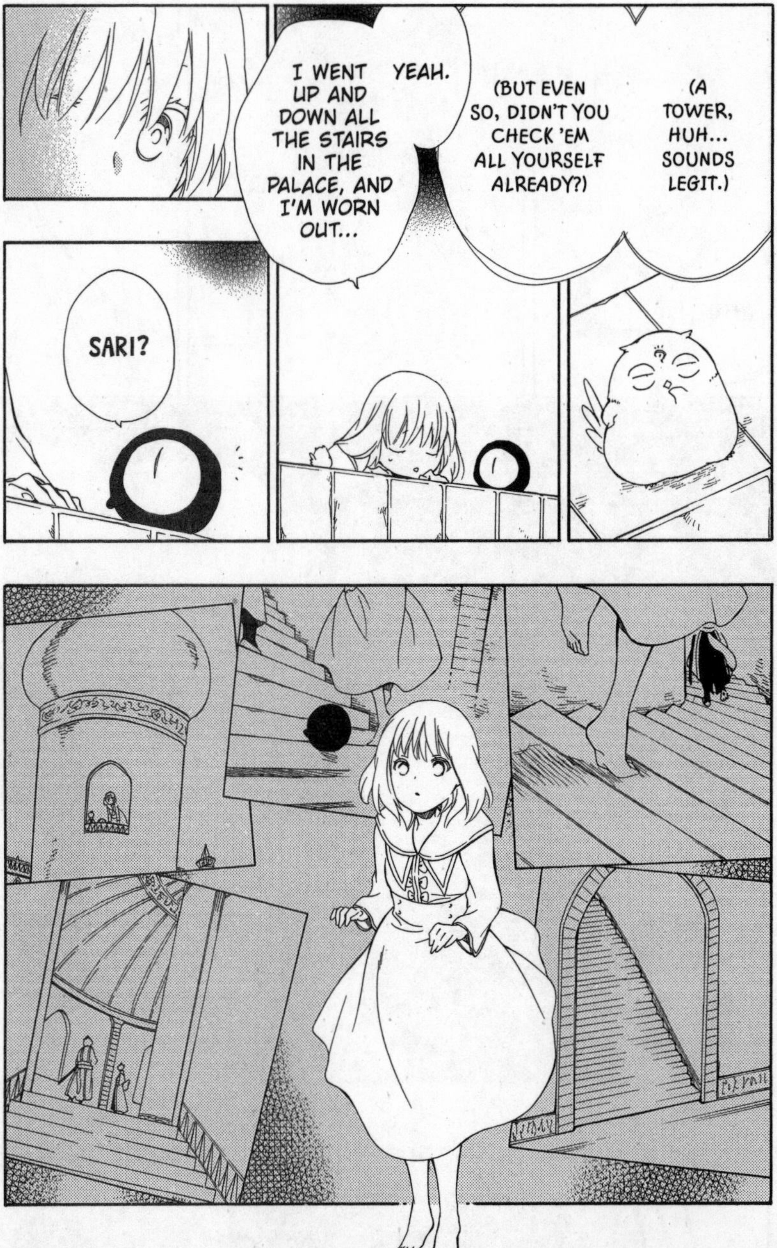
(A TOWER, HUH... SOUNDS LEGIT.)
(BUT EVEN SO, DIDN'T YOU CHECK 'EM ALL YOURSELF ALREADY?)
YEAH.
I WENT UP AND DOWN ALL THE STAIRS IN THE PALACE, AND I'M WORN OUT...
SARI?

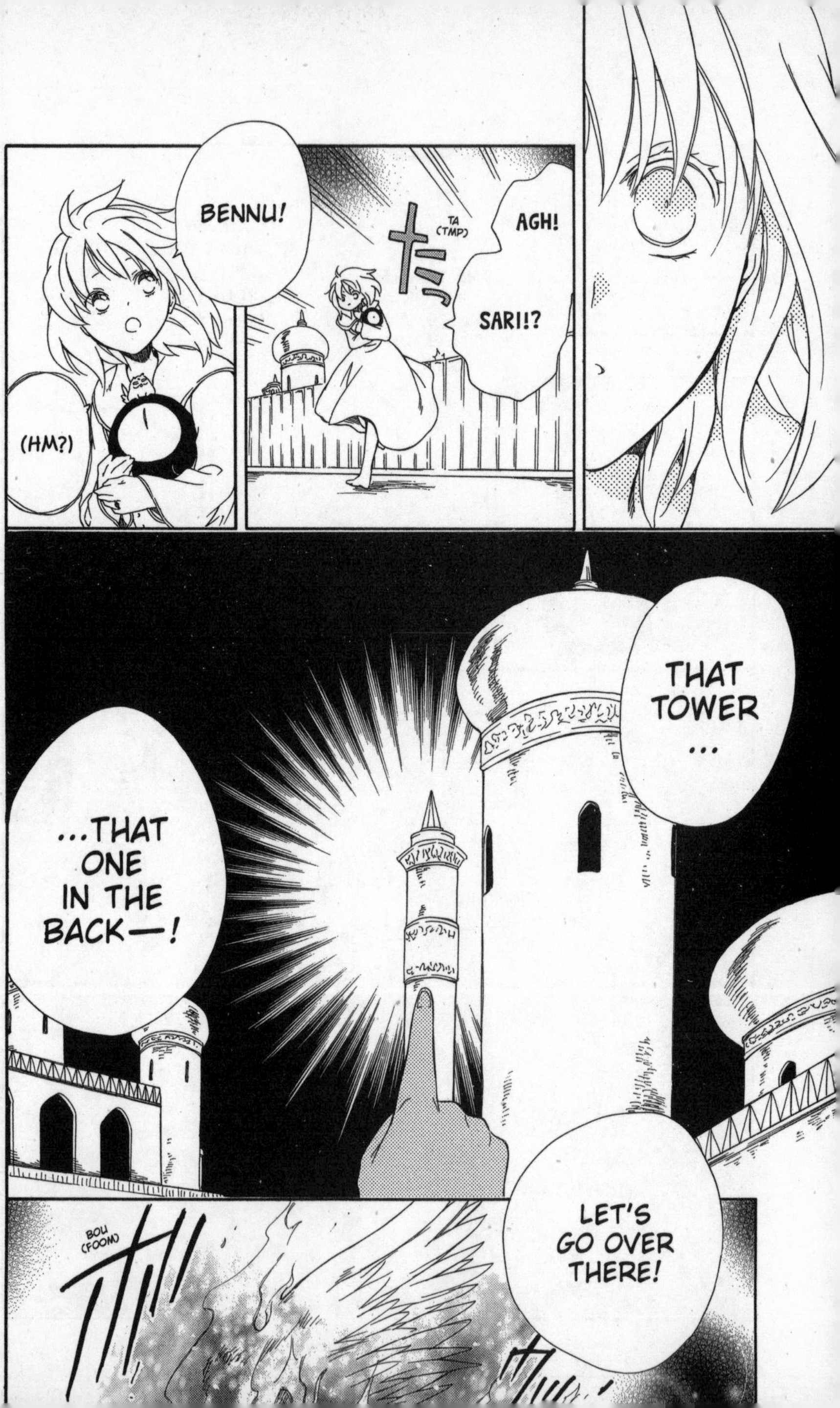
AGH!
SARI!?
TA (TMP)
BENNU!
(HM?)
THAT TOWER ...
...THAT ONE IN THE BACK—!
LET'S GO OVER THERE!
BOU (FOOM)

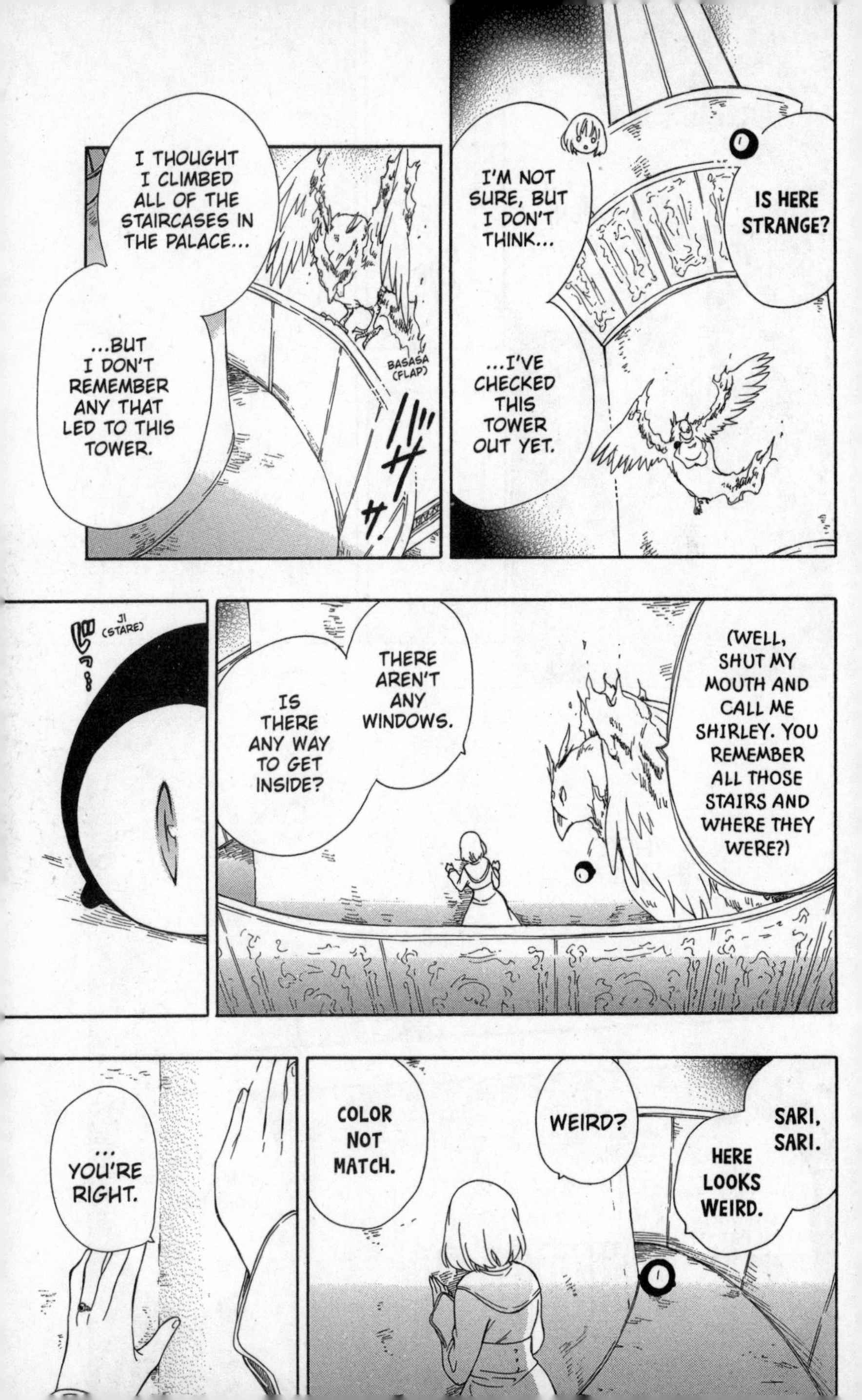
IS HERE STRANGE?
I'M NOT SURE, BUT I DON'T THINK...
...I'VE CHECKED THIS TOWER OUT YET.
I THOUGHT I CLIMBED ALL OF THE STAIRCASES IN THE PALACE...
...BUT I DON'T REMEMBER ANY THAT LED TO THIS TOWER.
BASASA (FLAP)
(WELL, SHUT MY MOUTH AND CALL ME SHIRLEY. YOU REMEMBER ALL THOSE STAIRS AND WHERE THEY WERE?)
THERE AREN'T ANY WINDOWS.
IS THERE ANY WAY TO GET INSIDE?
JI (STARE)
SARI, SARI.
HERE LOOKS WEIRD.
WEIRD?
COLOR NOT MATCH.
... YOU'RE RIGHT.

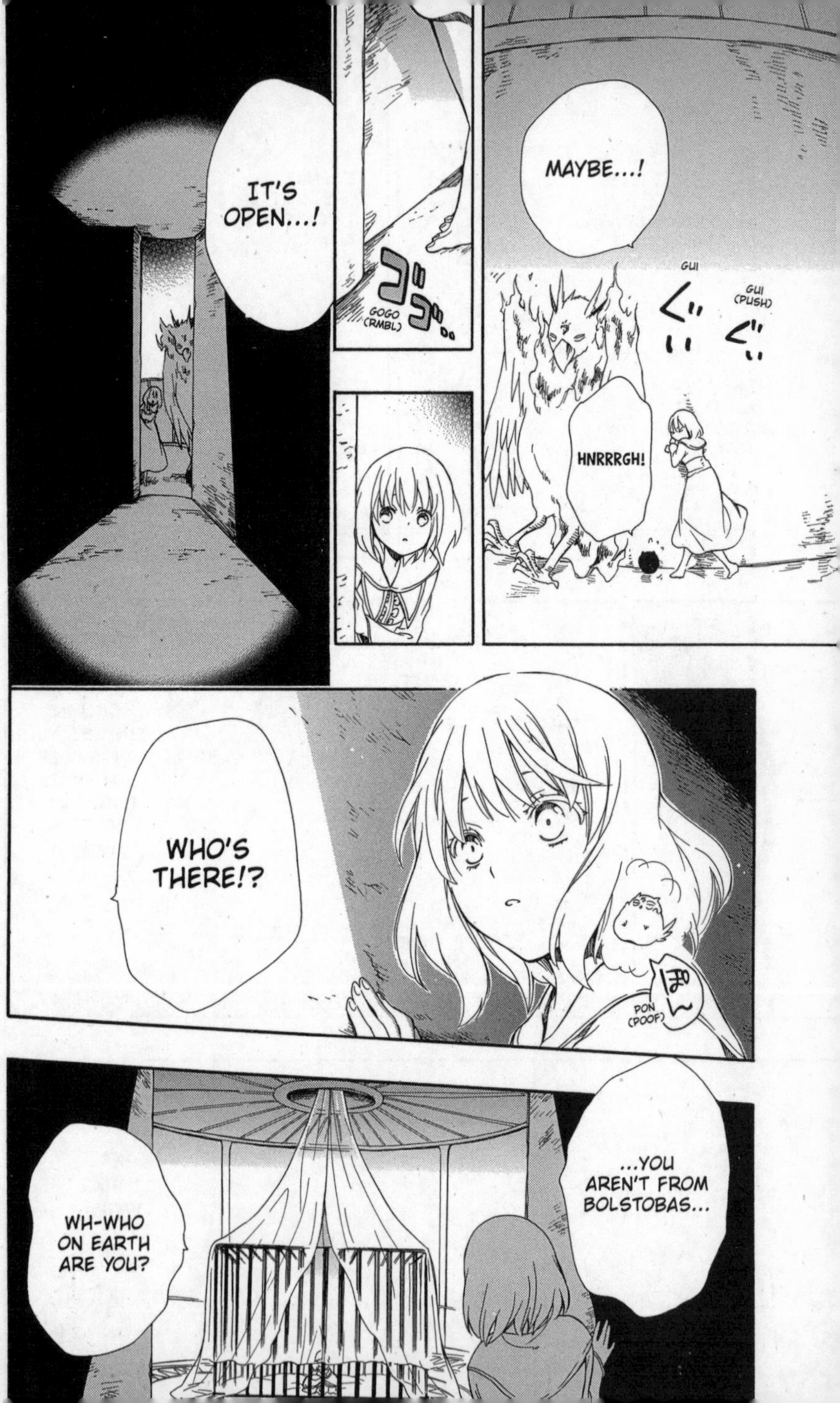
MAYBE...!
ぐい GUI
ぐい GUI (PUSH)
HNRRRGH!
ゴゴ GOGO (RMBL)
IT'S OPEN...!
ぽん PON (POOF)
WHO'S THERE!?
...YOU AREN'T FROM BOLSTOBAS...
WH-WHO ON EARTH ARE YOU?

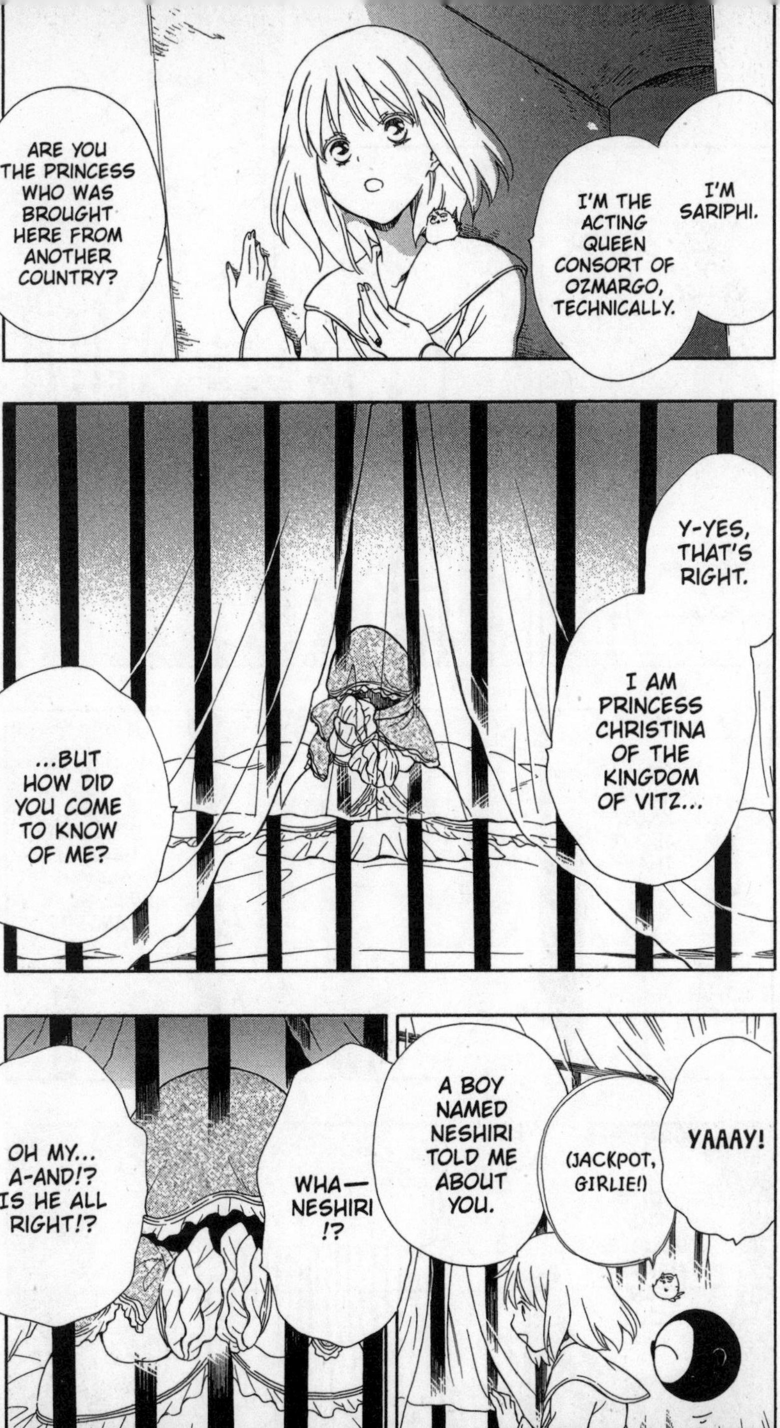
I'M SARIPHI.
I'M THE ACTING QUEEN CONSORT OF OZMARGO, TECHNICALLY.
ARE YOU THE PRINCESS WHO WAS BROUGHT HERE FROM ANOTHER COUNTRY?
Y-YES, THAT'S RIGHT.
I AM PRINCESS CHRISTINA OF THE KINGDOM OF VITZ...
...BUT HOW DID YOU COME TO KNOW OF ME?
YAAAY!
(JACKPOT, GIRLIE!)
A BOY NAMED NESHIRI TOLD ME ABOUT YOU.
WHA— NESHIRI !?
OH MY... A-AND!? IS HE ALL RIGHT!?

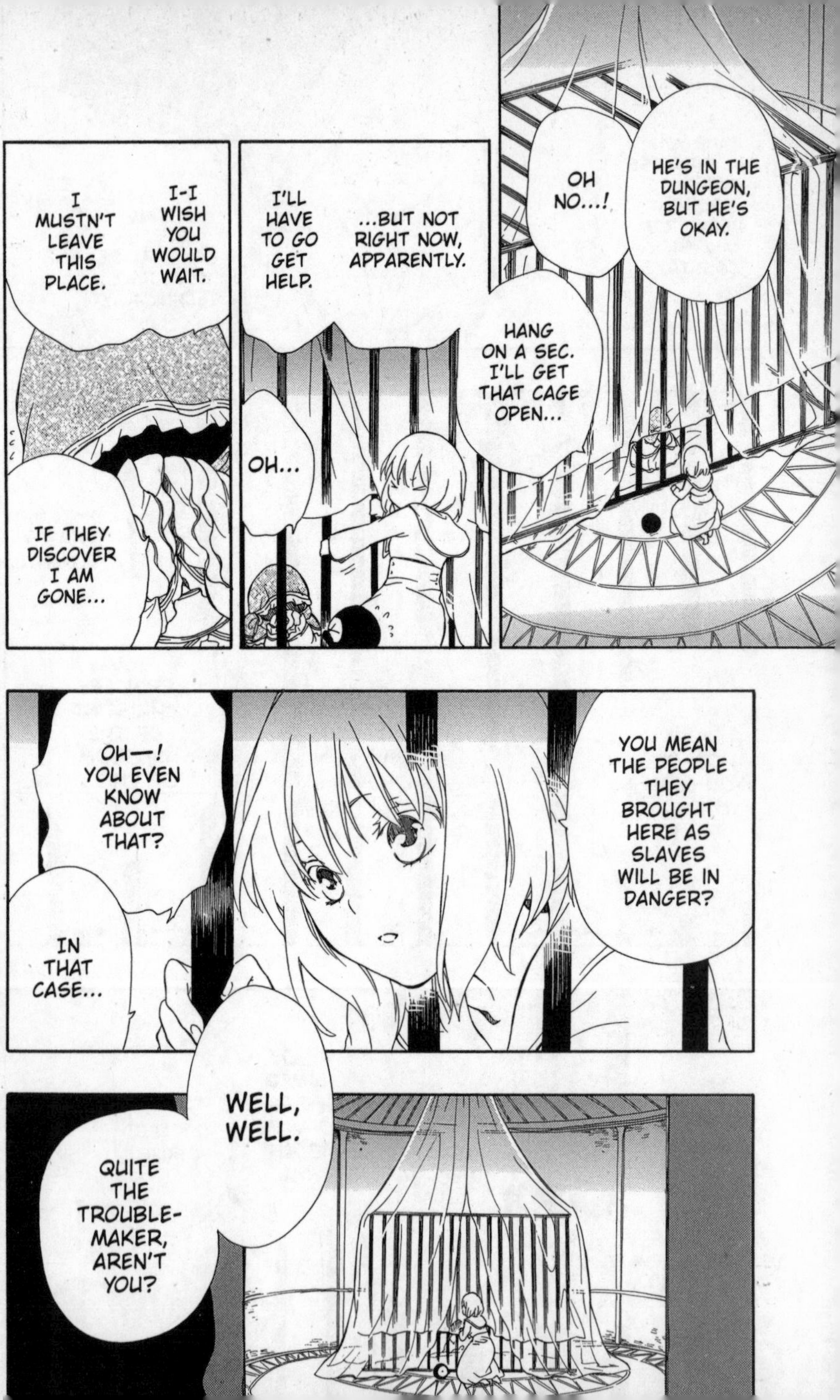
HE'S IN THE DUNGEON, BUT HE'S OKAY.
OH NO...!
HANG ON A SEC. I'LL GET THAT CAGE OPEN...
...BUT NOT RIGHT NOW, APPARENTLY.
I'LL HAVE TO GO GET HELP.
OH...
I-I WISH YOU WOULD WAIT.
I MUSTN'T LEAVE THIS PLACE.
IF THEY DISCOVER I AM GONE...
YOU MEAN THE PEOPLE THEY BROUGHT HERE AS SLAVES WILL BE IN DANGER?
OH—! YOU EVEN KNOW ABOUT THAT?
IN THAT CASE...
WELL, WELL.
QUITE THE TROUBLE-MAKER, AREN'T YOU?

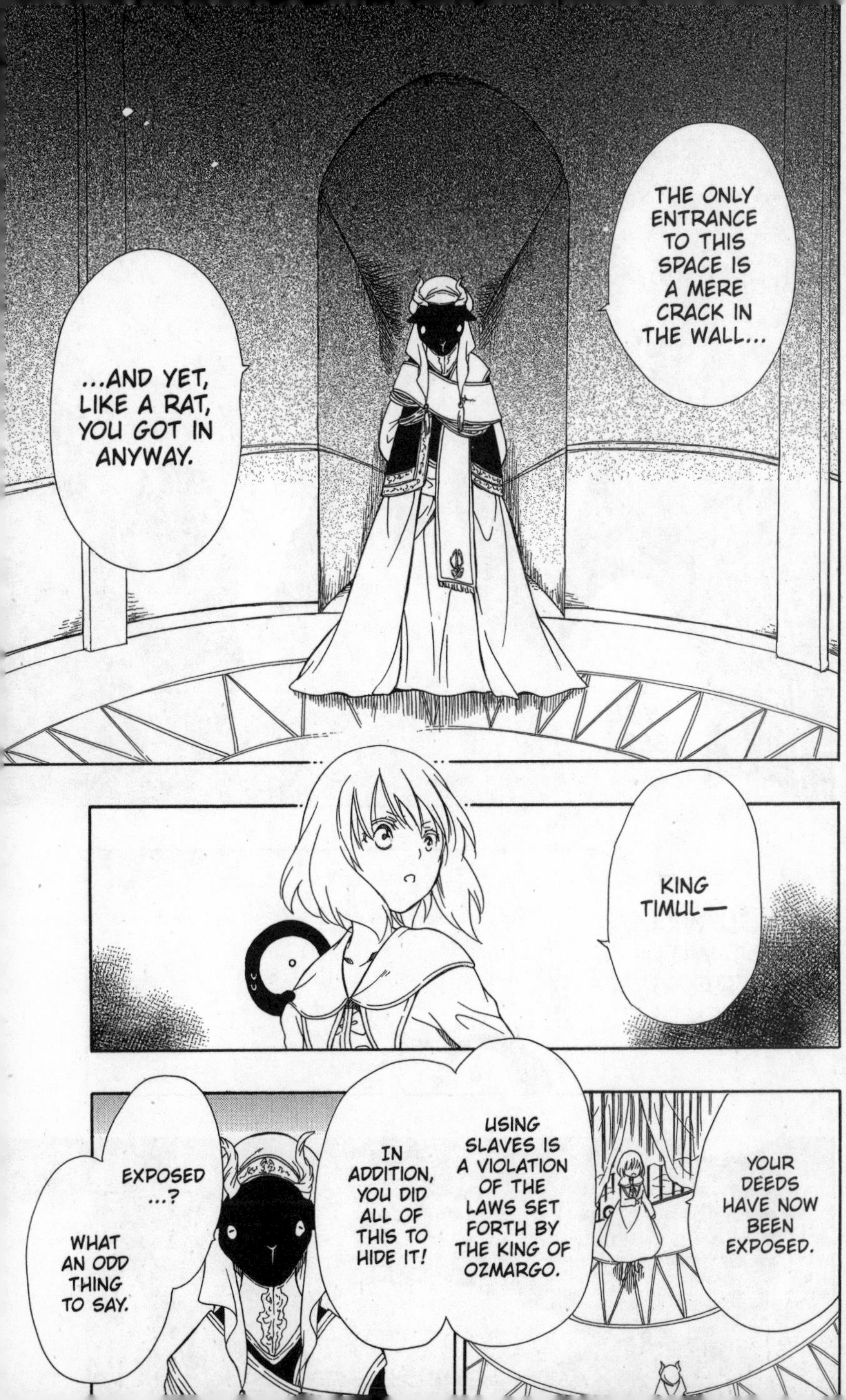
THE ONLY ENTRANCE TO THIS SPACE IS A MERE CRACK IN THE WALL...
...AND YET, LIKE A RAT, YOU GOT IN ANYWAY.
KING TIMUL—
YOUR DEEDS HAVE NOW BEEN EXPOSED.
USING SLAVES IS A VIOLATION OF THE LAWS SET FORTH BY THE KING OF OZMARGO.
IN ADDITION, YOU DID ALL OF THIS TO HIDE IT!
EXPOSED ...?
WHAT AN ODD THING TO SAY.

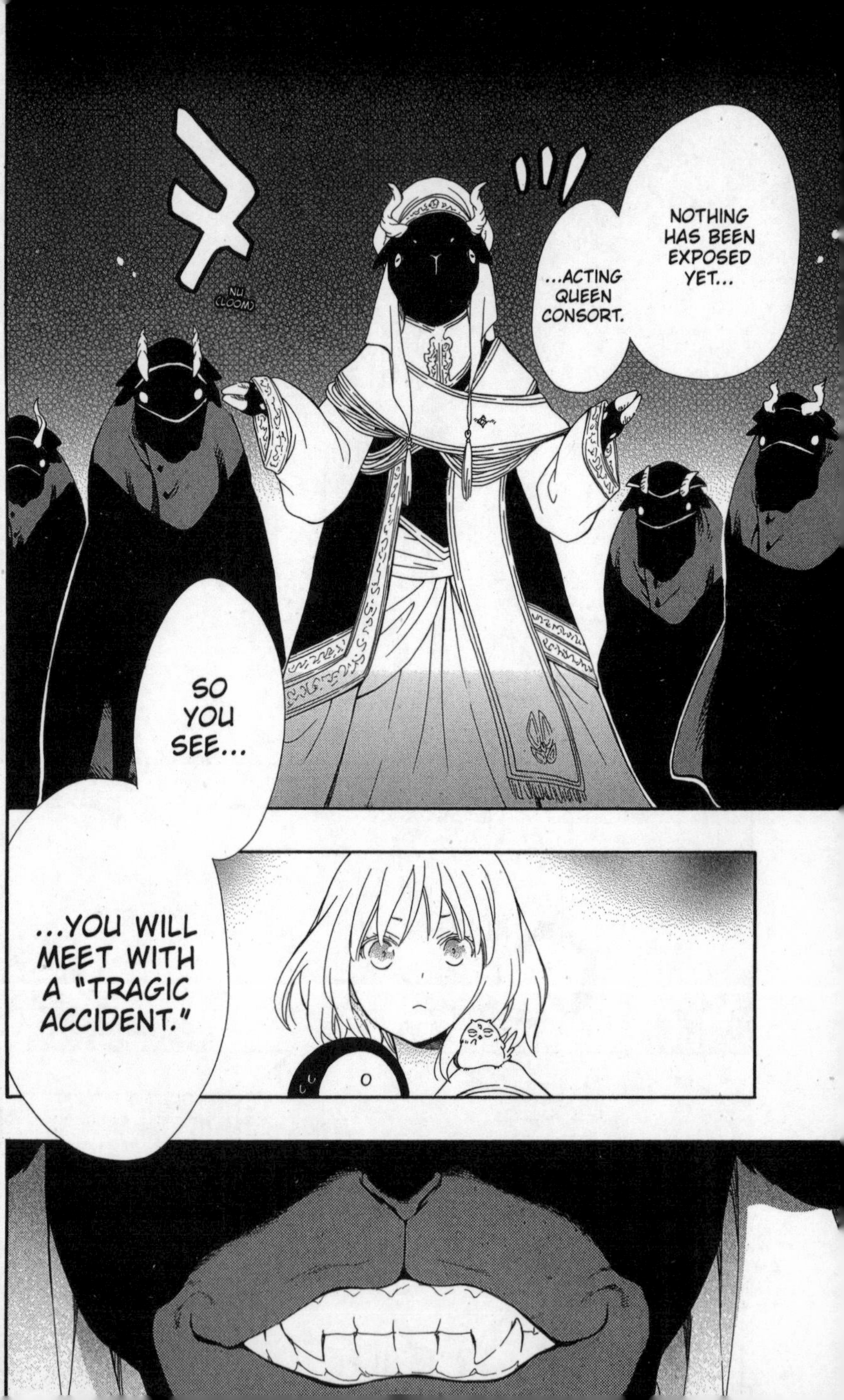
NOTHING HAS BEEN EXPOSED YET...
...ACTING QUEEN CONSORT.
ヌ
NU (LOOM)
SO YOU SEE...
...YOU WILL MEET WITH A "TRAGIC ACCIDENT."

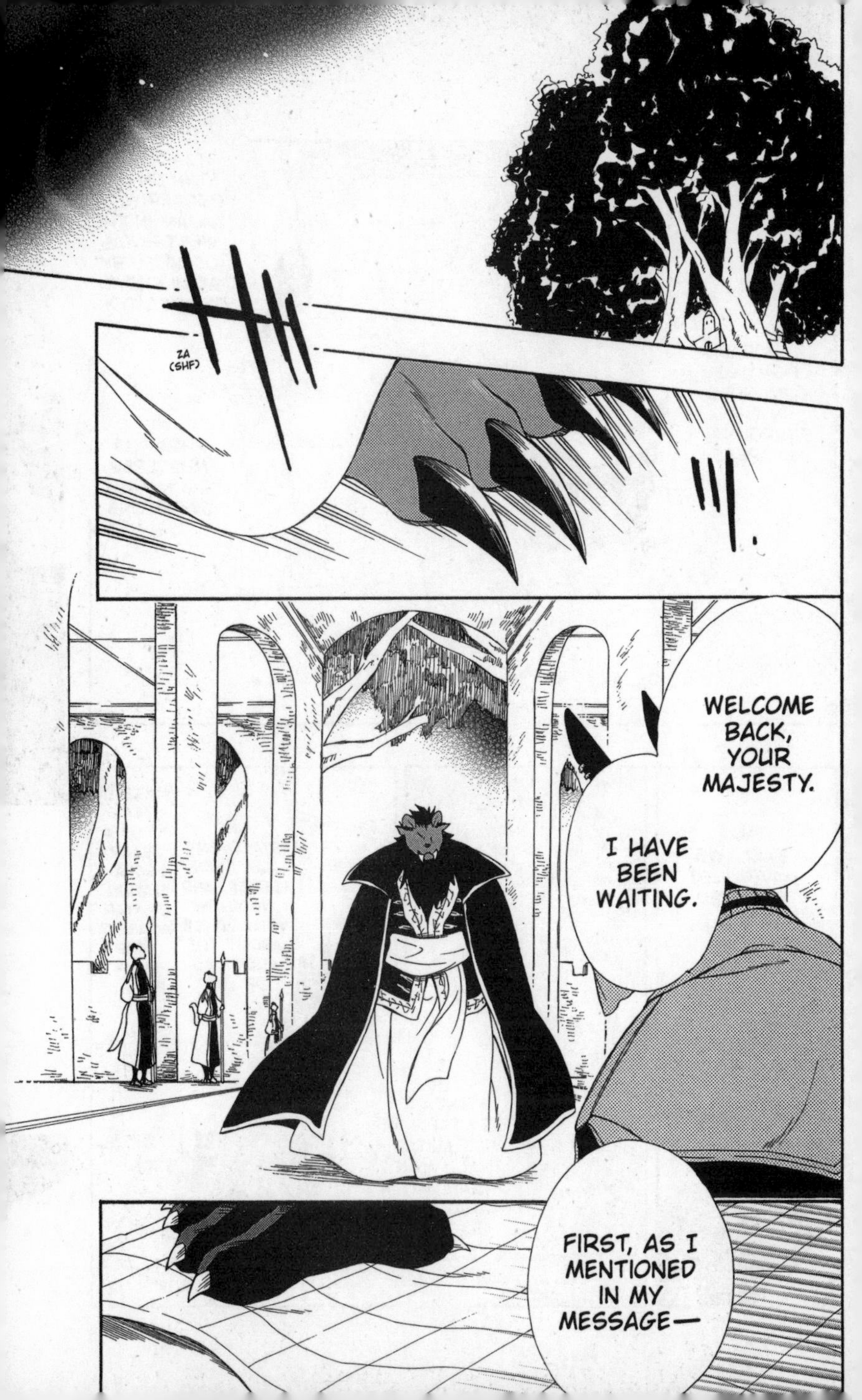
ZA (SHF)
WELCOME BACK, YOUR MAJESTY.
I HAVE BEEN WAITING.
FIRST, AS I MENTIONED IN MY MESSAGE—

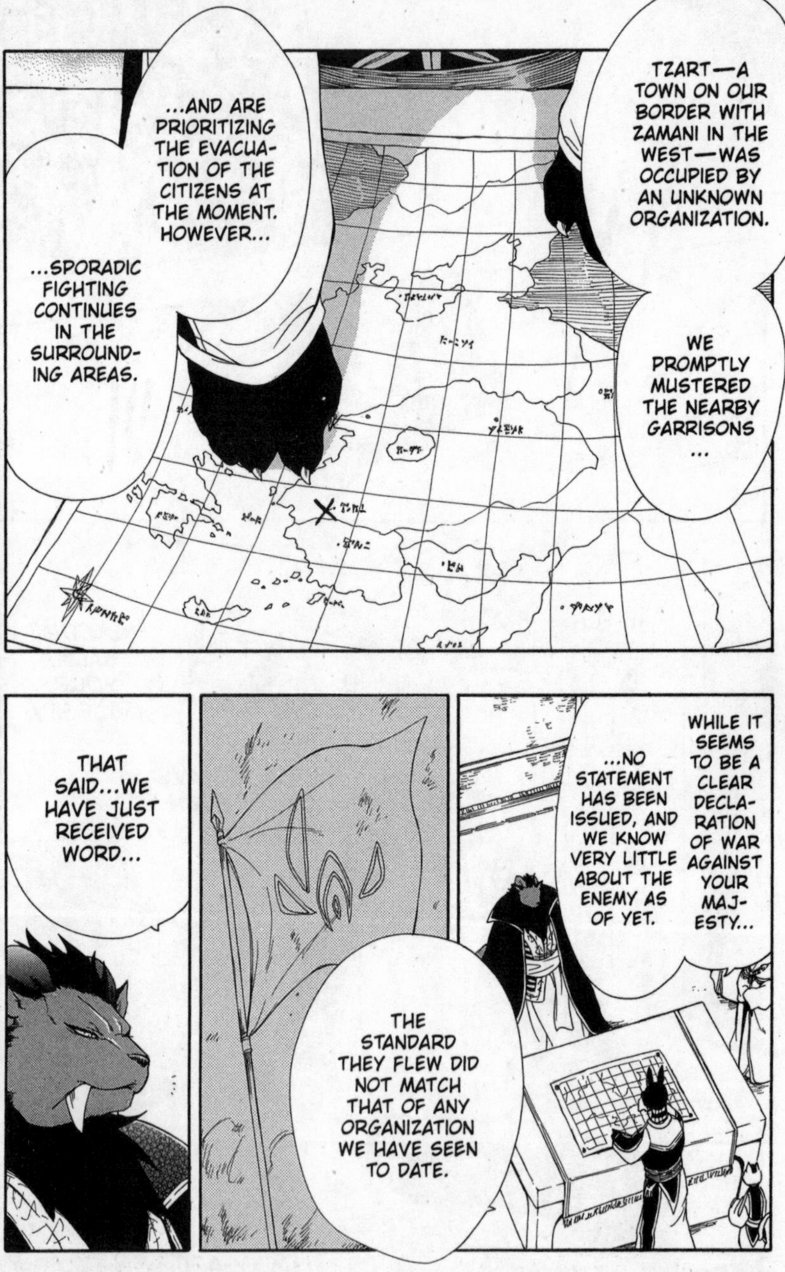
TZART—A TOWN ON OUR BORDER WITH ZAMANI IN THE WEST—WAS OCCUPIED BY AN UNKNOWN ORGANIZATION.
WE PROMPTLY MUSTERED THE NEARBY GARRISONS ...
...AND ARE PRIORITIZING THE EVACUATION OF THE CITIZENS AT THE MOMENT. HOWEVER...
...SPORADIC FIGHTING CONTINUES IN THE SURROUNDING AREAS.
WHILE IT SEEMS TO BE A CLEAR DECLARATION OF WAR AGAINST YOUR MAJESTY...
...NO STATEMENT HAS BEEN ISSUED, AND WE KNOW VERY LITTLE ABOUT THE ENEMY AS OF YET.
THE STANDARD THEY FLEW DID NOT MATCH THAT OF ANY ORGANIZATION WE HAVE SEEN TO DATE.
THAT SAID...WE HAVE JUST RECEIVED WORD...

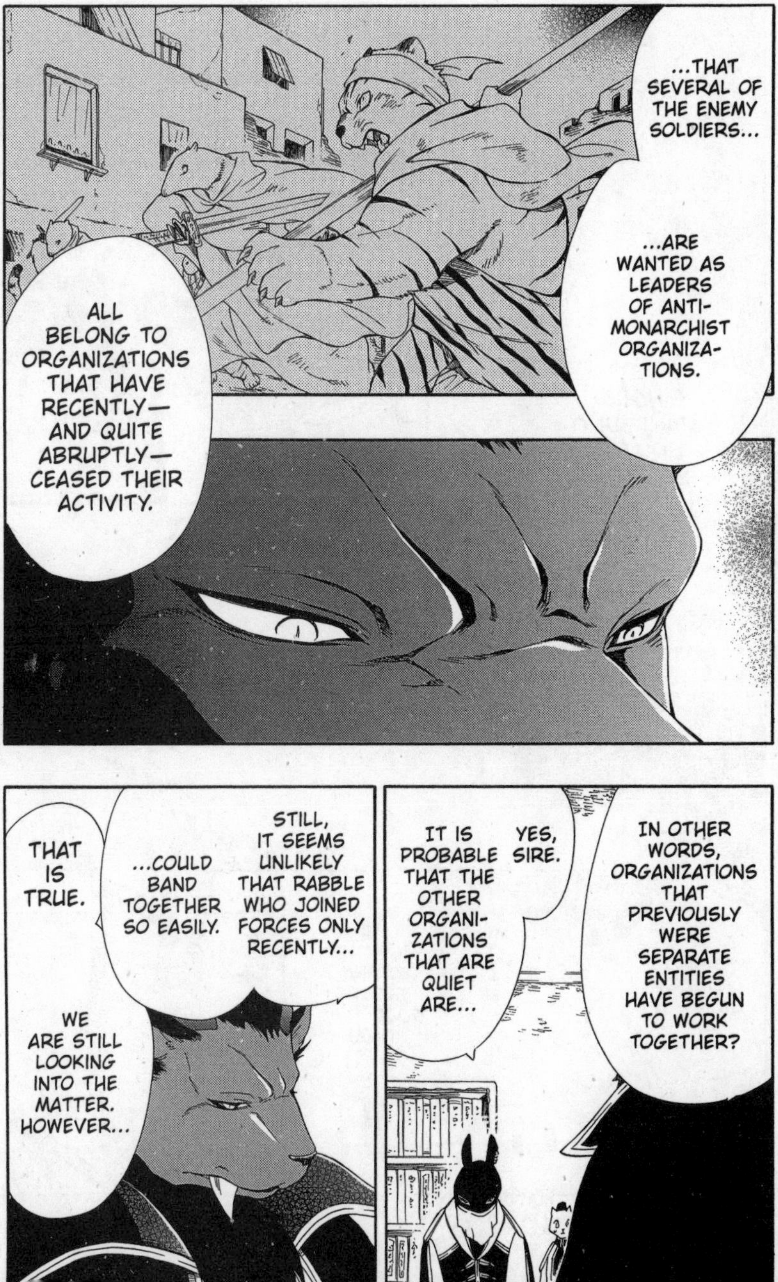
...THAT SEVERAL OF THE ENEMY SOLDIERS...
...ARE WANTED AS LEADERS OF ANTI-MONARCHIST ORGANIZA-TIONS.
ALL BELONG TO ORGANIZATIONS THAT HAVE RECENTLY—AND QUITE ABRUPTLY—CEASED THEIR ACTIVITY.
IN OTHER WORDS, ORGANIZATIONS THAT PREVIOUSLY WERE SEPARATE ENTITIES HAVE BEGUN TO WORK TOGETHER?
YES, SIRE.
IT IS PROBABLE THAT THE OTHER ORGANI-ZATIONS THAT ARE QUIET ARE...
STILL, IT SEEMS UNLIKELY THAT RABBLE WHO JOINED FORCES ONLY RECENTLY...
...COULD BAND TOGETHER SO EASILY.
THAT IS TRUE.
WE ARE STILL LOOKING INTO THE MATTER. HOWEVER...

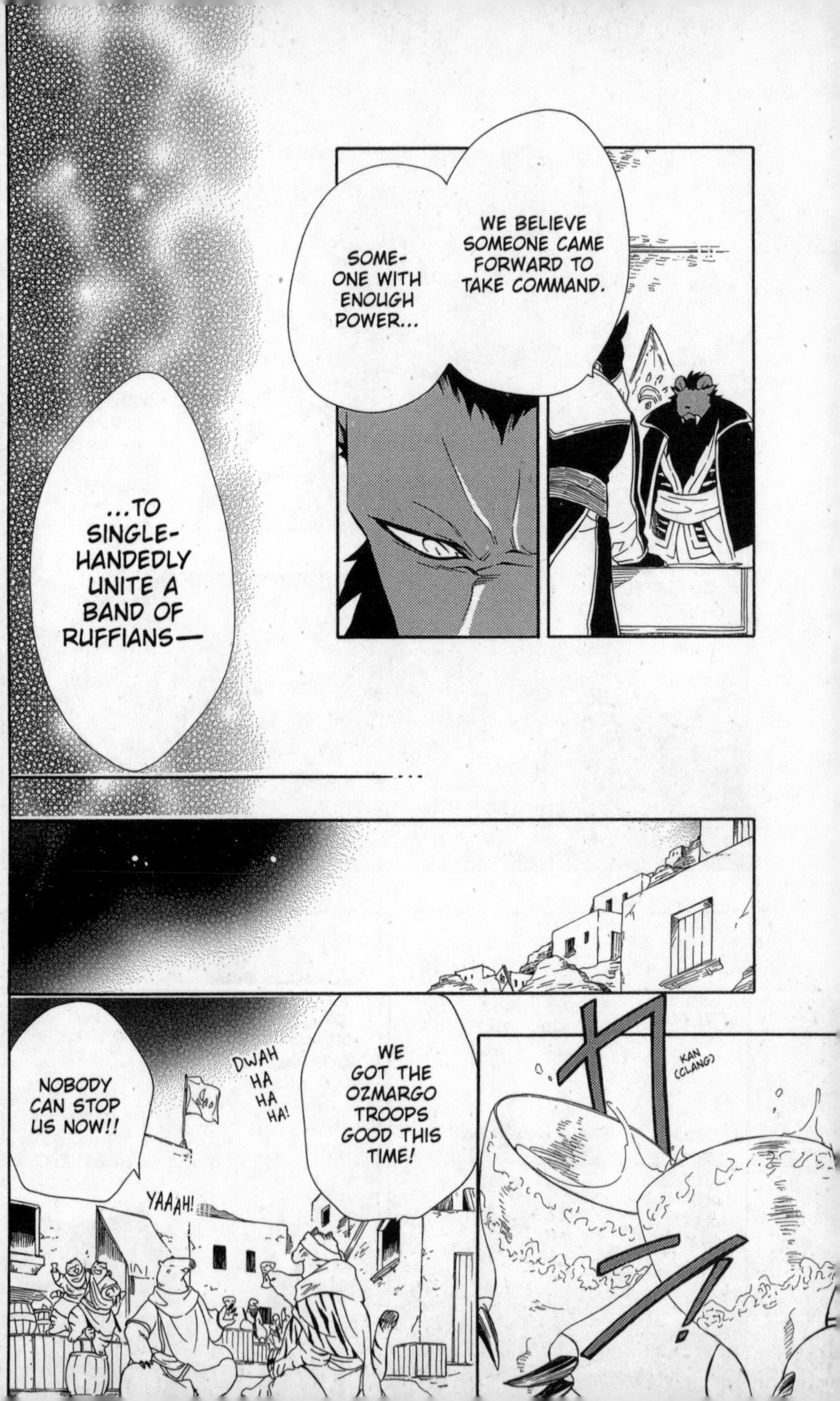

WE BELIEVE SOMEONE CAME FORWARD TO TAKE COMMAND.
SOME-ONE WITH ENOUGH POWER...
...TO SINGLE-HANDEDLY UNITE A BAND OF RUFFIANS—
KAN (CLANG)
WE GOT THE OZMARGO TROOPS GOOD THIS TIME!
DWAH HA HA HA!
NOBODY CAN STOP US NOW!!
YAAAH!

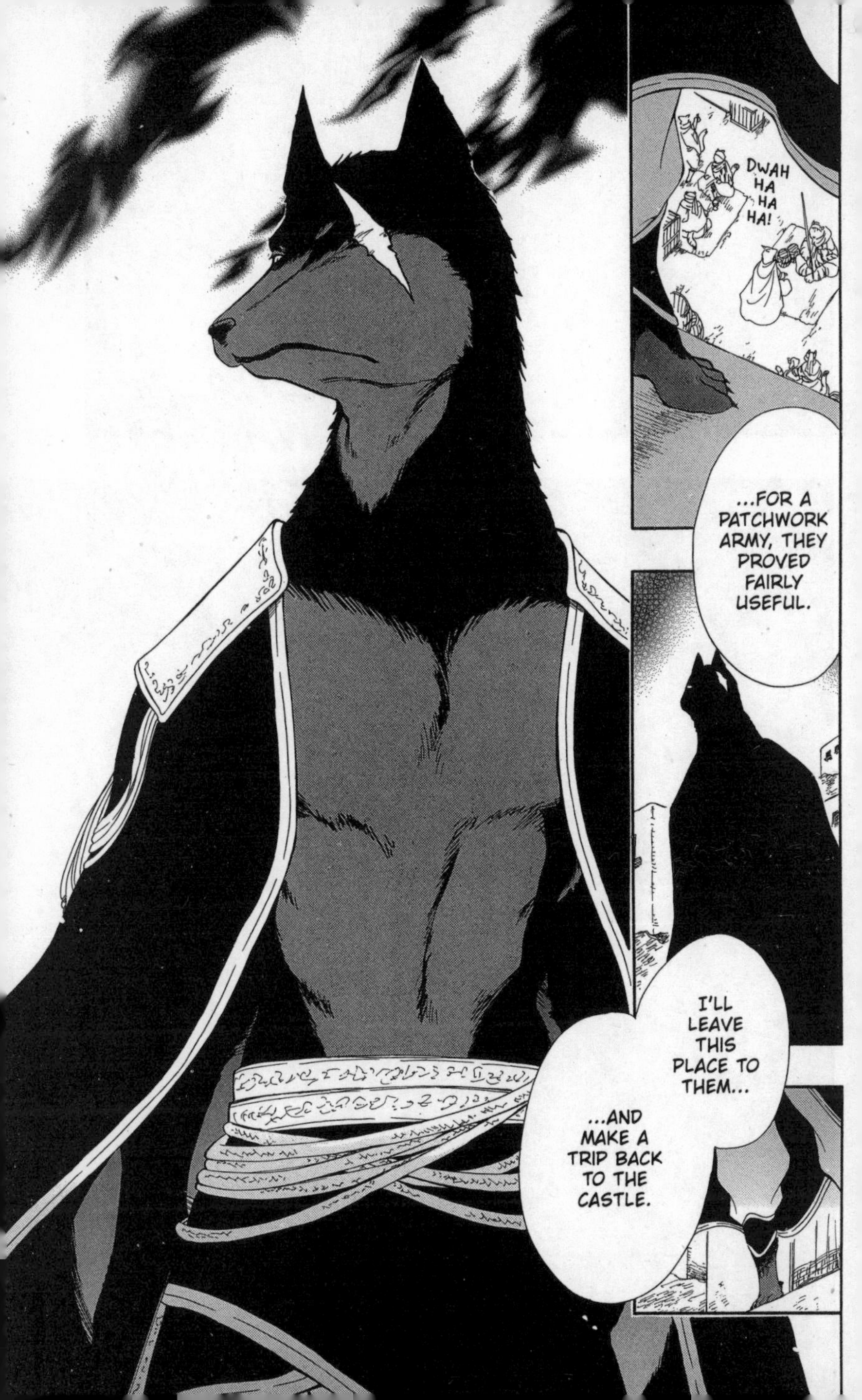
DWAH HA HA HA!
...FOR A PATCHWORK ARMY, THEY PROVED FAIRLY USEFUL.
I'LL LEAVE THIS PLACE TO THEM...
...AND MAKE A TRIP BACK TO THE CASTLE.

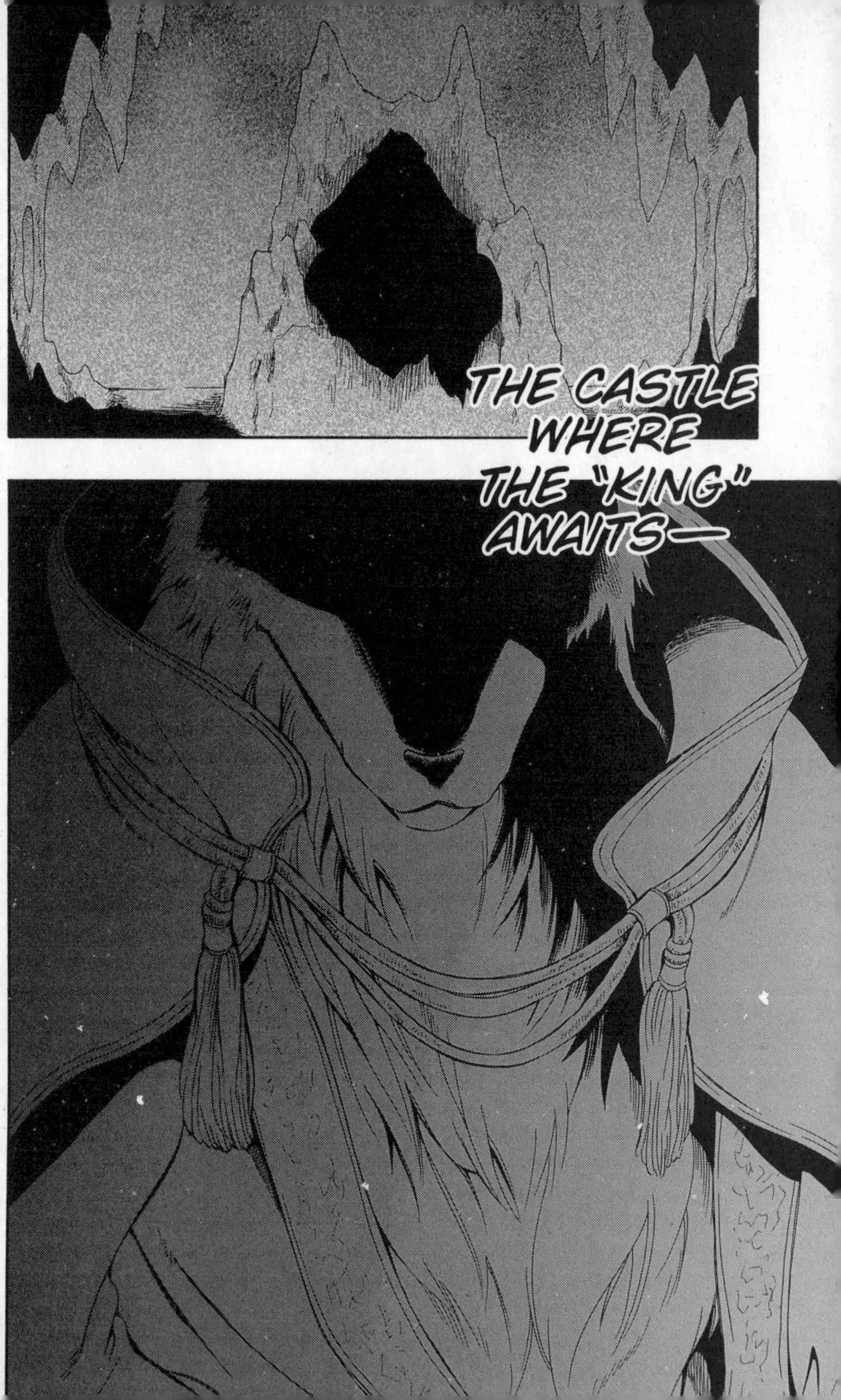
THE CASTLE WHERE THE "KING" AWAITS—

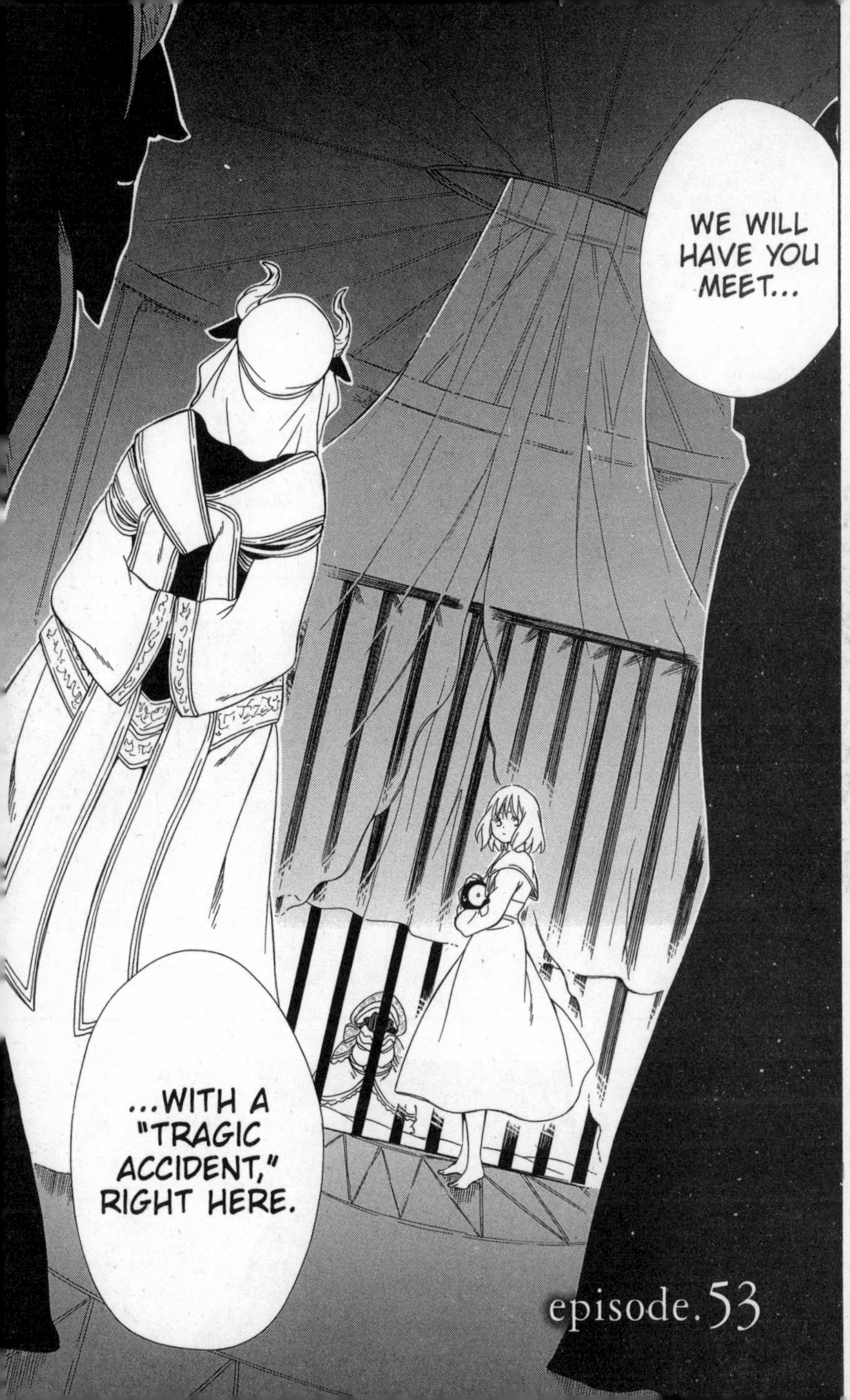
WE WILL HAVE YOU MEET...
...WITH A "TRAGIC ACCIDENT," RIGHT HERE.
episode.53

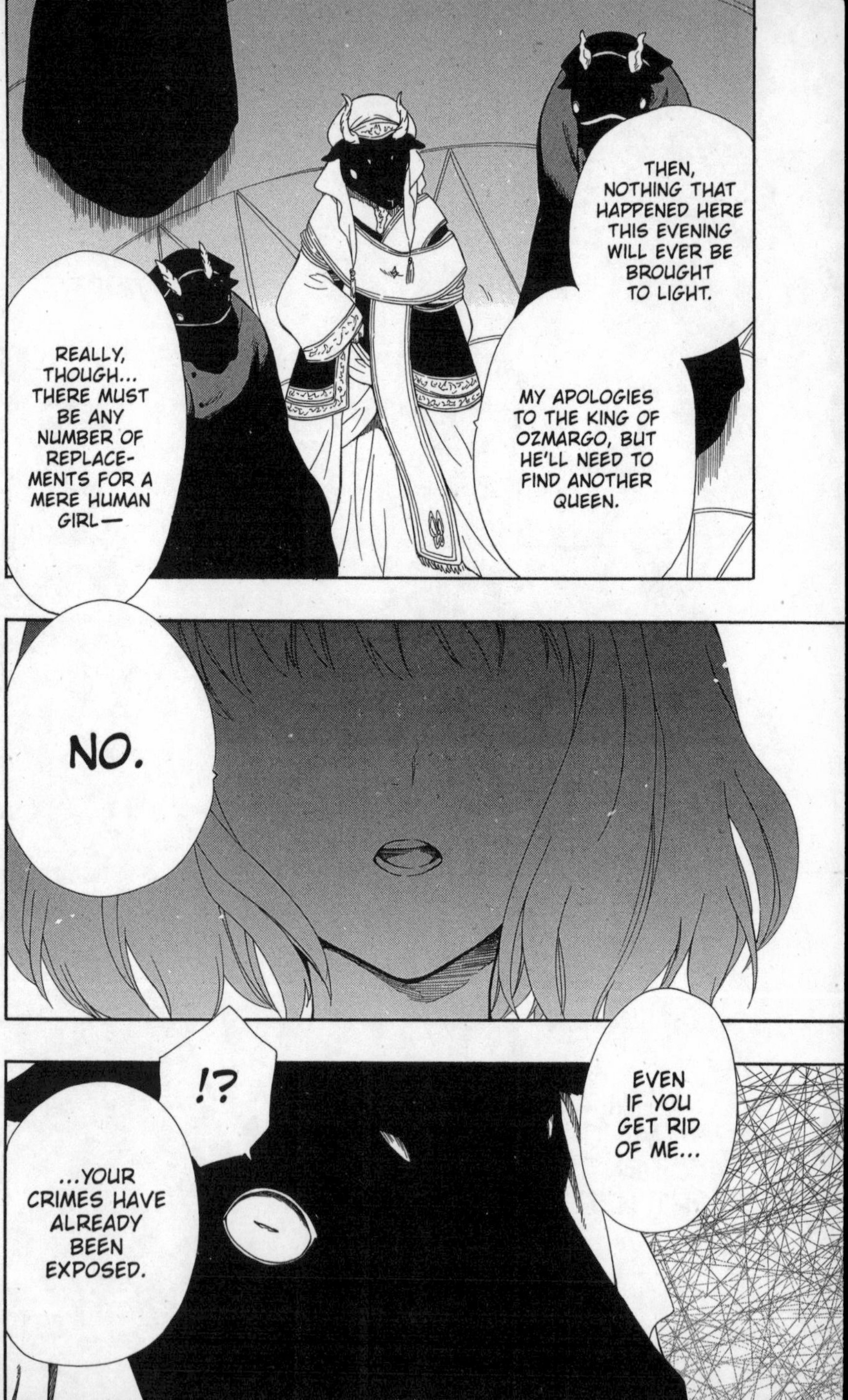
THEN, NOTHING THAT HAPPENED HERE THIS EVENING WILL EVER BE BROUGHT TO LIGHT.
MY APOLOGIES TO THE KING OF OZMARGO, BUT HE'LL NEED TO FIND ANOTHER QUEEN.
REALLY, THOUGH... THERE MUST BE ANY NUMBER OF REPLACE-MENTS FOR A MERE HUMAN GIRL—
NO.
EVEN IF YOU GET RID OF ME...
!?
...YOUR CRIMES HAVE ALREADY BEEN EXPOSED.

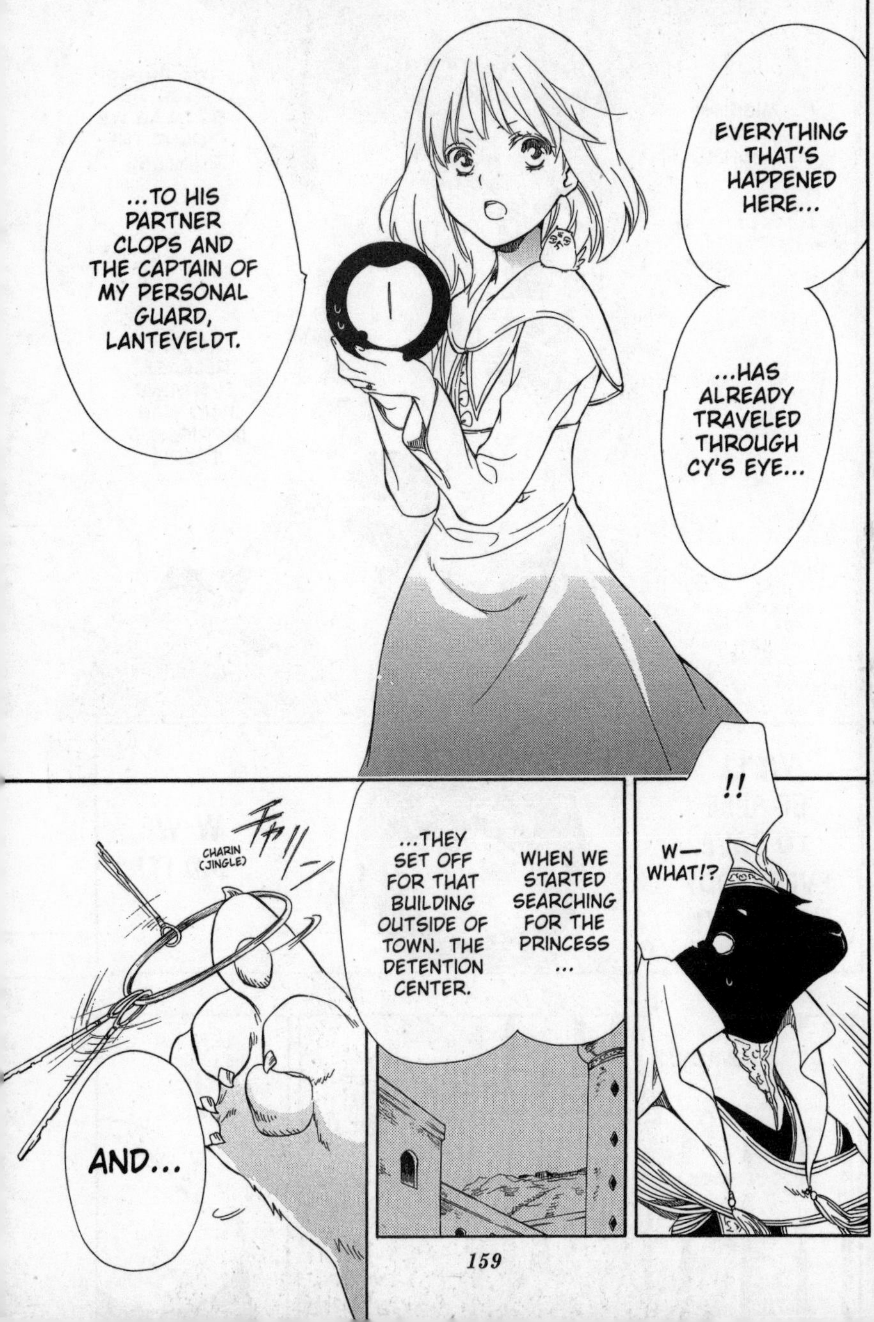
EVERYTHING THAT'S HAPPENED HERE...
...HAS ALREADY TRAVELED THROUGH CY'S EYE...
...TO HIS PARTNER CLOPS AND THE CAPTAIN OF MY PERSONAL GUARD, LANTEVELDT.
!!
W— WHAT!?
WHEN WE STARTED SEARCHING FOR THE PRINCESS ...
...THEY SET OFF FOR THAT BUILDING OUTSIDE OF TOWN. THE DETENTION CENTER.
チャリーン
CHARIN (JINGLE)
AND...

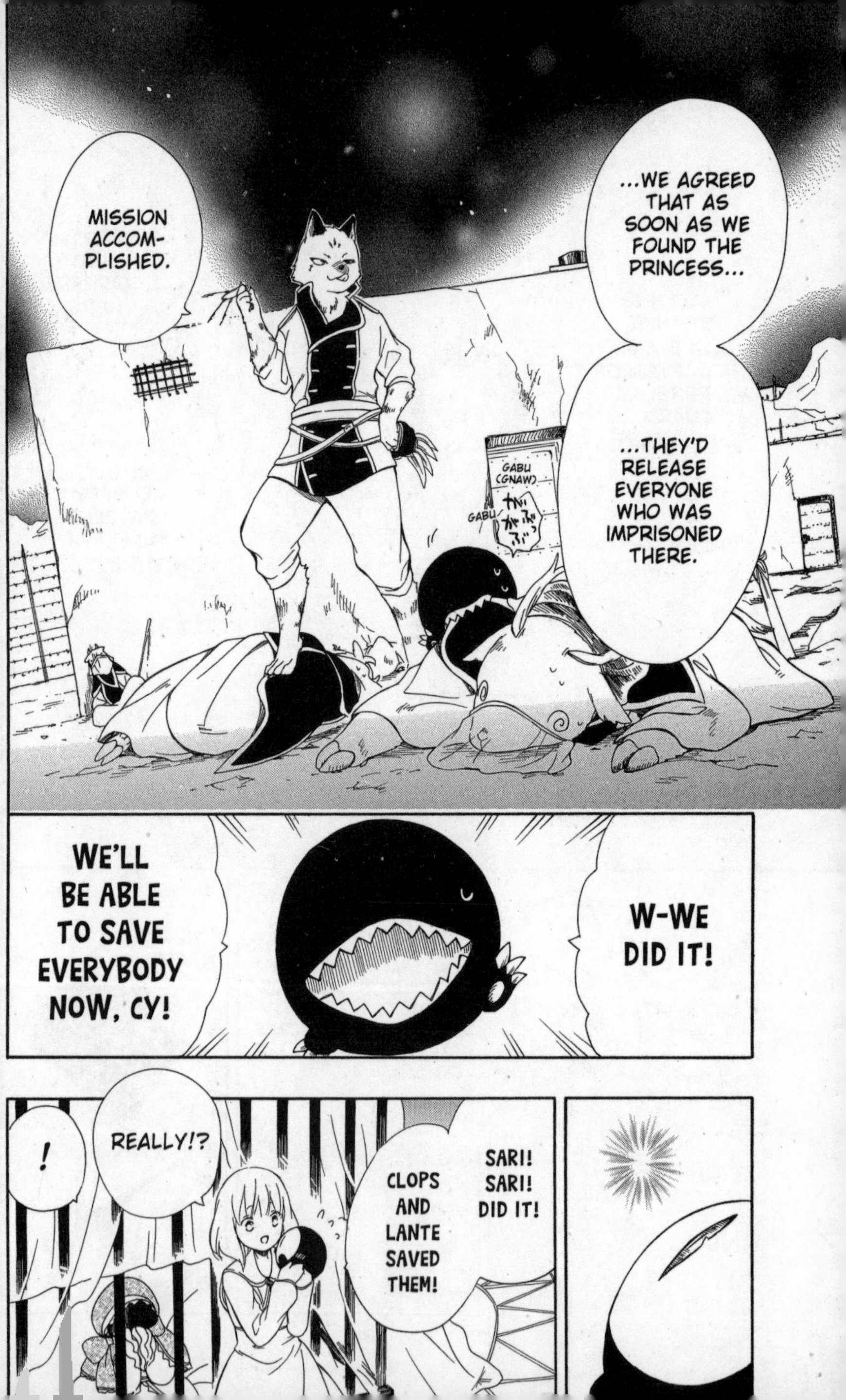
...WE AGREED THAT AS SOON AS WE FOUND THE PRINCESS...
...THEY'D RELEASE EVERYONE WHO WAS IMPRISONED THERE.
GABU (GNAW)
GABU
MISSION ACCOMPLISHED.
W-WE DID IT!
WE'LL BE ABLE TO SAVE EVERYBODY NOW, CY!
SARI! SARI! DID IT!
CLOPS AND LANTE SAVED THEM!
REALLY!?
!

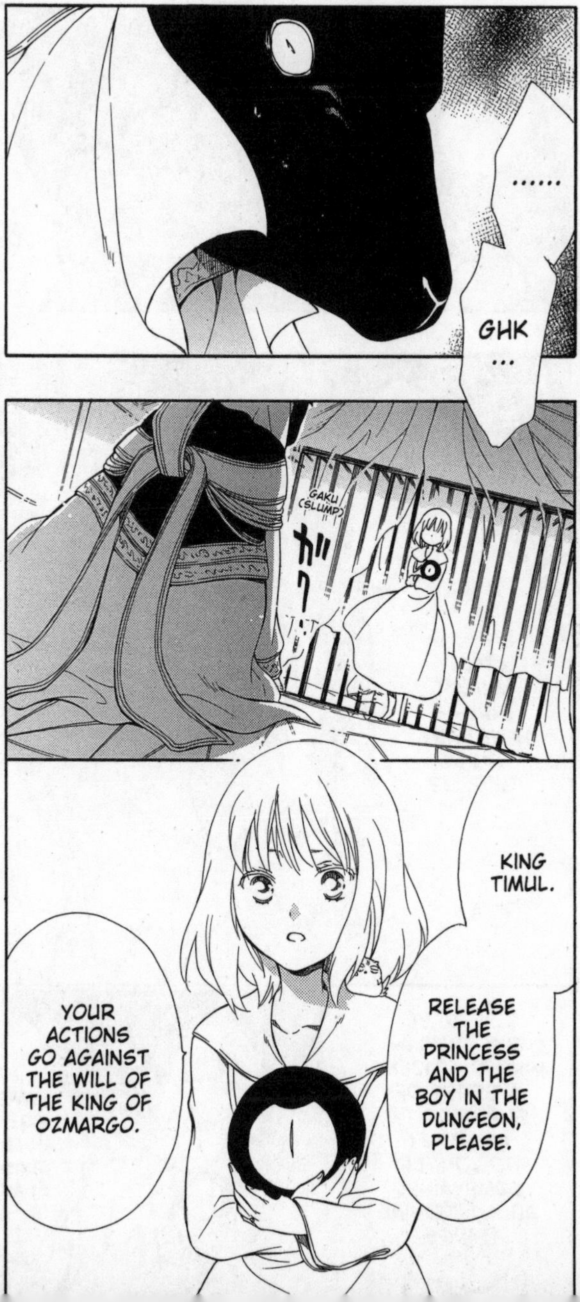
......
GHK ...
GAKU (SLUMP)
KING TIMUL.
RELEASE THE PRINCESS AND THE BOY IN THE DUNGEON, PLEASE.
YOUR ACTIONS GO AGAINST THE WILL OF THE KING OF OZMARGO.

AND THAT PRETTY MUCH BRINGS US TO THE END OF VOLUME 9. THE NEXT ONE WILL BE VOLUME 10! ...WHICH I'LL ADMIT MAKES ME THINK "YOU'RE KIDDING, RIGHT?" EVERY DAY, I DREW AND DREW. THEN BEFORE I KNEW IT, MY DREAM OF MAKING IT INTO DOUBLE DIGITS WAS ONLY A STEP AWAY.

I'M GOING TO WORK EVEN HARDER. AS I DO, I'LL CONTINUE TO BE GRATEFUL TO ALL SORTS OF PEOPLE. ALL RIGHT—HERE'S HOPING WE'LL MEET AGAIN IN THE NEXT VOLUME. GOODBYE!

THANKS TO MY ASSISTANTS S-SAN AND O-SAN THIS TIME TOO! PLEASE CONTINUE TO HELP ME OUT!

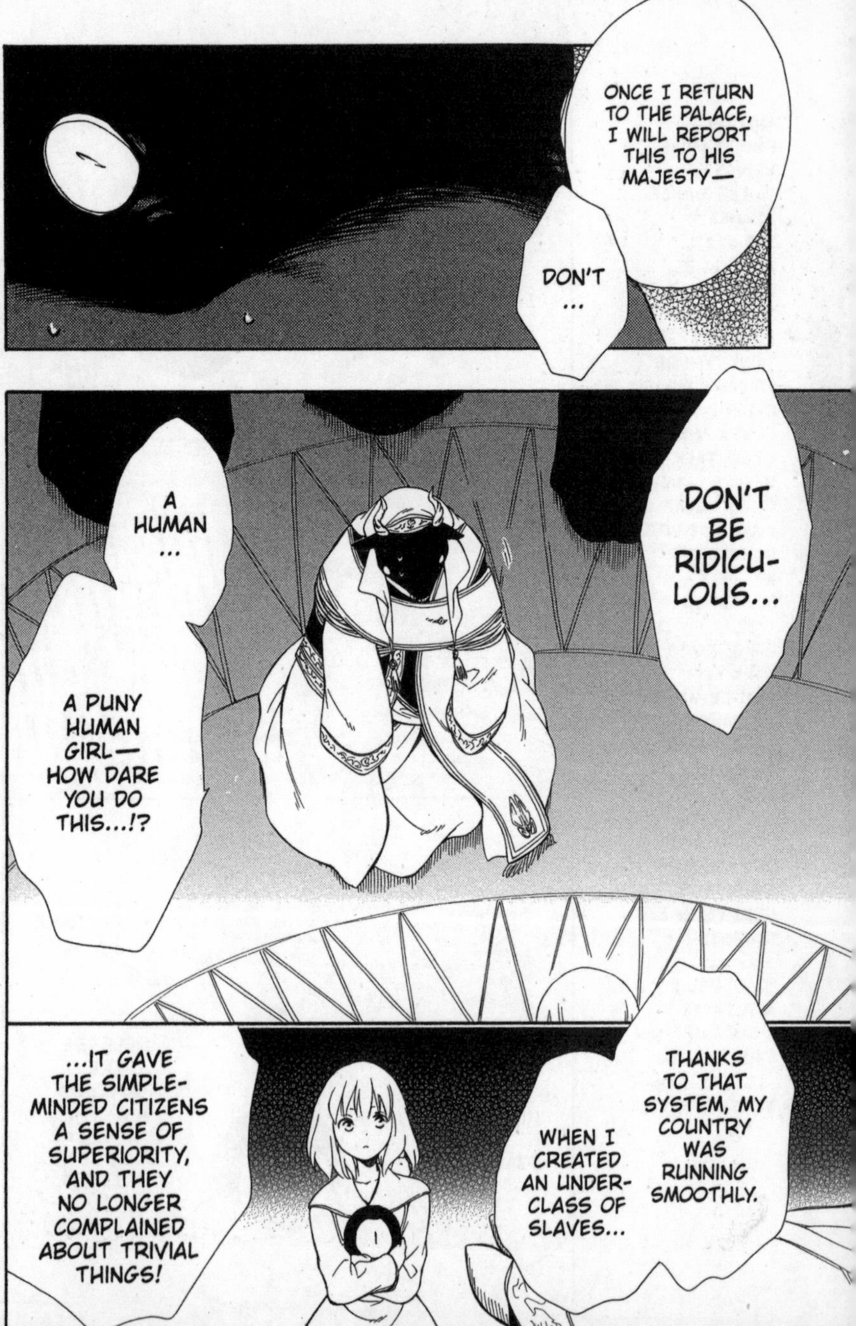
ONCE I RETURN TO THE PALACE, I WILL REPORT THIS TO HIS MAJESTY—
DON'T ...
DON'T BE RIDICULOUS...
A HUMAN ...
A PUNY HUMAN GIRL—HOW DARE YOU DO THIS...!?
THANKS TO THAT SYSTEM, MY COUNTRY WAS RUNNING SMOOTHLY.
WHEN I CREATED AN UNDERCLASS OF SLAVES...
...IT GAVE THE SIMPLE-MINDED CITIZENS A SENSE OF SUPERIORITY, AND THEY NO LONGER COMPLAINED ABOUT TRIVIAL THINGS!

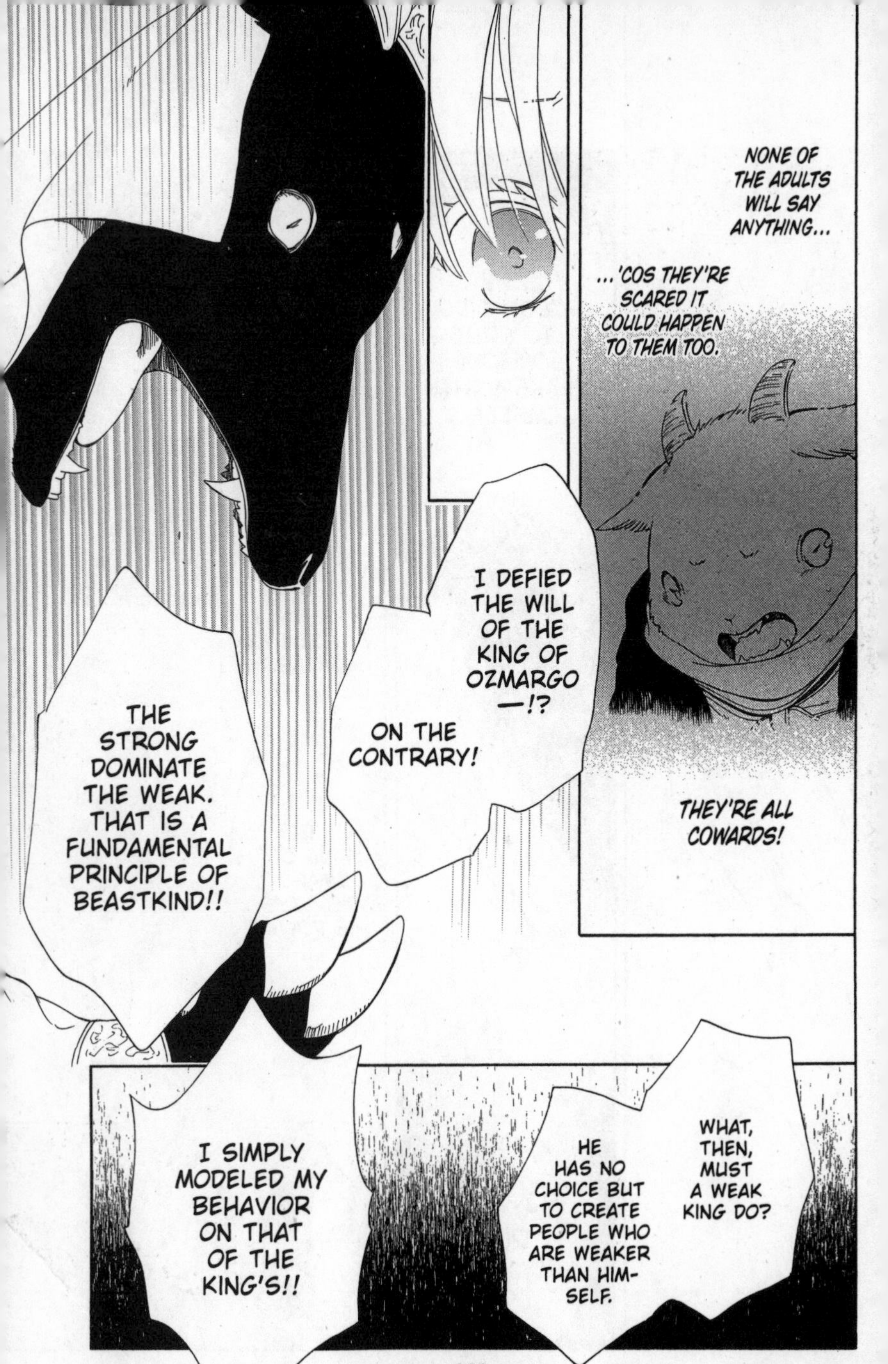
NONE OF THE ADULTS WILL SAY ANYTHING...
...'COS THEY'RE SCARED IT COULD HAPPEN TO THEM TOO.
THEY'RE ALL COWARDS!
I DEFIED THE WILL OF THE KING OF OZMARGO—!?
ON THE CONTRARY!
THE STRONG DOMINATE THE WEAK. THAT IS A FUNDAMENTAL PRINCIPLE OF BEASTKIND!!
WHAT, THEN, MUST A WEAK KING DO?
HE HAS NO CHOICE BUT TO CREATE PEOPLE WHO ARE WEAKER THAN HIM-SELF.
I SIMPLY MODELED MY BEHAVIOR ON THAT OF THE KING'S!!

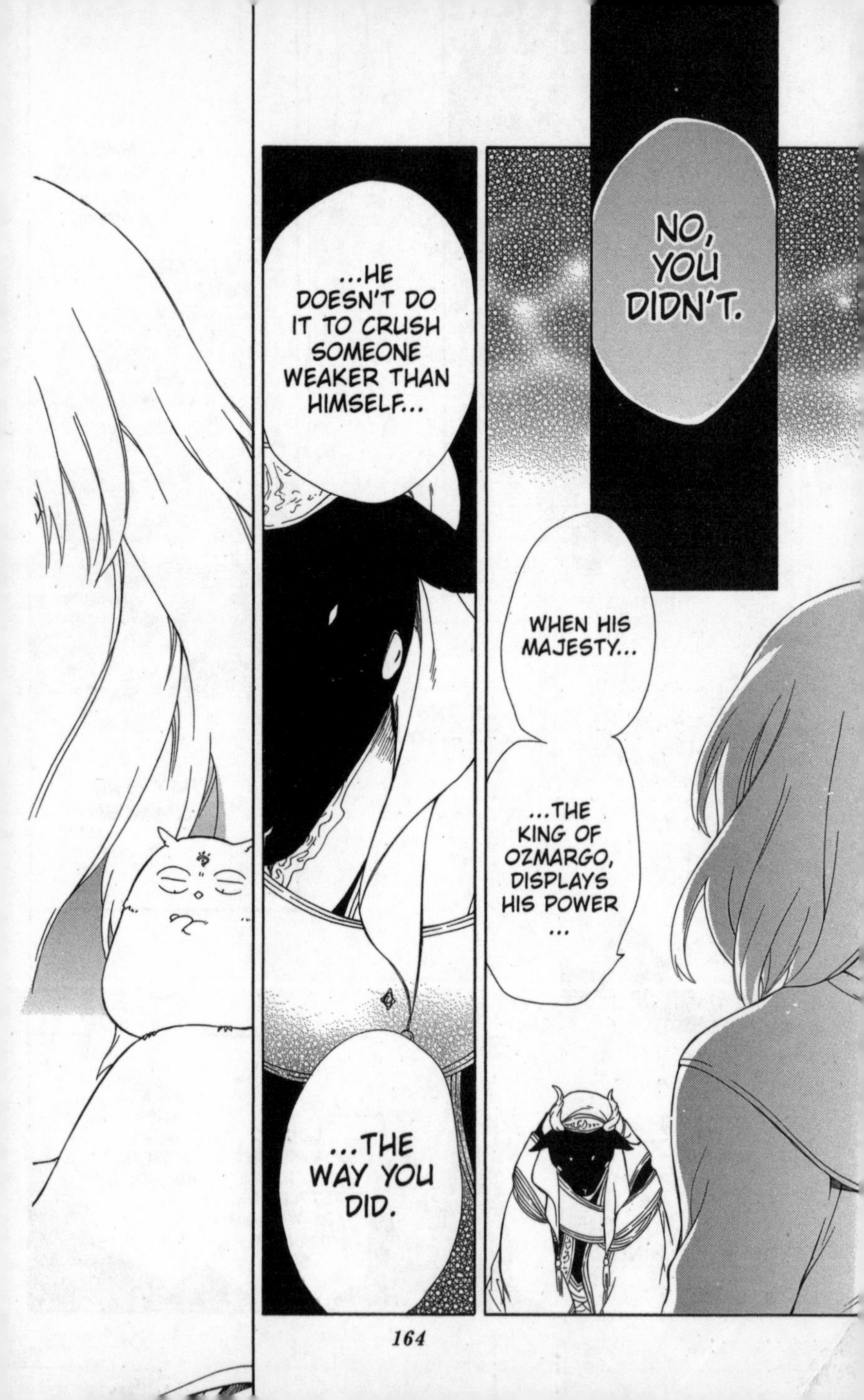
NO, YOU DIDN'T.
WHEN HIS MAJESTY...
...THE KING OF OZMARGO, DISPLAYS HIS POWER ...
...HE DOESN'T DO IT TO CRUSH SOMEONE WEAKER THAN HIMSELF...
...THE WAY YOU DID.

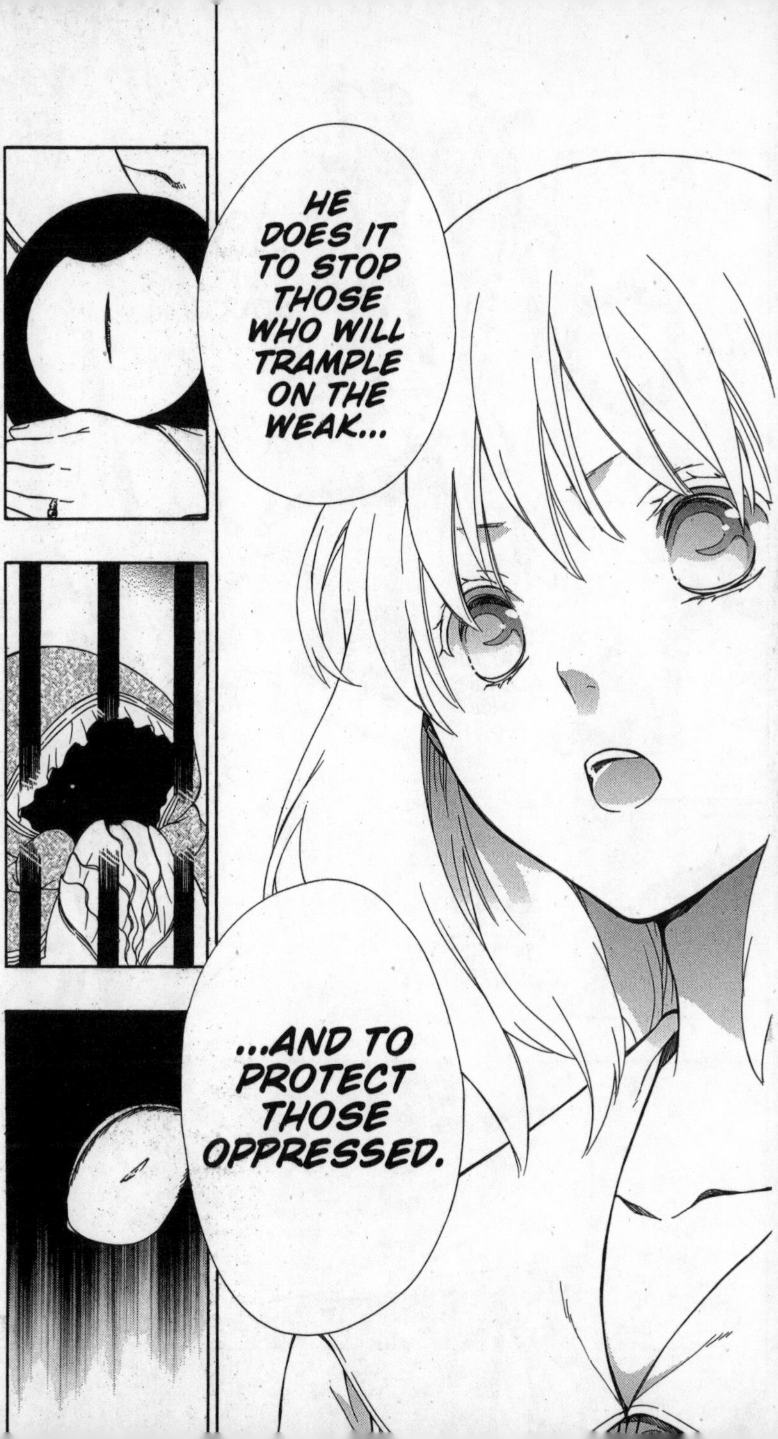
HE DOES IT TO STOP THOSE WHO WILL TRAMPLE ON THE WEAK...
...AND TO PROTECT THOSE OPPRESSED.

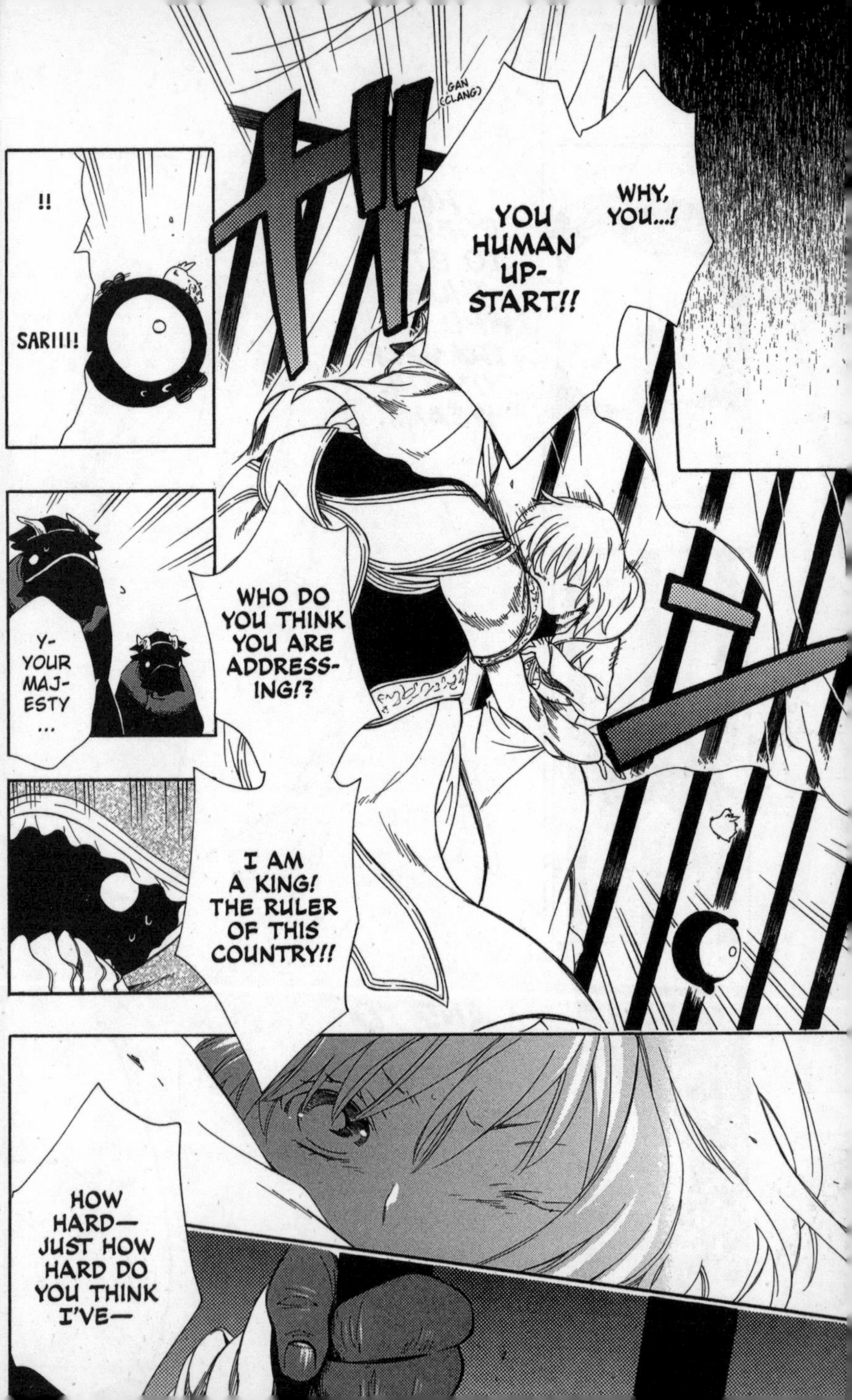
GAN (CLANG)
WHY, YOU...!
YOU HUMAN UP-START!!
WHO DO YOU THINK YOU ARE ADDRESSING!?
I AM A KING! THE RULER OF THIS COUNTRY!!
!!
SARIIII!
Y-YOUR MAJESTY...
HOW HARD—JUST HOW HARD DO YOU THINK I'VE—

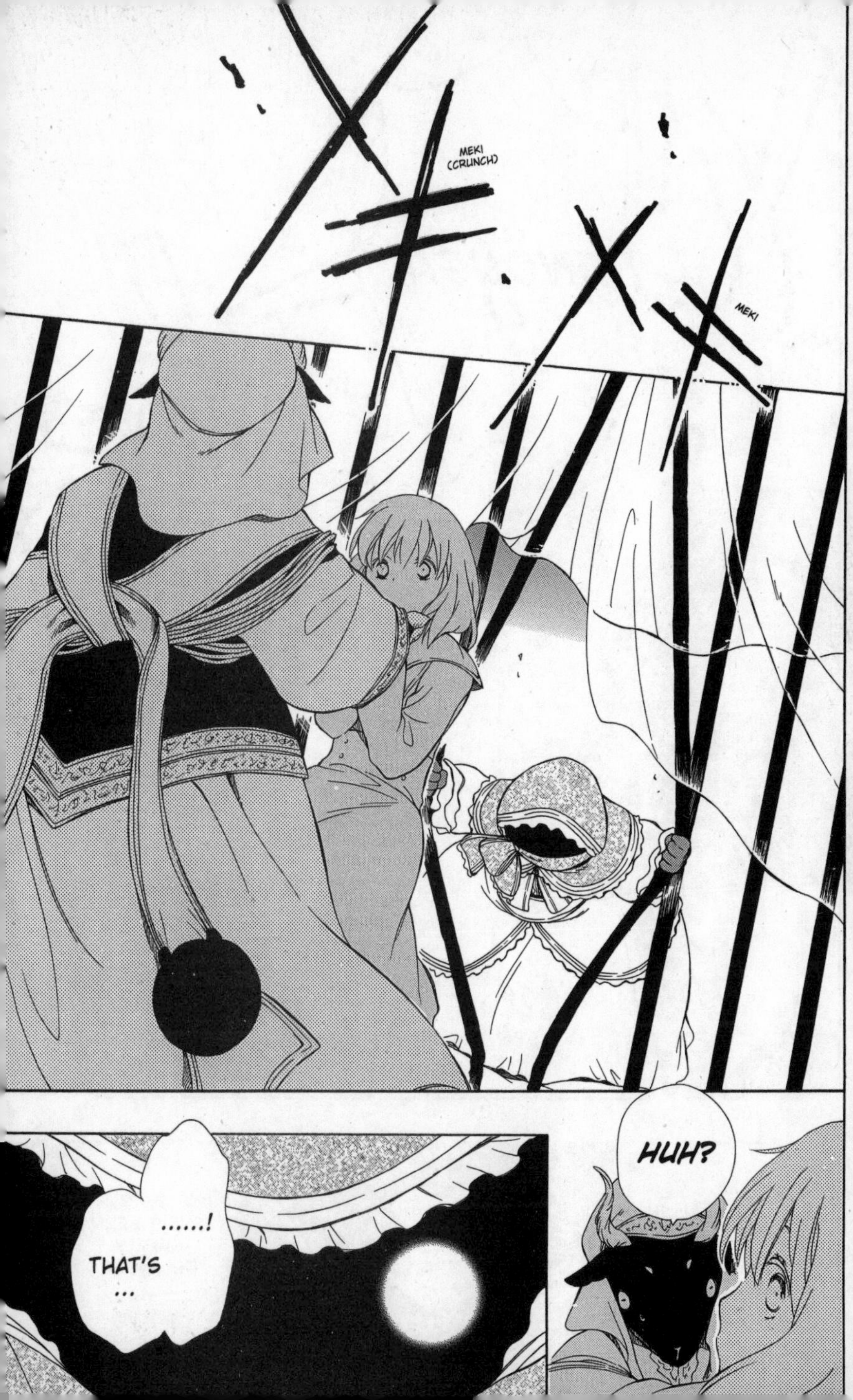
MEKI (CRUNCH)
MEKI
HUH?
......!
THAT'S ...

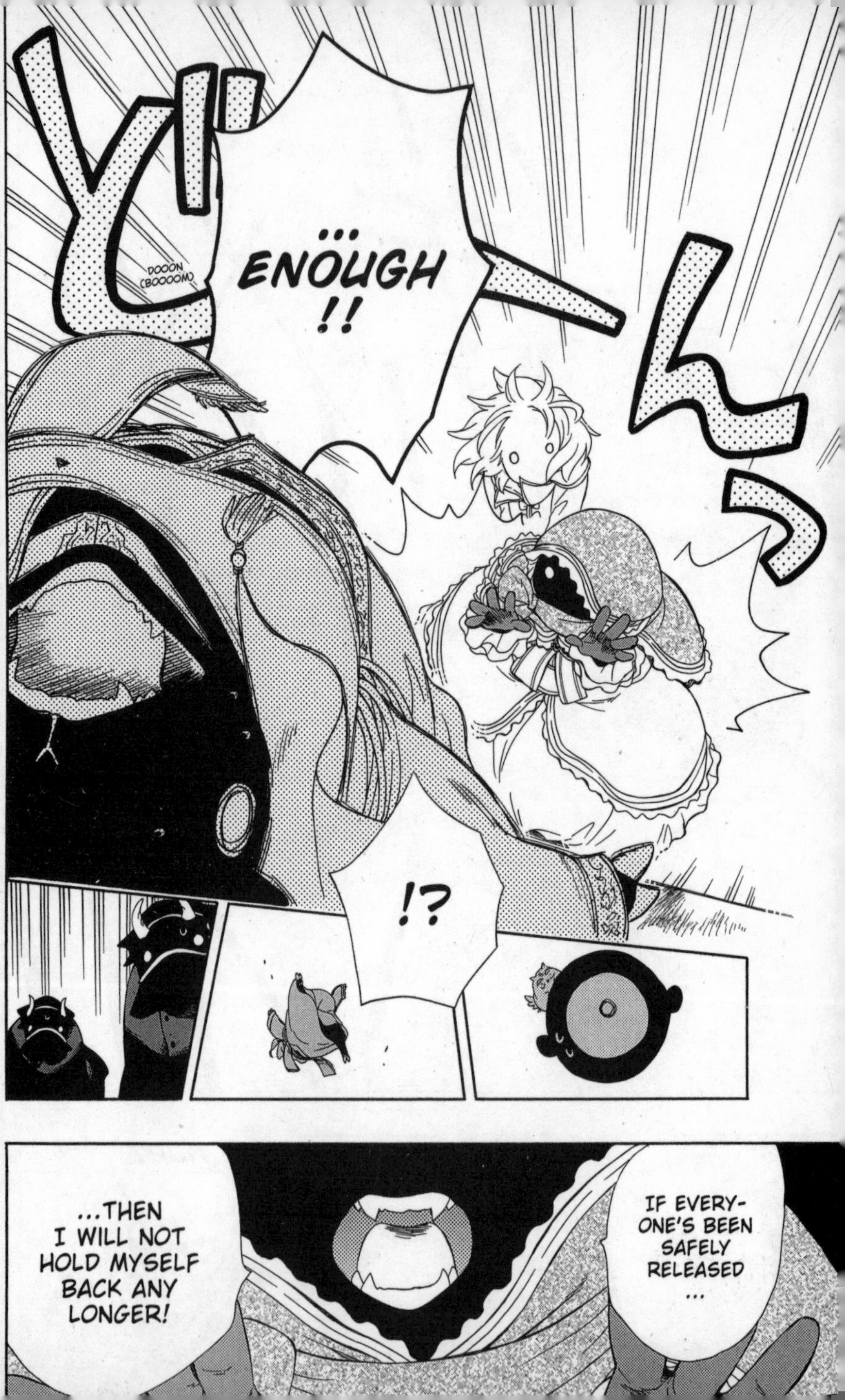
...ENOUGH!!
DOOON (BOOOOM)
!?
IF EVERY-ONE'S BEEN SAFELY RELEASED ...
...THEN I WILL NOT HOLD MYSELF BACK ANY LONGER!

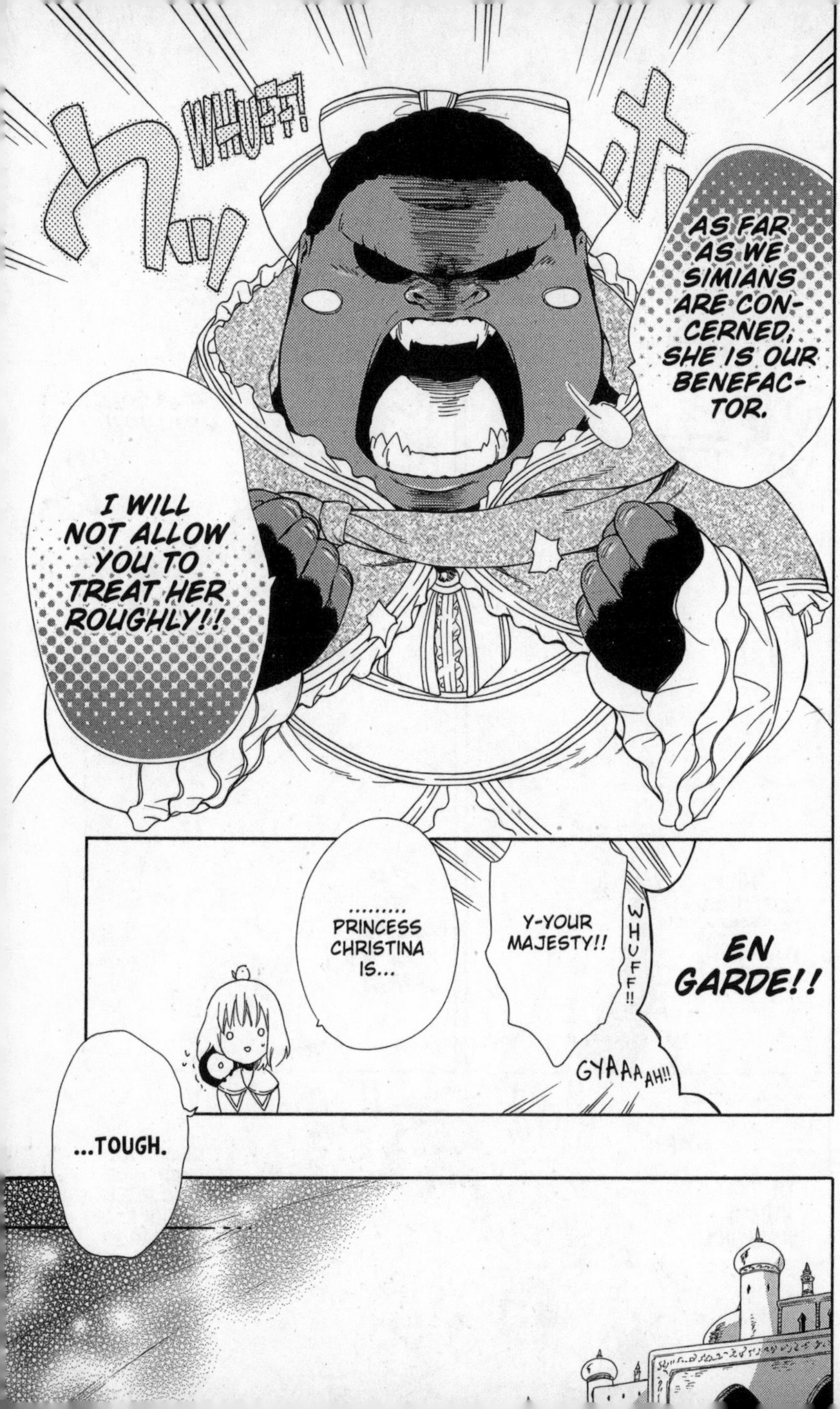
WHUFF!
AS FAR AS WE SIMIANS ARE CON-CERNED, SHE IS OUR BENEFAC-TOR.
I WILL NOT ALLOW YOU TO TREAT HER ROUGHLY!!
EN GARDE!!
WHUFF!!
GYAAAAH!!
Y-YOUR MAJESTY!!
.... PRINCESS CHRISTINA IS...
...TOUGH.

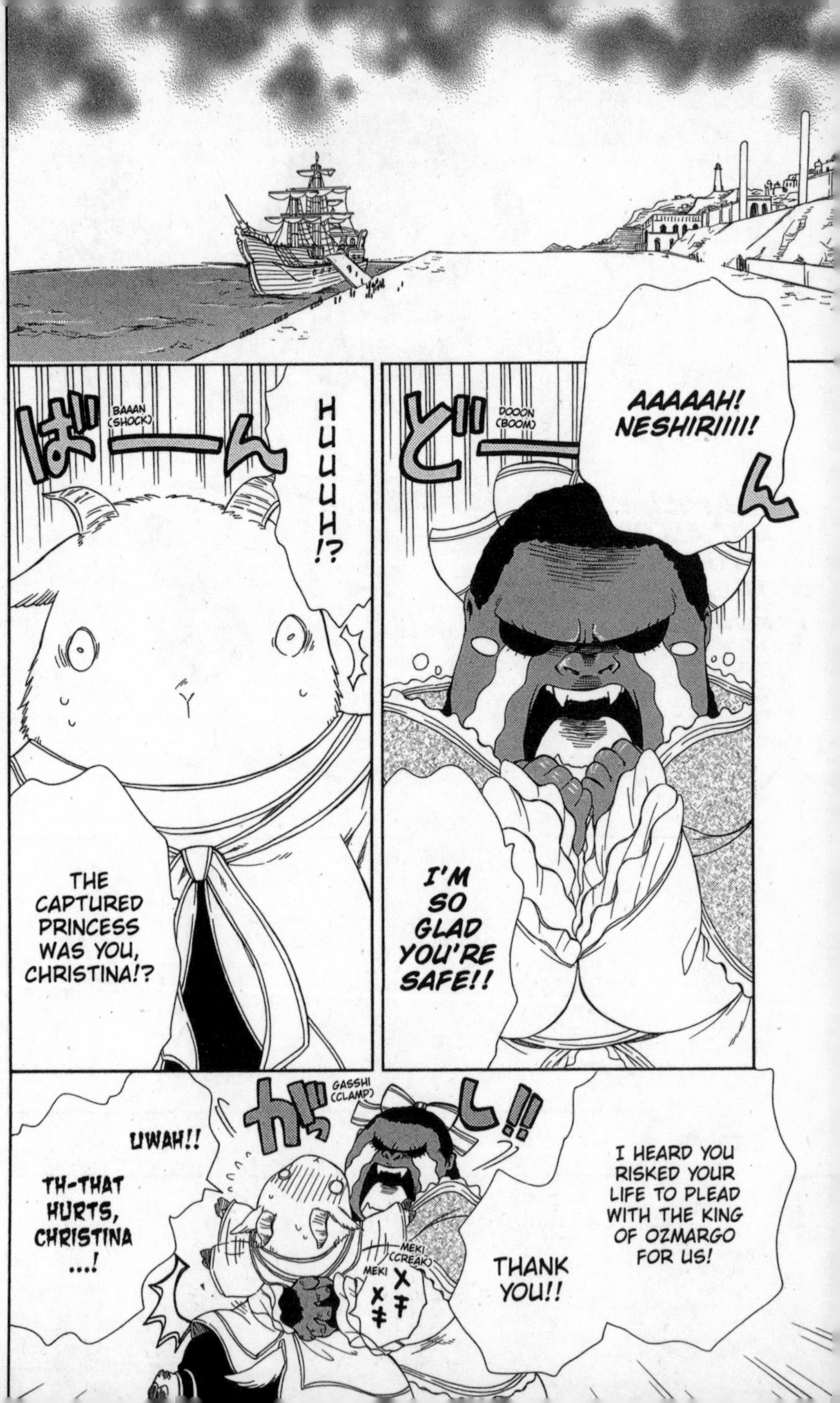
DOOON (BOOM)
AAAAAH! NESHIRI!!!!!
I'M SO GLAD YOU'RE SAFE!!
BAAAN (SHOCK)
HUUUUH!?
THE CAPTURED PRINCESS WAS YOU, CHRISTINA!?
GASSHI (CLAMP)
I HEARD YOU RISKED YOUR LIFE TO PLEAD WITH THE KING OF OZMARGO FOR US!
THANK YOU!!
MEKI (CREAK)
MEKI
UWAH!!
TH-THAT HURTS, CHRISTINA ...!

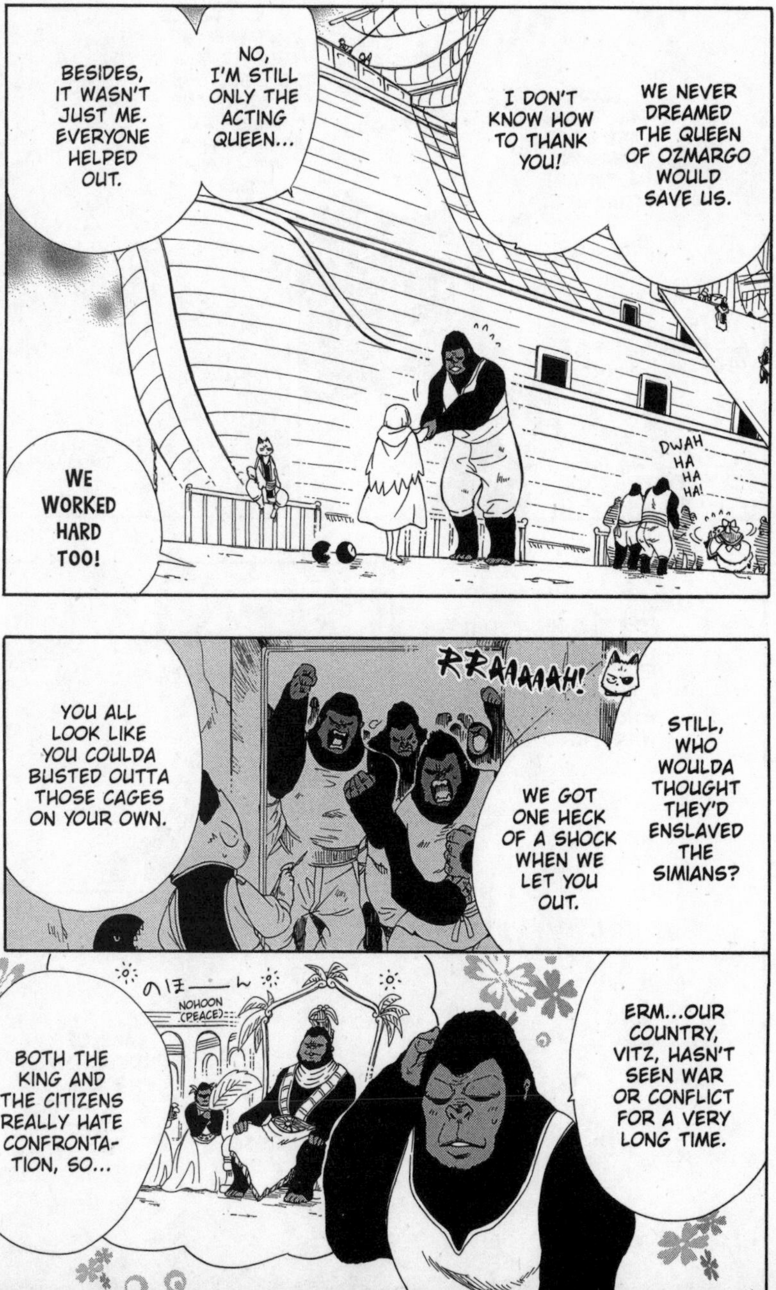
WE NEVER DREAMED THE QUEEN OF OZMARGO WOULD SAVE US.
I DON'T KNOW HOW TO THANK YOU!
NO, I'M STILL ONLY THE ACTING QUEEN...
BESIDES, IT WASN'T JUST ME. EVERYONE HELPED OUT.
DWAH HA HA HA!
WE WORKED HARD TOO!
RRAAAAAH!
STILL, WHO WOULDA THOUGHT THEY'D ENSLAVED THE SIMIANS?
WE GOT ONE HECK OF A SHOCK WHEN WE LET YOU OUT.
YOU ALL LOOK LIKE YOU COULDA BUSTED OUTTA THOSE CAGES ON YOUR OWN.
ERM...OUR COUNTRY, VITZ, HASN'T SEEN WAR OR CONFLICT FOR A VERY LONG TIME.
のほーーん
NOHOON (PEACE)
BOTH THE KING AND THE CITIZENS REALLY HATE CONFRONTATION, SO...

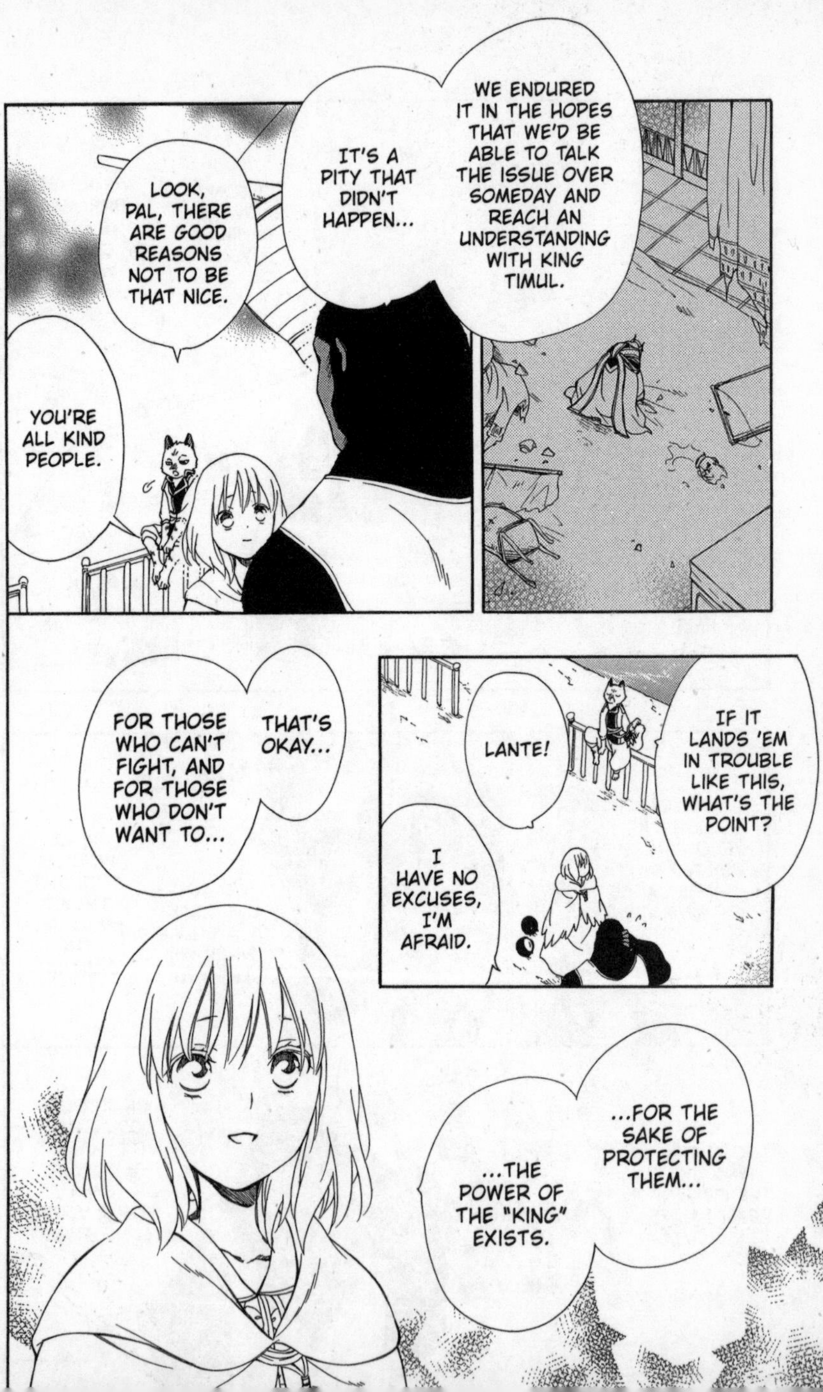
WE ENDURED IT IN THE HOPES THAT WE'D BE ABLE TO TALK THE ISSUE OVER SOMEDAY AND REACH AN UNDERSTANDING WITH KING TIMUL.
IT'S A PITY THAT DIDN'T HAPPEN...
LOOK, PAL, THERE ARE GOOD REASONS NOT TO BE THAT NICE.
YOU'RE ALL KIND PEOPLE.
IF IT LANDS 'EM IN TROUBLE LIKE THIS, WHAT'S THE POINT?
LANTE!
I HAVE NO EXCUSES, I'M AFRAID.
THAT'S OKAY...
FOR THOSE WHO CAN'T FIGHT, AND FOR THOSE WHO DON'T WANT TO...
...FOR THE SAKE OF PROTECTING THEM...
...THE POWER OF THE "KING" EXISTS.

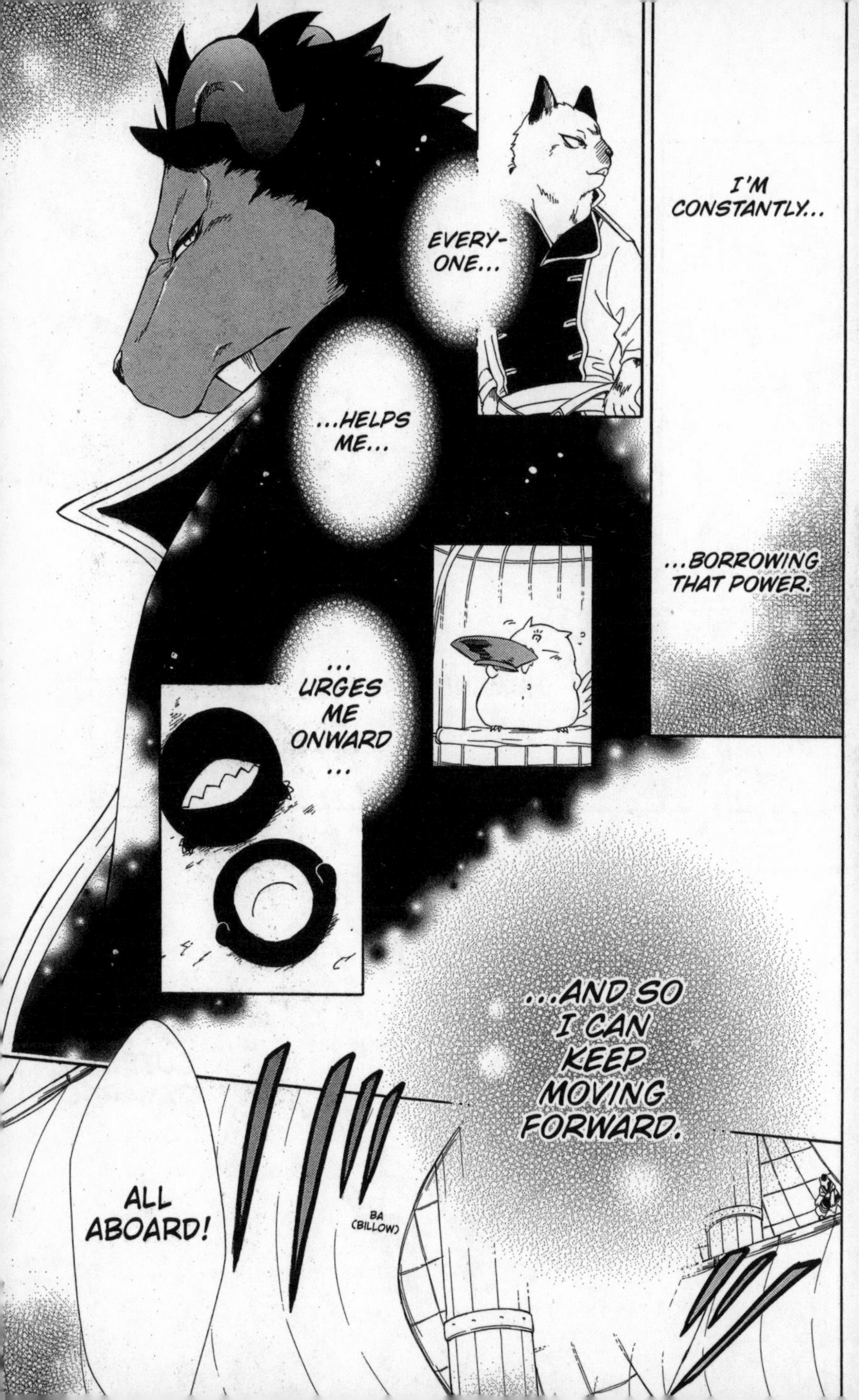
I'M CONSTANTLY...
...BORROWING THAT POWER.
EVERY-ONE...
...HELPS ME...
...URGES ME ONWARD...
...AND SO I CAN KEEP MOVING FORWARD.
BA (BILLOW)
ALL ABOARD!

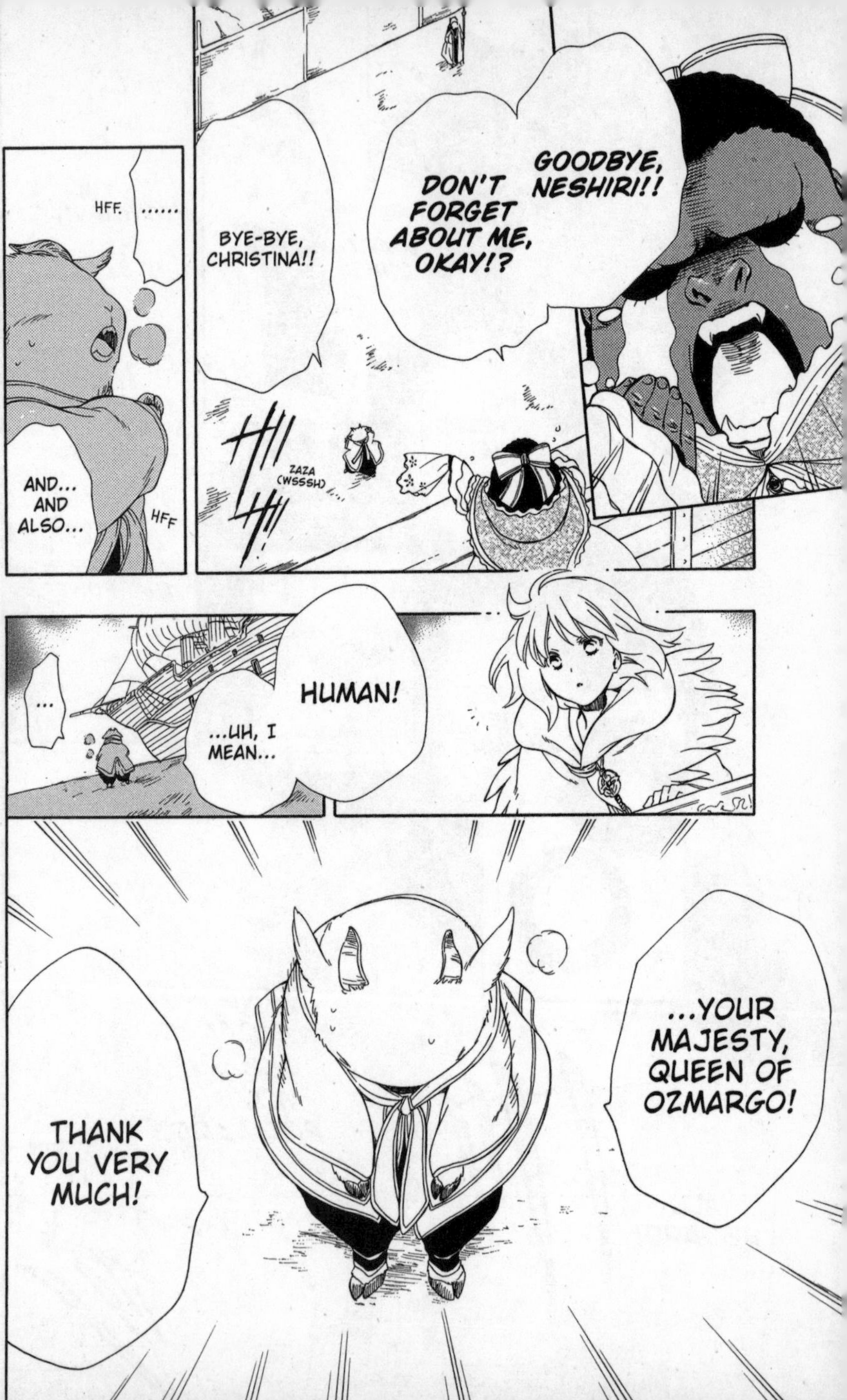
GOODBYE, NESHIRI!!
DON'T FORGET ABOUT ME, OKAY!?
BYE-BYE, CHRISTINA!!
ZAZA (WSSSH)
HFF. ......
AND... AND ALSO...
HFF
HUMAN!
...UH, I MEAN...
...
...YOUR MAJESTY, QUEEN OF OZMARGO!
THANK YOU VERY MUCH!

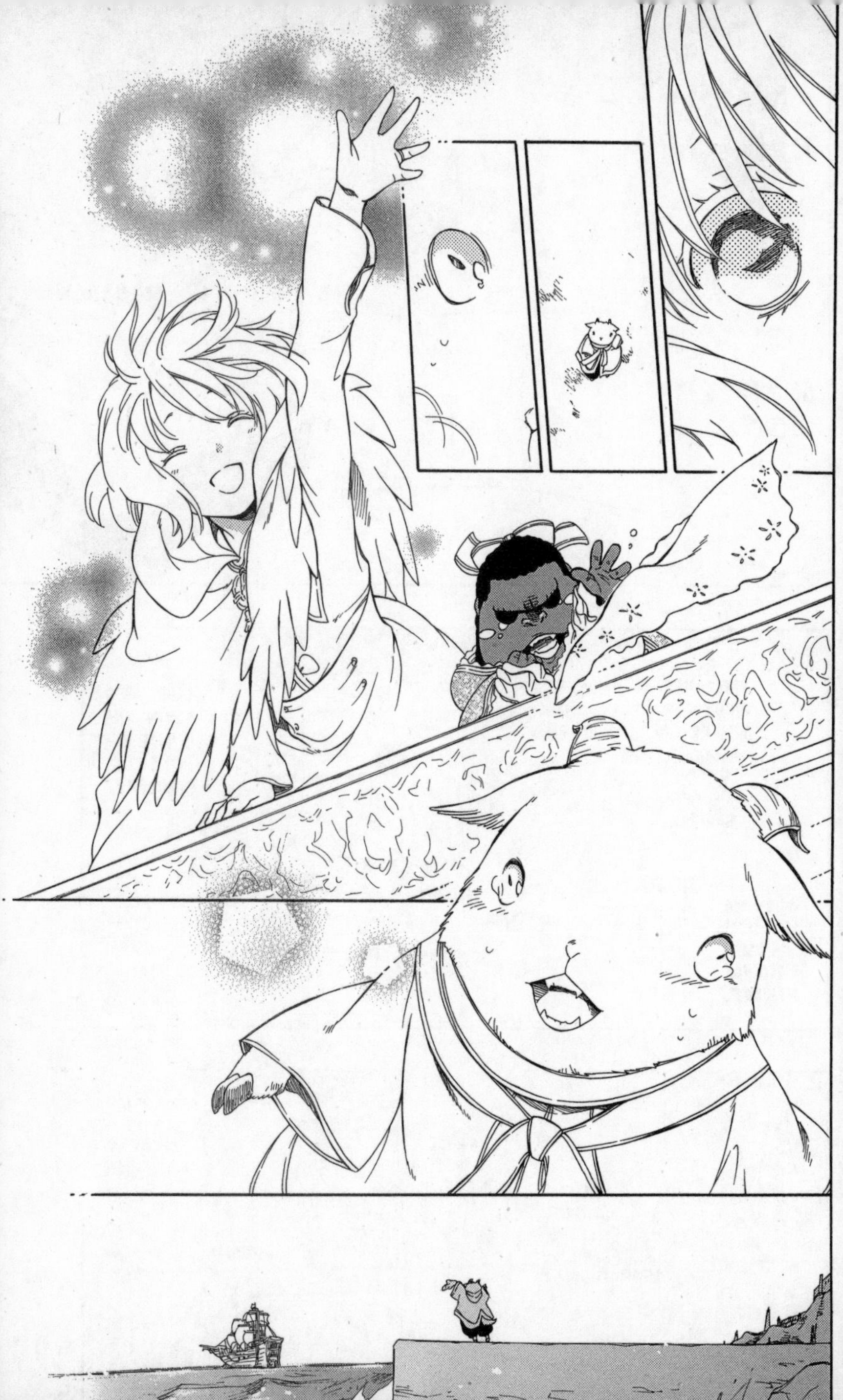

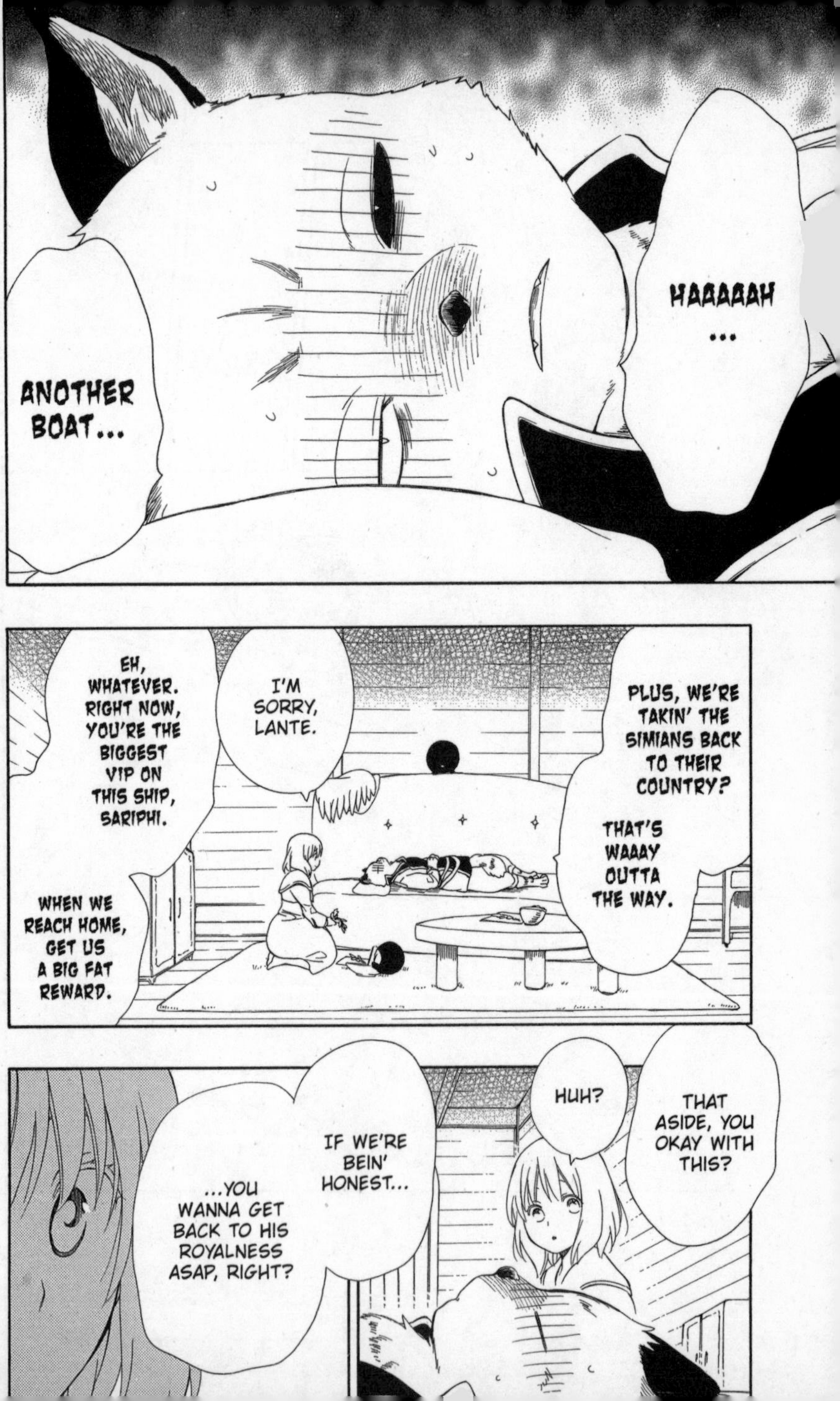
HAAAAAH ...
ANOTHER BOAT...
PLUS, WE'RE TAKIN' THE SIMIANS BACK TO THEIR COUNTRY?
THAT'S WAAAY OUTTA THE WAY.
I'M SORRY, LANTE.
EH, WHATEVER. RIGHT NOW, YOU'RE THE BIGGEST VIP ON THIS SHIP, SARIPHI.
WHEN WE REACH HOME, GET US A BIG FAT REWARD.
THAT ASIDE, YOU OKAY WITH THIS?
HUH?
IF WE'RE BEIN' HONEST...
...YOU WANNA GET BACK TO HIS ROYALNESS ASAP, RIGHT?

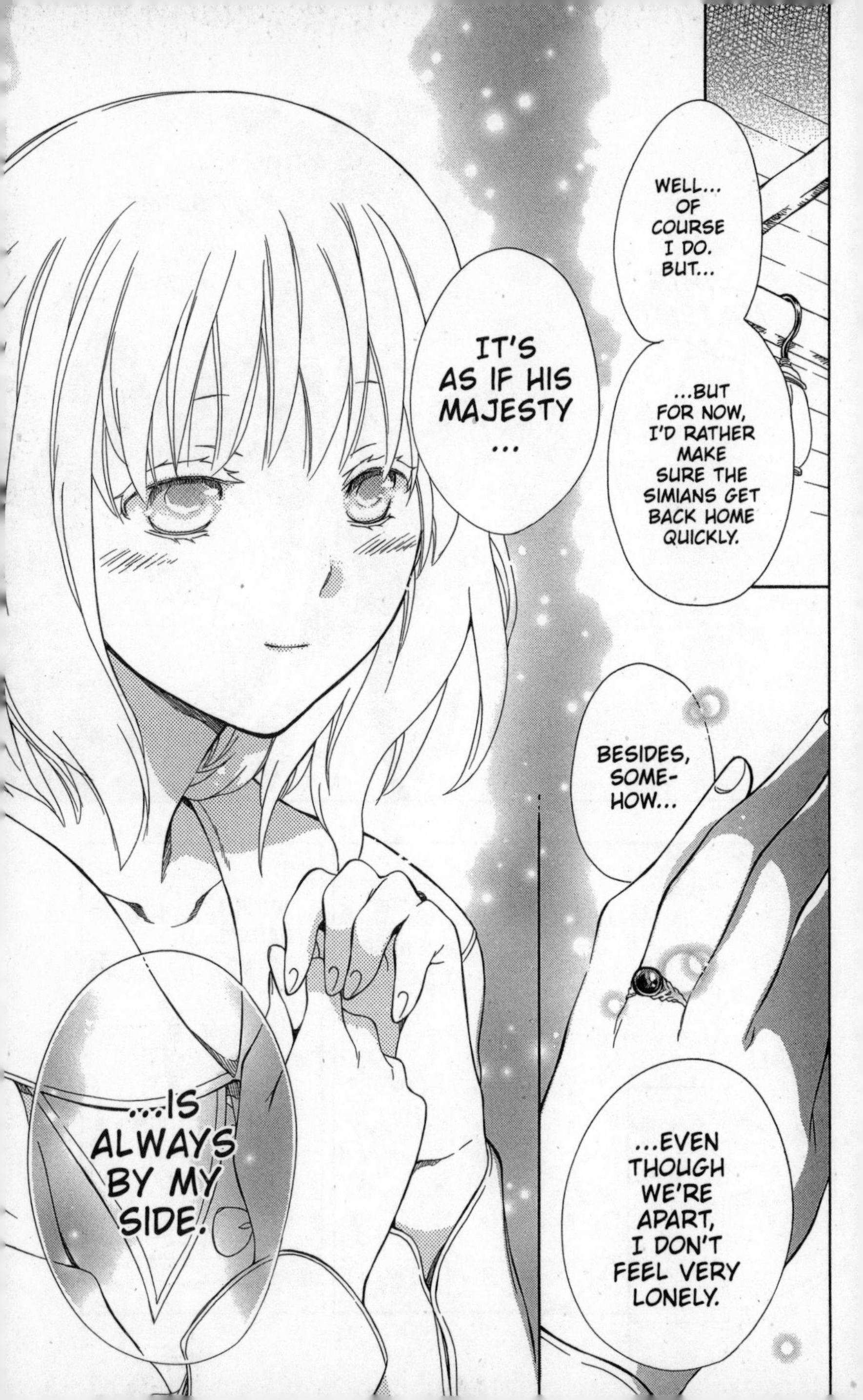
WELL... OF COURSE I DO. BUT...
...BUT FOR NOW, I'D RATHER MAKE SURE THE SIMIANS GET BACK HOME QUICKLY.
BESIDES, SOME-HOW...
...EVEN THOUGH WE'RE APART, I DON'T FEEL VERY LONELY.
IT'S AS IF HIS MAJESTY ...
...IS ALWAYS BY MY SIDE.

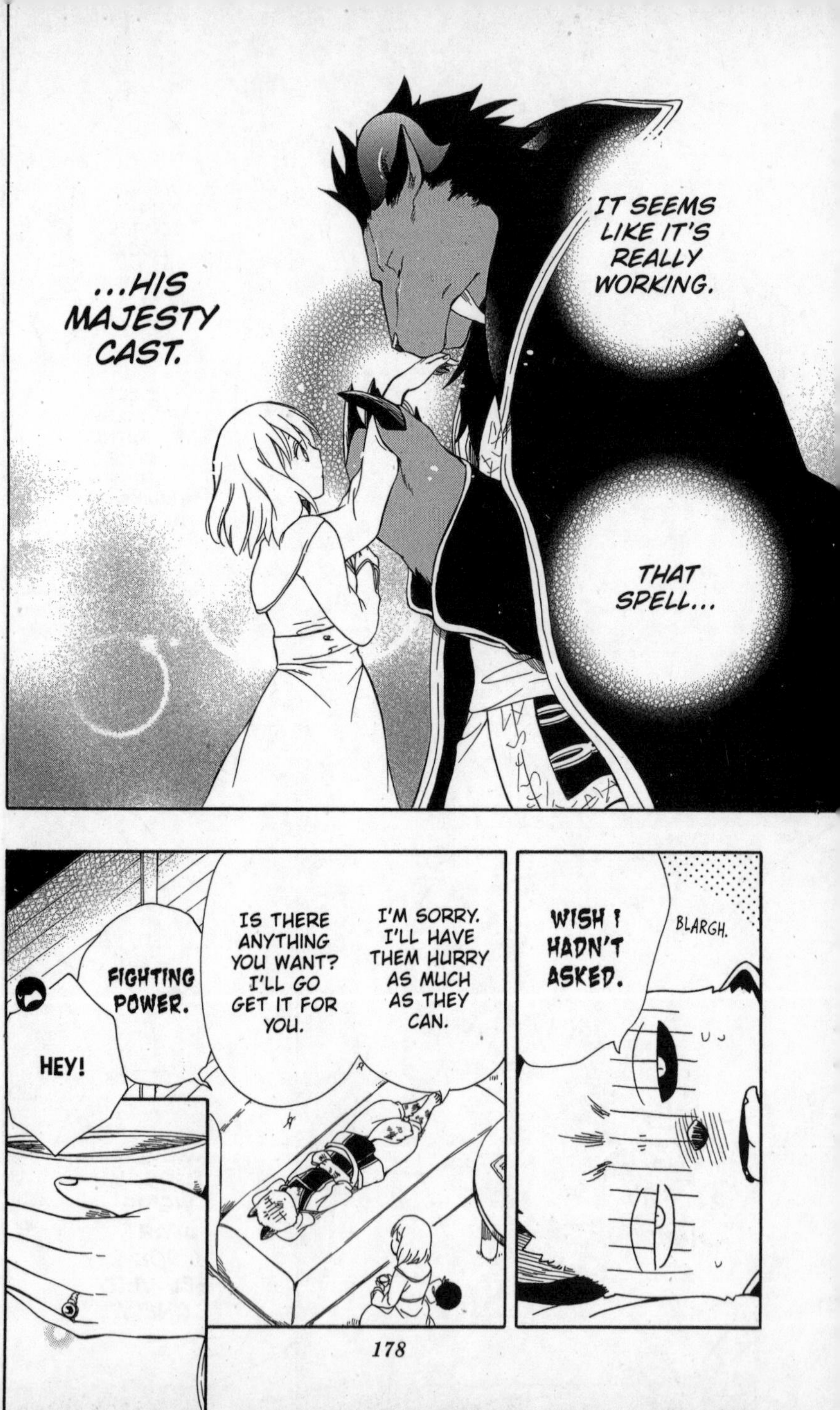
IT SEEMS LIKE IT'S REALLY WORKING.
THAT SPELL...
...HIS MAJESTY CAST.
BLARGH.
WISH I HADN'T ASKED.
I'M SORRY. I'LL HAVE THEM HURRY AS MUCH AS THEY CAN.
IS THERE ANYTHING YOU WANT? I'LL GO GET IT FOR YOU.
FIGHTING POWER.
HEY!

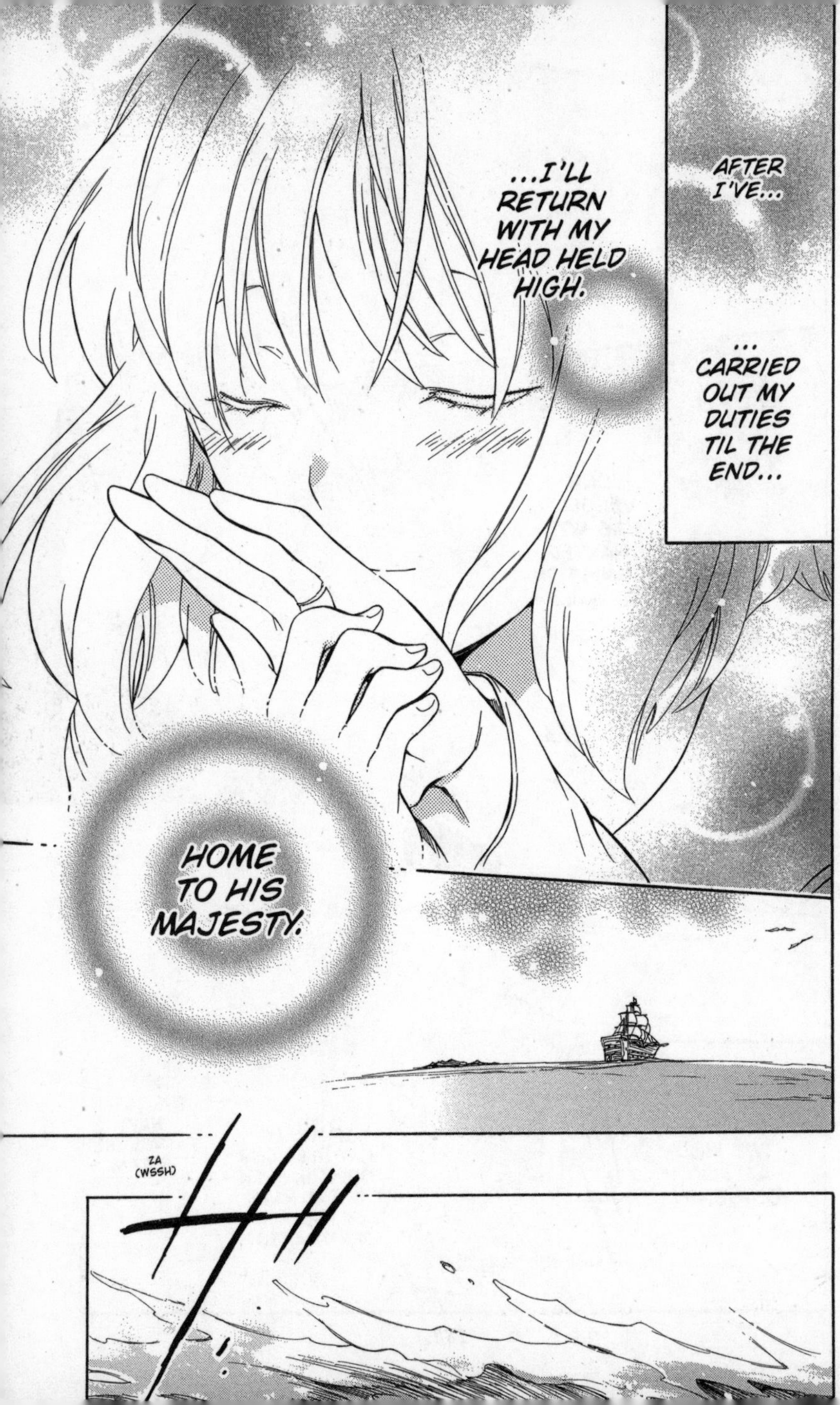
AFTER I'VE...
...CARRIED OUT MY DUTIES TIL THE END...
...I'LL RETURN WITH MY HEAD HELD HIGH.
HOME TO HIS MAJESTY.
ZA (WSSH)

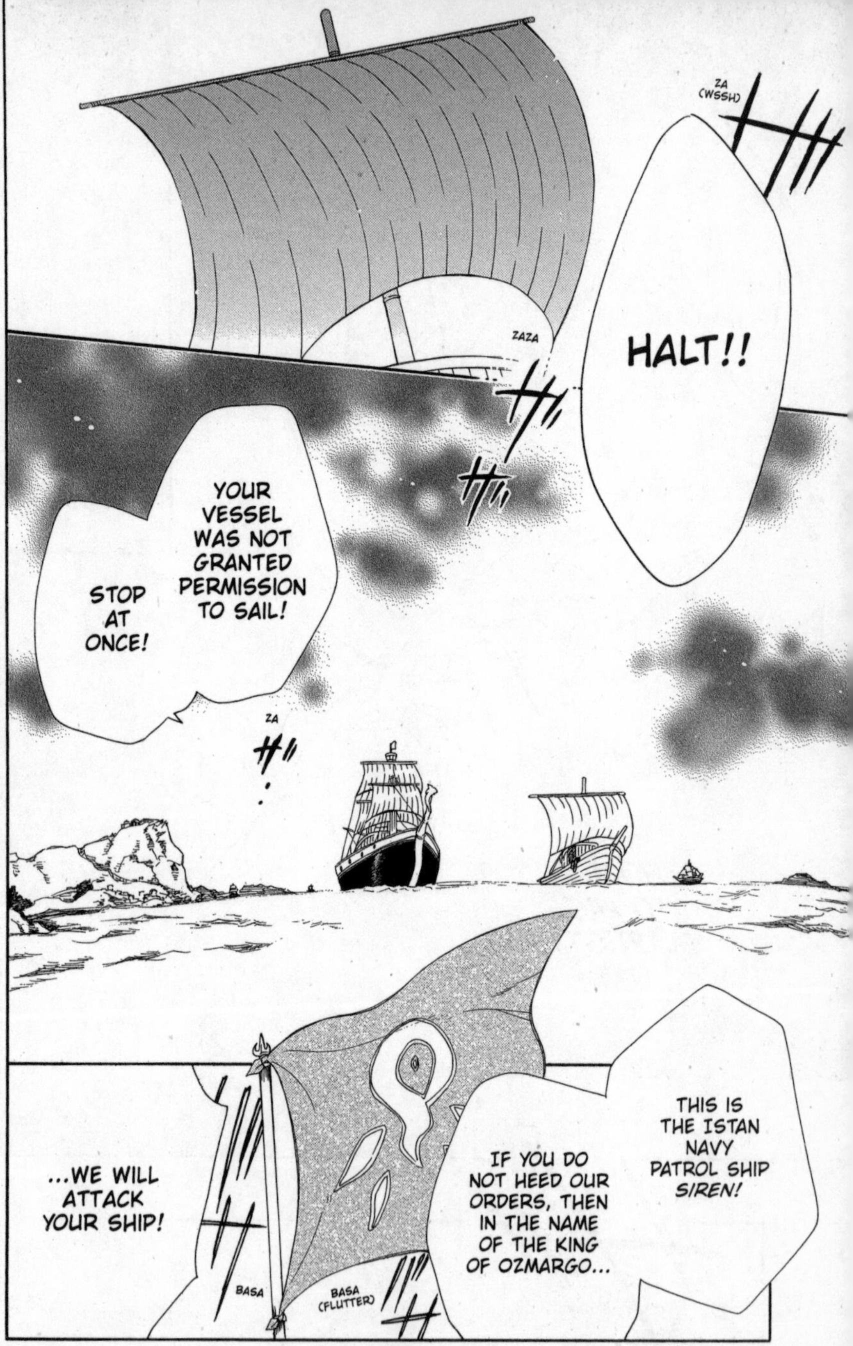
ZA (WSSH)
HALT!!
ZAZA
YOUR VESSEL WAS NOT GRANTED PERMISSION TO SAIL!
STOP AT ONCE!
ZA
THIS IS THE ISTAN NAVY PATROL SHIP *SIREN!*
IF YOU DO NOT HEED OUR ORDERS, THEN IN THE NAME OF THE KING OF OZMARGO...
BASA (FLUTTER)
BASA
...WE WILL ATTACK YOUR SHIP!

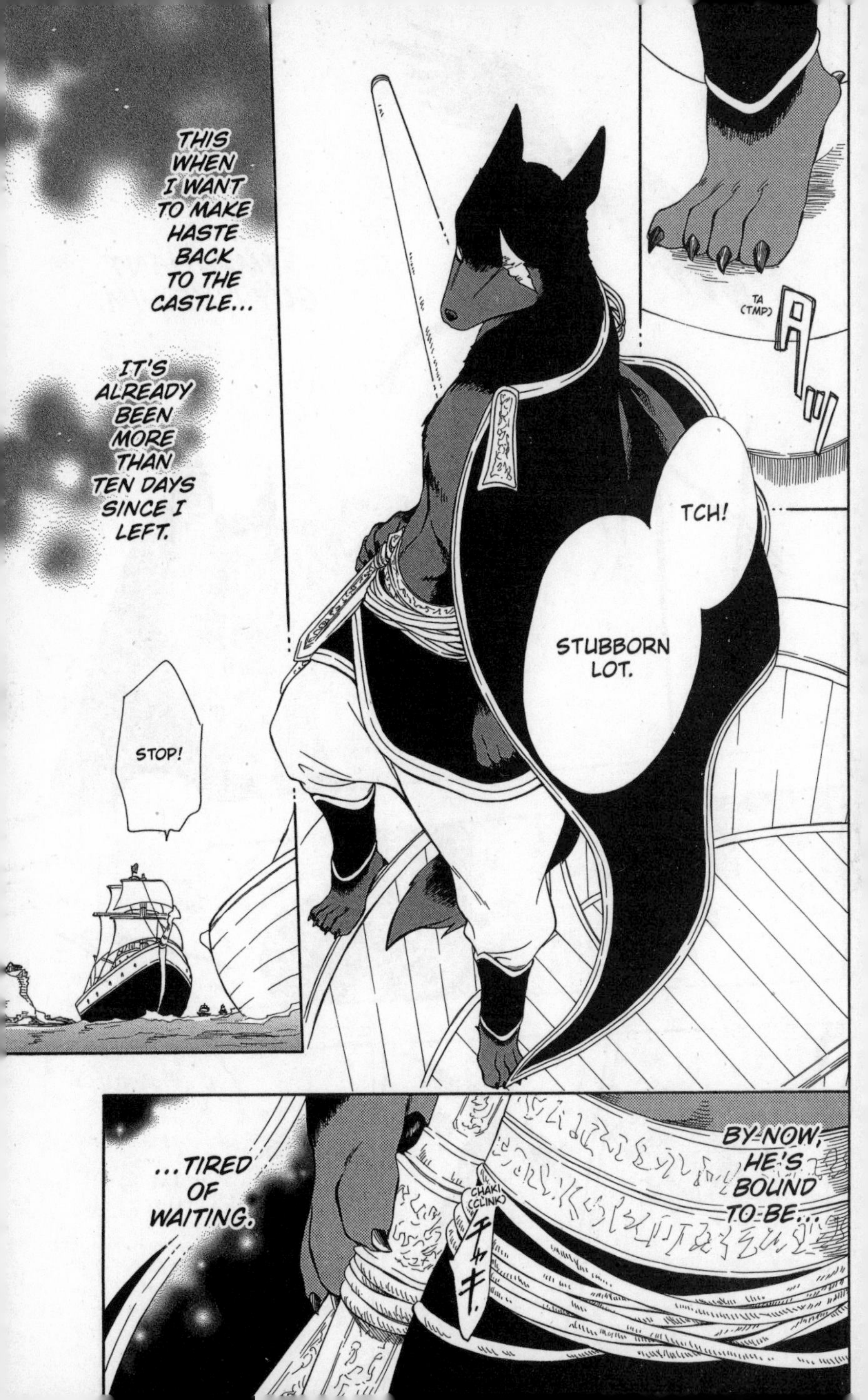
TA (TMP)
TCH!
STUBBORN LOT.
THIS WHEN I WANT TO MAKE HASTE BACK TO THE CASTLE...
IT'S ALREADY BEEN MORE THAN TEN DAYS SINCE I LEFT.
STOP!
BY NOW, HE'S BOUND TO BE...
CHAKI (CLINK)
...TIRED OF WAITING.

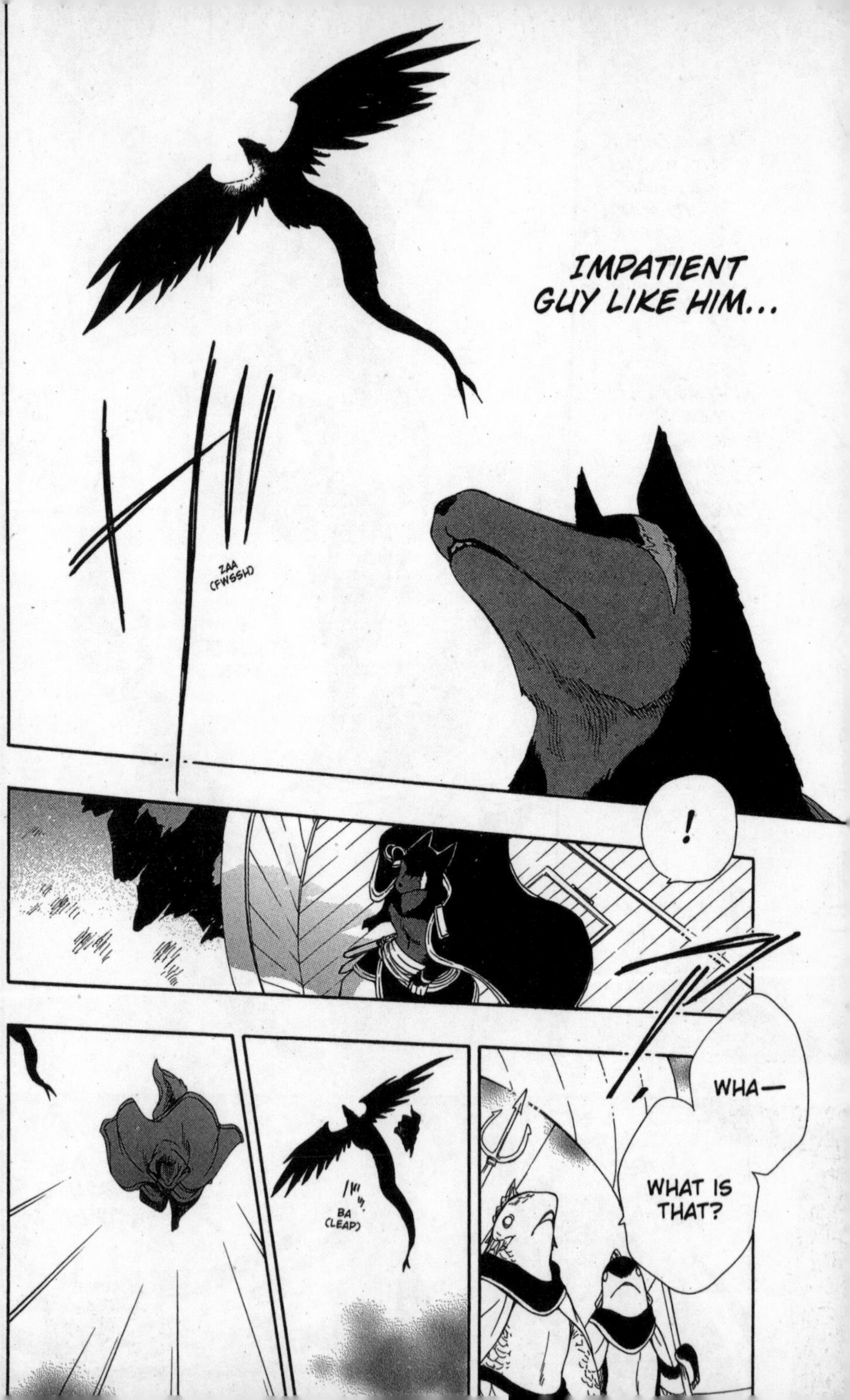
IMPATIENT GUY LIKE HIM...
ZAA (FWSSH)
!
WHA—
WHAT IS THAT?
BA (LEAP)

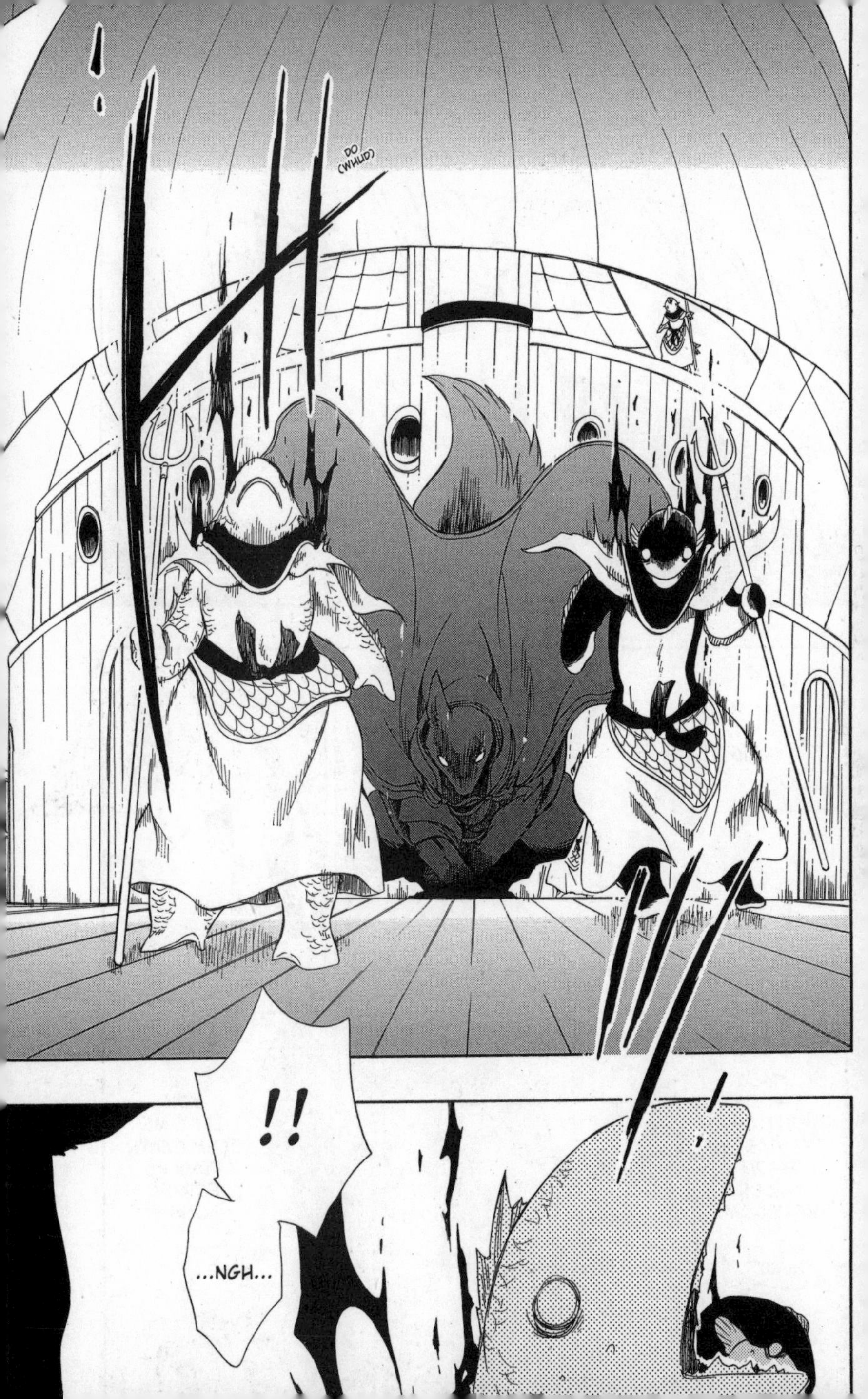
!
DO (WHUD)
!!
...NGH...

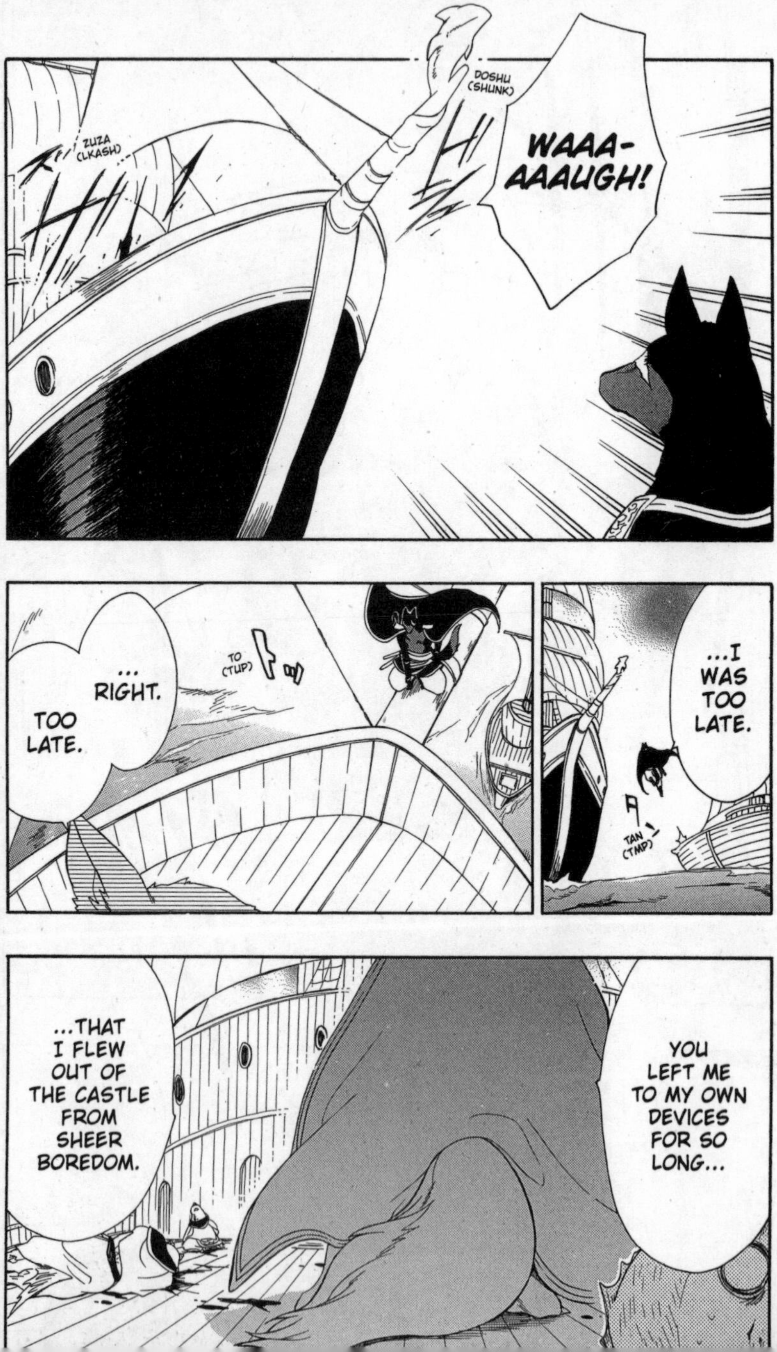

DOSHU (SHUNK)
WAAAA-AAAUGH!
ZUZA (LKASH)
...I WAS TOO LATE.
TAN (TMP)
TO (TUP)
... RIGHT. TOO LATE.
YOU LEFT ME TO MY OWN DEVICES FOR SO LONG...
...THAT I FLEW OUT OF THE CASTLE FROM SHEER BOREDOM.

GHK ...

Y-YOU SCUM... WHAT ARE...

NIR.

GLEIPNIR.

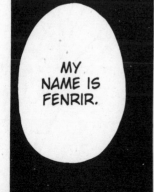

MY NAME IS FENRIR.

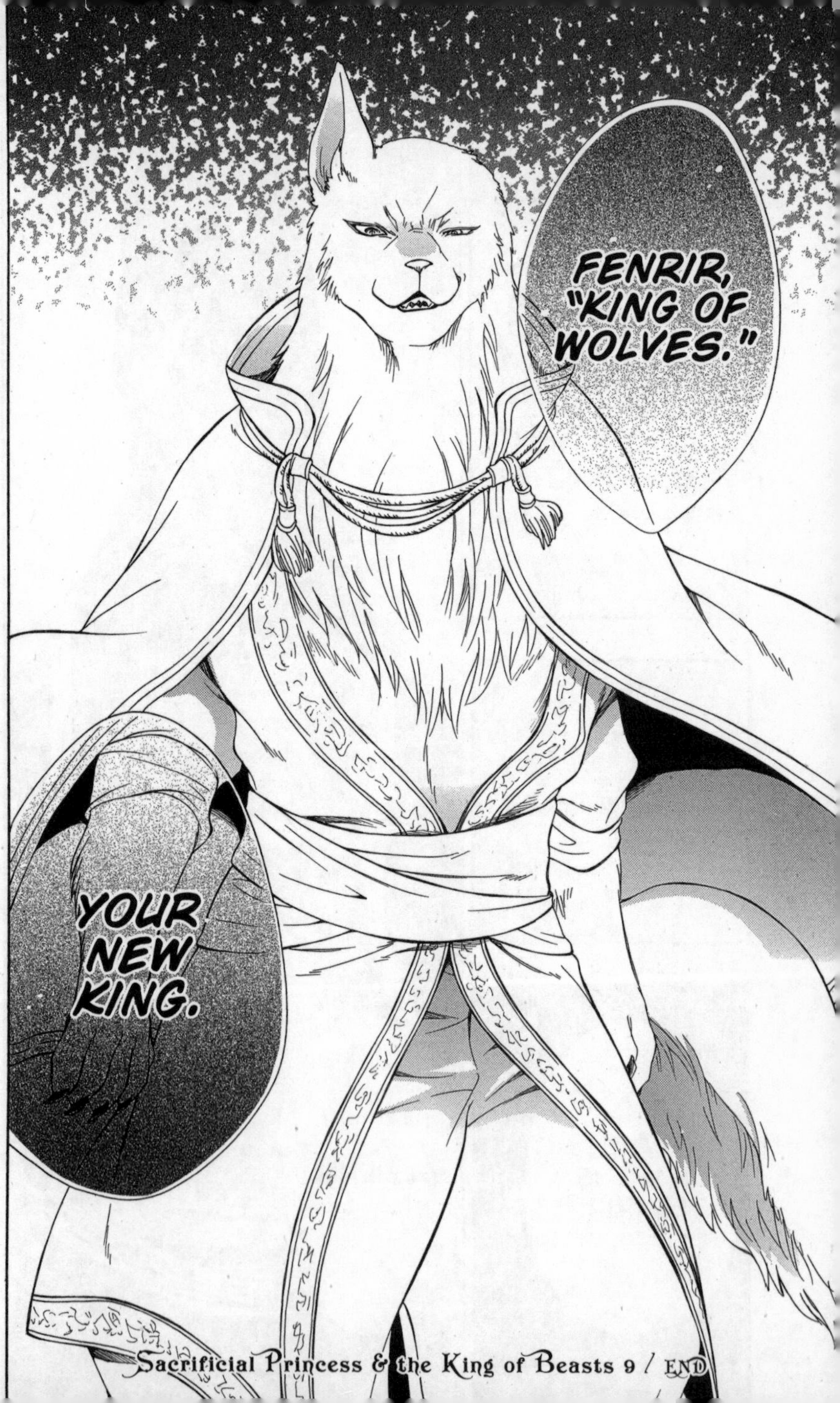
FENRIR, "KING OF WOLVES."
YOUR NEW KING.

Sacrificial Princess & the King of Beasts 9 / END

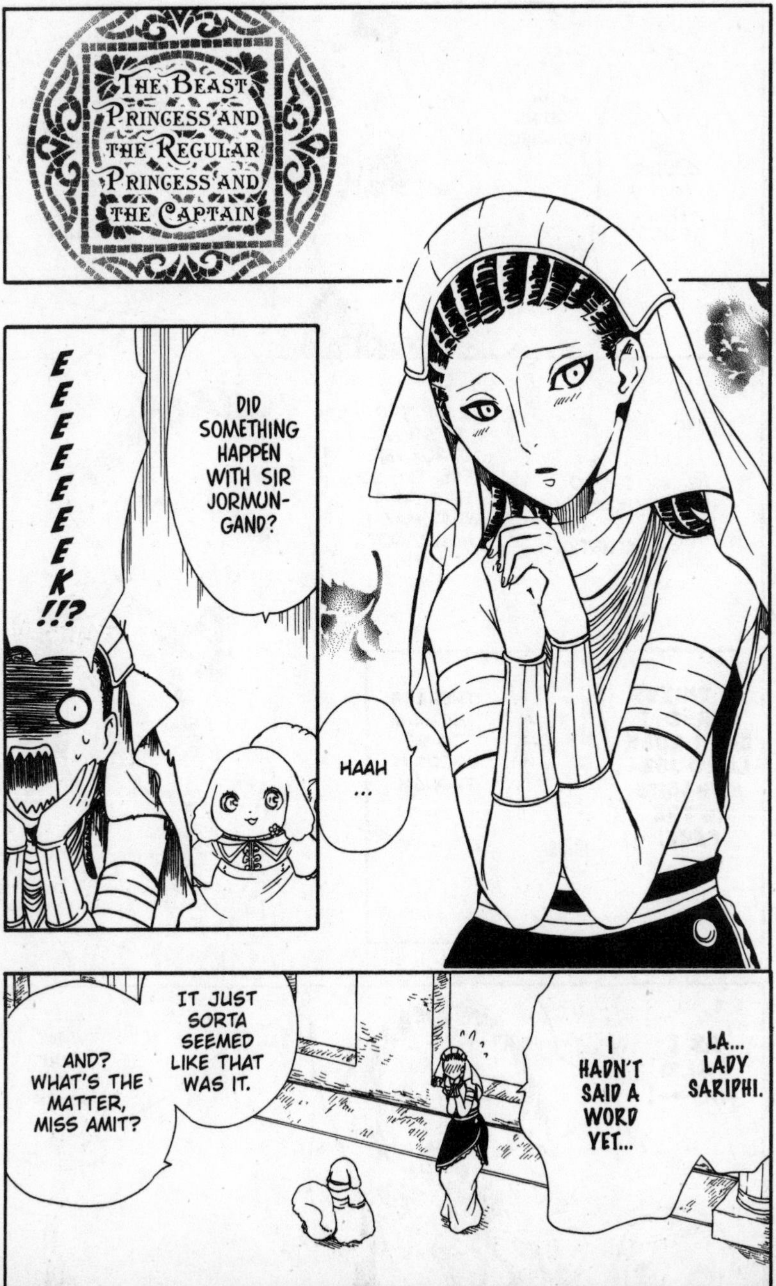
THE BEAST PRINCESS AND THE REGULAR PRINCESS AND THE CAPTAIN
HAAH ...
DID SOMETHING HAPPEN WITH SIR JORMUN-GAND?
EEEEEEEK!!?
LA... LADY SARIPHI.
I HADN'T SAID A WORD YET...
IT JUST SORTA SEEMED LIKE THAT WAS IT.
AND? WHAT'S THE MATTER, MISS AMIT?

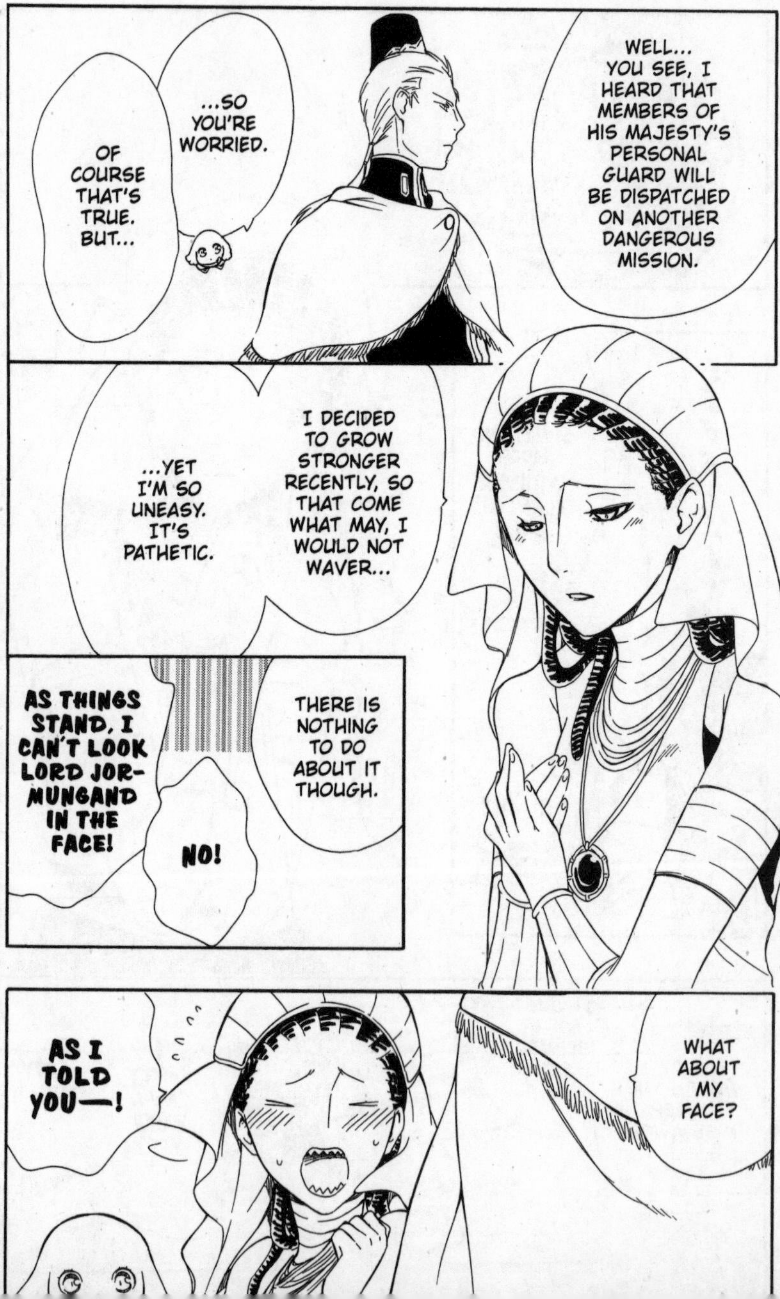
WELL... YOU SEE, I HEARD THAT MEMBERS OF HIS MAJESTY'S PERSONAL GUARD WILL BE DISPATCHED ON ANOTHER DANGEROUS MISSION.
...SO YOU'RE WORRIED.
OF COURSE THAT'S TRUE. BUT...
I DECIDED TO GROW STRONGER RECENTLY, SO THAT COME WHAT MAY, I WOULD NOT WAVER...
...YET I'M SO UNEASY. IT'S PATHETIC.
THERE IS NOTHING TO DO ABOUT IT THOUGH.
NO!
AS THINGS STAND, I CAN'T LOOK LORD JOR-MUNGAND IN THE FACE!
WHAT ABOUT MY FACE?
AS I TOLD YOU—!

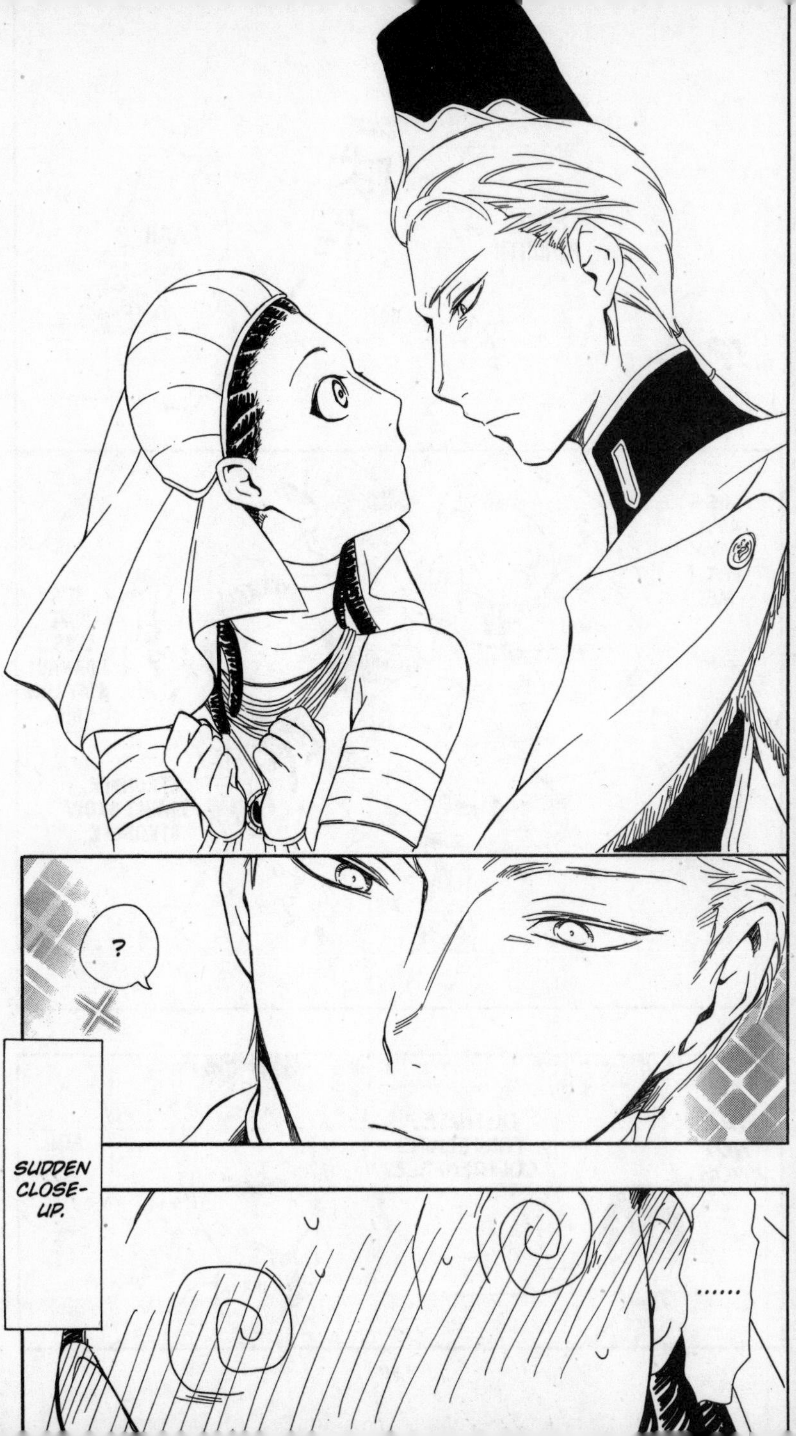
?
SUDDEN CLOSE-UP.
......

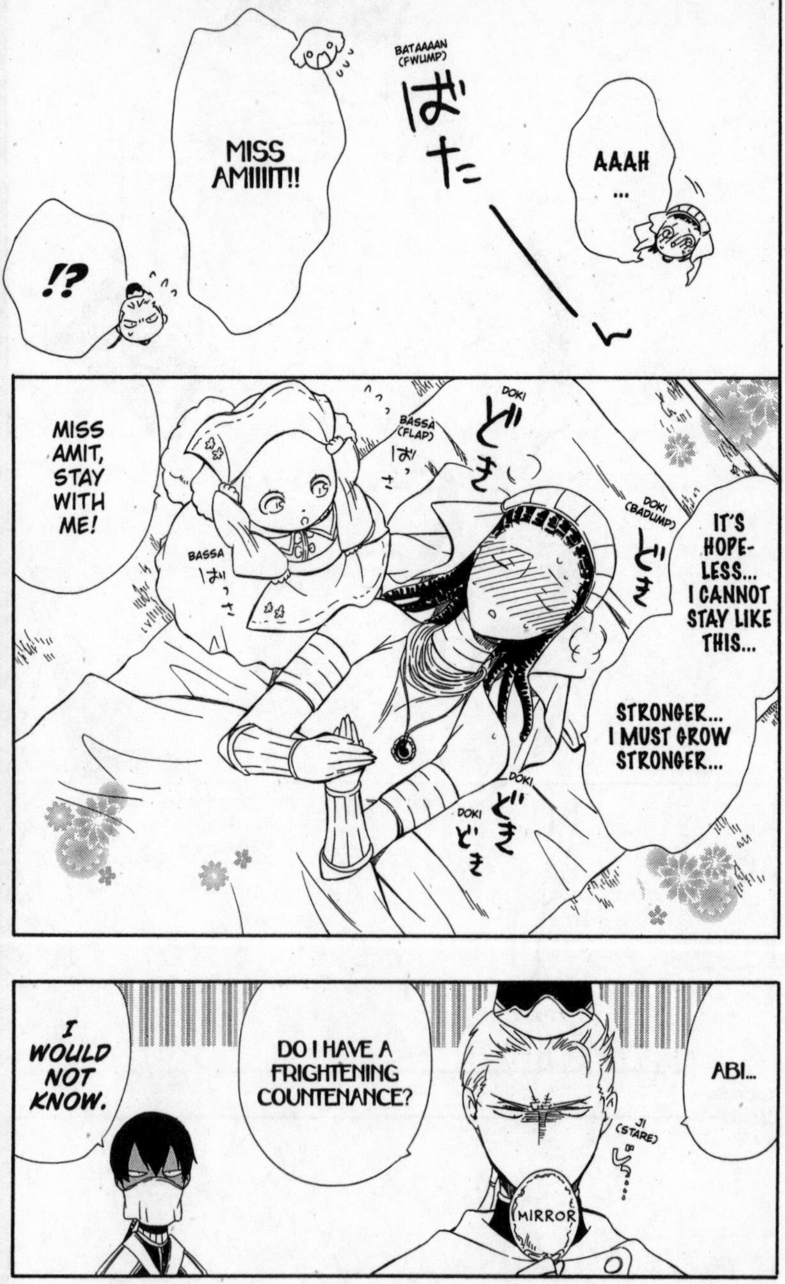
AAAH ...
BATAAAAN (FWUMP)
ばたーん
MISS AMIIIIT!!
!?
IT'S HOPE-LESS... I CANNOT STAY LIKE THIS...
STRONGER... I MUST GROW STRONGER...
DOKI (BADUMP)
どき
DOKI
どき
BASSA (FLAP)
ばっさ
BASSA
ばっさ
MISS AMIT, STAY WITH ME!
DOKI
どき
DOKI
どき
ABI...
JI (STARE)
じっ...
MIRROR
DO I HAVE A FRIGHTENING COUNTENANCE?
I WOULD NOT KNOW.

THAT'S IT FOR
VOLUME 9!

SACRIFICIAL PRINCESS AND THE King of Beasts

9

Yu Tomofuji

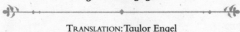

TRANSLATION: Taylor Engel

LETTERING: Lys Blakeslee

NIEHIME TO KEMONO NO OH by Yu Tomofuji
© Yu Tomofuji 2018
All rights reserved.
First published in Japan in 2018 by HAKUSENSHA, Inc., Tokyo.
English language translation rights in U.S.A., Canada and U.K. arranged with
HAKUSENSHA, Inc., Tokyo through Tuttle-Mori Agency, Inc., Tokyo.

English translation © 2020 by Yen Press, LLC

Yen Press
150 West 30th Street, 19th Floor
New York, NY 10001

Visit us at yenpress.com • facebook.com/yenpress • twitter.com/yenpress
yenpress.tumblr.com • instagram.com/yenpress

First Yen Press Edition: March 2020

Yen Press is an imprint of Yen Press, LLC.
The Yen Press name and logo are trademarks of Yen Press, LLC.

The publisher is not responsible for websites (or their
content) that are not owned by the publisher.

Library of Congress Control Number: 2018930817

ISBNs: 978-1-9753-9953-5 (paperback)
978-1-9753-0800-1 (ebook)

10 9 8 7 6 5 4 3 2 1

WOR

Printed in the United States of America